SNOW

SNOW

Townsend Kemp

For dear God without
whose Divine Guidance
this book would never
ever have been written.
xox
Townsend

Barrie & Jenkins,
London

First published in 1990 by Barrie & Jenkins,
20 Vauxhall Bridge Road, London SWIV 2SA

British Library Cataloguing in Publication Data
Kemp, Townsend
Snow.
I. Title
813'.54 [F]

ISBN 0–7126–3614–5

Printed in England by Clays Ltd, St Ives plc

Prologue

He glanced at his watch and saw that he had forty minutes in hand before the appointment, which suited him very well. He didn't in the least mind missing the royal carriage procession from Windsor. He was perfectly indifferent to the Royal Family in its entirety, their deportment, their wardrobes, their friends. Racing bored him to death. The statutory conviviality of an overcrowded, overdressed Royal Ascot meeting struck him as being both absurd and in some obscure way degrading.

It was excessively hot; Flaming June, indeed. He reflected maliciously that Ascot weather, hot or cold, and regulation kit decreed a state of intolerable discomfort for either all the men or all the women foolish enough to subject themselves to this fatuous annual endurance trial. In cool weather, silk-clad women shivered miserably, trying to ward off hypothermia in their chic new outfits more suitable to a drinks party, no doubt wishing they'd thought to put on thermals or, unthinkably, heavy tweeds. On hot afternoons such as this one, purple-faced men poured with sour, gin-scented sweat, ineffectually fanning themselves with race-cards and mopping with soaked handkerchieves. So traditional, so pathetic, so appallingly smug and English, he thought.

The car-park, one of the farthest from the entrances, was already deserted. Folding tables and chairs had been folded, giant picnic-hampers and wine-coolers returned to the backs of smart estate-cars and muddy Land-Rovers. There was a smell of hot metal and a layer of shimmering air danced above the multi-coloured roofs, the only movement in this automotive wasteland. He stripped off his tie and undid his collar. Then he removed his enclosure badge

1

and anchored it under the car-keys on the bonnet of his brand-new red XJ6.

If everything went according to plan, he would return to London by train, his car restored to him within twenty-four hours. There was the contingency plan, too, should the handover need to be aborted for any reason, but that would involve his having to go through the entire charade again on Gold Cup Day, traffic jams, heavy grey-wool camouflage hired from Moss Bros, enclosure badge, wineboxes, the lot. It was a distasteful prospect but, considering the staggering amount they were paying him, a burden to be borne philosophically.

He got a clean rag out of the boot and carefully dusted off a space on the Jaguar's hot bonnet. There was no point in standing about and sweltering, the sun beating down on the shadeless, scorched ground, dressed for the inclemencies of the North Pole. He was in the midst of struggling out of his tightish Moss Bros morning-coat when his captive arms were pinioned from behind.

'Let's have a full and frank discussion,' a familiar voice said into his left ear.

An agonizing kick to the back of his left knee made him collapse face down onto the ground, driving the air out of his lungs. A weight pressed down on his back, between his shoulder-blades, and he felt that he was suffocating, his nose pressed into the dusty grass. A powerful grip in his hair jerked his head back viciously and something tight and horrible was around his neck.

'Please,' he managed to croak. His eyes streamed with tears of pain and fear.

'You've pissed yourself, you scum,' the voice said, contempt and loathing only too plain. 'You'll breathe as much as I let you. Just enough air in you to tell me everything. Now *start talking*!'

He hesitated only briefly and the noose was jerked tight. 'All right,' he whispered, as red lights exploded behind his eyeballs.

PART ONE

1

She stopped to rest on a small spur and drink in the breathtaking view of the valley. The winter sun was low in the sky and blue shadows crept up toward the still-bright top of the mountain. The air shimmered with a strange light refracted from the great glacier above. She was somewhat surprised and obscurely gratified to note that the day had flown past quite pleasantly. Her skiing was showing signs of distinct improvement and she no longer felt insecure about being alone, even on this fairly taxing run. It was far from being the most difficult of Val Sainte-Anne's *pistes* but it was light-years away from the crowded bunny slopes at the bottom.

The sky and snow were beginning to take on the dazzling, delicate lavender hues of early dusk and she knew she mustn't dawdle. There was such a thing as becoming over-confident and running stupid risks but the beauty of the scene held her rooted to the spot. She had her camera with her, of course. For Camilla Sayle to be without her camera was unthinkable. Stuffing her mittens in a pocket and unzipping her anorak, she quickly checked to make sure she had a few frames left on the film. Good. She wanted a shot across a small ravine of the bare ridge a couple of hundred yards distant. It stood stark and pure against the improbable pastel hues of the late-afternoon sky.

As her deft fingers adjusted the Nikon for light and distance, a lone skier appeared at the top of the ridge and paused for a moment before continuing down it. She envied him his skill: the Paternoster was the most difficult and dangerous of all the runs. Camilla would never dare to attempt it herself, even with expert guidance. She caught the skier pushing off, stunningly silhouetted against the sky, and congratulated herself on her luck: it would make a far more interesting shot than the bare ridge, no matter how lovely. The skier was dressed in some silvery – grey material that gave a ghostly, mysterious quality to his presence. If she were very lucky indeed, she might even have a cover shot in this one.

She managed another two quick snaps of the lone skier before he (she had decided it must surely be a man) sank slowly out of view and then suddenly saw that he was not fearlessly alone, after all. A number of skiers had just topped the ridge and, like the first, were hesitating a moment before committing themselves to the tricky descent. They were wearing identical silver-grey ski-suits which must be made of some new, no doubt appallingly expensive, thermal concoction. The man who had gone ahead must be an instructor or local guide and his flock, undoubtedly a ski-club, would prudently follow strictly inside the tracks he had made for them. Spring was avalanche season. She felt absurdly pleased not to be the only person at the resort too timid to tackle that particularly difficult run on her own.

There was an eerie quality to the scene, a combination of the snowsuits being only faintly visible even at such close range and the absence of any cluttering trees, that she hoped her camera would capture. A few more shots of the main group of skiers silently pushing off and heading down in a disciplined, well-spaced crocodile and that would have to do for the day. The light was beginning to leech out of the sky and, although it was still quite bright so high up the mountain, she knew she would not reach the safety of the lower slopes until almost dusk. She didn't want Georgie to worry. He fussed over her enough as it was.

She had already negotiated the most difficult part of the run and, apart from a few scattered icy patches which she approached gingerly, there was nothing terribly challenging about the remainder. She was faintly aware that someone was behind her on the trail, occasionally audible as ski edges rasped over ice, and she hoped the follower wasn't one of those rude, impatient types, usually German, who insisted upon overtaking at the precise point where the trail was at its narrowest. But whoever was behind was obviously being

6

as cautious as she and maintained a respectable distance between them.

As the run opened out from the trees on the final stretch, she got her first sight of the village below; a few faint lights already switched on and promising the delights of a hot bath, a drink, an excellent dinner and early to bed. She was beginning to feel pleasantly tired, a slight ache starting in her thighs.

'Life,' she announced aloud to the thin, frosty evening air, 'could be worse.' She was smiling as she swept to a halt. The bleak months of the past, every day seeming as grey and featureless as an Arctic winter, were behind her; she suddenly knew it in a welcome burst of intuitive awareness. The ghost-haunted, sleepless nights might not disappear all at once; the tears might continue to engulf her at uncontrollable and often embarrassing moments but she hadn't the least desire to ignore her sense of well-being.

Some of this might be fairly attributed to the change of scene, the supremely tactful and undemanding company of Georgie and the combined physical effects on her body of high, pure Alpine air, the deep satisfaction of simple French cookery and a good deal of unaccustomed exercise. She was going to bed early because she was tired, not because she was too paralysed by guilt and misery to do anything else. She smiled again as she propped her rented skis against the hotel's rack. All the primeval clichés to do with the healing properties of time's passage turned out to be simple truth.

'And bloody well time, too,' she said.

'My dear, when you start talking to yourself it's the last and final straw. I shall have you committed.' Georgie was standing on the little hotel's broad wooden steps, a cigarette glowing in his hand.

'Georgie! You startled me!' Camilla scolded, somewhat taken aback that her out-loud musings had been overheard. Then she laughed. At least it was Georgie and not some complete stranger who would likely scuttle nervously away, as people do when confronted with muttering souls in London streets.

7

She hooked her arm through his as they went up to the door. 'Admit, Georgie, that you were beginning to miss me.'

'Well, darling, the thought had crossed my tiny mind that you might be lying neck-deep in snow, gently freezing, a quivering mass of broken bits and bobs, praying that your devoted old friend might come looking for you.'

'Georgie, darling, you really were worried about me,' Camilla said contritely. 'I do apologize for being so late but I got fired up with the light up near the top and the view and a group of skiers against the sky and it all looked almost like a mirage . . .'

'Frankly, my dear, before you go wittering on about the beauties of nature, I must confess that I wasn't excessively concerned about your safety. Well, a *little* concerned but, you know, not crazed with anxiety.'

Camilla burst out laughing. 'You really are the limit! Let's go in. I'm freezing! We can sit in front of the fire, defrost and have a drink before changing for dinner.'

'I *am* changed,' Georgie said severely. 'I'm wearing my best butch outfit.'

Camilla giggled as they settled into the deep sofa before the fire in the hotel's cosy bar-cum-library. Georgie was wearing a heavily ribbed black cashmere sweater, definitely Burlington Arcade rather than Oxford Street, over a pale pink silk shirt open at the throat and obviously bespoke, Jermyn Street and not Hong Kong. His corduroy trousers were a bright pillar-box red and he wore patent evening shoes unlikely to be from anywhere but Lobb's. His Cartier watch was circa 1920, if not earlier.

'Ah, Jean-Charles,' he said, waving to the serious-looking young barman who had just come in with a tray of clean glasses. 'Can we get drinks or is it too early?'

'Certainly, Monsieur Lacey. Whisky and soda no ice?'

'Yes, please. Two.' George removed his glasses from the top of his head, dislodging a carefully-combed lock of fine but sparse ash-blonde hair, the colour, Camilla suspected, the result of professional assistance and not unvarnished nature. He smiled at her. 'I do like this place, Camilla. How on earth did you sniff it out?'

'The Michelin, of course.'

'Oh, silly old me not to remember. I doubt you pee without consulting the Michelin as to where.'

'Wouldn't dream of it.'

Someone behind them began to laugh. 'I do beg your pardon,' a man said as they turned to look. 'It's superfluous to point out that I really couldn't help overhearing.' The man, tweedy, tallish and friendly-looking with dark, grey-streaked hair, was leaning against the bar, a large suitcase at his feet, watching Jean-Charles put their two drinks on a tray. 'Could I have one of those, too?' he asked Jean-Charles, 'but with ice, if I may.'

'Certainly, monsieur,' Jean-Charles said. 'Would you like me to show you up to your room first?' he asked worriedly, 'and bring your drink up to you?'

'As you know virtually all our darkest secrets,' Georgie asked, 'would you like to join us, either now or when you've parked your things? You've no option, really, unless you prefer to run away with your drink and hide in your room. This is the only sitting-room, you see,' he pointed out pragmatically, 'so you are forced to listen to our sparkling conversation unless you prefer keeping to the purdah of your own room.'

The man laughed again and nodded his acceptance. 'He is evidently American,' George informed Camilla in a stage whisper, 'with those pearly rows of absolutely perfect teeth. How on earth do they *grow* them, do you suppose?'

'Ice in their whisky,' Camilla whispered back.

She spoke with exaggerated courtesy to the newcomer. 'Please do sit down. This is George Lacey and I'm Camilla Sayle. George is appallingly rude but I am often quite polite.'

'My name's Brook Moseley.' He lowered himself onto the low sofa and Camilla's throat squeezed painfully. There was something very like Jeremy about him. Or had she simply been spending far too much time in the too-familiar company of undemanding friends like Georgie? Tears pricked the backs of her eyes, tears that she furiously recognized sprang from nothing more uplifting than self-pity.

Bugger, she thought savagely, although managing to say, 'Back in a tick,' fairly clearly, putting her glass down on the table. She walked briskly to the cloakroom on the half-landing, not wanting to risk going into mortifying floods of tears waiting for Jean-Charles to hand over her room key.

George's speculative glance followed her up the stairs. 'Tell me, Mr Moseley,' he asked politely, 'are you a skiing enthusiast or are you, like me, a lounge lizard?'

'I think I fall somewhere in between. Fall being the operative word. I enjoy skiing and do it very badly but most of all I love the Alps. Picturesque as hell and so clean.'

'This is a really pleasant little resort. Did you just happen upon it or have you been here before?'

The American said, 'The reason I laughed so hard is that I'm a Michelin freak just like Miss? Mrs? Sayle, who is obviously as wise as she is beautiful.'

'Mrs,' George said severely and then added, 'a widow,' more helpfully. 'A *recent* widow,' he amended, 'and I'm her duenna.'

The American laughed again and shook his head, either to disclaim any improper designs on Camilla, no matter how beautiful and wise, or to deny any impropriety of whatever sort.

George warmed to him. He was an appreciative audience and it was rare, at least in George's experience, that the ordinary run of straight men were entirely at ease in his company. They chatted of this and that, the American explaining that he was a history professor on a year's sabbatical leave.

'Are you here on your own, Professor Moseley? I don't mean to be nosey but I wonder if you might join us at dinner. Meeting new people is what resorts are *for*.'

'It's very kind of you and I'd love to. I'm here alone and I can think of no pleasanter way to spend my first evening. Shall I tell Jean-Charles to lay a table for three and get you another drink while I'm at it?'

'Oh yes, please. How kind of you.'

'Do you suppose I should get one for Mrs Sayle, too, or has she gone upstairs for good?'

10

'I imagine she'll be back in a minute. She's left her things. Yes, one for her, too, there's a clever chap. Do her good to get tight.'

The American went off to find Jean-Charles in the dining-room and was back in a moment. It was before six and they had the place to themselves.

George cleared his throat and said, 'Just a quick word in your shell-like: Camilla's had a rough time, a very rough time, and if she suddenly darts out of the dining-room in the midst of dinner the best thing is to carry on as though nothing were happening. She's still prone to occasional fits of tears that she absolutely cannot control and it is, I need hardly tell you, dreadfully shaming for her. I tell you this only to avoid any possible embarrassment for either you or her.'

Moseley nodded. 'I take it her husband recently died.'

Fairly, yes. Last June.'

'Was he very much older? I mean, did she have to go through one of those long, drawn-out illnesses?'

'No, not at all. Jeremy was a young man, mid-thirties, I think.' George sipped at his drink. 'Sayle is actually her maiden name, which she's kept professionally. Like actresses,' he added helpfully. 'Her husband was called Jeremy Hamilton. Major in the Scots Guards. He'd been on active duty in Northern Ireland and was murdered by the IRA.' George shrugged. 'Or so it's assumed. They never, in that so-charming phrase, "claimed responsibility". She was a soldier's wife and these things happen. All soldiers' wives know this. But the indelible horror of it was that he damned nearly died on television.'

'Good God!' Moseley's eyes were a cold grey. 'Of course! The man who was murdered at Ascot last summer.' He shook his head. 'The camera crews got there before the cops did. Ghoulish. I could only hope that it cost Noraid a fortune in lost contributions, although maybe it had the reverse effect.'

'There's far too much support for the IRA in your country, if you'll forgive my saying so.'

'We don't all have the brains of fleas and I agree with you entirely, Mr Lacey. Please do go on.'

'The television crews were out in force, as always for Royal Ascot. Some poor bugger – I forget his name – was feeling the heat dreadfully and decided to go home after the second race, I believe; possibly the third. He was inching his car forward to leave and it sort of bumped up onto something. Felt like he'd run over a tyre, he said. He got out to investigate and found that his wheel was on top of a man's back. Lost his head completely, the driver I mean, and ran screaming and waving towards the paddock.' He took a minute sip of his drink. 'It later became clear that he had drink taken. Shouldn't have been trying to drive at all, really, but the forensic chaps were in no doubt at all that Hamilton had been killed, strangled by his own tie, well before this poor, tight, old sod managed to run over him.'

Moseley's expression was grim. 'And his wife saw it all on television. Even I remember it clearly and I didn't even know the man. Did they ever catch the murderer? I suppose that would help a bit. I mean, it would go some little way to getting rid of all the helpless anger she must feel. Vengeance.'

George shook his head sadly. 'Not yet. The IRA never actually said they did it. Not their usual style, either. They tend to favour murder at a remove; bombs and bursts from a machine-gun.' His hands trembled with anger and he put his glass down. Then he continued in a calmer tone, 'This was more Godfatherish. It all sounds so vulgar and operatic, doesn't it?'

'The police had nothing to go on? It seems so unlikely somehow. I mean, *Ascot*, for God's sake. So many people milling about, not to mention the tightest possible security, what with the Queen . . .'

'And all the men in a sort of uniform, you know,' George reminded him. 'Thousands of men, sweaty but law-abiding, dressed exactly the same. Acres of parking with people constantly coming and going about their lawful pursuits. But,' he asked with a shrug, 'who ever looks down at the spaces *between* parked cars?'

He took a healthy pull at his drink before going on. 'In any event, the forensic lot came up with bugger-all

12

of any use. The murderer was strong, almost certainly a man, unless a homicidal lady weight-lifter. He would've had Hamilton face-down on the ground. Bruising showed that the murderer knelt on Hamilton's back, knee between shoulder-blades, precisely as taught in any army's unarmed combat course. It's an efficient, silent method of killing a man, so long as you can take him by surprise.'

'Surely they must have pieced *something* together. Witnesses galore. Someone must have seen Hamilton talking or having a drink or . . .'

'Fortunately or unfortunately in this instance, race meetings are nothing like our splendid football matches, where the police are out in full force to dissuade the loyal fans from mutual mass-murder. I expect,' he said with a rueful smile, 'you've heard of that quaint English custom in America?'

Moseley shrugged. 'Some of our tribal customs are pretty quaint, too, you know. A sight-seeing tour of Miami can be fairly lively.'

'Just so,' said George with an answering smile, briefly lightening the sombre conversation. 'In the Hamilton case there's simply nothing to go on.' He sipped morosely at his drink. 'I doubt the police are still looking, quite frankly. Unsolved murder. File kept open, just in case anything at all turns up.'

He glanced quickly over Moseley's shoulder. 'God, here's Camilla coming. Say something funny!'

Without a blink, Moseley burst out laughing. 'I love vampire jokes! Do you like parrot jokes?'

Camilla looked washed-out but calm. Her skin, George noticed, had a tight, shiny look. Cold water, he thought. She tweaked his cashmere sleeve. 'What vampire joke? Georgie, I don't think you've ever told me your vampire joke.'

'There are some things, my dear, your little Georgina would balk at uttering in your overwhelmingly distinguished presence.'

'I do wish you'd put a sock in it, Georgie,' Camilla said with conspicuous lack of distinction. 'Oh good. Is that drink for me?'

13

'It is, through the kindness and generosity of Professor Moseley. He will be giving us the pleasure of his company at dinner, what is more.'

Camilla looked uncertain for a moment and it was on the tip of the American's tongue to disinvite himself, out of consideration for her feelings. She was probably disinclined to be forced into making polite conversation with a stranger.

Sensing this, George quickly headed him off by scolding Camilla. 'And do pull yourself together, old thing. You look *shiny*. Shiny women put me off my food,' he explained confidentially to his new friend. 'Shall we take the few pitiful drops left in our glasses upstairs and make ourselves beautiful for this evening? Not, of course, that I can be improved upon but you, Camilla, are a disgrace to our sex.'

When Camilla came back downstairs sometime after seven, the American had changed and was ensconced in his former chair. Georgie was once more (or still) curled up on the sofa, an old Eric Ambler thriller lying face-down beside him. Both men had fresh drinks at their elbows. Georgie was entertaining Moseley with a highly-coloured account of the vicissitudes of life spent working for a magazine. A tantalizing smell wafted out from the small, wood-panelled dining-room, making Camilla feel suddenly ravenous. There were two men and a woman she'd not seen before sitting at the bar and Camilla got a long, appreciative look from both men, which made her feel for the first time since Jeremy's death that the hour spent bathing, changing and paying some slight attention to her face and hair had not been completely wasted.

She even earned an approving smile from Georgie when she sat down, which he covered up by saying, 'About time, too,' rather crossly.

The American beamed at her like a fond elder brother. 'Drink, Mrs Sayle?' he asked.

'I think I won't, thank you,' she said, 'I'm famished and I'd prefer to get stuck into something to eat and wine with. And do call me Camilla, by the bye.'

She was feeling considerably restored by the time they finished their *consommé d'écrevisses*. They chatted amiably of this and that. Moseley confessed that although he taught modern European history at his small New England college, his guilty secret passion was for the Renaissance. He was currently taking his sabbatical year off to indulge both his passion and his obligation to a New York publisher for a book on economic developments during the early eighteenth century.

'The Renaissance is too violent for me,' Georgie said. 'All those wars, my dears, and the invention of syphilis and gunpowder. I far prefer the eighteenth century. I really feel quite at home there. Such pretty clothes, superb music and the houses.'

'The *fleas*,' Camilla said, to annoy. Then she felt herself blushing idiotically. Out of the corner of her eye, she had seen that one of the men previously at the bar was staring at her from two tables away. The woman who had been with them before had disappeared. She must have had some overwhelmingly pressing engagement, Camilla thought, for the man was extremely, almost extravagantly handsome. At the advanced age of thirty-one, Camilla felt it would be ludicrous to ask Georgie to exchange places with her. Besides, it would give him a golden opportunity for a tease of epic proportions. She was uncomfortably aware that her dark-blonde hair was too long, her burgundy silk shirt unnecessarily severe in cut and her simple twill Jaeger skirt bagged because of all the weight she had lost since last summer. She made a firm promise to herself to do something about this depressing state of affairs the first thing upon returning to London.

Brook and Georgie mercifully failed to notice her pink cheeks, having got into an animated conversation, fuelled by an admirable Dôle and a succulent *poulet de Bresse*, about the magazine business. When Brook innocently inquired if *The Epicure* were generous about expense accounts and allowances, Camilla and Georgie fell into gales of helpless laughter. *The Epicure's* editor-in-chief was notoriously mean and the only people who could afford to work for the magazine virtually subsidized it by working for risible salaries. Their expense sheets were subjected to the most minute scrutiny. They were allowed a *per diem* allowance that would be thought insulting on any other publication. 'Thrift,' said Georgie in summation, 'takes on new meaning. There are only three telephone lines in the editorial section. I rest my case.'

Camilla suddenly remembered that she hadn't had a chance to tell Georgie much about the pictures she'd managed to get that afternoon. 'We'll have to see how they turn out, of course,' she said, 'but I wouldn't be greatly surprised if one of those snaps made a fabulous cover. We're here to do a piece on the up-market ski resorts,' she explained to Brook. 'I do the snaps and Georgie does the text.'

'I'll look out for it. When will it run?'

'Next November or January, I should think. Maybe Feb.'

'You work that far in advance?'

'Well, think of it this way: we can't do snaps of ski resorts in May or October and Georgie can't write up the hotels and restaurants and nightclubs and Beautiful People because they're all either closed or elsewhere. Our actual lead time is only three months.'

Brook laughed. 'Dumb question. Sorry.'

'Give me the films you've done, Camilla, and I'll trundle off to the PTT in the morning and mail them in with our expense chitties. We bung all our bits in the post,' George explained to Brook, 'pretty frequently. If, God forbid, we should lose our expense sheets, we'd *never* get reimbursed.' He pushed aside the scant remains of his *soufflé au Grand Marnier*. 'I wonder if the expense account would be stretched beyond endurance if I were to order the tiniest thimbleful of Calvados.'

'Here, George, you could get fired for such an extravagance. I couldn't bear to have that on my conscience. Let me do it. Same for you, Camilla?'

Camilla shook her head sleepily and stubbed out her cigarette. 'I'm caving in. Too much today, I think.' She yawned. 'Sorry, chaps. Not even any coffee.' She stood up, feeling pleasantly weary all over. 'No, please don't stand up. Shall we dine again tomorrow night? Do say yes, Brook. It's our last night here.'

'I'm sorry you're leaving so soon and I'd love to join you for dinner tomorrow. Good night. I see there's no need to say sleep well.'

Camilla nodded with an apologetic smile and went off to get her key. She had forgotten about her new admirer, who looked thoughtfully after her as she passed his table.

'Nice girl,' Brook said after he'd ordered their coffee and Calvados. 'It all seems so unfair when some really ghastly thing happens to a thoroughly decent person.' George nodded agreement without speaking. 'I must say, it shows almost superhuman strength or commonsense or plain spunk, if you'll forgive an Americanism, to go right on working.'

'Best thing for her,' George said. 'She started working for *The Epicure* several years ago, a year or so before she was married. I've only been working for the rag for the last few months so I can't claim to know all that much about her and I never knew Jeremy at all. When she was very young, she'd been a staff photographer for one of the American women's magazines, I forget which, and she really learned the trade in New York. A bit of location work but mostly studio stuff. How to tart up your hubby's den and put some oomph into your sex-life with a few simple exercises as illustrated above. You know the sort of thing.'

Brook grinned and shook his head. 'Being divorced man and boy these many years I seldom get a crack at anything more instructive about dens or exercises than *The Economist*. Skimpy on oomph and sex. I take it she's good.'

'Oh absolutely,' George said. 'She'll never be an Avedon or a Beaton or a Parkinson. I mean, I don't fancy there's much likelihood of her having an exhibition at the Tate, or anything like that, but she's terrifically competent as an all-rounder. Anything from flower arrangements to a bunch of camels having a zizz in the shadow of the Pyramids. She's got a good eye for the unexpected and the incongruous.'

17

'A sense of the ridiculous.'

George laughed. 'Got it in one. The very keystone of life, isn't it?' He made a put-upon face. 'I don't suppose you could be cajoled into a mini-pub-crawl, could you? On expenses, of course, with you standing in for Camilla.' He sighed and looked at his watch, squaring his shoulders. 'To work. It's almost ten. The great and the good will be trooping the colour at Hortense's.'

'Would we have to stay long?' Brook asked guardedly.

George waved a dismissive hand. 'Just long enough to bribe the bartender to tell me who's there, who's been there during the season and who might reasonably be expected. Camilla's already softened him up by taking some snaps and complimenting him on his profile. One drink's worth, I promise.'

'Anything for a friend, of course, but we won't have to dance will we? I'm a joke on the dance-floor. Strong men collapse in hysterics.'

'Never mind, duckie,' Georgie said with a wink, 'I'll let you lead.' He poured the last of his Calvados into the last of his coffee and drained the demi-tasse at a gulp. Then he sat wearily back in his chair and shut his eyes. 'God knows it's not easy for an old queen to admit but I *must* be getting even older than I thought. What I'd really *like* to do is to crawl into my bed with a hot-water bottle and Eric Ambler.'

'It's not your age; it's the altitude,' Brook said firmly.

Georgie hauled himself to his feet and blinked. 'I cannot *think* how your ex-wife ever let you go,' he said with deep feeling, as they left the dining-room. His eyes fell on Camilla's camera-bag on the floor by the fireplace. 'I'll just run that stupid girl's outrageously expensive equipment up to my room. Back in a tick.'

2

There was a little dish beside the bed, fashioned for the use of a seventeenth-century Chinese poet or artist as a paint-pot. Now it held cocaine and from time to time she would take a bit on her tongue and bend over him again. He briefly considered begging for mercy and his fingers were entwined in her hair, flexing to pull her head away with whatever strength remained in the rest of his body, but his subconscious must have cancelled the order and he came with such force that he could easily have turned himself inside out. Perhaps he had.

When he was finally able to speak, all he could manage was, 'God almighty'. Even that came out in a croak. He eventually summoned enough strength to reach across her and take a long pull at her drink, now watery with melted ice. His hands shook slightly as he fumbled for cigarettes and matches. He waited for his heart to start up again before attempting to strike the match and switch on the pink-shaded bedside lamp.

Her amused gaze was on him, the kindly-looking, myopic brown eyes holding his own as she took the cigarette from his nerveless fingers and puffed at it in the comically tentative way she had, as though an early experiment with smoking had turned out to be a great disappointment. Freckles dappled her face and body, her nipples so pale in the rosy light as to be only a faint discoloration at the tips of her breasts. Her head and pubis were adorned with fawn-coloured hair and she had the disposition of a rattlesnake.

'Well,' she said with finality.

He fumbled for the bed's control-box and the electric motor whirred softly, angling their heads a foot or so above the horizontal. Despite the lamp's reflection on the plate-glass window, they could see a few lights in

Val Sainte-Anne still sparkling below in the thin, frosty air. He remained silent as he finished the cigarette.

'I take it that you have no complaints,' she said softly. There was an implied question in her words and he wondered, with a slight spasm of irritation, how it had come to pass that American women almost invariably demanded a post-coital review once the curtain came down on their performances.

'That's right,' he agreed amiably, knowing perfectly well that she wanted, demanded, more than a laconic acknowledgement of her expertise. Skipping a rave notice would infuriate her but he didn't much care.

'I think I'll get a whisky,' he continued in the same companionable tone, as though they were old friends meeting in a pub after work. 'What shall I bring you?' He could have simply brought her a whisky or, better still, opened a celebratory bottle of the peach-flavoured champagne that took up an entire shelf in the huge refrigerator of the rented chalet. If it were any other woman, he would have done just that. With Nedda, however, it was an elementary precaution to keep one's distance, even down to such fine points as pretending not to know, or to have forgotten, her tastes, both preferences and strong dislikes, in drink as in copulation.

Her kindly brown eyes narrowed slightly as she tried to focus sufficiently to read his expression. 'Well?' she said again, this time as a definite, unignorable question.

He smiled vaguely and arched his eyebrows in interrogation to show his complete willingness to answer any question she might put. He knew this would annoy her and it did.

'How did you like it?' she demanded querulously.

He shrugged. 'It – *you* are incredible.' That was Delphic enough to keep her off-balance, he thought, recognizing in himself a childish determination to tease. 'What shall I bring you?' he repeated, this time brushing her palm with his lips.

She snatched her hand away and waved him off irritably. 'I don't care. Anything. Whatever you're having.' It was on the tip of her tongue to add something waspish but she held back. "Incredible" was acceptable as an adjective, if only borderline.

He padded off naked to fetch their drinks and she twitched the fat eiderdown up to cover herself. She was feeling rather flat and glanced at the cocaine in the little Chinese bowl. Perhaps later, when they had finished with the business that remained to be discussed.

Ruffo always had the same effect on her, the same effect in subtly differing shades. It was basically a matter of not being in complete control of him and their complex relationship, which was not at all the same thing as being out of control. Even as he spurted into her cocaine-numbed mouth and she knew he was damned near dying from pleasure, she was uncomfortably aware that she didn't exercise the total mastery over him that she had always sought. She had him in the palm of her hand on a financial level, undeniably, which was something, but he continued to elude her in small ways.

The business side of their relationship was almost the most satisfying part of it. At least he had to report to her. A terse phone call to say that the money was being moved, that the cocaine shipment had arrived, that he would await further instructions. She knew she ought to be grateful that she didn't have to do his thinking for him, as she did with so many of the others, but somehow she felt cheated. Flat. Her thoughts had come around in a complete circle and she eyed the little heap of snow again.

She looked at him expectantly when he came back with their drinks. Sure enough, her scotch was loaded with ice and his contained none. 'Why do you have to be so fucking English?' she demanded, not for the first time.

He laughed as though he thought she had made a joke and pushed the button that elevated the top of the bed further before settling himself in beside her.

'I mean it, Ruffo,' she insisted furiously. 'Why the fuck do you have to behave like a goddamned stage Brit? A stupid dago Henry Higgins.' She scooped two cubes of ice out of her own drink and plopped them into his, splashing

21

scotch onto the eiderdown. Ruffo as quickly fished the ice out of his glass and deposited it in the Chinese bowl, his fingers dripping lavishly onto its contents.

'Asshole!' she screamed. 'That's *pure*! That's the best blow on earth!' The cocaine visibly metamorphosed into an unappetising greyish paste under the catalysts of water and alcohol. She fished the ice out and hurled it across the room but the damage was done. Her rage flared up again. 'You stupid childish son-of-a-bitch!'

He looked at her calmly, feeling a faint tug of pity for her. There was a hint of softness in her jawline that hadn't been there the last time he had seen her. Actually, it wasn't unattractive. There was a certain vulnerability about her pale body, perhaps due to the incongruity of ferocious sensuality camouflaged by the dusting of Bambi-like freckles. But her face was improved by this new touch of softness, which accorded well with the deceptively benign, cow-like brown eyes. He knew that she must hate it when she studied her profile in the mirror. She was a few years older than he and would soon be looking forty in the eye. She would be afraid of that first hint of age, of incipient sag, of weak flesh bowing to the inexorable force of gravity. There were still things that lay beyond her power of control and manipulation and she was not one to give in to them gracefully.

Her eyes met his and flinched away from the sympathy she saw there. She despised any form of pity and any form of weakness capable of commanding it. She chose to believe that he occasionally felt sorry for her because of her strength and her flashes of honest Celtic temper, which he parried with his imperturbable, English-aping *sang-froid* and a lingering hint of patrician distaste for public displays of emotion. Sometimes she hated him. Quite often, in fact. She had frequent recourse to promising herself that one fine day she would bring him to his knees. He was a slippery bastard. For the moment, however, she needed Ruffo in a great variety of ways.

'Do you feel up to a little business?' she asked.

'Shoot,' he said, grinning.

'Oh for God's sake, Ruffo.' She sighed and gazed at him reproachfully.

'Sorry.' He grinned again, unrepentant. He kept forgetting that she had absolutely no sense of humour. 'It all went fine this afternoon. I told you that. There's nothing Jacki doesn't know about these mountains. And he collected a damned good bunch of chaps . . .'

'Bunch of chaps,' she mimicked, annoyed again.

'Top-hole!' he continued. 'I met them where we'd agreed and came down on a run that marches parallel with the Paternoster a good bit of the way and *despite* their carrying God knows how many kilos on their backs and *despite* your bloody guns,' he punctuated each 'despite' with a playful pat on her shoulder to add to her evident irritation, 'they made excellent time. Without the aforementioned bloody guns and a ton of ammunition in their rucksacks, it'll be a doddle.'

'So Alexis did his part okay, too. I mean, he was on time at the meet and everything.' Alexis sometimes displayed a cavalier attitude towards punctuality which infuriated her. It could be dangerous, too, besides being inexcusable in this sort of operation.

'Bang on time. Of course, he's worked with Jacki before and he damned well knows that timing is everything when you're humping stuff across the frontier on skis. In any event,' he said, glancing at his watch, 'your sample dozen guns and matching ammo should be arriving at the Gare de Lyon about now. The TGV is always on time. My end of things is done and it's up to your boys to deliver the payload across the Channel.'

He stretched and yawned. 'I must say I enjoyed the whole business. God, what a beautiful afternoon it was!' He patted her shoulder again, as though she were one of his damned horses, Nedda thought. 'You should take up skiing, my dear. Marvellous exercise and it's never too late to . . .'

'And you're reasonably sure it will work as smoothly when we set it up seriously? I mean, on a scheduled basis and not just a trial run.'

'Even easier, I should think, without all the hardware complicating the proceedings.'

Ruffo normally never touched the arms side of things. That was strictly between Alexis and Nedda or whatever other IRA *capo* was handling the purchasing, probably that prize lunatic Gillon. He didn't understand guns or explosives, wasn't interested, didn't need to know about it and didn't want to know. He had only consented to set up this thing because Nedda's chums were dead keen for these new machine-pistols, or whatever the hell they were, to be tried out before Alexis found another buyer for the rest. Besides, Ruffo had wanted to test Jacki's route for future cocaine-runs. He was a devotee of the principle of having as many baskets as possible for one's eggs. If a mule got caught, if a route was blocked, if a pipeline clogged, one could switch immediately to an alternative. That way, there was no risk of merchandise building up at any one staging-point. It was simply a matter of common-sense, a commodity in remarkably short supply amongst Nedda's colleagues, judging from all available evidence and newspaper accounts of arms caches being found littering the British Isles. IRA eyes swam when they spoke of "The Cause" and they were immensely keen on blowing things up, including themselves, but their grasp of logistics in any form was derisory.

'You're absolutely sure about Jacki? I mean, you've never used him before and . . .'

He snorted and almost did the nose trick with his mouthful of scotch. 'My dear Nedda, Jacki was probably smuggling before he could walk. His father's a smuggler; his grandfather was a smuggler; his remotest ancestors were smugglers. They very likely smuggled Hannibal *and* his elephants across the flaming Alps! He's from the Val d'Aosta and they are to smuggling what the Irish are to getting pissed as newts.'

She didn't look entirely pleased at the analogy. 'All Gillon's idea. I don't trust mercenaries,' she said sulkily.

He burst out laughing again and she scowled furiously. 'And you're in bed with *me*? You trust Alexis enough to pop between the sheets with him whenever given the chance, too.'

'Why must you always be so goddamn childish, Ruffo? What's sex got to do with anything? What I'm talking about is Jacki and his group.' She made a disgusted face. 'They're completely lacking in political commitment.'

Exercising patience to the fullest, he contented himself with a gentle reminder. 'Alexis is in it for the money, Nedda. You know that. You also know that I'm in it because you've left me with no choice. You made me an offer I couldn't refuse. Neither of us has ever pretended to be anything but a mercenary or a reluctant subject of blackmail but we haven't let you down yet or even tried to cheat you. Admit.'

'But a complete outsider . . .'

'Jacki's a businessman, too. Your "politically committed" playmates,' he added, unable to keep a note of contempt from creeping into his voice, 'are so committed that they make stupid mistakes instead of watching what they're doing. Thank God you've got what system there is compartmented off, otherwise the whole committed bunch of you would have been rolled up years ago.'

He mentally braced himself for a storm but none came.

'You don't trust either Alexis or me to handle paying the staff so you, my dear Nedda, had to settle up with Jacki. You can't have it both ways.' He enjoyed needling her and went on before she could interrupt him. 'To be on the safe side, we can't be seen together very much. Not enough to appear connected in any way. You know that. You made the rule. And,' he reminded her, 'you chose the hotel you're staying in. But as for tomorrow, I'd better find out who exactly was behind the camera up there this afternoon.'

'But you did find out. She's here with that faggot doing some sort of fashion layout or something for some dumb English magazine. What the hell else can there be to find out? She's no cop, for God's sake. Even cops look smarter than she does. Even stupid *English* cops.' She calmed down a little. 'Let me know tomorrow night.'

25

She collected her clothes and stormed out of the bedroom without turning out the other light or a backward glance. By the time the front door of the chalet slammed behind her, Ruffo was half asleep. He smiled in the dim light; she had forgotten to take her snow.

3

'God I'm sore!'

Georgie leered. '*Must* you be so public about it, darling? Someone could hear, you know, and draw entirely the wrong conclusion.'

Camilla decided that the wisest course was to ignore him completely, although she had decided too late to avoid making a horrible face at him. 'I must admit, my angel, to a slight hangover,' Georgie continued irrepressibly, 'and it is definitely not improved by your pulling hideous faces. It makes you quite plain, which is depressing and unnecessary.'

'I'll ask for more coffee.' She waved the empty pot and the waiter vanished into the kitchen for more.

'Do that. Ah, here's young Brook. Good morning.'

Brook sighed deeply and dragged a chair to their table. 'Did I hear you say coffee, Camilla? I had some sent up but then I fell asleep again and when I woke up it was stone cold.' He glared at George. 'Your idea of a nightcap isn't anything like what we consider to be a decent, God-fearing nightcap in Amherst, Mass.'

'Well,' Georgie shrugged philosophically, 'Hortense's is famous for its cocktails. I couldn't very well write anything about brandy-and-soda that would transfix our esteemed readers. Do be reasonable, Brook.'

'You two ravers certainly *have* been through the wars. Georgie, you're babbling and poor Brook is moribund,' Camilla said with a touch of asperity. 'I believe my room is beside yours, Brook. I hope I didn't wake you up crashing about this morning.'

'No no no. I was awake when you left your room. Shaving,' he explained, touching a small cut on his chin. 'I'm afraid I jumped when you dropped your key.'

Camilla said, 'poor you' automatically and then looked

perplexed. 'I didn't drop my key.'

'Well, then, someone else did in the passage outside our doors. It doesn't matter. It's only a small cut and my hand wasn't what you'd call rock-steady. My life isn't in any danger from the amount of blood I lost.'

Camilla stood up. 'I can't possibly drink any more coffee without getting the shakes myself. I'll go up and get my things.'

She was back in no time, her face ashen. 'Georgie,' she whispered, 'someone's been in my room!'

Georgie leapt to his feet, almost upsetting the table. 'What's missing?'

'My camera-bag is gone! I didn't look to see if . . .'

Georgie slumped back into his chair, looking considerably annoyed. 'For God's sake, Camilla, pull yourself together. You've given me a frightful turn. You left everything in the sitting-room when you went up to change last evening and I dragged your bits and pieces up to my own room. Very careless of you.'

Camilla, still shaken, sat down as well. 'Perhaps I will have some more coffee. Brook, please pour me out some. My hands are shaking.' She laughed nervously. 'Sorry to be such an ass but my door was ajar when I went up and then when I saw that my camera-bag wasn't there . . .'

'Oh, stop your talk, woman,' Georgie cut in. 'Sorry I barked at you, old dear, but I'm in no fit condition for alarums and excursions this morning. The chambermaid must have been . . .'

'She wasn't though. The door was ajar and there was no one there and my bed hadn't been made and then I didn't see my things and . . .'

Brook patted her hand. 'It's okay, Camilla. Calm down. The maid probably forgot soap or something. She could've gone to get some fresh towels.' He continued to hold her hand. 'Anyway, your stuff's in George's room so that's okay.'

'Actually,' said Georgie, 'it's not. I brought the bag down with me so I wouldn't have to negotiate those damned stairs again.' He looked contrite. 'My fault, really. I should've

28

told you when you said you were popping upstairs to get it. Forgot I had it with me. Apologies all round.' He prodded at a piece of croissant on his plate. 'Frogs are all right in their own way but their marmalade is a national disgrace.' He gazed moodily out the window. 'All this wretched snow unhinges the mind. Very boring stuff, snow.'

It didn't take him very long to do his morning chores. First, he went upstairs to find the chambermaid, an apple-cheeked girl who proved to be both anxious to co-operate and embarrassingly effusive in her thanks for the modest hundred-franc note George gave her. Humming a few bars of *The Barber of Seville* aloud, he went to his room to scribble a brief note and then crunched along the snowy road to the village *papeterie*, buying a padded envelope and *Le Figaro*.

He had been warned that the resort would begin to fill up today, being the Friday before Palm Sunday, as people began to arrive for the Easter holiday. There was only a small queue at the PTT, however, exclusively composed of village people posting letters and clutching pension books. He had a weakness for French post offices. He liked the way everyone arriving broadcast a general '*Bonjour, Messieurs, -dames*' without first having a crafty look round to see if there might be anyone there they actually knew. The English would shrivel in mortification at such comprehensive politeness. He eavesdropped as he addressed the envelope and popped in Camilla's films, their expense chits and his single sheet of notes: it would appear that the Mayor's daughter found herself in an interesting condition.

What with one thing and another, George thought with considerable satisfaction, his assignment was among the simplest and most congenial to his own tastes he'd ever had.

His little chores done, he addressed himself to the principal business of the day and carefully negotiated a slippery patch to Val Sainte-Anne's most esteemed restaurant, *Le Dauphin*. He was a few minutes early for his appointment with the chef/owner, Antoine Maure, but the great man was sitting peacefully in his empty dining-room with a newspaper.

His kitchen was a peaceful scene, the strong Alpine sunlight gleaming on stainless steel counters and an army of copper pans hanging from their overhead racks. A large pot simmered gently on the immense stove, surrounded by its own delicious-smelling nimbus. M. Maure was reducing something and George's mouth watered, despite having finished his breakfast only an hour or so earlier. His stomach rumbled perversely. M. Maure burst out laughing and beamed upon George in evident approval.

'It is,' he announced, 'the hour of the *apéritif*, Monsieur Lassie. May I offer you a Pernod?'

George grinned. 'With pleasure. It is impossible to be in France without constantly longing for something to eat or drink, I find.'

'Ah, monsieur, so you are a francophile? So many of your compatriots are quite the opposite.'

'It is, I assure you, dear sir, based on nothing but bile. We English cross the Channel and our souls curdle with jealousy.'

M. Maure laughed appreciatively and was about to say more on this interesting topic when he heard a discreet tapping at what George assumed to be the back door. He excused himself and was back in a moment, leading in a young man who looked somehow familiar. George realized that the newcomer was the younger of the two men he had briefly glimpsed dining at the hotel last night.

The *patron* busied himself producing glasses, Pernod and a pottery jug into which he put several cubes of ice and cold water from the tap. The three men sat down at a large square table – this would be where the staff ate in relative calm before the evening stampede – as Maure poured out the drinks. 'I excuse myself, Monseigneur,' he apologized before lifting his glass, 'I have forgotten to present Monsieur Lassie, who is here to interview me for an English magazine. Prince Cavallesi di Monteavesa.'

The prince was one of the handsomest men George had ever seen, with features of almost cold, classical purity and a profile that would send any sculptor stampeding off to find the best block of Carrara marble available. He had thick, curling auburn hair, greenish eyes and the body of an athlete.

The prince pronounced himself enchanted to meet George and at once turned a formidable blast of charm on the chef, whom he addressed as "Maestro". M. Maure blossomed and pottered about producing *amuse-gueules* to accompany their drinks.

'M. Lassie, may I, without impertinence, express my admiration for your lovely companion at dinner last night? You must insist, Maestro, that M. Lassie present you to the exquisite lady he was fortunate enough to dine with at the hotel.' He popped a canapé into his mouth. 'Perfection,' he declared.

There was no mistaking the prince's curiosity about Camilla. And why not? George thought. She was too young to mourn Jeremy much longer. The proprieties had certainly been satisfied by now. 'My esteemed colleague from the magazine. She does the photographs. Miss Sayle,' he added helpfully.

George put up only token resistance when the chef pressed him to stay and have "a simple lunch", composed exclusively of leftovers and likely to be fit only for the pigs and most certainly unworthy of such distinguished connoisseurs of food and wine. George, who would have very much enjoyed becoming a connoisseur had he been able to afford the learning process, avidly looked forward to sampling a typical French pig's diet.

Monteavesa politely quizzed George about his proposed article on Val Sainte-Anne, laughed over Hortense's photogenic cocktails and modestly disclaimed any great expertise in skiing, pleading lack of both time and any inclination towards violent exercise. They chatted amicably in the manner of people seated together on airplanes as M. Maure prepared, put before them and tucked into one of the best meals George had ever had in his life.

Everything was simple and incredibly good: an omelette with fresh chervil, followed by trout, followed by venison with *cèpes*, followed by a small salad, followed by cheese, followed by profuse apologies that there hadn't been sufficient time to prepare a fitting dessert. George knew that there was no point in laying himself open to ridicule by attempting to rise from his chair and accepted a second cup of coffee to accompany his *digestif*. He was piously grateful to Divine Providence that he had completed his small errands before coming, thus allowing what was left of the afternoon to be spent on his bed.

'Maestro,' said the prince, belching with oriental punctilio, 'you have surpassed yourself. I haven't eaten so well since my last visit.'

M. Maure rolled up his eyes. 'Please, Monseigneur, do not tease an old man. But I have forgotten to ask how it goes with your vineyard?'

'Much better, thank you. I shall send you a case, dear Maestro, and I would be delighted, no, *honoured*, if you would be good enough to try it and tell me, absolutely frankly, what you think of it.'

He rose to his feet. George, too, managed somehow to stand upright. They were effusive in their thanks and left.

George was thinking sleepily about the delights of his solitary bed as they squeaked down the road.

'Do you,' the prince asked, 'by any chance have a business-card about your person? I've got none with me. I shall be in London soon and I should be delighted if you might be free to dine some evening.'

Rummaging in the pocket of his Puffa, George fished out a card. The prince read it and laughed. 'I *thought* "Lassie" sounded unlikely. Winsome. I ought to have guessed it was Lacey. Your offices are in Hanover Square. That's handy.' He looked up. 'This is my turning. Well,' he said, putting his hand out, 'it has been an unexpectedly delightful day. I do hope we shall meet again soon, Mr Lacey. Good bye.'

Alexis tugged irritably at his moustache as he talked. 'Bloody woman! She's always meddling in our end of things. Sometimes I'd very much like to kill her.' He laughed and said, 'Now I think of it, I can't imagine why we haven't.'

'The goose that laid the golden egg? Come on, Alexis. You'd starve or perish from boredom. I have far more reason to kill her than you have and I'm too chicken to have a go. That's a big organization.'

Alexis made a growling noise in his throat. 'I won't starve, Ruffo, and you'd have a go, just as I would, except we both know perfectly well that Gillon the Villain would take an extremely dim view and our pleasure in being Nedda-free would be nothing if not short-lived.'

He splashed a modest amount of whisky into his glass and added ice, glaring at Ruffo with his one good eye. 'She's getting worse, in case you haven't noticed. Can't you keep her really charming and excellent nose out of the coke? She's so unpredictable nowadays and those wild shifts of mood make the simplest conversation tricky as all hell. I don't know.' He paused. 'I do wish she wouldn't meddle,' he repeated irritably. 'Why did she have to be here at all? It's not as though Jacki didn't know his business, for God's sake.'

'My dear old friend, you know perfectly well that this trial run provided her with a perfect excuse to see you.' Ruffo chuckled and said, 'Then she found she had to make do with me instead. She wasn't best pleased.'

Alexis threw his head back, seeking enlightenment from the dusty rafters. 'Dear God, Ruffo! You still can't pass up a chance to pop into bed with her, even after all these years.'

'Well,' Ruffo countered, somewhat stung, ' I don't see you pitching her out of your bed either.'

4

Willie Hibbert, rumpled and harassed-looking as always, bent over the lightbox. 'You've got some really good stuff here, Sayle. Well done. Nice shot, this one. Not too athletic; nothing too strenuous. Bugger makes it all look easy.'

Camilla was surprised and flattered. Willie didn't normally scatter rosepetals upon his staff's submissively bowed heads. 'Oh, Willie, do you really think it will make a nice . . .'

Willie had already lost interest in her. 'Quentin,' he said to the art director, 'have a look at this. Unless we get something better, I think this shot might make a good cover. What do you think?'

'Colours are good. I'll do a dummy if you like, Willie. Heaps of time to decide. How many pages did you have in mind for the piece?'

'Eight, I should imagine; four full spreads. No jump pages if poss. Give Lacey an exact line count. Lots of white space to go around that menu he got from the restaurant. Just reading his copy gives me indigestion. Make it chichi as hell. Precious, even. With every sodding royal on earth flocking there like a bunch of coronetted lemmings it's the in place.' He rolled his eyes up and communed silently with the great editor in the sky, which he always did in moments of stress. Willie disapproved of sports, both blood- and non-blood, that weren't hedged round with tradition and plenty of photogenic trappings.

'Let us hope the bleeding place won't have gone *out* of fashion before the piece runs,' he grumbled. His most strenuous disapproval was reserved for anything subject to the arcane laws of fashion; *The Epicure* should maintain a lofty position far above such mundane and ephemeral considerations. *Vogue* was anathema to him, a point of view not improved by the fact that Condé Nast Publications were *The Epicure*'s landlords and Vogue House the address.

Camilla and George wisely kept silent. For a travel piece, their expenses had been remarkably low. After Willie had left, James Quentin said sympathetically, 'He really hates travel pieces, ladies, which means that this one is particularly good if he's going for eight pages. And you're fully aware that he loathes anything smacking of physical exercise.' He shooed them out of his office.

Walking to Oxford Street to catch the number 10 bus, Camilla's sunny mood began to dissipate in the cold, grey London air. She had forgotten to bring something to read and stared sightlessly out the window as the bus inched along in heavy traffic. She leapt off at Queen's Gate and walked through Kensington Gardens, somewhat cheered by the carpet of buttery daffodils but, taking to the pavement again at the High Street, the throng of shoving pedestrians depressed her all over again. She trudged up and down the aisles of Marks and Spencer to restock her empty fridge and went back to her flat to finish unpacking.

It was Tuesday and they had arrived back in London the previous evening, going straight from Heathrow to Hanover Square to drop off Camilla's last rolls of film and George's fat manila envelope, bulging with his final collection of notes, menus, postcards and expense sheets.

They agreed that their two days at Courchevel had been a bit of a letdown after their first stop; it lacked Val Sainte-Anne's atmosphere of *luxe, calme et volupté*. They had also missed the cheerful presence of Brook Moseley and Camilla had found herself abandoning the ski-slopes after only a few runs, bored without his funnily inexpert but game company. At least he had faithfully promised to look them up when he was next in London. He had been nagged into promising to come soon.

She looked around her flat with distaste, going from room to room putting things away. It all looked so dingy and she lacked the energy to remedy the situation. She felt bad-tempered and fretful, wishing she had somewhere else to go. She had come to dislike the place and thought she really must get around to doing something about it, either plunge into a complete overhaul or sell. Everything looked faded and unkempt, not slovenly so much as neglected. Her mother had sensibly suggested letting it for a year, which would give her time to decide one way or another, but Camilla lacked the stamina to look for somewhere else to live. Then there was the daunting prospect of clearing out cupboards and drawers to make room for her putative tenant's things. She knew she could get a whacking great sum should she decide to rent but she already had more money than she needed, an enviable situation to be in but one which never ceased to surprise her. Jeremy had always been so improvident, splashing money about with wild abandon.

Flopping into a chair, she sifted listlessly through the post that had accumulated in her absence. To add to everything else, or, more accurately, subtract from the small but precious feeling of contentment she had built up over her working holiday, there was nothing but a bank statement, junk mail and a reminder postcard from her gynaecologist that she was overdue for a check-up.

She resisted a strong temptation to feel sorry for herself. The time for that was past and she simply had to begin to look forward, to plan for, at least, the immediate future. Her mother was returning from Kenya on Friday. Camilla brightened as she thought about that. She would meet her mother at Heathrow and go down to Bath with her. The long Easter weekend would give them a chance to catch up on each other's news and she knew her mother would be glad of her company.

The phone rang and Camilla jumped to pick it up before her answering machine cut in. 'I thought you might be feeling sniffy,' Georgie said.

'I was, a bit. And fairly angry with myself on top of it all.' She laughed, happy that he had rung her. 'Are you psychic?'

'No, bored. I had thought of having a look round the bars but I don't even feel like that, although goodness only knows why. Old age, I imagine. Loins all ungirded.' He sighed.

'Look, I've just Marxed and I've got a fair assortment of bits and pieces. If you're really bored and not simply being kind and fussing about my being on my own, would you like to come round to me for some modest nosh?'

'Tcha,' he said in disapproval. 'I do wish you'd learn to cook, Camilla. You are an idle slut. As to your kind offer I think I won't, thanks. I really must get some shirts ironed and catch up on *The Archers.*'

He paused and Camilla guessed that he had really rung her up to ask her a favour. 'I was wondering,' he began diffidently, 'if you might meet me at the office tomorrow, late morningish.'

'Oh Georgie, why? You know I've got masses of boring little chores to do before the weekend. I've got to bung some clothes in to be cleaned and . . .'

'I know, darling,' he interjected before she could enumerate the boring chores, 'but I'm afraid I've made something of a muddle over my notes for our skiing piece. I'm unable to say with any degree of conviction which caption should go beneath which snap.'

'Can't it wait till next week? I'll be in on Wednesday morning.'

'By next week you'll have forgotten, too. Do say yes, darling,' he cajoled. 'Willie can get so *unreasonable* if one has firmly captioned a snap of the Wimpy Bar at St Pancras as being the Palace at St Moritz. If you would be absolutely angelic and help poor old me, you will be given a delicious luncheon. If you are a wicked girl and refuse, an evil fairy, myself for instance, will cast a spell on you and your lovely golden hair will go black at the roots.'

Camilla laughed. 'All right, you blackmailer!'

She arrived at the office in a thoroughly bloody-minded state.

Sometimes, when these fits of irritability seized her, she felt obscurely that it was all somehow Jeremy's fault. He had been a charmer, entertaining company and such a superb lover. Now he was gone. She frequently woke up at ridiculous, spooky hours of the night in the middle of ferociously sexual dreams that refused to be exorcized by a half-hour's concentrated reading of some uncompromisingly cerebral work on history or politics. Just thinking about Jeremy made her ache painfully. And how often, when he was alive, had she hated him. How often, when he entered her, had she wanted to be free of his dominion over her, her craving for his body despite her certainty that another woman had been shuddering beneath him just hours before.

'Okay,' she fumed, stripping off her old mac as she strode into the office, 'show me the muddle. Let's get it sorted out and then I can paddle back home.'

Georgie calmly peered at her over his half-spectacles. 'Oh, it's you.'

She gave her streaming umbrella a violent shake. 'You were perhaps expecting the Prime Minister?'

'Your stately ironies are as nothing compared to the gratitude I feel towards you, dearest wet person.' He rolled a chair up for her next to his own in front of the lightbox. 'D'you happen to recall *precisely* where it was you took this little series of snaps?'

'Course I do. That was at Val Sainte-Anne, late afternoon our first day there. That little group were with an instructor or guide on the Paternoster Run, near where it begins up by the glacier. *Precisely*. You're doing your caption copy already?' She sat down grudgingly. 'It's the toughest *piste* they've got out there. I was too chicken to take it on; I was on an easier one that marches parallel to it for the first bit.'

Her filthy temper evaporated as she thought of that beautiful afternoon. 'It *is* a hell of a shot, isn't it? Though it's me who says it and shouldn't. Purest luck, actually, but don't tell Willie that.'

'Wouldn't dream of it.' He leant over and pecked her on the cheek. 'Credit where credit is due, darling.'

Camilla was pleased. 'Why are you working so hard? Is Willie up to something?'

Georgie shrugged vaguely. 'I don't know, my angel. You know how they all are in this place. Quite mad,' he said, tapping his forehead, and then turned to a few other transparencies for verification of his notes. 'That's the lot, then. Can't think how I got my knickers in such a terrible twist over this bunch. Couldn't remember which resort it was. Not that it matters all that much, I suppose. One mountain-top looking rather like any other. Silly of me to fuss.'

'Hungover, I expect,' Camilla suggested unsympathetically. 'You might have described them over the phone, you know.'

'Sorry, old thing, but I had to make absolutely sure. You sound bitchy and hungry. C'mon,' Georgie said, 'scramble back into your soggies and I'll buy you some decent grub.'

'Can we make it dinner tomorrow instead? That is, if you're at a loose end and not seeing to your loins,' Camilla suggested. 'I really must clear the decks before I meet my mother at Heathrow on Friday. I've only got today and tomorrow.'

'Course, darling, and bless you for coming in. I'll cook us something delicious for dinner.' He gave her an owlish look and patted her damp hair. 'You look terrible.'

She clenched her teeth and said, 'I look terrible because I came within a hair's breadth of having to swim all the way here. Now I'm swimming back. *Your* lovely golden hair, as we're on the subject, is going grey at the roots.' She grinned evilly at him. 'Shall I come to you at around half-past seven?'

'Yes, do. Bye for now and thanks again.'

Having checked her own desk to see if there were any messages, she glanced back at George before leaving. He was bent over a transparency with a large magnifying-glass in his hand, checking it against the numbered contact-sheet. He didn't look up as she left.

George switched off the lightbox and rubbed his eyes. He had been sorting carefully through every photograph Camilla had taken and now he had a splitting headache.

Dots danced before his eyes as he gazed at the restful rain sheeting down the window. A telephone rang unanswered in a nearby room and finally stopped.

The offices were almost completely silent and he realized that everyone was still out to lunch. He rummaged in his jacket, fished out his diary and found a telephone number under S marked 'solicitor: conveyancing'. He picked up the phone and slowly punched the number, spoke briefly and rang off. The short conversation had had nothing to do with the buying or selling of property.

He was hungry. It was almost half-past two and he heard the lift doors open, followed by a woman's voice asking for messages at the reception desk. The pub crowds would be thinning out around now. He lit a cigarette and was thinking unenthusiastically about a pint and a Scotch egg at the local when the phone rang. It was Camilla.

'Georgie!' She was crying. 'Thank God you're there!'

'What is it, darling?'

'My flat's been broken into. Everything's strewn all over the place and . . .' She began to sob.

'Camilla, listen to me. I'll get a taxi and come to you straight away. Have you rung 999?'

She took a deep breath, evidently forcing herself to be calm. 'Yes. They said they'd be here as quickly as . . . Oh, Georgie, *please* come, please,' she wailed. 'I'm so frightened!'

'Shhh, darling. All right. I'll be with you soon. Now, Camilla, do as I say. You mustn't touch anything at all until the police arrive. Do you understand?'

'Yes. Yes I do. I won't. Fingerprints.' She began to hiccup gently.

'Camilla, I'm ringing off now to run for a taxi. Lock yourself in the bathroom until the police arrive. I'm sure you're in no danger whatever but it will make you feel safer. Have you got that?'

'Yes.'

'Good girl. I'm on my way. Goodbye.'

He put the phone down and rushed to collect his coat and umbrella. He thriftily switched off the overhead light and was about to go out the door when he had a sudden thought. Turning on his desk lamp, he got out his diary again and impatiently stabbed out a telephone number. It seemed to take forever to answer but finally someone picked up on what seemed to George to be the hundredth ring. He barked out orders and tapped his foot in frustration as his instructions were read back to him.

Another voice came on the line, crisp but polite, saying, 'That will do, Williams, thank you.' There was a click as Williams put his phone down and the voice said, 'You still there, Georgie?'

'Yes.'

'I take it you think this business follows upon our earlier conversation?'

'I don't know. It could be a simple burglary, of course, but . . .'

'Quite. Or it could be that other business. I'm putting you on hold for a tick.'

There was a long pause on the line and George waited with considerable impatience. 'Sorry. It took longer than I thought to get things in hand . . .'

'Look,' George cut in without apology, 'Camilla's in a bad way and I've promised to get there as quickly as I can.'

'Yes, yes, I'm with you. I won't hold you up and this is an open line. We'll talk on the way there. Go downstairs and wait for me. I'll collect you in five minutes.'

'How do I explain *you*?' This was not the time, George thought furiously, to clutter up Camilla's flat with mysterious strangers. 'Or do you want me to . . .?'

'We'll cook up something in the car. I'm moving. Five minutes.'

He was as good as his word. The rain had strengthened to a downpour and George scuttled across the pavement into the waiting black Jaguar. He nodded briefly to the driver and huddled in the back seat, grateful that the heater was on.

'I'm getting too old for this sort of thing, Maurice,' he said, his teeth chattering slightly, whether from the cold, his wet feet or simple nerves he neither knew nor cared. He'd been in this game far too long, he thought bleakly.

'I brought you a bun. Here. Didn't think you'd have had time for any lunch. Flask, too. Chisky. Do you good.'

George took a long pull of the cherry brandy and whisky mixture. The taste instantly recalled long, happy shooting weekends in Norfolk with Rupert, the great love of his youth. He felt warmed by both the alcohol and the memory and thanked Maurice before biting into the bun.

Maurice spoke as George chewed. 'I won't come up to the girl's flat for the moment. Leave you to sort things out there and I suggest that you take her home with you. That is, unless you have other, ah, encumbrances on the domestic front.'

'Sadly not,' George said before taking another bite.

'Good. I mean good in the sense that the present situation is made easier. Get the girl . . .'

'Camilla,' George said with a touch of reproof in his tone.

'Yes. Take Camilla home with you. Pack her a nightie, toothbrush, teddy bear, clean knickers, what-have-you and have her to stay. Probably jump at the suggestion, poor thing. Grounds: she'll feel safer, flat-footed coppers not barging in and out. You know the form. I've ordered a car for you with Mayhew as driver. He's a good man and will keep an eye out for followers. You can pretend you called a radio cab. Leave all the details to you.'

'Any ideas?' George took another sip of chisky and decided regretfully that it would have to be the last.

Maurice shook his head. 'This thing's a mess. There's simply no *pattern*. At least, nothing I can see.' He reached out and took the flask from George's hand, took a demure sip, screwed the cap back on and deposited it in a side-pocket of the car door. 'The Paris Embassy got another letter this morning.'

The radio squawked, announcing the arrival of the police and two of their own men at Camilla's flat. 'Did you hear all that, Sir Maurice?'

'Yes, thanks, Chapman.'

The driver acknowledged the message, turning left into Park Lane, and George's heart sank when he saw the heavy traffic inching along. Where did everyone go in the middle of a rainy April afternoon? It would take them days to get to Kensington at this rate. The driver caught his eye in the rear-view mirror. 'Not all that bad, sir. I'll nip along through the Park. We'll be there in about ten minutes.'

'Splendid, Chapman, thank you. Quick as you can.' George turned back to Sir Maurice and said, 'I think it's best we save the Paris letter for some other time. And I agree with you, by the bye, about the lack of pattern. It's been driving me potty, too.' He glanced with considerable annoyance at a bus belching black smoke from its exhaust. 'I think this renewed burst of activity concerning Camilla has nothing to do with the original search. Different hand, don't you know. From what she said on the phone, it sounds as if the place was pretty thoroughly tossed. No attempt at subtlety there. Didn't give a shit about the police, obviously.'

'Different hand. I agree. So you make it a new set of pieces on the board?'

'Possibly a whole new game. For one thing, I find it hard to believe that Camilla was involved in any way with her husband's, ah, activities but – and this is a major but, Maurice – she is *very* evasive on the subject of the late unlamented Hamilton.' He flapped his hand from side to side. 'If she did know something, she also knew that her own continued existence would depend on keeping quiet about it.'

'I take it you still believe that Hamilton was killed before he turned over the putative It to his contact?'

'If he had handed It over, why should his executioners have searched his flat with such exemplary thoroughness so quickly after the event? Sorry to answer a question with a question and all that but so far we've boobed badly in this thing. Instead of letting him run and having him under surveillance, we ought to have pulled him in and subjected him to an extremely thorough grilling. I doubt that he would've proved a tough nut. He would be alive and we would know a hell of a lot more than we do now about the IRA set-up in England. And, quite apart from other considerations, we'd at least know what It is, or was.'

'Information? Passed along at Ascot?'

'Then why the search? Floorboards up, bath panels dismantled, the whole bang shoot. From the way the place was searched, I had a feeling that the baddies were looking for something largish. By that I mean not just a twist of paper. They clearly ignored all of his papers, in fact, and Camilla's films, too. That struck both of us as being odd at the time, if you recall. If Hamilton had photographed documents, you'd expect anything even remotely suggesting film would've been nicked.'

He hissed softly, a sure indication of anger. 'You do see, Maurice, that even dead the good Major has us chasing our own tails around in circles.' He fell silent and took a final look at the Park's carpet of daffodils before the car turned into Kensington Gore. As soon as he was able, he would retire and buy a cottage somewhere in the country. Perhaps even in France if those-who-would-be-obeyed could find it in their hearts to permit such frivolity on the part of an elderly civil servant.

Sir Maurice said, 'She never let on to you that she knew her flat had been turned over?'

George shook his head. 'No, I'm positive she didn't know and that she has no idea that her phone's bugged, rather that it *was* bugged, to be pedantic. It was, let's face it, a very professional job. Good God, Maurice, if we hadn't had a man watching the place, we'd never have known!'

'And it's entirely possible,' Sir Maurice added dryly, 'indeed probable, that she would have met with a fatal accident by now.' He glanced out the window. 'Look, Georgie, we're just about there. Some of our chaps shuffled in with the coppers, needless to say, but they'll need a tiny bit of direction. Do we take it as given that the baddies were after the photographs she took in France?'

'I don't know but it's the only thing I can think of. It's the only new factor in the game and until the lab boys do their stuff we're no further. I strongly suspect that they had a brief sniff round in her hotel room at Val Sainte-Anne.'

The Jaguar pulled into the kerb behind a police car. The rain had slackened somewhat and the sun slanted in from the west, angling under the black cloud directly overhead. George opened the door before Chapman had a chance to do it for him. 'I'll go up first, shall I? Get her out of your way as quickly as possible. I think you'd best be a police Inspector, if you can fix it with our colleagues in the Met. Unless you can think of anything more suitable to your age and station in life, that is.'

'It'll have to do for the moment. I'll wait five minutes before I come up. Oh, and Georgie, don't forget to chat up the constables a bit. Within reason, of course. You're not being nancy enough. Cover is everything in this game.'

'When straight old men begin telling queer old men how they ought to behave it's the last and final straw,' Georgie said with a laugh. He blew a kiss to Chapman, who visibly paled from embarrassment.

5

Georgie's small house in Seymour Walk was exactly to Camilla's taste, far more so than her own, somewhat larger, flat. She looked around with envious admiration. The little square rooms were deliciously scented with beeswax polish and flowers. They were furnished in an eclectic mish-mash of periods and pieces, French and English, Italian and Dutch. Portuguese tiles surrounded the little iron fireplace, glowing with hexagonal lumps of smokeless coal. There was an air of ordered, comfortable and comforting clutter which was the sort of thing that happened, she thought, when a lifetime was devoted to the single-minded pursuit of beautiful things, lovingly maintained.

She wandered down to the kitchen and filled the electric kettle. Outside, a tiny patio had curved steps leading up to a modest west-facing garden, beautifully kept and smelling fresh after the intermittent spring rains. Brilliant scarlet early tulips stood out bravely against the dark, ivy-covered brick walls, small guardsmen defying winter to attempt any stealthy return. Damp, newly-turned earth steamed slightly in the warmth of the late-afternoon sun. She sat at the kitchen table, drinking her tea and taking tiny mouse-like bites out of a ginger biscuit as she'd done in childhood, to make it last longer. She was somewhat surprised at herself for being so calm. Georgie was a gentleman of the old school: tea and a ginger biscuit would see you through any crisis.

She heard him pottering about upstairs, getting sheets and towels out of the airing cupboard and swearing as he eventually managed to prize open a long-unopened window. It was so kind and thoughtful of him to insist that she stay. He had even thought to telephone and arrange to have "a couple of boys" of his acquaintance go in and set her place to rights, once the Old Bill had left with their fingerprint powder, chattering radios and muddy boots.

Nothing could have been more welcome than Georgie's insistent invitation.

The amiable senior policeman who had ambled in not long after George had seen her distress over the horrible mess the flat was in and tactfully allowed her to leave, detaining them only long enough to make a note of Georgie's address and telephone number. There was nothing she could do around there in any event, except get underfoot. What little jewellery she had was in the bank and the silver had, so far as she was able to tell, remained untouched. She didn't blame the burglars: it was mostly plate and showing an indecent amount of copper. Her elderly television set was, apparently, equally beneath their consideration but they had taken a camera and some photographic equipment. Thank God, she had told the police, it was all insured.

The phone rang and she heard Georgie clattering down the stairs to answer it. She heard him laugh delightedly and then he shouted for her to come up to the sitting-room.

'It's Brook,' he said as she came in. 'He's here. In London, I mean.'

'Oh.' Her face lit up.

'I've told him why you're here, just to keep him from getting too jealous. I don't fancy being horse-whipped on my own steps. At least, not by him.' He handed the telephone to her. 'And over a woman, of all the silly things.'

'Brook! How lovely. You *are* a ray of sunshine.'

'Camilla,' he said anxiously, 'are you okay? George told me your apartment had been burgled. Flat, I mean. Jesus!'

'At least I wasn't in it at the time, Brook. And, yes it's awful and thank God Georgie has taken charge both of me and of getting the mess sorted out. But let's not talk about it. How long are you in London for? When shall we see you? That's a far nicer thing to talk about.'

'Can I take you two out to dinner?' Brook asked at the precise moment George said, 'Ask him to come round here to dinner.'

Camilla laughed. 'Brook, Georgie says can you come here to dinner. Why don't you come here and we can all have a drink and then you and Georgie can fight it out as to whether he cooks or you buy.'

'That sounds eminently reasonable. I'll be there within the hour.'

He was actually there in rather less than an hour, carrying not one but two bottles of champagne. 'I know,' he explained, 'that people normally drink this to celebrate but I see no reason why we shouldn't have some to buck us all up.' He dealt with the cork as George produced pretty Baccarat flutes from a walnut corner cupboard.

'To drowning all sorrows,' George said, lifting his glass, 'in Louis Roederer's vats.'

They drank the first bottle in the sitting-room and opened the second in the kitchen, Brook and Camilla sitting at the scrubbed pine table watching George dither purposefully here and there, putting together what proved to be an admirable dinner. They managed to get through two further bottles of wine with dinner and Brook declined an Armagnac with a furtive, worried look at the empty wine bottles standing by the door.

George walked him down to the Fulham Road. 'Do come again soon, Brook. It's been fun this evening and really awfully good for Camilla. Takes her mind off things.'

'How long will she be staying with you?'

'Not long. She's going down to Bath this weekend with her mother but I'll be here, should you find yourself at a loose end. Please feel free to ring me, Brook. I've devoted the weekend to sloth and you wouldn't be interrupting anything more urgent than the crossword puzzle or pulling up a few weeds, according to the vagaries of our curious climate.'

'Thanks, George, I may take you up on it. I'll give you a ring.' He took a notebook out of his breast pocket. 'Here's the address and phone number of the flat I'm borrowing for the moment. The owners won't be back for another ten days or two weeks. Just in case you're feeling bored.' He said, 'Thanks again for a delightful evening. Good night.'

She caught the end of the bulletin on the BBC World Service as she stepped out of the shower: O'Neill and

Molloy had been convicted and sentenced to twenty and seventeen years respectively. 'Conspiring to cause explosions.' She forced herself to block out the newsreader's odious English accent and concentrate on the sense of what he was saying. How the flaming hell had that cache of weapons and explosives been found in the first place? The voice droned on dispassionately. 'Scotland Yard's Anti-Terrorist Squad, acting on an intelligence tip, mounted a long-term surveillance . . .'

She punched the radio's off-switch and towelled herself down vigorously, working off some of her anger. It was all very well setting everything up for them, doing all their thinking for them, working night and day getting everything into place at the right time. There were plenty of volunteers to replace this brace of morons who had somehow managed to get themselves caught before striking a single blow. There were hundreds more people to continue the struggle; well, dozens, but it was a question of investment.

It took time and money to train people and more time and money to equip them. Did those blarney-merchants in Dublin and Belfast think that she was capable of magically transporting more stuff to what they would *insist* on calling 'the front line' by a simple act of prestidigitation? Magic wands didn't kill the English; bombs and bullets did and they had to be purchased, cash on the barrelhead, and put into the hands of the soldiers. No weapons, no war. How many times had she to repeat that? The speechifiers were really only capable of providing the soldiers; she and Gillon did all the rest, or anyway most of it. Putting in new workmen was no problem; replacing their tools was the hard part.

Thank God Gillon had begun the process of hiving off their own operations from the control of the posturing hard-liners in Ireland. They were all morons.

Wrapped in her towel, she strode down the passage and into the office to switch on the television. She didn't give a shit that Costelloe was sitting there. He hardly even counted as a man. Most of the men she had worked with over the years were little better than eunuchs. She had once heard someone talk about "the terrible purity of the Irish" and the concept

49

had struck her as being meaningless, even ridiculous. She had then discovered for herself that it was true. She didn't mind at all, so long as all that pent-up sexual energy was properly channelled into a need for vengeful destruction. She didn't want it dissipated at the goddamned pub and in their endless ideological wrangling about means and ends.

Killing the English colonialist murderers was all that mattered.

Costelloe ogled her, as he often did. 'You're a lovely woman, Nedda,' he said thickly.

'Shut up, Liam,' she explained, 'there's news from London.'

There was a satellite dish on her terrace that picked up a bewildering number of television transmissions. Costelloe seemed too thick to use it properly, spending most of his time glued indiscriminately to cretinous soap-operas such as *I Colby* dubbed into Italian. She snatched the remote-control out of his hand and got the six o'clock news from London. There was some footage from last autumn, when O'Neill and Molloy had first been picked up: a serious-faced young pig from Scotland Yard's Anti-Terrorist Squad gloating over a few samples from the cache in Cheshire. Nedda hissed, sucking the air between her teeth like a Japanese. The bastards had unearthed another cache last week in the Midlands. Supplies on the mainland of Britain were getting dangerously low.

'Thank God the machine-pistols we bought from Alexis got through,' she said aloud, not directly addressing Costelloe, who was currently engaged in thoroughly exploring the contents of each nostril. 'Find anything useful?' she enquired sweetly.

'Ah, Nedda,' he said, 'leave off, for the love of God.' He smiled at her ingratiatingly, his pallbearer features rearranging themselves into an expression of bogus camaraderie.

She looked at him with loathing. She needed someone sharp, someone capable of quick assessment and a decent measure of initiative to help her out. Why had she been saddled with this mindless nose-picker? At least he looked

50

the part, Nedda thought: serious, benign and more than a little stupid. Profile so low as to be barely visible. He fitted his cover if not his actual function.

There was nothing more of interest on the news and she switched off the television, taking the remote-control with her. She needed complete silence to think everything through and Costelloe would have to forgo a few minutes of *I Colby*, no matter how vital to future plot developments they might be. Naked in front of the floor-to-ceiling mirrors in her big dressing-room, she half-heartedly went through a brief session of exercises, only vaguely recalled from winter afternoons in the school gym. Ruffo's aside about skiing as beneficial exercise had stung her, as she knew it was meant to do. Even after all this time, they still couldn't help sniping at one another, scoring random hits here and there.

She was nearing forty but she had had no complaints about the way she looked. A bit of loose skin around the eyes; nothing more. She stared into her own reflected eyes and thought how very innocent they still looked: brown, roundish eyes, as trusting and loving as a dog's. In early adolescence she had been ashamed of her pale, freckled skin but it hadn't taken her long to discover that some men, many men found her deceptively helpless-looking body irresistible. She stared complacently at her reflection and smiled. Sex was the only exercise she needed. Fuck Ruffo, she thought, both literally and figuratively. He had his uses but he was hardly indispensable.

Thinking of Ruffo's body made her catch her breath. She needed sex *now* and briefly toyed with the idea of summoning Liam but the thought of what his body was likely to be underneath his accustomed layers of evil-smelling clothes made her reject the idea immediately. Her hand moved of its own volition into her pubic hair, stroking herself softly before moving farther down, but she stopped reluctantly and stood up. There was time for that later. Perhaps she would ring Alexis and have him talk to her, saying all the things he knew would bring her to a quick, violent orgasm.

She dressed without calculation or pleasure, struggling impatiently into an Armani silk shirt and the skirt from

51

a Saint-Laurent suit, then stepping into a pair of Chanel sling-back shoes, not caring what she put on. Women who spent hours going from shop to shop and fitting to fitting were absurd, beneath contempt. She had work to do. There were so many things to be seen to, that only she could see to, lacking as she did a really good back-up.

'Any further news on Patrick Devlin?' she asked Liam Costelloe, who was on the terrace, sulkily staring out at the grey, foam-tossed sea, no doubt wondering what interesting things *I Colby* were getting up to without him.

He smiled his lugubrious undertaker's smile, exposing mossy, greenish teeth. 'Got right away, Nedda. Showed the bastards a clean pair of heels.' He rubbed his hands together, making a dry, papery sound. 'That was brilliant, it was, the good judge throwing out the extradition order. Fucking English and their fucking extradition orders! Anglo-Irish Agreement be damned!' He laughed happily, exposing an additional number of eccentrically-distributed teeth. 'Lucky to get a beak who knows right from wrong these days.'

'The judge's decision had nothing to do with luck, ass-hole,' Nedda said furiously.

'Is the lovely beak one of ours then?' Costelloe had acquired a weary familiarity with all of Nedda's forms of address.

'He is now. There are photographs in our possession that the good judge would not at all like anyone to see.' She smiled sweetly. 'It was an offer he couldn't refuse, if you follow my meaning. Choirboys, I believe, or child pornography. Anyway, something to do with kids. I think you get my drift.'

'Oh, I do, I do.' Costelloe nodded but he felt acute disappointment: a good Irishman, be he judge or tinker, should know without coercion where his loyalties ought to lie.

'Get me Gillon on the phone,' she ordered, heading for the kitchen to see what, if anything, there was to eat. She was hungry. She was really hungry for a man but food would have to do. There was no man within easy reach

52

but the deeply unappetising Costelloe. There was about half a glassful of milk left in the carton and she downed that while searching for something more substantial. She eventually found an apple well past the first blush of youth but still edible. She bit into it savagely and threw the rest into the dustbin. Costelloe could damned well do some shopping, as he seemed underoccupied. She would make a list and send him up to the nearby Codec for a major re-stocking.

'Ah, here's herself now,' Liam said chattily to Gillon, passing her the phone.

'What's the position?' she asked, using her generalissimo voice for Liam's benefit. Gillon never noticed.

'Two for their side with the convictions – I gather from Liam you got that on the television – and one for our side with Patrick trickling through their grubby fingers. We owe them one.'

'I know all that,' she snapped, 'and I want to make it a big one. I want them to know that when we settle scores we settle them with interest.'

'It's a fine thing we've got Patrick back,' Gillon went on, unperturbed by her tone. He was too thick-skinned to resent Nedda's brusqueness and it left more time for him to talk. Economy of speech was not, in Gillon's view, either necessary or virtuous. 'He and Ginger Reardon are the best we have with the explosives after our little setback in Gibraltar,' he continued cheerfully enough.

Gillon's insouciance frequently made Nedda want to chew the carpet. 'We've been betrayed again! There was no reason whatever for the pigs to find the goods in the Midlands,' Nedda said furiously, 'unless your boyos have been bragging in the pubs. Christ, Gillon,' she exploded, 'can't you keep them away from the booze when there's an important operation in the running stage?'

He chuckled merrily. 'Ah, darling, and how d'you think I'd do that thing? Sew their mouths shut and they'd just be finding another orifice . . .' His laughter increased as he expatiated on this novel idea. 'Rig up an enema filled with Guinness and use the tradesmen's entrance!'

Nedda tapped her foot in annoyance until Gillon's fit of humour had subsided to titters. 'I don't care what you do. Antabuse implant. Make the stupid fuckers so sick after the first pint that they stay off the stuff.'

He roared with renewed laughter. 'Ah the wonderful ideas you have, to be sure, Nedda! We'd have a serious recruitment problem on our hands. Antabuse,' he repeated with a further giggle. 'Such fine things they have in America. Scientific.' When he managed to control his hilarity he said, 'As to the boys, I'm in charge of operations and I've no lack of mercenaries for any operation of any sort. I would remind you, my dear, that your brief extends to finances only. You are the Exchequer. I am the Chief of Staff.' To ease the tension between them, he said, 'Must ⁱ remind you how beautifully expendable the mercenarie ﹀ are?'

Nedda controlled her urge to slam the phone down. 'How *can* you trust these mercen es you've recruited? Goddammit! One of them could have sold out for more money! They said on the news that Scotland Yard were following an "intelligence tip". That's what did for O'Neill and Molloy. Someone talked, Gillon!'

'And it's the Yard you're putting your faith in nowadays, Nedda,' Gillon said reproachfully. 'You Yanks have a touching faith in the coppers. Now you know they're not above saying whatever comes into their heads just to make us worry. Just to make us distrust one another, Nedda.' His voice held a warning note.

'Well,' she said reasonably, 'Patrick or no Patrick, we've got to protect our supply routes at all costs. Patrick and whoever Patrick trains can't go out into the field empty-handed, now can they?'

'Dear me, no. We've still got that dump in the New Forest and a grand supply of Semtex, about a hundredweight as I recall, at the house in Brixton. Always assuming the bogies haven't stolen it yet,' he added, vastly amused by the possibility.

Nedda waited for a fresh outbreak of hilarity to subside before continuing. 'Gillon,' she eventually said, rigid with anger, 'I wonder if you've discussed matters with our friends in North Africa. They're not asleep on their feet at Scotland Yard, you know.' She forced herself to be calm. 'If we don't get re-stocked soon by the Colonel . . .'

'Well, as to that . . .' Gillon was evasive.

'Gillon,' she said with extreme patience, 'I'm not trying to poach. You know I would never do that. You've got a pool of foreigners supposedly working for us, but establishing new routes is becoming more and more important, both for re-supply and for moving our own merchandise to pay for it all. We've got to explore more ways to get re-stocked on the British mainland and that has to be our first order of business. We're losing stuff too quickly. There's another shipment of you-know-what from Brazil expected soon so we'll have all the money we need for re-stocking. But we're getting dangerously low on the stuff that goes bang. It's time to see what else Alexis has in his cupboard.'

He chuckled appreciatively, although he seldom found her at all amusing, except inadvertently. 'I like the new toys Alexis bought for us. Those Israelis make a fine product, you have to hand it to them. Small, light, just the ticket. I'll give him a ring and arrange for more. You'll fix the finances, as usual?'

'No,' Nedda cut in hastily, 'don't you call Alexis. I've got to speak with him about a payment so I'll get him to ring you. Stay by the phone.' She paused. 'I may have an assignment for your happy little band stationed in London, Gillon. I'll talk to Alexis first about getting more of what you want but the new route over the glacier may have been blown already.'

Gillon's voice was cold when he said, 'I thought you reported that it was all tickety-boo, Nedda, my dear. No one said anything to me about a problem when Jacki's lads pitched up with their rucksacks in Paris.'

'To tell you the truth, I'm dubious about Jacki. I don't like using mercenaries, as you know. But there's another factor, too. There was a dim-looking English bitch at the top of the run, taking snaps with her little camera, supposedly for some dreary London magazine. The films aren't at her apartment – Connolly gave the place a good going-over – so they could

55

only be at the magazine's offices. I'm considering sending the team into the office to have a thorough search. There's no risk with a holiday weekend coming up. The English take their holidays very seriously and the place will be deserted. I want to think about it for a bit, Gillon.'

'Do that,' he said icily. 'I'll be interested to hear how you intend to proceed. Reardon's our best bomber and I can't have that team compromised in any way.' He chuckled again. 'It's good to know that you make mistakes, too, my darling girl. It had better not be yet another costly mistake, like your biddable old drunken priest from Boston.'

'I don't see how you could conceivably blame me if the bitch with the camera turns out to be a cop. If the films *are* at the magazine, then it's just coincidence. Reardon and Cahill search and destroy while the two others stand guard. There'll be plenty of time.'

'So long as it doesn't interfere with Monday.'

'And as to Boston,' she went on, 'how can I find out what happened to the missing stuff,' she asked defensively, 'if you won't let me have our friends there haul him in and make absolutely sure he talks?'

'Never mind, dear. It's not important enough to bother with. If the cops in America nobbled him, he doesn't know anything to tell them. Don't worry your head about it.'

Nedda didn't want to know what had happened to the priest. She hated any sort of failure. 'But what if that new route across the Alps is already blown?'

'Now calm down, m'dear. My, you are in a prickly mood. Tut tut. Female rattiness, I daresay.' Then he laughed. 'Ah no, I beg your pardon, Nedda. It's not your hormones giving trouble it's the holiday. How bad-tempered you become when the markets shut down and your telex falls silent!'

He paused and she heard a slight rustling sound as he covered the mouthpiece with his hand, clearly speaking to someone with him, probably one of the Altdorfers. 'Good news to come. I think we could all do with some good news, don't you?'

'Yes,' she said.

'Well, then, if you can tear young Liam away from his soap-operas and get a fair crack at the television, I can assure you that you will see sights very much to your liking. Ta, love.'

Gillon was right: the scene was very much to her liking. At Wolfenbüttel, six men of the Queen's Royal Lancers had been killed and several more were in hospital, some of them in critical condition. Their transport had been hit by an RPG-7 rocket-launcher. The IRA had claimed responsibility. The West German police were looking for two Irishmen, recently resident in Amsterdam, suspected of association with the IRA and thought to be connected with the atrocity at Enniskillen, and two other persons, one possibly a woman, who were seen nearby parked in a silver-grey Volkswagen Golf.

Nedda felt much better than she had in days. She also felt like having a small private celebration and peremptorily ordered Costelloe to go to his own flat for the evening. He looked wounded but did as she told him. When she heard the front door slam shut behind him with unnecessary force, she found her supply of snow and smiled with proprietorial happiness as she felt it hit. It really was the best blow on earth.

Then she picked up the phone and dialled Alexis' number. She felt so good that she was only mildly disappointed when she got nothing more than his answering tape. Just the sound of his voice made her tingle.

PART TWO

6

It was abnormally quiet in Regent Street. At a little before eight o'clock on a sunny Good Friday morning there was virtually no traffic and WPC Helen Tarrant strolled slowly towards the Savile Row Police Station, savouring the mild spring weather and knowing she had plenty of time in hand.

When the brittle, staccato sound of shots arrived from a long way off to her ears, she was gazing into Liberty's extravagantly-dressed Easter windows and she could not, at first, believe what she had heard. Surrounded as she was by echoing concrete, stone and plate glass, it was impossible for her to judge exactly where the burst of gunfire had come from. Regent Street itself was deserted but for an empty-handed man walking at a normal pace up by Oxford Circus. The stillness of the whole area made her doubt that she had heard anything at all but her training and instinct overrode her hesitation and she began to run. Being a young woman who believed in fitness, it took her far less time to cover the short distance from Liberty's to the Savile Row Police Station than it would have taken to find an unvandalized telephone.

She arrived only slightly out of breath and told the desk sergeant, the butt of endless jokes because his name was Fluck, what she had heard. He looked at her dubiously. Behind him, WPC Joanna Davies caught Helen's eye and, with a glance at her street-map, began to radio, instructing drivers to investigate a report of gunfire in the area. Helen joined her, concentrating hard to try narrowing the possible target area, and made a circle on Joanna's map with her finger. Joanna relayed the co-ordinates and waited for the cars to report in.

Sergeant Fluck moodily picked his teeth with a wooden match as they waited. As the minutes ticked by, Helen had begun to doubt that there had ever been anything real to shatter the morning's peace. Then the radio crackled into life. There were bodies in Hanover Square near the corner where it joined St George's Street.

Joanna radioed immediately for an ambulance and directed cars standing by or investigating the area to seal off all entrances to the Square. Stanley Fluck scrambled quickly to find Inspector Prescott, barked out orders and checked the duty-roster to see who had weapons-training. Two men wearing flak-jackets and carrying rifles pounded into the street at a run while Inspector Prescott, who had just come on duty, cursed richly and followed them at a determined dog-trot, thinking for the millionth time that it was imperative that he stop smoking sometime in the very near future.

No one actually told her *not* to go, so WPC Tarrant followed, maintaining a discreet distance well behind Prescott's wheezing jog, for fear of being ordered back to Savile Row. The people lying unmoving on the pavement and the profound stillness of Hanover Square, broken only by the cackling of police radios and some small birds engaged in an acrimonious territorial dispute, lent an air of unreality to the morning. Less belligerent birds sang exuberantly in the bright spring sunshine. The square gardens looked just on the verge of greenness, a hint of pale-green leaves surrounding some of the trees like a nimbus. She caught a glimpse of daffodils beyond the railings. The entire scene before her had a hard-edged, surreal quality as though two television sets were tuned to different programmes at wild variance with one another in the same room. Although it seemed to her as though a week had passed between hearing the gunfire and seeing its result, less than a quarter of an hour had actually elapsed.

The police photographer got down to cases before anything was touched, recording every aspect of the three bodies lying crumpled on the pavement amid congealing pools of blood. Helen approached no closer than the corner of St George's Street, keeping as much distance as possible between herself and the hypnotic, dark-red lake. She had never realized that the human body could contain so much blood and there was no doubt whatever in her mind that the victims couldn't possibly be other than stone dead. A Chanel shoulder-bag of quilted black leather stood absurdly upright near the kerb, the interlocked Cs of its clasp clearly visible and an Hermès scarf still neatly tied to its brass-and-leather chain. The bright cover of an A–Z could be seen lying in one of the blood-pools, its pages a solid rusty red. A tightly-furled man's umbrella leant at a gentle angle against the kerb, as though sun-bathing, its smart wooden handle in the gutter. It was all too absurd.

The ambulance was already pulling up, having encountered no traffic, and Helen stood rooted to the spot as the ambulancemen bent over one body, a man's, examined it briefly and moved swiftly to the next, conferring inaudibly. The second body was carefully placed on a stretcher as was the third, both women. The ambulance took off at speed toward Regent Street, a police car pulling back into place to block off Hanover Street immediately the ambulance passed. Another ambulance pulled up and the remaining victim, obviously beyond earthly help, was removed at a more sedate pace. Helen continued standing where she was, staring at the impossible blood and surprised to feel the cool tracks of tears coursing down her cheeks. Finally, she could bear the oppressive atmosphere of the square no longer and retreated back towards the police station.

It was at this moment that a small, frail, elderly man emerged timidly from the dim interior of St George's church, blinking in the sunlight. 'It's all right, my dear,' he said softly, peering up into her face. 'It's the shock. Saw it during the War. All you need's a cup of hot, sweet tea.' He looked about approvingly and said, 'Very impressive, I must say. Efficient. I only rang nine-nine-nine a few minutes ago.'

Unaccustomed to a free conversational rein, he was still talking, all traces of shyness evaporated with the golden warmth of an unusually tractable audience, five minutes later. He finally lapsed into silence when Inspector Prescott detached himself from a group of constables and came towards them, checking his tape-recorder and patting his pocket to establish that his notebook was to hand, in case of mechanical failure. A belt-and-braces man, Prescott had a profound mistrust of all machines.

Having released a stunned but grateful WPC Tarrant with a direct order to return to Savile Row, he firmly herded the old man back into the church, away from the multiplicity of distractions on offer in the street. He started the tape, establishing his own identity and the witness's name, address and a few other details before beginning to ask questions. The witness, Mr Albert Fawnbrake of Braganza Street, Kennington, was acting as a temporary verger at St George's, Hanover Square during the absence of the regular holder of that office, currently absent in his native Herefordshire to ease the final days of his moribund mother. Mr Fawnbrake was forthcoming to an overwhelming degree, despite his pre-emptive admission that he had not actually seen 'the outrage' being committed. It was very plain that he deeply regretted this.

'Now, sir, you're absolutely sure that it was automatic fire you heard and not a rapid series of single shots?'

'Positive. In the Infantry I was. I was standing right there by the columns there – that's a porch, you know, classical, *Georgian* – and I served with the Eighth Army in North Africa; corporal and would've made sergeant if I hadn't got hit in the leg at Alamein, and I know the difference between . . .' He fell silent.

'Quite, Mr, ah.' Prescott glanced up from his notebook, where he'd copied name and address for future accuracy in spelling, and the verger had vanished. He looked down and saw that the old man was sitting in the nearest pew, carefully rolling up his trouser leg, thus exposing an area of bluish, puckered skin. 'No need, sir, to show me your wound. May we continue please, sir?' He longed for a cigarette but thought it could appear disrespectful to be seen puffing away in a church, Georgian or otherwise. On Good Friday, at that.

'Well, here I was, you see, early as I always am on account of not being able to sleep very well, as I've already told you,' the old man gestured impatiently, rather piqued by the policeman's evident lack of interest in his medical history, 'and it being Good Friday with people wanting to get their devotions over and done with early – Stations of the Cross don't get done in five minutes, young man – when I heard these shots. From up the road there. So naturally, I thought to run along and have a look. Well, limp would be more the case, on account of my wound and not moving all that quickly . . .' He waited hopefully for a belated spark of interest, giving this policeman a fair chance to change his mind, but no. He sighed.

'What precisely did you see, sir?'

'When was that then?'

'When you went out to have a look round.'

'I didn't go, did I? Not then, at least. I *thought* to go, is what I said. But then I thought better of it, I don't mind telling you, young man. I hid is what I did, behind that first pew there. Good, solid English oak that pew is. I don't say a bullet wouldn't go through it but they'd have to see me first, if you follow . . .'

'All right, sir,' Prescott said, thinking God give me strength. 'You heard the gunfire. You hid. How long did you stay behind the pew?'

'Ho ho. I bloody well stayed until I heard 'em go away, that's how long I stayed. Bravery's all very well when you've got Jerry in your sights and your mates at either elbow.' He glared at Prescott. 'And you'd've done the same if you was me. I'm no spring chicken but I've got a few good years in me left and I'm not going to get a mess more of holes in the old carcass, not if I have anything to say about it . . .'

'Quite. Very sensible, sir. No heroics, ha ha.' Prescott tried a winning smile but the temporary verger was staring gloomily out of the church door, refusing to meet his eyes, no doubt brooding darkly on the police's lack of compassion for the tribulations suffered by ordinary, law-abiding citizens who had served King and Country. 'How long would you say, sir, between taking sanctuary, if I may put it that way, and getting the all clear. That is to say . . .'

'I know what you're getting at, young man. Let me think. Two minutes, maybe three.' He took Prescott's elbow and led him onto the church porch the better to illustrate his account.

'I heard 'em walk past my church, talking they were, arguing more like, so I go and lean round the door and there they both go walking down towards Conduit Street, calm as you please but for the arguing, and I hide behind this column here so I can get a look and then they turn the corner. To the right, towards Bond Street, maybe Berkeley Square. I know they can't see *me*, not once they've turned the corner unless they can see through walls, so I go quick as I can up St George's Street,' he pointed, 'that being the direction they had come from, and I go round into the square and I see the fallen and I come back and ring nine-nine-nine.'

He folded his arms and glared at Prescott, as though challenging him to pick any holes in his story. 'I saw them bodies so I came back into the church and through that door there, here's the key here on my chain, which leads into the vestry and rang nine-nine-nine. And that's all I have to say to you.'

'Mr Fawnbrake, did you see anything other than the bodies when you went out to look?'

'Before or after I rang nine-nine-nine?' the old man asked exasperatingly.

'Before.' Prescott took a deep breath. 'You think you saw the gunmen walking away? What exactly made you think it was the gunmen you saw and not simply passers-by?' He felt faint from pure exhaustion. It was like pulling teeth.

Fawnbrake gave the Inspector a sly look. 'Couldn't swear to it in a court of law, like. Didn't actually see the gun, did I? Bags they were carrying, maybe full of tennis rackets for all I know. Maybe done their shopping in Berwick Market.' He laid his finger alongside his nose like a Victorian villain. 'But if they wasn't, weren't, the assassins, why just walk away? I mean, you and I wouldn't, would we? We'd ring nine-nine-nine, wouldn't we?' He nodded vigorously, his spectacles flashing in the sun like signals. 'If it was you and me, one of us would be running to find a copper. Course you *are* a copper, hum, so the situation wouldn't be quite the same.'

The force of Mr Fawnbrake's logic was overwhelming. 'And these people, you say, were just walking away?'

'I already told you that. Why don't you listen, young man? They weren't dawdling, mind you. They were walking smartish and having a good old chin-wag.'

'Can you give me some sort of description, sir?'

'What they were wearing, general height and build sort of touch. That much I can tell you. I had the impression them bags they had was heavy, too. But they were walking *away*, like I said. Anyway,' he added complacently, as though settling an argument, 'they were foreigners, weren't they?'

'Foreigners?'

'Jabbering to beat the band in some foreign language and it wasn't Arabic, so you can put that right out of your mind, just for a start. None of them Lesbianese wearing tea towels on their heads. I know a bit of Arabic, see. Picked it up in Cairo. During the War, that was. Won't tell you how, though,' he teased with a roguish wink, implying sumptuous brothels with unimaginable delights on offer to the discerning.

'Why didn't you come forward with this information straight away?' Prescott asked in a soft voice, thinking how easy it would be to throttle the old man.

'Nobody asked me,' he answered sulkily. 'Too busy you all were sweeping up them cartridge cases and that.'

'Shit,' Prescott said with deep feeling and lit a cigarette, choosing to ignore the indisputable fact that he was standing on a Georgian porch.

'All right. Let's go over what we've got so far,' Commander Richard Goudhurst said. 'Hard only for the moment. We'll get to conjecture later.' It was by now plain that his Anti-Terrorist Squad would be landed with this thing.

'Three Japanese tourists. Three Japanese tourists! Why the flaming hell would anyone gun down three bloody Japanese tourists? Or any species of tourist, come to that.' Fry's detestation of terrorists was so bitter that it was widely rumoured around Scotland Yard that he had refused to head the Anti-Terrorist Squad when the post was offered him. Richard Goudhurst, with his cooler temperament and ruthlessly logical mind, was altogether more suitable.

Fry's people had fielded the 999 call, handling the forensic side of things and letting Prescott's people get on with interviewing witnesses. It was their manor and they knew the local form.

The precise time of the murder had now been pinpointed, somewhat belatedly, by a new witness: Eric Ballard of Mile End, who happened to be en route from the Oxford Circus tube station to his place of employment, the Eastland Hotel in Conduit Street. Mr Ballard had heard the gunfire just as he reached the top of the tube stairs at the south-east corner of Oxford Circus. He had then checked his watch and scuttled along without stopping, narrowly averting a collision with two men.

Prescott looked upon this new witness with favour. Now two witnesses, other than WPC Tarrant, had stated positively that they had heard machine-gun fire, both credibly enough: one an old soldier and the other a middle-aged Rambo freak.

The bottom line, Prescott thought, was that the entire messy business could be shoved not only onto Scotland Yard, but more specifically onto the Anti-Terrorist Squad. His only remaining task was to collect any further information from witnesses on the manor who, once the media triggered their memories and got their blood up, might come forward with something entirely new, elaboration on the small bits already collected from Fawnbrake and Ballard or, at least, corroboration of same. Ballard had not only produced the precise time but, prompted by Prescott, had recalled seeing two men. His description, although disappointingly sketchy, ruled out their being the same pair the verger had spotted walking down toward Conduit Street. This gave added weight to his own and Detective Chief Inspector Fry's theory that the murderers were terrorists. Nothing else made any sense at all.

In the meantime, Prescott had garnered some gratifying kudos for his team at Savile Row, due entirely to WPC

Tarrant's sharp eyes and keen awareness of the finer things in life. No sooner had the names of the victims been established than she had wasted no time and headed smartly for Claridge's, to enquire if Mr, Mrs and Mrs Shigekawa were, by any chance, registered. They were.

Within the space of an extremely productive half-hour, various employees – waiters, the housekeeper and chambermaids, commissionaires and an epicene young Swiss who dealt with travel arrangements – provided a mosaic of information concerning the Shigekawa family.

They were, to begin with, father, mother and daughter-in-law. The son, "Young Mr Shigekawa", was expected from New York the following night, Saturday. A car had already been booked to collect him at Heathrow off the BA flight scheduled to land at half-past nine. They were occupying a two-bedroom suite on the third floor; had arrived from Tokyo the previous day at tea-time; had dined early in the Causerie; had had a simple breakfast served in their suite at seven o'clock, accompanied by *The Daily Telegraph*, *The Times* and *The Independent*.

Offered a taxi by the commissionaire, they had declined. His impression was that they were simply striking out for a walk, no particular destination in mind. On this important point he was firm: they gave no sign of people setting out for an appointment. There had been no checking of watches; no communion with the A–Z held at the ready; no purposeful striding out in a set direction. He had, for lack of other employment, watched them walk slowly along Brook Street and had lost interest when they had paused lengthily in front of Colefax and Fowler's window. The time was somewhere around a quarter to eight.

The suite had been booked in December by letter from Kyoto. Claridge's had confirmed the three-week booking and had promptly received a cheque for a thousand pounds, drawn on Messrs Coutts & Co, as a deposit. Quite unnecessarily, in the event, for Mr and Mrs Reejiro Shigekawa (senior) had been frequent guests at Claridge's over the years. Mr and Mrs Toshmichi Shigekawa (junior) had spent the first fortnight of their honeymoon there,

69

almost three years before. The elder Shigekawas lived in Kyoto; "Mr and Mrs Junior" in New York. Mrs Junior's Christian name was Mari, her maiden name was Suehiro; she was an American citizen, born in Honolulu.

She telephoned all of this information to Inspector Prescott, slowly spelling everything out for the benefit of his tape-recorder. In return, she was told, depressingly, that a call had just come in from the Middlesex Hospital: the elder Mrs Shigekawa had died. Some faint hope, tentatively expressed, had been held out for Mari's chances of survival. The surgeons considered her to be critical with all visits strictly forbidden; she was in Intensive Care. She was a healthy young woman of twenty-six but it had to be borne in mind that she had also lost a great deal of blood. She had miscarried of a fourteen-week male foetus and was still under heavy sedation.

Helen put the phone down, feeling all the elation drain out of her, as though a plug had been pulled. She meekly thanked her morning-suited auxiliary for his help and the prompt and complete co-operation of the staff. She trailed slowly down the marble stairs and out the revolving door, thinking inconsequentially that she was a year younger than Mari and would never hanker after a Chanel bag again.

As she walked, head bent, along Brook Street, pretending to look at the shop windows so that passers-by wouldn't see her tears, she bitterly regretted having abandoned Marks and Spencer's admirable training programme in favour of the Met. Her parents had been right, after all.

7

Sir Maurice Lyall, Bt., OM switched off the television and resumed his place at the table. His fingertips drummed an irritable tattoo on the folder before him. 'I'm sorry but I don't buy it: "an attempt at kidnapping gone tragically wrong".' He shook his head emphatically. 'Doesn't smell right.'

'No more do I buy it. Nor does Denis Fry, if it comes to that. The idea stinks. However, it's only one of the possibilities and the most obvious, given the circumstances. Clearly, we had to give the press something to chew on and Denis is hoping that media coverage will flush out some more witnesses.' He pushed the plate of sandwiches across the table. 'Speaking of chewing, have another.'

'Yes, thanks, Dickie.' Sir Maurice bit into his sandwich. 'How much of what Fry just gave on television was established fact?' he mumbled indistinctly.

'Pretty nearly all of it. But then we have so little. Fact, I mean, as you gathered from the folder. Guesses are another matter. We haven't uttered a squeak about a possible IRA connection, about which more later. What we were trying to do is to get anyone who might have seen the murderers to come forward and, at the same time, prevent the buggers themselves from doing a flit. We can't let them get out of the country. There's far too little evidence, as things stand for the present, to manage an extradition warrant, so we feed just enough to the press to winkle out a witness or two without putting the wind up the killers. It's a balancing act.'

He ground out his cigarette, almost lit another and instead flicked the packet aside in a peevish and futile gesture of rebellion. 'Fry and I agreed that we would feed the reptiles with what the killers themselves already know and nothing more. The kidnapping angle is a red herring; the logistics are all wrong. Three victims plus four captors cannot simply march around Mayfair until they manage to whistle up an empty taxi. There was positively no car. Every vehicle has been checked for a radius of a mile, right down to tiny, clapped-out Minis.'

Sir Maurice stirred in his chair and said, 'Mightn't they have had a van, even a minibus, with a driver who took off at the first sign of trouble? I don't say that's likely but not altogether impossible.'

Goudhurst said, 'We considered it but it isn't, as you say, very likely. There was almost complete silence in the area, given the hour and the holiday, and Fawnbrake, at least, would've heard any good-sized vehicle starting up and driving off. He's a silly old fart but there's nothing wrong with his hearing.'

He glared at the packet of Silk Cuts and said, 'WPC Tarrant would have been aware of it too, despite her pounding to the police station at flank speed. She was wearing rubber-soled shoes and wasn't making much of a racket herself. We're keeping an open mind, of course. But apart from the gaping holes from a logistical and transport point of view, common sense says the pattern's all wrong for an attempted snatch. You wouldn't bag all three. You'd take one or both women, leaving the man free to meet the demand for money. Someone's got to go to the bank.'

He caved in and lit another cigarette before going on. 'The kidnapping angle provided us with an excuse to withhold the names of the victims. You'll notice, too, that Fry gave a very gloomy view of the girl's chances of pulling through; nor did he furnish the name of the hospital, just as an added precaution. In fact, when last heard from, the Middlesex told us that they are altogether more hopeful than they were an hour or so ago. She's still in Intensive Care, of course, and she's being guarded. Strong as an ox, that young lady.' Then he added softly, 'Thank God.'

He unscrewed the flask on a tray beside him and peered into it. He picked up his telephone and asked that more coffee be brought in.

Sir Maurice gave him a quelling, headmasterish look.

'Now then, that farrago that Fry so stolidly delivered just now: what is fact and what is your fine Italian hand at work? I mean, apart from what is designed to confuse and lull the enemy. What, actually, is there to go on?'

He poured out for both of them. 'The witness Fawnbrake,' he said, jabbing his finger at the folder, 'kept insisting to Prescott, the first chap who interviewed him, that the two people he saw walking away from the scene of the crime were foreign. He was firm, altogether voluble one might even say, in his conviction that they were not speaking Arabic.' He peered donnishly at Sir Maurice over his half-spectacles, as though instructing him on the finer points of sixteenth-century methods available to the Inquisition for establishing evidence.

'Two factors come into play here. We know that the IRA have got the odd foreigner on the payroll, thanks to your mysterious informer. And we've also got a chap called Stancliffe who's a genius when it comes to interviewing witnesses. Fawnbrake, with much hemming and ha-ing, finally admitted that the pair he saw brought to mind Gurkhas.

'Stancliffe is a man of extraordinary patience – he has a passion for fly-fishing, makes those little fiddly whatsises they use, so it would appear to be something built-in – and the result of all his delicate probing of Fawnbrake's psyche is that he is quite sure that the two people the old geezer saw are,' he put up a single finger, 'one: Oriental, very possibly Japanese or Korean – that's my own guess – and,' second finger, 'two: a man and a woman. The hitherto unsuspected female-ness,' he grinned, 'established by a vague impression of an anatomical jiggle when observed at closish range in the process of turning the corner into Conduit Street.' He stubbed out his cigarette. 'The Gurkha-ness was catalysed into an overall impression of short-legged, black-haired beings, the one that jiggled having, I quote, "a low-slung bum".'

He sat back in his chair and waited for Sir Maurice to comment. He was slightly disappointed if not unduly surprised when Sir Maurice simply nodded and asked, 'And the other pair?'

'There again. Ballard, this chap who works as a porter at the hotel, said that his were definitely two men and that one was on the tall side (Ballard himself an inch or two below six foot), the other podgy and smaller. With Stancliffe's peculiar style of brain-scanning, Ballard revealed that the shorter one brought to mind a very much younger Arthur Scargill.'

This time, Sir Maurice had prudently waited for the revelation before attacking his coffee. 'Interesting. In what way?' He sipped in complete safety.

Goudhurst looked through the papers in his folder and summarized. 'Incipient beer-belly. Gingery hair elaborately arranged to cover bald pate.' He once more peered owlishly at Sir Maurice. 'Ballard specifically said that his hair looked like "a trap-door".'

'Apt.'

'I quote further: "long, pointed, rat-like nose and not much chin", what chin there was apparently propped up by further chins.'

'A portrait to the life,' Sir Maurice commented without irony.

'A portrait to the life of one Desmond Reardon, commonly known as "Ginger", a really lamentable lack of originality there. The computer portrait's in the file. He is credited with being an explosives expert, wanted for questioning in connection with the bombing early last year in County Fermanagh, in which three schoolchildren and an off-duty policeman . . .'

'Were killed and two further children had their legs blown off. I remember it well, Dickie.' He snorted with disgust and looked away. 'I take it you would very much like to know if the IRA have been beefed up by having at least two Japanese Red Army seconded to them, always assuming your guess as to their nationality is correct. Not a pretty thought, is it?' He tapped sharply on the folder. 'The opinion in here that the weapon was a Uzi leads you to think Jap not Paddy. Paddy favours the AK-47.' He turned

74

his ice-blue gaze back to Goudhurst. 'And what about the taller chap?'

'Reardon's minder, very likely, one Eamonn Cahill. "Scruffy-looking", I am quoting again, "greasy, collar-length hair dark-brown, jeans, bomber-jacket, looked like he belonged on a motorcycle." He's a gunman, picked up by the RUC in Belfast but released for lack of evidence and dropped out of sight about two years ago. As did Reardon. The Garda have been on the watch for him, too; Cahill I mean, but on suspicion of drug-dealing in Dublin, oddly enough. Had a word with Dominic Ryan. Cocaine, to be precise, and that fairly recently.'

Sir Maurice's eyebrows shot up again. 'Interesting,' he said.

'And surprising,' Goudhurst said. 'Drugs are not un-common in the Republic but, I am told by Ryan, the problem there, although fairly widespread, has heretofore been limited to the filthier varieties, heroin for the most part. Cocaine-users tend to come from a more elevated social and economic milieu. Bloody stuff costs the earth. Bankers not wankers. They haven't got to steal to get their hands on the stuff so the traffic has a low profile. It's considered a "fun drug", whatever that may mean – I gather something you take on occasion rather than daily; more Pimm's or pink champagne than medicine, in other words – and acquires a certain cachet for being astronomically expensive. Like driving a Roller, I imagine. Conspicuous consumption. Not my line of country at all, drugs,' he finished somewhat lamely.

'Your contacts amongst the esteemed Gardai couldn't be of more help with Reardon and Cahill?'

'Alas, no more than that, for the moment at least. If, by some miracle, we were to pick them all up in the next five minutes, we'd have to release them almost as quickly for lack of evidence. Even if Ballard picked them out in an identity parade, walking up Regent Street is not a criminal offence, even on Good Friday. There's no warrant out in the Republic for Cahill's arrest so we couldn't even extradite. The Gardai would simply like to have a chat and, I quote Ryan, "frighten the shit out of him". The Orientals, especially, could be pulled in for questioning if we stumbled across them but, failing their shooting up the china department at Harrods, we couldn't hang onto them.' He prodded morosely at a curling tomato sandwich.

'Quite a lot forrader than seemed possible this morning, Dickie. My congratulations. Nothing worse, I know, than a motiveless murder.' Sir Maurice looked at his watch. 'If we're going to be hanging about here a while longer, do the amenities of the Yard stretch to drink? I confess I could do with a whisky.'

Goudhurst stared fixedly at the baronet, choosing, for the moment, to ignore his request. 'Now then, Maurice, with these identifications, admittedly tentative in the extreme, and the ballistics report, how can you help the police in their enquiries?'

Sir Maurice's smile was wintry. 'Quite a lot, Dickie, but first I must telephone for reinforcements. Thereby,' he added helpfully, 'allowing you the necessary time to arrange for some liquid refreshment.'

'Connection or coincidence. Is that what you're asking me?' George Lacey put the folder back down on the table. 'You know perfectly well, Maurice, that I believe in coincidences roughly as much as I believe in the Essential Goodness of Man.'

'Which is precisely why I hauled you out of your nest, Georgie.'

It had stopped raining and George would have far preferred to have the last hour or two of daylight to himself, working in his garden and enjoying his solitude, now that Camilla was off his hands, gone to her mother's in Bath.

He was desperately worried about Camilla. The previous day, he had been contentedly pottering around the garden when she had joined him, offering to help. He had set her to doing some light pruning of his weeping cherry, whose blossoms had just dropped, and left her to get on with it as he shopped for their luncheon. He had returned to the house to find Camilla raving and crying, screaming her hatred of

76

Jeremy as she hacked viciously at his Fusillier tulips with a hoe. Cradling her in his arms, he had finally succeeded in calming her, but she refused to be dissuaded from collecting her mother at Heathrow and accompanying her to Bath. She had vanished before he was up, leaving fifty pounds on his kitchen table with a touching note begging him to forgive her "tantrum".

George had never met Lady Juxton and prayed that she was the sort of woman who would instinctively realize that her daughter had been subjected to vastly more horror than she could be expected to cope with.

His mind was on everything other than the business at hand. They were looking at him, waiting for him to answer. George smiled apologetically and said, 'Sorry, I was just turning over various possibilities in my mind. Maurice,' he began. 'Have you put Commander Goudhurst in the picture about our conjectures to do with Major Hamilton's activities?'

'Yes. I told him all about that. I've also sent for the enlargements of Mrs Hamilton's photographs from that skiing place you went to.'

'Now that, I think, really *is* a coincidence,' George said, thankful to Maurice for providing a focal point around which to marshal his thoughts. 'Her being on station, as it were, when those men were pushing off down the mountain. We've had everything sifted by experts at the MoD. They're the ones who boast that they can read the headlines of Ivan's newspaper in Red Square from a snap taken by a satellite.' He laughed. 'As luck would have it, the photogenic skiers weren't reading *Pravda* so all the experts could tell us was that they were carrying heavy loads in their rucksacks. Apparently whipped out their slide-rules and worked that out in the twinkling of an eye, arriving at this conclusion by estimating the depth of the tracks the skis made in the snow.'

Sir Maurice said, 'I'm sure we all agree that what is most unlikely to be pure coincidence is the presence of heavily-armed persons suspected of IRA connections in the immediate vicinity of the office where the films were presumed to be. Mr Lacey has reason to think that someone searched Mrs Hamilton's hotel room at the skiing place. Luckily, she had forgotten her camera and accoutrements in the hotel sitting-room, Mr Lacey then taking the precaution of keeping them in his own room, merely to avoid their being misplaced, damaged or nicked. He then posted the films to London. Again, this was done from habit rather than suspicion.

'Having found nothing in Mrs Hamilton's flat, our friends would assume the films to be at the magazine's offices in Hanover Square. They would further assume that they could search with impunity early on a holiday morning. The area is, as you know, largely composed of office blocks and therefore deserted as the moon on any holiday. The guns were, I imagine, either in transit from one place to another or simply carried as insurance against the unexpected.'

'Which you posit is what happened to the Japanese family?' Goudhurst asked.

'Yes, poor buggers.' Sir Maurice sipped delicately at an extremely pale whisky-and-soda. Goudhurst, who hadn't previously met George, tried not to look embarrassed at the word "buggers". 'It's entirely possible, of course, that *if* the IRA duo were paired off with Japanese Red Army reinforcements, for reasons we shall guess at later, one of the Shigekawa family might have recognized them or spoken to them for some entirely innocent reason. To ask directions, for example, or simply ask the time.' He stared moodily at his glass. 'Pure bad luck on their part.'

Goudhurst shook his head, unconvinced. 'The IRA have made some pretty appalling mistakes of late. Blowing up civilians, blowing up themselves. Blowing up entirely the wrong people and then saying they're sorry, it was a mistake. But these killings are an overreaction even for them.'

George and Sir Maurice kept silent as Goudhurst continued to think aloud.

'We've picked up a lot of their most senior and experienced men. They've been making some pretty spectacular cock-ups of one sort or another, like that half-baked attempt to spring one of their best explosives men out of prison. But it's too absurd that they'd go to such extraordinary lengths to protect a supply route. Pissing about in the Alps like that, even with the most expert skiers, an entire Olympic team, they couldn't transport very much.'

Sir Maurice stopped him. 'You did say Uzi, Dickie? That was the murder weapon?'

Goudhurst nodded. 'That's what the ballistics chaps think. I take your point, Maurice. Something entirely new, not part of the IRA's usual arsenal and you're wondering if the young lady's snaps were of a team smuggling them into France. Pop them into a heavy goods lorry with a load of hot-house grapes and presto here they are in London.' He measured out a space between his hands. 'A Uzi is smallish, with a folding stock. Easily concealed, nicely balanced. Weighs around five kilos, as I remember. But the magazines are heavy. A normal magazine is thirty nine-millimetre rounds.'

'So,' George said, 'a very limited number of guns and ammunition humped down a mountain in rucksacks.' He shrugged. 'The returns are simply too small to make an elaborate and expensive set-up such as that pay for itself. A dozen or so guns and two or three magazines apiece – it's too mad even for the IRA.'

Sir Maurice leant back in his chair. 'Not if what they're moving about is compact and extremely valuable. If what Mrs Hamilton witnessed was a trial run . . .' His voice trailed off.

'Diamonds, you mean, bearer bonds, nuclear secrets on microfilm and suchlike?' George asked, doodling on the notepad in front of him. 'For that sort of thing you need just one courier with a briefcase, or even a moneybelt or a lady's handbag.'

Sir Maurice nodded impatiently. 'Well, the bastards were carrying something and they want to protect that supply route, otherwise why go after the film. Ah, we're chasing our tails again!' He slapped the table hard enough to cause George to drop his pencil.

'Look,' Goudhurst said, 'the Provos have been concentrating for the past two years on killing as many British

79

soldiers as they can, when they don't make a complete balls of it. They call this "the long war" and wars are fought with weapons and weapons cost money. A great deal of money. Lately, they give every indication of having money to burn.'

He lapsed momentarily into silence, fiddling with his glass.

'They're concentrating more on Europe, too,' Sir Maurice said, 'and that's a shift.'

Lyall stood up and walked up and down the ugly little room to restore circulation. He moved to the end of the table to recharge his glass. 'Drink anyone?'

Goudhurst said, 'Not just for the moment, thanks,' then changed his mind. It had been an extremely long day and it wasn't over yet. 'Is it my imagination or were you not utterly taken by surprise at the putative involvement of Japanese terrorists?' He was aware that Lyall and Lacey exchanged a quick look.

'We get letters, Dickie,' Sir Maurice said softly. 'They are addressed to "Security", just that, at our Paris Embassy. Always typed and on three or four different typewriters, cheap paper and envelopes available at any stationers, various postmarks: Italy, France, Switzerland, Germany. West Germany,' he amended. 'Not much hard information but useful snippets. That's the informer I told you about.'

He seemed reluctant to go very far into the matter so Goudhurst said, 'And you were tipped off that there was a non-IRA connection?'

'Yes. There's a Red Brigade connection, too, besides the Japanese.'

'Those Italians who shot their Prime Minister?'

'Amongst others,' Sir Maurice said blandly. 'They go in for kidnapping in rather a big way, too.'

'I don't get it.' He held up a hand. 'I don't say your information's not valid but why would the IRA bring in outsiders?'

We think they're professional mercenaries. Ragtags. Unreconstructed leftovers from the Baader-Meinhof gang,

Red Army Faction, people of that sort. People who've developed a taste for killing, people with a habit of violence. The Middle East is an excellent source for them these days. People looking for an excuse to murder, looking for a cause in whose name, under whose banner they can go on killing.' His expressive eyebrows betrayed his contempt. 'They acquire the habit and they'll do anything, take on anyone's crusade, to support it, like a craving for drugs or women or gambling or danger. They probably get paid little enough over and above their expenses.' He fell silent.

'But it's very, very expensive nonetheless,' George added softly. 'It all costs money. We think they've got small cells stashed here and there. Keep in mind the recent business in Germany and the sergeant who was openly gunned down at Ostend in the car-ferry queue. The killers went to ground immediately. That means an elaborate and efficient organization underpinning the hit teams. People going about renting flats and houses, providing cash for food and transport, forged passports and driving licences, what-have-you. To support any sort of large-scale operation involves having large reserves of cash on tap without having to resort to bank transfers and other traceable paperwork.'

'It all costs money,' Goudhurst repeated as softly. 'That, as our American colleagues would say, is the bottom line. Is that the particular line of country you're following?'

George merely nodded and cleared his throat. He was thinking.

8

It had all been rehearsed many times and went like clockwork. The two Japanese got on the Piccadilly Line at Green Park, changed to the Circle Line at South Kensington and left London from Paddington, taking a train to Reading. Its link with Heathrow guaranteed that foreigners, suitably festooned with the paraphernalia of travel, were unremarkable and went completely unnoticed, especially in the midst of the bustling Easter weekend.

Reardon and Cahill went to Oxford Circus and returned by tube to Brixton, collected the car and drove to Reading in traffic that was not particularly heavy, given the holiday. Reardon hated driving with Cahill, who proceeded so cautiously that Reardon was sure that they would attract attention. He had explained many times but Cahill seemed to be incapable of grasping the fact that the hundredweight of Semtex in the Cortina's boot was as harmless as Fairy Liquid without a detonator. Reardon promised himself for the thousandth time that he really must do something about learning to drive and getting his own licence but he knew he never would. He was as wary of the internal combustion engine as Cahill was of explosives.

The Japanese were waiting at the appointed spot in the railway station car-park and scrambled into the back of the Cortina without a word. Their command of English was beyond eccentricity, limited as to syntax and vocabulary, yet made up largely of words of such shocking impropriety that Reardon preferred to keep conversation to a minimum.

Cahill kept the car at a sedate, steady sixty as they went along the M4. They drove to the safe house in almost complete silence, Reardon saying only that he would telephone for further instructions. The Japanese merely nodded their understanding, not at all curious about what arrangements, if any, had been made in the event of postponement or outright failure. They spoke softly to one another from time to time, staring out at the Berkshire countryside without interest. When it began to rain, they dozed off, leaning against one another like puppies, lulled by the monotonous swish of the windscreen-wipers and the gloomy, dripping landscape as the car turned off the M4 in Wiltshire.

Cahill pulled the car into the shed near the house. He knew nothing could be seen from the road but he shut the rickety doors anyway, out of habit. The safe house was cold and uncomfortable. Reardon went from room to room switching on the single-bar electric heaters. A large patch of damp in a corner of the sitting-room supported a luxuriant growth of mildew, the smell of it combining with the smell of mouse-droppings to remind him of home, a cottage in County Cavan. With some recourse to sign language, he conveyed to the Japanese that he would go to the call-box on the road just outside the village and ring their control at five o'clock. Before that, they would have something to eat and then they could sleep if they felt like it.

Cahill set about heating up a large tin of Heinz baked beans and sliced a brown loaf to make toast. The kitchen was filthy, mice clearly audible behind the skirting-boards. The Japanese, watching this operation with unconcealed distaste, nibbled a few mouthfuls, nodded briefly and took themselves off to one of the poky, dank little bedrooms upstairs. Cahill wondered enviously if they would have a fuck. He had been thinking of nothing else since the shells from his Uzi had ripped through the soft, yielding flesh of the three jabbering people in Hanover Square.

Although he found the woman, Reiko, overwhelmingly plain, he was feeling keyed up and would have fancied a go himself but he was more than a little frightened by Mitsu's blank inscrutability, which Cahill sometimes felt masked a deep contempt. He and Reardon spoke softly to one another in stilted Irish liberally salted with English, not at all convinced that the Japanese were as unfamiliar with ordinary English as they pretended. It was better to take no risks. Reardon's answers to his questions were curt, verging on hostile, but Cahill was accustomed to that. He knew Reardon didn't like him and didn't care.

The Japanese still hadn't come back downstairs when Reardon left to walk the half-mile to the call-box on the road and make his report to Gillon, leaving Cahill to sleep or, unnecessarily, stand guard. First he stopped at the shed. Although it had stopped raining, Reardon fished his Wellingtons out of the Cortina. He carefully set the two time-delay fuses attached to the Semtex explosive in the smart crimson carrier-bag emblazoned "Salvatore Ferragamo" and the more sober navy nylon suitcase of carry-on size. That left considerably more than half of the remaining Semtex in the boot to be wired up when the time came.

He then squelched across the muddy field to the copse where they had buried the new Uzis, checking for signs of intrusion. He and Cahill had dug another deep hole in the soft earth a few days before, following Gillon's instructions, and he made sure that the light camouflage of branches was still in place. It was likely they would need it, given the unforeseen complications of the morning. With the approach of warmer weather, the guns would soon have to be moved to avoid the risks posed by picnickers, bird-watchers and courting couples, but for the moment all was well. There were no fag-ends or other bits of rubbish strewn about the copse. If people had been there they hadn't stayed long.

The call-box stank of urine and Reardon paced about out-side it waiting for the telephone to ring. He knew that Gillon would not blame him that things had gone wrong. When the phone rang, Reardon picked it up instantly. As expected, the conversation with Gillon was brief and without recri-mination. He didn't need to go into an elaborate explanation that killing the Oriental people who had materialized from nowhere, babbling incomprehensibly at Reiko and Mitsu until Mitsu had pulled out his machine-pistol, had been a necessary precaution to forestall possible complications and identifications, and thereby protect the principal operation.

That was the splendid thing about Gillon: he had the sort of mind that was capable of grasping a situation immediately without Reardon's having to justify or explain every move. Gillon was possessed of a formidable intelligence, a fact that Reardon appreciated but frequently made him afraid. He was immeasurably relieved that their failure to destroy all film and photographs to be found at *The Epicure* didn't appear to cause Gillon much annoyance. It had, apparently, been a mere precaution rather than a life-or-death matter, for which Reardon was at once both grateful and obscurely vexed. The alternative part of the plan, he was told, should go ahead without delay, really only a matter of shuffling component parts of the overall scheme into a slightly different sequence, discarding the jokers. It was essential that the Monday schedule, although perforce now abbreviated, should go smoothly.

Reardon didn't pass through the copse on his way back to the house, wanting to avoid unnecessary footprints in the damp earth. Cahill raised a questioning eyebrow as Reardon returned and they had a brief, whispered conversation.

Going to the foot of the stairs, Cahill called up to the Japanese to start getting ready. They would be pushing off at nightfall. After a moment or two, they heard footsteps above.

Cahill shot Mitsu first as he turned at the bottom of the stairs to go along the passage towards the lavatory at the back. He had used both a silencer and a tattered velvet sofa-cushion to muffle the noise and Cahill helped him lower the body soundlessly to the floor before going upstairs and killing Reiko. She had gone back to sleep and died almost without waking, a single shot through the heart. He twitched back the disgusting blanket and smiled when he saw that she was wearing nothing but a jungle-green teeshirt illuminated with an alligator and the single word "Florida". So they had had a fuck. Her bladder had voided in death and there was a sharp smell of urine. It made no difference whatsoever to him.

He quickly took off his jeans to avoid getting blood on them. He didn't want Reardon to know about this, for some obscure reason he didn't bother to worry about.

As he pumped into her, he purposely looked away from her acne-pitted face, especially her eyes, opened in frozen disbelief during the last second of her life.

Nedda felt superb, sharp in her perceptions and omniscient. The cocaine supercharged her body and brain and she tingled with multiple sensations, all wonderful. Her nerve-endings took on a life of their own as she dealt with the second rail. She was magnificently aware of her own power and the headiness that came over her when she knew everything would go exactly right, even as she had always predicted.

The war was taking a new direction under her influence, an influence she felt was growing exponentially. Immense amounts of money were now available because of *her* ideas and *her* management. More money than the stupid, gullible Irish-Americans could ever have been coaxed or shamed into producing; more money than the highminded windbags of Sinn Fein could ever dream of or promise in their soaring flights of platitude. Only she knew how much money there was and where it was and how it was made to grow and work for The Cause.

Soon the war would cease to be a piddling, nickle-and-dime affair, a local bush war with half-crazed ideologues potting away at one another in the hideous housing estates and backstreets of Belfast or Derry. Nedda wanted a world stage and her elation was due to the certain knowledge that soon she would have it. Bang in the centre, where she belonged. Bang! She laughed aloud.

The beauty of it was that only a handful of people would know who it was pulling the strings. She had no use for the trappings of power, only its reality. In this way, and so many others, she was very similar to Gillon. When the British were finally defeated, when Gillon seized power in a united Ireland, the political puppets of Sinn Fein would dance, perhaps only dimly aware that their movements were controlled by a jovial ex-Jesuit and an Irish-American woman with a genius for international financial management and an MBA from the Harvard Business School to prove it.

Gillon would see to it that the politicians who wouldn't or couldn't dance were eliminated. She laughed again. The remainder would be given unmistakable incentives to emigrate.

Nedda was currently pulling in more than thirty million pounds a year in clear profit, more than double what the IRA were grossing from their assorted rackets in Ireland, North and South. Contributions from America were gradually drying up – last year, the tired old harangues had only pulled in a derisory sum, maybe two per cent of the targeted five million dollars – and Nedda had more than taken up the slack as paymaster. It followed that she would increasingly call the tune. She had no patience for the IRA's ponderous councils endlessly debating strategy, tactics, means to ends and how many broken eggs were required to make a respectable omelette. They were only useful as front-men, for dealing with other ranting tub-thumpers in Australia and America.

The mercenaries that Gillon scavenged for on some sort of international human dung-heap were working out far better than she had thought they would. It had been a clever move on his part. She didn't begrudge him the credit for having thought of it, freely admitting that she had been short-sighted in initially opposing his plan. The advantage lay in their being totally expendable. They lived in the shadows and no one would raise the alarm when they disappeared. By using them and then killing them when they were no longer needed, Gillon was doing no more than what they themselves ultimately yearned for.

What she was unwilling to admit, even to herself, was that Gillon sometimes frightened her. She found him the most fascinating man she'd ever known and was powerfully attracted to him, something she knew he was aware of, and, what was worse, she also knew she would never dare to try seducing him.

She paced aimlessly around the large flat, seething with energy but at a loss for something to do. There was nothing to look at but the grey sea, trailing pennants of polluted foam in the wind, and crashing monotonously onto the artificial beach far below. The telex sat silent. There lacked even the background noise of Costelloe mooching about trying to stay out of her way. She had dismissed him for the weekend: he got on her nerves. He was likely to be in Nice with a whore.

She had to get out, find some release for all her pent-up energy. On rare occasions such as this, she missed having any friends. She made a decision and dialled.

'*Pronto*,' a woman's voice answered.

'Hello, Margareta,' Nedda said.

'Oh, it's you,' the woman said, with a marked lack of enthusiasm.

'Yes,' Nedda agreed. 'Is Ruffo there?'

'No, he isn't.'

All right, you old bitch, Nedda thought. 'Do you expect him?' she asked politely.

'He's abroad.'

'I see,' Nedda said, not allowing a trace of her disappointment to colour her tone. She could have simply rung off but she wanted to get even with Ruffo for not being there when she wanted him and she could vent a fraction of her frustration on Ruffo's mother instead, in the absence of any better target. She knew that Margareta was afraid of her.

'How's Ottavio?' she enquired in a friendly manner.

'My husband is well, thank you.' Her voice, with its light Swedish accent, was glacial.

'I'm so glad,' Nedda said with great warmth. 'Manfredi? All the family? Everyone ticking over nicely?' Then she put the knife in and twisted it. 'And my adorable little Guido, Margareta, how is *he*?'

There was a sharp intake of breath, as Nedda had known there would be. The old bag's scared shitless, Nedda thought with vicious satisfaction. She derived immense pleasure from having the entire family jump to her bidding whenever she snapped her fingers. They'd all be driving taxis if it weren't for her, anyway, and she wasn't above reminding them of it.

'Getting bigger, Nedda. You wouldn't recognize him,' Margareta said with an ingratiating, placatory note.

Don't you just wish I wouldn't, Nedda said to herself with a smile. The Principessa sounded like a potential victim trying to wheedle a homicidal maniac into putting down his axe and accepting a soothing cup of tea instead.

'I can't wait to see him,' Nedda said, knowing that the cow would be shaking with combined fear and impotent rage by now.

'He's become something of a handful, Nedda,' Margareta said desperately. 'I'm sure you wouldn't have time to . . .'

Nedda laughed gaily. 'But I mustn't take up *your* time with chit-chat, Margareta. Do tell Ruffo I called and don't forget to tell my sweet little Guido – but I must stop thinking of him that way; he'd be so *embarrassed* – that I'll come see him soon. Eton is such a pretty school. So historic, so traditional, so very *English*!'

'I won't forget, Nedda,' Margareta promised and Nedda knew the message had been received and understood.

She slammed down the phone again and ran into her dressing-room. Throwing things about and letting everything fall where it might, she chose her costume for the evening with unaccustomed care, selecting a simple Lagerfeld in midnight-blue velvet to accentuate her dappled, pale skin. There didn't seem much point in bothering with anything underneath but she went to the safe and took out a diamond necklace and matching earrings from Boucheron.

When she left the flat she was in a much-improved mood. An hour later, she had forgotten that the conversation with Margareta had ever taken place.

Ruffo had chosen well, Gillon was pleased to note. The bar at the Lorient railway station, although not terribly crowded, was noisy enough, with regulars shouting greetings to one another and the usual departure and arrival announcements coming through loud and clear on the speakers. Strangers would attract little undue attention in such a place. They settled themselves at the quieter tables towards the back.

A morose-looking man with a tanned, deeply-lined face and the characteristic rolling gait of seamen made his way through the crowd at the bar. It was clear from the way he peered about uncertainly, his expression a fine mixture of apprehension and bravado, that he was their man. Ruffo drew himself up to his full six-foot-four, dwarfing Gillon, to beckon him over.

'*Capitaine* Kerrien?' he asked.

The man nodded without speaking and glanced nervously at Gillon, who was wearing his cassock, its front, as usual, liberally sprinkled with cigarette ash in true Jesuit fashion.

'*Mon père*,' he said, evidently taken aback at finding himself in the company of a priest. Gillon beamed and motioned the Breton to join them, urging him, with Ruffo as interpreter, to have a drink. Ruffo ordered for all three of them and introduced Gillon as Father Falvey, a name not very far away from the one enshrined in his British passport, and himself as Guy Ruffino, citizen of Marseille, calculating that a Breton wouldn't know the difference between an Italian and a Marseillais accent.

'It was I,' he said with engaging humility, 'who deranged you in the midst of your siesta yesterday when I permitted myself the liberty of telephoning to make our appointment.'

Yann Kerrien thawed visibly, disclaiming any derangement caused, his two quick gulps of cognac, judging from the tremor of his hand, warming his mood rather a lot. It was good to be treated with respect again.

He was in no hurry to get down to business. Perhaps, if what one heard about the Irish was true, this affable priest might enjoy a drink or two amongst, if not yet friends, then natural political allies and potential business associates. He glanced shrewdly at Gillon to assess his fondness for the bottle.

'Tell him it's a cold day and on a cold day a drop of cognac is good for the circulation,' Father Falvey said, piously adding, 'and a gift from the Good Lord.'

Kerrien got the general drift of this remark before Ruffo had finished its translation and dutifully drained his glass. He didn't wish to appear rude or ungrateful, certainly not to a beneficent God. Ruffo caught the barman's eye and signalled for another round.

Not taking any chances that Kerrien's ignorance of English was as total as he claimed, Gillon said, 'My son, you must tell him that his reputation as a fighter for Breton autonomy is much admired in Ireland. We Celts are a warrior race and our folk memories of injustice and persecution stretch back into the mists of time. We admire the perseverance of our distant cousins, the Bretons, driven out of their native lands, lands that bear their tribal name to this day, by the usurping Saxons.' His dark face wore an expression of fanatical dedication.

Kerrien listened to Ruffo's translation and nodded solemnly. He mumbled a few words in Breton and the good father smiled broadly.

'Tell him that I recognize the sound of his ancient and beautiful language, so heart-breakingly similar to our own, but not its sense. Tell him I apologize most humbly that we must communicate in the languages of our common enemies, Saxon and Frankish.'

They finally got down to business and the logistics of the operation came easily enough, Gillon deftly extracting information on the trawler's normal crew and judging to a nicety the speed with which the Breton's glass ought to be refilled. Kerrien's small eyes grew misty again when the good father repeated his assurances that heroic deeds would be celebrated again soon, in Breton and in Gaelic, as they had been by the bards of old.

Their arrangements were sealed with a single valedictory drink, a thick sheaf of five-hundred-franc notes passed under the table – for expenses and anything over to be contributed to The Cause of Breton Autonomy – and mutual assurances of esteem and victory.

9

Sir Maurice interrupted the argument between George and the American. 'Mr Moseley,' he said with little patience, 'whether you are in favour or not is, I'm afraid, quite beside the point. Lacey and I wish to speak with you. Here in the lobby, if you insist, although I think we'd have a bit more privacy in your flat. There is nothing to be gained by being abusive.'

With extreme bad grace, Brook led the way to the lift and punched viciously at the call-button. 'Look. I don't want you to get the wrong idea. Camilla's up there. She's not in very good shape.'

'I thought she'd gone to her mother's,' George said, genuinely surprised.

'She did. They had a discussion about Jeremy, if you must know, which became rather heated. Camilla got very upset and she was still upset when she got up this morning. She tried to call you, George, but you weren't at home. I gave her my number the other night at your house so she got me instead. She needed someone to talk to.'

The elderly lift grumbled as it crept slowly up. 'There were further high words over breakfast and Camilla called for a taxi and went straight to the station. It's a holiday weekend, not that either of you seems to have noticed that, and she had to wait ages for a train. She was still upset when she got to Paddington and she called me from there. All her other friends are away, she said,' he explained sheepishly, clearly anxious that the two older men not think that he had unchivalrous designs on a distraught, lonely and very attractive woman.

He opened the lift gate more gently and ushered his unwanted guests down the passage. The frozen pizzas he'd gone out to buy for dinner were starting to seep water through the paper bag. He rummaged for his latchkey and unlocked the door, calling to Camilla as he did so. 'It's Brook, Camilla, with George and a friend of his.'

She stood in the doorway that separated the small entry from the sitting-room. Her face was taut. 'You were so long, Brook. I thought you'd been set upon by revolting tribesmen.'

'Set upon and waylaid by us,' George said smoothly. Her face was tight with strain. 'This is Sir Maurice Lyall, my dear. Tribesmen we may be but, I trust, not quite revolting.'

'Georgie, don't play the innocent with me,' Camilla said coldly, looking considerably annoyed. 'You and your playmate didn't just stumble over Brook as he was counting his change at Europa. I'm sorry about your garden but I assure you that I'm perfectly all right now and I won't have you checking up on me. I suppose he's a head-shrinker,' she said, teeth clenched and nodding in the impassive Lyall's direction.

'Now, Mr Moseley,' Sir Maurice said, settling himself into a chair without invitation. 'Perhaps you would be good enough to explain why it is that you have made spurious claims to being a professor of history at this university in America, Antwerp.'

'Amherst,' Brook corrected, 'after Jeffrey, Lord Amherst. An English Field Marshal of the eighteenth century. Small but excellent. The college I mean; I don't know if the Field Marshal was either small or excellent.'

'I am waiting, Mr Moseley, to hear what you might have to say,' Sir Maurice said patiently.

'Sir Maurice, I'm afraid I have no idea by what right you are putting any questions to me at all,' Brook said with equal politeness. 'I've broken no law.'

George held up a warning hand, like a schoolmaster confronting a roomful of unruly boys. 'This sparring could go on forever, Maurice. Brook, you'll simply have to take my word for it that we are civil servants with a security brief.'

Brook opened his eyes very wide, mocking George's pomposity. Before he could open his mouth, Camilla flopped onto the sofa and said, 'Golly! You're James Bond and he's M? Very bad casting, Georgie. Do you actually expect us to believe that you, of all people, are a policeman?'

'Please be patient, Mrs Hamilton,' Sir Maurice said severely. 'Mr Moseley, I have the power to have you deported. Tonight, if necessary.' He looked evenly at the American who merely sighed.

'Sorry. I don't suppose you are the sort of civil servants who carry warrant cards, or whatever they're called here. I am a civil servant, too, and I don't have anything on me that proves it. So it looks like we're at an impasse.' He returned the baronet's even stare.

Sir Maurice wearily levered himself out of his chair and looked about. 'If I might use your telephone?' he asked Brook.

'In the bedroom. First left.' He heard Sir Maurice shut the door behind him and smiled reassuringly at Camilla, who glared back. 'I suppose common courtesy requires me to offer you a drink, George, while your buddy checks up on me.'

That *would* be kind, Brook. Whisky-and-soda for me, please. Do give poor Maurice one, too, there's a clever fellow. He's not a bad old thing, you know. Just doing his job.' He smiled up at Brook as he accepted his glass. 'Blessings on you. I'm just doing mine, too, in point of fact.' Turning to Camilla, who pulled her tongue out at him, he said, 'I'm glad you're here, dear girl, despite your childish devotion to flouncing in and out of rooms. We would've had to have a little heart-to-heart chat soon, in any event. This will save a good deal of explaining and beating about the bush.'

'I don't believe any of this,' she said mulishly.

'You don't believe that a silly old queen like me could be in the security services, do you?' George asked with a slight smile. 'One thing we silly old queens are good at is detail. Think about it, my dear. Maurice, who is *not* a silly old queen, is good at overall pictures and I worry away at the fiddly bits.

94

'Think of me,' he ordered gently, 'as your wicked Uncle Augustus who does the most beautiful embroidery and lives in Tangier on money provided by your late father's estate to keep him living anywhere except here.'

'Christ! You really *are* a policeman or a spy,' Camilla said, once she'd recovered from the surprise.

'Well, yes. You can think of me as a snooper or you could, if you were inclined to do so, look upon Maurice and me as guardian angels, in a way. Jeremy was involved with some *very* unsavoury people Camilla, who wouldn't have had the slightest hesitation in dusting off the thumbscrews if they believed you had an inkling of what your late husband was getting up to.'

Sir Maurice came back and looked at the drink Brook handed him with surprise and gratitude. 'That's uncommonly decent of you, Moseley. Thanks very much.' To George he said, 'Jay Rodman says he's okay.' He sipped, said, 'That's better,' and sat down again.

'I was just,' George said a bit defensively, 'saying to Mrs Hamilton that we had in any event intended to speak with her . . .'

'I know you,' Camilla suddenly said, scowling at Lyall. 'You were the policeman, an Inspector you said, who came to my flat the day it was broken into. I thought when you arrived just now that I'd seen you somewhere before.'

Sir Maurice nodded slightly. 'I assure you, Mrs Hamilton, that I was there for your protection, not for any sinister reason. As Lacey told you, we had every intention of being rather more straightforward with you in the near future. I'm afraid that, until Mr Moseley's position in all of this has been clarified, we cannot discuss matters directly concerning you in his presence.' He bestowed upon her the sort of avuncular half-smile normally associated with family solicitors. 'I am quite certain that we can get this sorted out . . .'

'Did Rodman tell you why I'm here?' Brook interrupted. He was becoming impatient with the fencing.

'He only told me that you weren't one of his,' Sir Maurice said guardedly, both men aware that Camilla remained an unknown quantity and Jay Rodman was the CIA's Head of London Station.

George cleared his throat and got everyone's attention. 'I see no point in continuing in this vein. If we are to get Camilla's co-operation, which we very much need at this point, we can't flit about behind carnival masks. I am fully prepared to vouch for her. She's no babbling idiot any more than she's an IRA sleeper and the pricking of my thumbs tells me that Mr Moseley's quite all right, too. Now, Maurice,' he said, turning with marked lack of deference to his superior, 'why don't we simply lay down our hands?'

'Fair enough,' Sir Maurice said equably, to Camilla's surprise. She had thought him rather forbidding.

'I'm not at all sure that I *want* to hear anything, Sir Maurice,' she said.

'Hoity-toity,' George teased. 'Come on, Camilla. No one's waving the Official Secrets Act in your face. Just listen.'

'As Mr Moseley will have gathered, Mrs Hamilton, Georgie and I are civil servants concerned with security. We now know that Mr Moseley is similarly engaged on behalf of the American government but we would like to know which government department and why he is here, on our turf, and why he was in France, conveniently in place where a situation arose about which we would like to know a great deal more.'

'Does this have some bearing on the break-in at my flat?' Camilla asked, somewhat chastened.

'We think so. But for the moment we're whistling in the dark.' Sir Maurice looked at her evenly. 'Going back even further, Mrs Hamilton, we also think there is every likelihood of a strong connection with your husband's murder.'

'I see,' Camilla said, barely audible. 'Please continue, Sir Maurice, and please forgive my rudeness.'

'Nothing to forgive, my dear young lady. Mr Moseley?'

Brook's stomach rumbled loudly, breaking the tension in the room. He grinned. 'Two minutes while I put the pizzas

96

in the oven and bring out some ice. We can get more to eat later, but for the moment I'm not in control of myself.' His stomach rumbled again to substantiate his claim and Camilla, feeling unaccountably more relaxed than she had thought possible, busied herself with refilling everyone's glasses.

Brook immediately set about the challenging task of dividing the two pizzas, one sausage-and-onion and the other a prosaic cheese-and-tomato, into four equal pieces, using the single blunt instrument provided by his landlord. As the oven heated, he got the last tray of ice out of the tiny fridge and returned to the sitting-room. The pizzas eventually got hot enough for the cheese to melt and were hungrily consumed whilst he told his "snow story".

He worked for the Drug Enforcement Agency and was following up on some extremely tenuous leads, little more than rumours picked up here and there about a relatively new traffic in pharmaceutical-quality, unadulterated cocaine. His field of expertise was primarily concerned with what he called "black economics" and lay in following the often very faint trails left behind by money on the move.

Brook inclined towards a theory, by no means the only one kicked about in Washington, that the main distribution-point for this new cocaine, with its own distinctive chemical fingerprint, was in Europe and that there was an organization behind it that they hadn't previously encountered. There appeared to be no connection whatsoever with Colombia, nor, indeed, any other Caribbean country. The quantities available in America were minute and the price was correspondingly astronomical.

'I'm an economist by training and education and this new organization began to fascinate me,' he explained without apology. Sir Maurice and George nodded their understanding.

The DEA had nothing but rumours to go on until a mule, in this instance a Catholic priest from Boston, was picked up in Rome. His suitcase had a false bottom containing five kilos of cocaine, unadulterated, top-quality snow.

'Was this priest by any chance Irish-American?' Sir Maurice asked.

Brook smiled and nodded. 'I gather it's the Irish angle that interests your, ah, government department, so the fact that Hanratty's Boston-Irish isn't mere coincidence.'

'Yes,' Sir Maurice said economically.

Father Joseph Hanratty had lately been interviewed in Boston by Brook's colleagues. A tape-recording had been made, a copy of which he said Sir Maurice and George could have if they wanted it. Hanratty's story was a fascinating one and he was, Brook assured them, far, far too stupid to have invented a single word of it. 'Jonathan Kirkwood, who did all the interviewing, swears that Hanratty has the reasoning-power of a young gerbil,' he said.

Father Hanratty was also very frightened that his bishop might learn he'd been mixed up in shady goings-on, although he was left in a state of perfect ignorance that his suitcase had once contained cocaine, although he was aware that it had contained something of interest to officers of the law. The DEA hadn't bothered to enlighten him on the grounds that it might prove more productive to wait and see who, if anyone, might scuttle out of the woodwork. Hanratty was too birdbrained to keep his mouth shut, even in his own interest.

He said he had been telephoned in Boston by a man with an Irish accent who asked if the priest might be willing to perform a service vital to The Cause. Father Hanratty had willingly agreed. He had been given an Alitalia ticket New York–Milan, Rome–New York and a ticket for the Boston–New York shuttle flight, plus a new suitcase, with instructions that he keep his packing to a minimum. An envelope was in the suitcase, containing three hundred dollars and a thick sheaf of lire, a second-class single railway ticket Milan–Rome and the name of a large hotel in Milan, the Executive, opposite the Porta-Garibaldi railway station.

He was to check into the Milan hotel and go up to his room, staying no more than ten minutes. He was then to go out for no less than one hour, leaving his door slightly ajar and his room-key on the bed. He was to make no telephone calls from the hotel. His room was paid for and he was to continue on to Rome the following day and spend four days there, returning to New York and taking the shuttle back to Boston.

The programme had an elegant simplicity, the instructions neatly laid out and numbered chronologically. It would have worked admirably if Hanratty hadn't been robbed on the train. He had fallen into conversation with a youngish couple who were fellow-occupants of the compartment, both speaking fairly good English and anxious to improve it. They had companionably offered him some of their wine. Never one to pass up a drink, the priest had accepted with alacrity. He had been shaken awake by the conductor when the train was approaching Rome.

He had an awesome hangover, a condition not altogether unknown to him, but the conductor was suspicious and had asked him to check his belongings, there having been a recent plague of robberies on the Italian railways. Sure enough, his money and passport were gone and the conductor radioed ahead to the Carabinieri. In the course of checking the still-dazed Hanratty's suitcase to see if anything were missing and dusting it for fingerprints, they discovered that its false bottom contained five kilos of pure cocaine of exceptionally high quality. Even the police lab had been impressed.

The DEA man attached to the Rome Embassy enjoyed the most cordial relations with the Carabinieri. Brook flew out to lend a hand. It had been decided to let Hanratty run to see where he would lead them, the Carabinieri having substituted baking soda for the cocaine in his suitcase. They were unmoved by the idea that the Mafia, or whatever organization owned the shipment, might kill the priest on the assumption that he had diverted the goods for his own ends.

Brook's DEA colleague posed as a solicitous US Consulate man and escorted the befuddled priest through the police formalities, depositions as to the amounts of money lost and descriptions of the suspected thieves. Everyone had tut-tutted over the sinful state of a world in which a blameless priest could be duped by cynical young persons whose only thought was of immoral financial gain. He was eventually bowed onto his Alitalia flight with a replacement passport and further effusive apologies and reassurances that the malefactors would be caught and harshly dealt with.

There had been no "meeters" waiting for the priest in Rome, New York or Boston. Two policemen posing as building inspectors had gained admission to the South Boston rectory the day after Hanratty's return but the fake cocaine had already been removed. There were no new fingerprints. With all the to-ings and fro-ings at the rectory, inhabited by no less than three other priests and a female housekeeper, all of whom had armies of friends, family and parishioners constantly in and out, the Boston Police couldn't pinpoint who actually did the removing. Red-faced, they had explained that they hadn't counted on a crowd-scene. It was at this point that Hanratty was hauled in for questioning, there being nothing to gain by keeping him in the dark and hoping stark terror might jog his sluggish memory a little. There was no doubt he knew he'd been smuggling but he wasn't told what had been in his shiny new suitcase.

Brook was teamed with an English-speaking policeman in Milan and they had a stroke of luck: a hotel employee, actually a reservations clerk, named Mario Buozzi had been waiting for his wife, due to arrive on a suburban train from Rho. Buozzi was killing time in the bar of the Porta-Garibaldi railway station opposite the hotel. It was his half-day and he and his wife intended to shop for some furniture.

He recognized the man who had made an unusual booking, "Mr Castle", clearly waiting for someone at the station's main entrance. Buozzi was curious about him because not only had Castle come to the hotel in March to book no fewer than fifteen single rooms for one night, as well as a sixteenth for two nights, but he had mentioned

100

something about a sales conference, without, however, inquiring about any of the hotel's many conference rooms. Such block bookings were normally done by telex in any event.

Buozzi watched as Mr Castle stood about for a while, occasionally glancing up at the station clock. Within a few minutes, a car pulled up, driven by a woman, and Castle piled in with his two suitcases. Buozzi had time to note that this car was a dark-blue Renault saloon and that it had French number-plates. The Renault was fitted with a roof-rack holding a single pair of skis. Buozzi had thought at the time that Mr Castle didn't at all look the skiing type, rather more the sort of person one might see driving a hearse. He hadn't paid much attention to the woman and his description of her was sketchy. He remembered only that she was wearing a dark fur coat, probably mink, with a matching, turban-style hat completely covering her hair. She looked decidedly unpleasant, as though she'd been held up in heavy traffic and regarded the inconvenience as a personal insult. She and Castle had hardly spoken before driving off.

A second stroke of luck came as a result of the Carabinieri's quickly-circulated description of the Renault and its occupants. A bored frontier-guard at the Italian entrance of the Mont Blanc Tunnel clearly remembered the car because it bore French number-plates and its occupants, a man and a woman, had an Irish and an American passport respectively. The car's papers had been in order, however, and he had waved them through, unfortunately unable to recall either of the two names. Being older and longer-married than Mario Buozzi, he had a pronounced interest in the entire female sex; thus he was able to elaborate upon Buozzi's description of the woman, saying that she had pale, freckled skin. Smartly-dressed, rather arrogant in manner but on the whole quite attractive. She smelled, he added, very expensive.

Brook had promptly rented a car on the off-chance of stumbling across this ill-assorted couple and having in any event nothing better to do with himself.

Interpol had been alerted but there was no shortage in France of dark-blue Renaults containing a solemn-faced man and ill-tempered looking woman, both in their mid-to-late thirties.

'So when we met in Val Sainte-Anne, I take it that you were hoping to pick up a trail gone cold?' George asked.

'That's about it,' Brook agreed. 'I was just stooging around on the off-chance.' He shrugged. 'I was getting underfoot at the Rome Embassy but I didn't feel like just calling it a day and hopping on a plane back to Washington.'

Sir Maurice, who had made careful notes throughout Brook's recital, said, 'Thank you very much, Mr Moseley. That has been most helpful. Now, to prove to you that this is not a one-way street,' he smiled, 'we have reason to believe that some photographs Mrs Hamilton took by lucky chance on top of a mountain show what could possibly be another aspect of your cocaine distribution.'

He leant back in his chair, looking rather donnish. 'Let us posit that a consignment came in by sea somewhere along the Italian coast and that Milan was chosen as a staging-point for the cocaine to be divided up and smuggled out in small, manageable quantities. Milan's a clever choice: excellent communications, large, industrial city, not immediately associated in police or customs minds with drug-trafficking.'

Brook nodded. 'Agreed. An unusually clever choice, we thought. As you say, an industrial city with freight rolling out constantly bound for unlimited destinations. Freight containers that can conceal almost any quantity of cocaine, suitably disguised.'

'Mr Castle,' Sir Maurice went on, 'has his fifteen mules and a schedule for the arrival of each. The mule goes up to his or her room, tips the porter, inspects the plumbing, adds or subtracts clothing and leaves again, according to the instruction sheet. Castle pops in and doctors the mule's suitcase. The mules *expect* their suitcases to be heavier when leaving. Can you,' he asked Brook, 'find out how much baggage Castle had when he arrived? Or if a parcel was left for him at the hotel before he checked in? It's quite a lot, isn't it? Five kilos apiece for fifteen carriers is seventy-five kilos, at the very least. Some of the mules may have carried more if they were travelling by road or even rail, not to mention concealment in ordinary freight. The hotel's proximity to a railway station is interesting. *And* it seems possible there was some over, which got put into rucksacks and skied across the frontier. But more of that later.'

He looked at George. 'My feeling is that Castle and the woman passed on the drugs before crossing into France.'

'Quite. I had the same thought. I wish we had some maps,' George said plaintively.

'I've got a road-map of the area,' Brook said, 'if I can lay hands on it.' He went out and Camilla followed him. Sir Maurice listened briefly, then quickly whispered, 'What's your feeling, Georgie? How far can we go with him on the IRA involvement?'

They heard the loo flush. 'I think he's fine. I think, Maurice, we don't hold anything back. As Jay vouches for him . . .' He fell silent as Camilla returned and meekly sat down without speaking. They heard Brook rummaging about in another room, muttering to himself as he opened and shut drawers.

He returned, already unfolding a big Michelin map. 'Castle and Co could've unloaded anywhere between Milan and the Mont Blanc Tunnel but I'd go for somewhere in the Val d'Aosta, here.' His finger traced the road on the map. 'Here is where France, Italy and Switzerland all meet.'

'We have reason to believe,' Sir Maurice caught George's eye and began again. 'We seem to have acquired a mystery informer of some sort who tipped us off that the IRA has had one shipment of Uzis and may buy more. We'd very much like to find them. One of them has already been used with tragic results.'

'The murders in Hanover Square? You think the IRA did *that*? Why, for God's sake, would the IRA want to kill Japanese tourists?' Brook asked with unfeigned astonishment.

'Another of their little slip-ups,' Sir Maurice said evenly. 'We think it's possible they found out about Mrs Hamilton's snaps and were either intending to ransack the magazine's offices or firebomb the whole place, which is rather more their style. The tourists simply blundered along, we assume.

'As to the Uzis being smuggled, the timing is right to bear out the tip from our source and our guess is that Mrs Hamilton's skiers brought them across the Alps from Italy or Switzerland. Airport metal detectors make it a great deal more difficult to smuggle arms by air than drugs. We think the guns could have been brought into England by lorry, along with something perfectly straightforward like machine parts, through any of the Channel ports.'

'But it's entirely possible,' George said, 'that the skiers moved both arms and cocaine. A bit of both, if you follow, possibly even as a dress rehearsal for a later exercise or an entire series of runs. Groups of jolly skiers attract no attention at airports and railway stations. There's glacier skiing up there in summer, too, which gives the place an extended season. Nothing remarkable in humping heavy rucksacks about. Uzis aren't frightfully heavy but their magazines are. Brook,' he said after a slight pause, 'I'm really just thinking aloud. I'm afraid I know nothing of drugs but will you bear with me on one or two points?'

'George, I know nothing of guns and explosives, so let's just agree to ask dumb questions as the need arises.'

'Your Mr Castle and the lady in mink have organized things very well indeed. The hotel-room wheeze is excellent. Mules simply disperse to airports, railway stations, what-have-you, with their loads, never having glimpsed the distributor. If caught, as was your Boston priest, not a great deal can be sweated out of them. Had it not been the happy circumstance of Signor Buozzi skulking about with nothing better to do, Castle would have come and gone unnoticed. I assume that the Milan hotel was a large one?'

'Vast.' Brook consulted a notebook and added, 'Four hundred-plus rooms. Frequently used for conventions and that sort of thing.'

'Payment?'

'Cash.'

'What are you sniffing after, George?' Sir Maurice asked.

'It smells like a one-off to me. The mules themselves are likely one-offs, too, and not on any black-list. The hotel is a one-off and, at a guess, Milan itself is a one-off.'

Brook nodded his agreement. 'I'm with you, George, but what does all that tell us?'

'A small organization and not set up on the usual IRA lines. They tend towards self-contained cells, each running about in its own territory and doing its own thing. This is quite, quite different. Plenty of arms and legs to perform specific chores but only one head, like a creepy-crawly. Small is beautiful,' he explained, thinking aloud. 'Reducing the spread reduces the risk of leaks. The priest, for example. Got pulled in but couldn't do more than lead you back up the pipeline to Milan. And in Milan there's nothing left to discover. Impasse. The brains behind this have structured the operation beautifully: any leak is self-sealing, to borrow an automotive metaphor.'

Brook steepled his fingers. 'The small fry, the mules, are used once, paid and that's all. If they talk they haven't much to say. But are you gentlemen of the opinion that the IRA, or some part of it, is behind this cocaine ring?'

Sir Maurice said, 'I am certainly leaning heavily in that direction. George?'

'I, too. We've seen in recent operations of theirs that a different hand seems to be controlling them, a different mind, if you will. But that mind is directing principally their activities on the Continent. In Ireland, both the Republic and Ulster, they continue to make a terrific balls-up of bloody nearly everything they try.'

'Whereas in Europe they've bagged a respectable number of British soldiers over the last year or two. *And* got clean away with it,' Brook said as he stood up. 'I'm for a drink. I'll just get some cold soda out of the fridge. There isn't any ice left but I don't suppose you weird Brits want any.'

The buzzer sounded and Brook went to speak on the intercom. 'It's Jay Rodman, alone. Feels like talking shop, he says.' He laughed. 'I must be psychic that my powerful mind turned to drink a split-second before Rodman's hand touched that bell.'

Sir Maurice laughed. 'I rather think it was Jay's powerful mind willing your errant thoughts along the proper channels.' He looked hopefully towards the door. 'I wonder if he's psychic enough to have thought we might be hungry and brought us some sandwiches.'

Camilla, who had been listening intently to every word, rose slowly out of her chair. She really was, George thought, a remarkably beautiful woman.

'At the risk of sounding pushy or even, God forbid, *whimsical*, I still don't see what any of this has to do with me and unless you are intending to keep me here or in the sodding Tower of bloody London I am going home.'

PART THREE

10

Lord Nicholas Millardale watched as the plane lost altitude and settled gently onto the runway. It turned within a few dozen yards onto a taxiway to allow a big charter jet to take off, stuffed with holiday-makers doubtless bound for some unpleasant Spanish resort. The plane approached Lord Nicholas who waited at the cargo end of Stansted Airport, a thorn in the flesh of those who lived under its approaches but a blessing to Millardale and other Newmarket trainers. The pilot cut the engines after making a final slow turn and waved, his cap set at a rakish angle and his dark, deeply-tanned face lit up with a broad smile. Beside him sat Ruffo, grinning from ear to ear. Millardale wondered if he had begun taking the flying lessons he was forever rabbiting on about.

He turned away and walked to the horse-box to help his daughter get Glissade down the ramp. It was Easter Sunday and father and daughter had insisted on doing the short run themselves to avoid taking one of the stable-lads. They had little enough free time in any event and, with the onset of the flat-racing season, the lads had their hands full. Evening stables would be starting by the time they got back to the yard with this new yearling of Ruffo's, Chianti Classico, and his mare, Échappée, who was due to foal within the month.

Glissade was a lady. She stepped daintily down the ramp like a prima ballerina taking a fifth curtain-call. She was a seasoned traveller and looked inquisitively about, her soft nostrils twitching with fastidious distaste as they encountered the unaccustomed reek of jet engines and asphalt. Another giant charter plane ran up its engines for take-off and Diana Millardale tightened her hold on Glissade's halter but the mare simply watched as the machine lumbered up into the clear afternoon sky, its engines trailing black vapour. She got bored and lowered her head to explore the tarmac for something nice to eat.

'Afternoon, Lenfant,' Millardale said, shaking hands with the pilot, who had got out to stretch his legs. A Gauloise, as usual, was stuck to his lower lip, despite no-smoking signs liberally plastered everywhere. There weren't any fuel bowsers about and he wouldn't have paid the least notice even if there had been.

'*Bonjour*, Milord,' Lenfant said.

'Diana,' Millardale said to the girl, 'this is Captain Lenfant. My daughter, Diana.'

Lenfant kissed her hand and she blushed. 'Mademoiselle,' he said, 'pr'aps you will give me the pleasure of your company on the return journey? Luca must stay with this beautiful creature in the business end of my aircraft, lucky man,' he kissed Glissade's burnished chestnut neck, 'and I have no company in the cockpit. Besides, Luca is not pretty, not very good-tempered and not such a lovely travelling companion as you.'

Ruffo, having helped Luca, his travelling head lad, to get the skittish colt into the Millardales' horse-box, now joined them, kissing first Diana, then Nicholas and finally Glissade. 'I'm certainly not intending to kiss you, *mon vieux*, so you can stop backing up,' he told Lenfant.

'A terrific amount of kissing seems to be going on here. So evocative at the end of a runway, don't you find?' Lord Nicholas framed the scene with both hands. 'Quite like the end of *Casablanca*.'

Ruffo laughed. 'With Glissade in the Ingrid Bergman part.' He rubbed his hands. 'I'll give Luca a hand with Échappée and then we can wave bye-bye to Glissade and then we can get these two poor exhausted equine persons to their new home and tucked into their beds and then we can settle down for a lovely drink. I brought you some wine, Nicky.'

He turned back to the pilot. 'Pierre, if you could tear your eyes away from my exquisite god-daughter and attend to your aeronautical muttons, you might hand the wine down from the cockpit to his lordship whilst I see to my children's happiness and well-being.'

All of these things were accomplished with a minimum of fuss and Lenfant clambered up into his aircraft again for the short hop back to Deauville.

Before starting up his engines, he called down to Ruffo in French. 'As it's Easter Sunday, will Madame Marie be cooking dinner?'

'No,' Ruffo shouted. 'The Maries are visiting their son and daughter-in-law in the Saintonge. But you won't starve, Pierre; my sister will feed you. Probably the leftovers from our lunch today.'

'And it was?'

'Lamb. Easter Sunday, what the hell else would one eat?'

Lenfant looked thoughtful. 'I'm not fond of lamb,' he whined. 'Pasta, too, do you suppose? If I were to ask madame la comtesse very, very sweetly?'

'If you ask *very*, very sweetly I suppose she might.'

'May I ask for your god-daughter's hand in marriage?'

'Certainly not! She's only sixteen, far too good for you and she's not the least bit interested in Frogs. She only likes horses.'

'How about,' Lenfant asked craftily, 'if I throw in some flying-lessons? For you, I mean.'

'I shall speak formally on your behalf with her parents,' Ruffo said.

Diana rode in back with the horses as Ruffo and Nicholas chatted comfortably in the cab. Nicholas drove at a sensible, leisurely pace, his mind half on the comfort of the horses, half on his plans for the other three Ruffo had in training with him. Two of them were doing remarkably well and this new colt entrusted to his care, Chianti Classico, looked like very promising raw material. A beautiful walker, the big, rangy bay was still growing fast by the look of him.

The mare, Échappée, had had a brilliant racing career under another trainer, winning both the Oaks and the 1,000

111

Guineas two years ago, and Ruffo had turned down an offer well in excess of a million pounds for her, according to the paddock grapevine. As a breeder, Ruffo was quickly climbing into the big leagues in such illustrious company as the Queen and the Aga Khan.

Échappée was a temporary house-guest at the Millardale yard, Penleigh Mill Farm. Ruffo was sending her on to a stud near Newbury, to drop her foal and then be covered by Repeat Pattern, whose fees, at £100,000 a go, had already recouped his selling price of $3,250,000 in America. The racing bush-telegraph buzzed with rumours of Ruffo's participation in the syndicate that had successfully bid on Repeat Pattern in Kentucky. Ruffo's sister and brother-in-law were having their own spectacular successes, too. Glissade's first foal would be the product of their great stallion, Vignoble. Keep it in the family, Lord Nicholas thought, or as much of it as you can.

There was no lack of money nowadays, which faintly surprised Lord Nicholas, although he was naturally pleased both for his friend and himself. His yard had the benefit of the fat training fees Ruffo paid punctually and without quibble. Lord Nicholas knew that Ruffo was sending him the cream of his exceptionally good annual crop of yearlings, with others going to the top trainers in France, England and Italy but none, surprisingly, to Ireland. Perhaps it was too inconvenient for Ruffo to visit regularly, Nicholas thought.

Penleigh Mill Farm had literally been put on the racing map by the Monteavesa string. With the potential winners bred by Ruffo and his father and entrusted to the then-small yard, Nicholas had worked hard and produced spectacular results. He and his wife, Barbara, had been unsurprised but nonetheless grateful that other owners had quickly fallen into line, almost queuing up to put their own horses into the capable hands of a man with such a record of classic triumphs. The Millardales, after much agonizing, had decided to back their winning-streak and double the size of the yard, which now housed sixty horses. Ruffo had again come to their aid when the banks had frowned upon such ambition. He had lent them the money.

'Think of it,' he had said, 'as an advance against training fees, Nicky. Besides, I am convinced that you will make a success of it.' He had laughed. 'I have a deep-rooted superstition that when one is having a run of good luck, as I am having, it brings bad luck if one doesn't share the good luck with one's friends. Let us not speak of it further.'

Nicholas and Ruffo had been both friends and racing colleagues for many years and it hadn't been so terribly long ago that Ruffo had had to throw in his hand on any yearling that notched up over five thousand guineas in the bidding at Newmarket. He had always had a good eye, though, and he had knocked down Glissade at the bargain-basement price of just over four thousand guineas, making her subsequent triumphs on the flat doubly sweet.

They chatted comfortably, Lord Nicholas full of praise for Ruffo's big two-year-old, Bardolino, who had, according to his proud trainer, trotted up to the finish in a recent six-furlong race 'through pissing rain' at Doncaster, leaving the other eight runners virtually in the stalls. Bardolino's jockey, a taciturn man not overgiven to enthusiasm when it came to his mounts, had burbled to Lord Nicholas that the colt was 'a real Christian, gov.'

Bardolino's elder sister, Valpolicella, was another matter. 'She is,' Lord Nicholas said, 'a cow. She's got the speed, Ruffo. When she's in the mood she can run the rest of them into the ground. I've got the videos to prove it which I'll show you later. But last time out, just cantering up the course, she managed to kick Steve Cauthen's mount a nasty swipe to the shoulder, part company with poor Pat Eddery who had the dubious pleasure of being up on her, and stand stock-still at the off. Wouldn't budge out of the stalls. Kicked two handlers and bit a third, who said he would've smacked her if he hadn't been afraid I was watching. I would've smacked her but I was afraid the Stewards might be watching. A real, no-nonsense flaming pig of a disposition!'

Ruffo burst out laughing. 'Remind you of anyone?'

'Your charming wife, d'you mean?' Millardale asked with a smile. 'I do see a family resemblance, now you mention it.'

'What do you think we ought to do with her?'

The trainer laughed again. 'I trust you're speaking of Valpolicella,' he said, with a sideways glance at his friend. 'My advice is to cut your losses, get her out of my yard before she chews up all the lads. God knows her bloodlines are irreproachable with Mill Reef as grandpa, so breed her. To a stallion with an extremely docile nature. It's a shame with her turn of foot but . . .' he shrugged, thinking of the unfathomable mysteries of heredity and Ruffo's wife and Ruffo's son and how completely opposite in temperament the latter was to the former.

'Funny old things, genes,' he finished, thinking less of humans than of horses, as was his wont. Vino Rosso, for example, who was standing at the Castello Monteavesa stud, had given Nicholas many sleepless nights wondering how The Great Stallion in The Sky ordained heredity. Vino Rosso's form, in the course of his relatively brief racing career in Italy and France, had been perfectly good. Nothing wrong with it. Ruffo and his father had decided to retire him from racing as a four-year-old, after he had pulled up lame in a race at Longchamp. But as a sire, Vino Rosso had proved to be pure magic. His progeny had won every single classic race amongst them, including the English, Irish and Italian Derbys, English and Irish 2,000 Guineas, English and Irish St Legers, the Goodwood, Coronation and Gold Cups, the Arc, everything, the whole bang shoot. Vignoble, Pinot Grigio, Bacchante, Champagne Katie, Échappée, Passeggiata, Red Sky, and now Silver Vine and Bardolino: all winners and all products of a single stallion's miraculous loins.

Nicky smiled at Ruffo, who was engrossed in the list of possible entries Fatima had thoughtfully typed up for him to cast an expert eye over: Lingfield, Ascot, Goodwood, Ayr, York, Epsom, Sandown, Newbury, Newmarket, The Curragh, Leopardstown, Phoenix Park, Longchamp,

Auteuil. Bardolino and his half-brother, a rangy three-year-old grey called Silver Vine, were going to have a busy spring and summer. *Insh'allah*, Nicholas reminded himself.

Ruffo hadn't bought a colt in more years than Nicholas could remember. He had spent every available penny on buying wives for his formidable Vino Rosso, a complete harem, in fact. Keep it in the family, Millardale thought again, glancing at Ruffo, who looked happy and relaxed as the horse-box slowed to negotiate the gate at the entrance to Penleigh Mill Farm.

As they pulled into the yard, Ruffo's son, Guido, shot out of the house to greet them. Of a sudden recalling his age and dignity, he reined in to a casual stroll. 'He's now firmly insisting that we call him "Guy" in the English pronunciation, Ruffo.'

Ruffo laughed. 'Thanks for warning me, Nicky. If I didn't remember so clearly about myself, I would be in a state of constant amazement at how determined children are to be no different from other children.'

Guido was in the same Eton house as the younger Millardale boy, Edward, who trailed at a respectful distance behind, in deference to Guido's seniority of just under one year. Ruffo squeezed his son in a great bear-hug, giving him all the latest family news in Italian with a wealth of detail and accompanying gesture. At fourteen, Guido was already at least six feet tall and still sprouting. He was wearing clothes his father didn't recognize, which must have been bought for him by Barbara Millardale, Ruffo thought with a slight pang of conscience. Barbara would be forced into confessing how much she had spent on the boy and Ruffo would discreetly settle up. The Monteavesa family hadn't been together since Christmas and Ruffo was aware that his son was now at the age when his lack of a mother was receding in importance and being overtaken by his need for a more attentive father.

Not that Guido ever complained. He was overjoyed to see his father and have news of the family. There was no hint of reticence about him; nothing that hinted at secret feelings of resentment or envy at the more conventional

115

upbringings enjoyed by his friends. One of the many splendid things about Eton, as well as his old school in Normandy, l'École des Roches, was that so many of the children came from far away. There were countless boys who lacked parents conveniently placed to give them lunch at weekends and the Millardales acted *in loco parentis*, just as Cristina and Antoine had done in Normandy. Nonetheless, Ruffo promised himself that he would have a long chat with Barbara about the boy, once everyone else in the house was safely tucked up in bed or down at the village pub for a final drink.

As Nicholas kept half a supervisory eye on the bustle of evening stables, tactfully allowing Ruffo to catch up on Guido's latest news, he realized with a start that Ruffo had been only two years older than Nicholas' eldest son, Gerald, when he had married and produced Guido. It would be nice and so wonderfully tidy if Gerald and Ghislaine were eventually to marry. He suddenly missed Gerald, who had grown into a friend. He was with Ruffo's brother, Manfredi, at the Castello Monteavesa, spending the Easter holidays there.

The thought of Gerald, Manfredi and his wine sent Nicholas scurrying back to the horse-box. He asked a passing lad to lend him a hand and between them they took the four ten-litre wineboxes into the kitchen. 'Thank you, Kevin,' he said to the lad. 'Help yourself to a mug of coffee if you like. Just leave the mug in the office when you're finished.'

The boy mumbled his thanks, poured himself some coffee and promptly spilled it, as he turned to look for milk and sugar, all over Barbara, who had wandered into the kitchen reading, a habit she had. She laughed. 'Never mind, Kevin, it's not all that hot. Sponges right out if you spill it before you've added the milk and sugar. Pour yourself some more and be off with you. I'll mop up.'

'Thank you, m'lady,' the boy whispered, scarlet with embarrassment.

'What have you done with Ruffo?' Barbara asked. 'I thought I heard you drive in ages ago.'

116

'I'm being diplomatic, darling, leaving father and son together for a bit of a catch-up. You know,' he said, shaking his head, 'I was thinking of the quirks of heredity on the way home and quite apart from being a flaming bitch, Guido's mother is such a fool! That boy is absolutely smashing and to be totally indifferent about him . . .'

'For God's sake don't speak of her, Nicky. I can't even bear to think about that odious bitch. I'm only glad she's perfectly content to leave him alone, with any luck for good.'

He took her in his arms, nuzzling her ear. She was conveniently only an inch or two smaller than he. 'You, on the other hand, do not fall very far short of perfection.' He held her at arm's length and looked into her amused eyes. 'Barbara, you know I love you more than any other woman in this kitchen?'

'But?'

'But I wonder why it is you are forever bumping into people because you are physically incapable of putting a book down. I only ask,' he added mildly, 'in the spirit of scientific enquiry.'

She perched on a stool at the huge kitchen table and considered his question. 'I have briefly put books down. I then spent many thousands of hours trying to find them again. Make me a gin and tonic, there's a decent chap. The reason for all of this, as you're in a scientific mood, is that everyone in this house reads. Fatima will wander in for some coffee and will pick up my book, thus providing herself with a refreshing change from *The Sporting Life* and the racing calendar. She apologizes three months later, when I've well and truly forgotten both plot and characters, and says, "Oh I didn't realize you were still reading it and isn't it *good*?" The children pick up my books; you pick up my books; Mrs French picks up my books when she's dusting and tidies them right into the bookcase in the library, where I never think to look because they've no right to be there until I've finished them.'

She sipped at the drink he handed her. 'Ah,' she said.

117

'I only asked,' he said with ruffled dignity, 'because people quite frequently think I'm mad, you see. My head lad hurls himself to the ground at regular intervals pointing towards Allah, who appears to live in Ipswich. My wife bounces off people because she has her nose in *The New Yorker*.'

'Do you propose to divorce us? You understand that I'm only asking in the spirit of scientific enquiry.'

'No. At least I don't think so. I'd have a very tricky time trying to replace you. Have you, dare I ask it, given thought to the picnic for tomorrow's point-to-point?'

She didn't deign to answer but pointed at The White Man's Burden, an immense and venerable hamper gaping open and already containing paper napkins, crockery, cutlery and other underpinnings for a large feast. Nicholas kissed her.

'Ruffo has brought us enough wine to keep us legless for a month.'

'That makes for a refreshing change,' Barbara said. 'Most of our owners drink us dry. Let's start charging them.'

'Let's run upstairs and have a quickie instead. You can bring your book if you like.'

11

Barbara rummaged about in the vast right-hand pocket of her Barbour. She found a broken dog-lead, a crumpled cheque with some unspecified person's telephone number scribbled on the back in her own writing and the American thriller she had begun that morning as Ruffo and Nicky had ridden out with the first string. She squelched slowly away from the noisy crowd, oblivious to the unrelenting drizzle, reading as she went. She managed to negotiate, on some sort of bat-like radar, the untidy ranks of parked cars in the now-deserted field. The mud sucked at her wellies, forcing her to bunch up her toes to keep from walking right out of them. She bounced off someone.

The bouncee whirled about, looking understandably surprised, and tipped his cap. 'Ah, Lady Nicholas. I'm afraid you've caught me out. Is this your motor?'

She smiled. 'Colonel Dalgleish. What a nice surprise. Would you like something to drink?' she asked automatically. Then the Colonel's question sank in. 'Oh dear. Yes, the car's ours.' She looked worried. 'Please don't tell me we've got a puncture.'

'No no no. I was admiring your giant wine box. I've never seen one that size.'

She laughed. 'Impressive, isn't it? One of our owners has a vineyard in Italy and he kindly provided it. Jolly useful for picnics, as you can see. They've got this ten-litre size in Europe, you know, but it's never caught on here. Can't think why. You must have a glass, Colonel,' she urged him, 'and something to eat if you like. Masses here.' She rummaged about in The White Man's Burden, producing an unused plastic glass which she filled from the spigot. 'We think the wine's rather drinkable and I can recommend the egg-and-cress sandwiches. Cheese and chutney are off, I'm afraid.'

'A small tot of wine will do nicely all on its own. Ah, how kind, Lady Nicholas,' he said, accepting the glass. He sipped. 'Excellent,' he said, leaning into the car to peer at the wine box. 'Castello Monteavesa, Torri del Benaco, Verona,' he read. 'Really very good indeed.' He took out a pocketbook and carefully copied down what he'd read. 'Excellent. I'll try to get some. An owner of yours, you said?'

'Prince Ruffo Monteavesa. He's here with us today. Don't you know him? He's played some polo in his time at the Guards' Club. Now I think of it, that's the last time we saw *you*, Colonel; last summer at Smith's Lawn. Ruffo Monteavesa was with us that day, too.'

'I don't believe we've ever actually met. Know the name, of course. High-goal player a few years back. Used to play on the Prince of Wales's team. Tall chap for polo. The tall ones never last long. They look so foolish on the ponies.'

Barbara smiled and nodded. 'That's the one. I doubt he'd mind looking silly but he hasn't much time to play these days. He and his father have a stud in Italy and what with breeding being seasonal and polo being very nearly the same season, and the family wine business, I should think he has little leisure during the spring months to get in any practice.'

'Pity. Very promising player as I recall. Well, Lady Nicholas, thank you again for the wine. Must beat the bushes to find my wife and children.'

'Would you like some more to take along with you on safari?'

'Thank you, no.' He neatly deposited his empty glass in the plastic-lined pail Barbara always brought along. He smiled and tipped his cap again, striking off towards the crowd of people and dogs two or three furlongs distant.

Barbara thought briefly what a nice, old-fashioned sort of soldier the Lieutenant-Colonel was. Scots Guards? Irish Guards? Grenadiers? She couldn't remember, not that it mattered. She set about tidying the debris of her picnic. She found the small transistor radio she carried in the car and switched on for company as she sorted everything out.

'On Easter Monday in the year 1916, at around mid-day, the curtain rose on another blood-stained scene in the history of Ireland. Dublin's General Post Office was seized by a group of armed men who called themselves patriots. They fired off their pistols and forced astonished postal clerks and ordinary citizens out of the building, a crowd quickly gathering in O'Connell Street outside. This not very remarkable event was the beginning of the Easter Rising.

'At the time, the people of Dublin saw this futile and eventually blood-soaked gesture as a typical piece of Irish buffoonery, but its consequences have reached down to our own day. Patrick Pearse, a bombastic schoolmaster, harangued the mystified crowd from the occupied Post Office, claiming to represent "the provisional government" of the Irish Republic and issuing a communiqué as "Commandant General of the Irish Republican Army".

'The uprising was suppressed by British troops within a few days, without much regret on the part of the civilian population who had, inevitably, suffered the most, caught in the cross-fire between the IRA and the troops. The leaders, who seemed not to have much of an idea what to do with the Post Office once it was occupied, were eventually rounded up, tried and executed. They met their fates in a defiant spirit of confidence, unshakably persuaded that posterity would remember them. That infamous confidence has been borne out today.

'The IRA have today demonstrated their own methods of reminding the world of the 1916 Easter Rising.

'Item: There has been a large car-bomb explosion outside a British Army of the Rhine barracks in West Germany, killing four soldiers and five German civilians, three of them children, who were passing in their car when the explosion occurred.

'Item: The British Embassy in a residential section of Athens has been fire-bombed, fortunately only slightly wounding two Greek cleaners.

'Item: In the Irish Republic, a judge who has recently granted an extradition warrant for a Provisional "soldier" wanted in connection with the murder of an off-duty Belfast policeman earlier this year has been killed, machine-gunned in his own garden and in plain sight of his wife and a visiting grandson.

'Item: A scheduled British Airways flight due to take off from London to Belfast exploded on the runway at Heathrow, either killing or severely injuring passengers and crew. The casualty figures are still not known. Names will not be released until the passenger-list has been thoroughly checked and next of kin notified. An emergency telephone number will be read out at the end of this bulletin. It is believed that the bomb placed aboard the aircraft was timed to go off when the plane was in the air. Take-off was delayed, however, due to bad weather and unusually heavy holiday air traffic.

'Item: A mortar attack on an RUC post in Northern Ireland failed when the home-made device misfired, killing three IRA men instead. They have yet to be identified.

'Item: In London, Piccadilly Circus has been cleared of all traffic and pedestrians as a team attempted to defuse a bomb left in a carrier-bag on the ground floor of Tower Records. An alert shopper spotted the apparently ownerless bag leaning innocently against a display and informed the uniformed private security man posted at the main entrance to the shop. Following standing orders, the guard immediately notified the police and the large shop, crowded mainly with young people, was partially evacuated. The bomb exploded, however, before the shop had been completely cleared, killing a Nigerian tourist and another security guard.'

'Item: Sir Gerald Benson, DSO, DFC, British Ambassador to Portugal was shot by a sniper as he . . .'

Barbara switched off her little red radio and sat unmoving, her face in her hands, unable to listen to any more. What had happened to so debase people that they were capable of planning and executing such atrocities and then boasting of them? Feeling suddenly very tired, she curled up under the new tartan rug on the back seat of the Volvo and went to sleep, too sickened by the gory news from the real world to read her thriller.

In Boston, too, Easter Monday was not without incident.

Besides being profoundly stupid, Father Hanratty was now thoroughly frightened as well. The same Irish voice that sent him to Italy had just telephoned, asking in a reproachful tone why it was that Father Hanratty had not returned his recent call.

'But I haven't . . .'

The man at the other end of the line chuckled. 'Ah, now, it was my mistake, to be sure. I left word that you were to ring "Professor Moriarty". I was just having my little joke and you not a great reading man, Father.'

The priest was too confused to say anything at all. 'Hello?' the man said, 'are you still there?'

'Yes.'

'That's better. I was ringing to ask you a little question and here it is, Father Joe. Are you ready?'

'Yes.'

'I was wondering now if there might be any connection at all between two little facts. One, that the brand-new suitcase we gave you for your pilgrimage to Rome is now empty, completely empty. Two, you have chattered away for some time with our brave Boston Police.' He chuckled again. 'The question is this one: do those brave boys in blue now have the contents of your expensive new suitcase?'

'I don't understand you,' the priest babbled. 'I unpacked when I came home . . .'

'Ah now, Father. And when you were unpacking the lovely new suitcase, did some small corner of it interest you enough so that you had a little peek? Curiosity killed the cat, you know.' He chuckled again and the priest shuddered. 'Now what is it, I ask myself, that you discussed so fully with the guardians of public safety. I ask myself what happened to our property. Good little priests shouldn't meddle in things that don't concern them.' The voice had become malicious.

Father Hanratty put the telephone down and realized he was crying. He ought to have told the man about what had happened to him in Italy, about those dreadful young people who had drugged the wine they gave him and then robbed him of all his money on the train to Rome. He stayed beside the phone in the hall for a few minutes, hoping that Professor Moriarty would ring him back so that he could explain everything. But the wretched thing remained silent. Then he remembered that the Professor had said he'd rung before.

He went off to find Mrs O'Shea in her lair at the back of the house. She looked surprised when she saw him. 'What's wrong, Father Joseph? You're crying, poor man. Here, sit down at my table and I'll fetch you a nice cup of tea.'

'No. No tea. Do you,' he asked, mopping impatiently at his eyes and trying to focus his attention, 'recall someone asking for me on the telephone, Mrs O'Shea? A Professor Moriarty?'

'Oh bless you, yes, Father. Did I forget to tell you? Is the poor man in need of you and I forgot to give you the message? What a silly old woman I am, to be sure.' She rummaged about in a large drawer, whose contents appeared to include everything that could conceivably come in handy in any sort of emergency, domestic or cosmic: bits of string, orphaned wooden matches, bent paper-clips, candle ends and enough scraps of paper to run off an entire edition of the Sunday *New York Times*. 'It's got to be in here somewhere, Father Joseph. I never throw anything away,' she explained unnecessarily.

'When you find it, Mrs O'Shea,' he said hopefully, 'would you please give it to me. I'd like to call him back, you see.'

In his heart, he knew that Mrs O'Shea would never find the right scrap of paper. The poor old soul had probably forgotten what it was she was meant to be looking for by now. He also knew that this was his punishment, a punishment he richly deserved for having succumbed to his fondness for wine, and that he should bare his neck and submit to whatever Divine Providence decreed for him. He was guilty of the sin of pride, too, for having been ashamed to tell anyone of his experiences in Italy, afraid of the ridicule and even contempt that he had earned.

He went to his room and shut the door. He felt an overwhelming need to confess. It took him no time at all to find his own scrap of paper, the one given him by the kindly, helpful policeman who had talked to him before.

Jesus, Mary and Joseph, he ought to have told the good man everything right then and there. Here was his name: Kirkwood. He had been so understanding about a simple parish priest wanting to do a small thing for The Cause, and the policeman not even an Irishman and likely a godless Prod to boot.

Mr Kirkwood had begged him to call if there were anything, no matter how small and unimportant-seeming, that came to him. He went out into the hall and listened before dialling the number on his scrap. He could hear Mrs O'Shea singing along with a televised advertisement for breakfast cereal and he knew his colleagues were unlikely to return to the rectory much before six o'clock. They always spent an hour at F. X. Drumm's Tavern ('Happy Hour 4:30–5:30 Weekdays, Unescorted Ladies and Tenors Welcome'), only a block away from St Malachy's.

He breathed out gustily as the telephone answered on the first ring and realized that he'd been holding his breath. Fear caught at his throat. 'May I speak with Mr Kirkwood, please,' he eventually managed to squeak, his voice sounding an octave higher than normal.

'This is Kirkwood. Who's speaking?' The man sounded irritable. Perhaps he was just about to leave for home.

Father Hanratty identified himself and then, to add to his shame, he began to cry once more. Mr Kirkwood was commendably quick to grasp that the priest was frightened out of his stunted wits. He promised to send a car to collect him and then, hearing the terror in the man's voice, promised to come himself.

Kirkwood's previous interview with Father Hanratty had been an unforgettable proof of the axiom that a person's interest in anything outside himself is in direct proportion to his own intelligence. Father Hanratty's horizons were, to be charitable, narrow in the extreme. Breaking the law was, to him, an utterly meaningless concept. For the priest to be jumping out of his skin he must have been overtly threatened. Probably ready to cough up some more information, Kirkwood reasoned, in exchange for protection. A lecture on the duties of a responsible citizen would have been an absurd waste of everyone's time.

Kirkwood got to the rectory as quickly as the rush-hour traffic would allow and saw a greyish nylon-lace curtain twitch in a front window, the priest appearing at the door before Kirkwood could get out of the car. He then shut the door behind him with exaggerated caution and looked furtively down the street before scuttling along the cracked concrete walk and into Kirkwood's car, a totally anonymous and elderly tan Ford. The DEA man did a U-turn as he pulled out from the kerb, heading back the way he had come and in the opposite direction from that in which Father Hanratty had seemed to look for approaching danger.

'Why don't you duck down until we clear the area,' he suggested helpfully. 'I'll tell you once we're on the Expressway and then you can come up for air. Want to tell me about it now or wait until we get downtown?' He checked his rear-view mirror for tags but the road behind was clear.

Father Hanratty began to talk compulsively, incessantly and not very coherently. Kirkwood was patient, letting him burble on without interruption but picking up key words here and there for later use. He would have the old man repeat every syllable into a tape-recorder once they were sitting in his office and he could calm him down with a stiff drink and a full pack of Marlboro Lights on the table in front of him. He had already barked orders that these lubricants should be procured as he left the office at a run.

What gradually became clear was that the silly, gullible old bastard had nothing to add about his recent adventures in Italy, apart from telling Kirkwood that the man who had set him up and had just phoned again in a distinctly menacing way was called Professor Moriarty. Could the police, *surely* the police could check Boston's profusion of colleges and universities and find the man. Kirkwood, without betraying the smallest hint of a smile, solemnly assured him that they would begin to do so right away.

But the priest did have one thing to add: in 1973, he had been contacted here in Boston by a young woman. She had claimed to work for Noraid and had given him a large, bulky manila envelope with detailed instructions about its delivery to a man in France. Hanratty was shepherding a group of his parishioners on a pilgrimage to Lisieux to celebrate the centenary of St Theresa's birth.

Arriving finally at the DEA's office and fortified with a slug of neat Canadian Club, Father Hanratty could give no description of the man who had collected the envelope in France, never having seen him, but he *had* retained a vivid impression of the young woman. In fact, he had seen her on television, a local news programme, a year or two after his Lisieux adventure. There had been a fund-raising dinner, either Noraid or the Democratic Party, he couldn't remember which it was, and she had been on the dais with Senator Edward Kennedy and other bright stars of the Boston-Irish political firmament. Clearly she held a position of some importance in the hierarchy of whichever organization it was.

As disgruntled underlings were re-routed away from their homes and dispatched to Boston's principal news-papers to browse through microfiche files, Kirkwood suggested mildly that he was in no position to guarantee Father Hanratty's continued safety unless he could convince his own superiors that here was someone who could justify such a lavish outlay of time and money by producing concrete results.

Hanratty lowered his voice. 'Well, I think – I don't know but I think, mind you – that it's the same thing. I think that envelope all those years ago contained money for The Cause. And I think my suitcase had money for The Cause. I couldn't swear to it but that's what I think. And the Italians on that train were looking for it but it was too carefully hidden for them and they didn't find it. Or maybe they did find it and stole it and Professor Moriarty thinks I stole it. But it was very heavy, you see. The suitcase was heavier when I left Milan than it was when I got there.'

Kirkwood didn't break the flow of the priest's theorizing by asking why The Cause should smuggle money into Boston when so much money was actually raised in Boston and sent with perfect legality on to The Cause's war chest in the Ould Sod.

'Ah,' he said. 'Interesting. And how did you discover that, Father?'

'The weight,' he said, nodding several times and topping up his glass. 'I unpacked all my things and the suitcase still felt very heavy. Maybe they had put gold in there.' A leprechaun's hoard, no doubt, Kirkwood thought. 'I put the suitcase in my closet.' His face crumpled again. 'That's all I did, Mr Ah.'

'Jonathan, Father. Please call me Jonathan.'

'They think I've stolen their money! That money goes to poor Irish families whose fathers and sons have fallen in the Great Struggle. I swear I never . . .'

'Is that what the Noraid fund-raisers say, Father? That the money goes to widows and orphans?'

Father Hanratty looked at Kirkwood with an expression of blank incomprehension. 'Well, naturally. Everyone knows that.'

Kirkwood hadn't the least intention of wasting time by arguing this particular piece of loony Noraid humbug with a backward, alcohol-soaked priest. He was reassuring instead. 'Once we get everything untangled and we find Professor Moriarty, I'll go and tell him myself that it was probably the Italian police who stole the money. Them or the people on the train. Took the money out of your suitcase and put something equally heavy in its place so that you wouldn't find out until it was too late to do anything about it.'

Father Hanratty looked a little more cheerful. This Jonathan might be a Prod but he treated a Man of God with respect and consideration. He lit a Marlboro with shaking fingers and felt better.

'Could you tell me a little more about Lisieux, Father?'

The priest screwed up his eyes in fervour. 'A wonderful sight! Candles everywhere in the basilica and we visited her birthplace. Her convent, too, so peaceful. Carmelites. Very moving it was, the simplicity of . . .'

'The envelope you took with you. How did you pass it along to the right person?'

'Oh that.' The priest had evidently forgotten why it was he had telephoned Jonathan in the first place. 'I just left it at the hotel we stayed in, Paris that was, on our way to Lisieux.'

'You left it at the desk or in your room? I mean, was it like this last time in Milan?'

'No no not the same thing. It had writing on it.' Useless to ask if he had read the writing; his lack of curiosity was boundless. 'The young woman told me to leave it at the desk first thing when we arrived and a man would pick it up. That's all I had to do, you see.' He sipped deeply and beamed at Kirkwood, pleased with himself for having carried off one responsibility without mishap.

Kirkwood looked up as young Ingersoll bounded in clutching a fat manila envelope bearing the logo of the *Boston Globe*, his tie over his shoulder and sweat beading his black face. 'Am I firstest with the mostest or what?'

Kirkwood grinned up at him. 'God knows, the firstest. Mostest we'll see.'

Ingersoll spread out the contents of his fat manila envelope, a stack of press photographs, neatly tagged glossies prominently featuring Senator Kennedy. Boston newspapers had no lack of Kennedy material.

Feeling very much the star attraction, the priest hung over the big table and carefully studied each photograph. 'That's her! That's the one there. I'd know her anywhere.'

With rising excitement, Kirkwood turned the eight-by-ten over and read the typed label. There were several people sitting ranged behind Senator Kennedy, who was speaking at a lectern. Some looked bored, others keen and one was asleep, possibly drunk. They were variously identified as Mrs Joan Kennedy, Mr Edwin Madden and his daughter, Edwina, the Archbishop of Boston, Cardinal Medeiros, and his secretary, Father Stephen Fahy, SJ. The occasion was, as the old man had promised, a 1974 Democratic Party fund-raiser, rubber chicken at five hundred bucks a wing.

As Kirkwood read and made notes, Father Hanratty looked through other photographs. 'Here she is again,' he crowed, pleased with himself.

' "Senator and Mrs Edward Kennedy with noted Boston philanthropist Mr Edwin Madden",' Kirkwood read the caption aloud, ' "and his daughter, Miss Edwina Madden. Mr Brendan Conklin of Sinn Fein (right) was the evening's speaker, seen here chatting with His Eminence Cardinal Medeiros." ' Kirkwood checked the date: October 1973. A Noraid event, most likely. Teddy Kennedy had publicly dissociated himself from Sinn Fein sometime in the mid 1970s, Kirkwood recalled.

'Ingersoll, you're a local boy, aren't you?' Jonathan Kirkwood was from Minneapolis and had been attached to the Boston DEA office for less than a year.

'I'm local all right, boss, but when these were taken I was just a snot-nosed kid.'

'Jesus!' Kirkwood said, laughing. 'I think the bad thing about getting old is that you assume everyone with their second teeth is the same age as you are. Someone around here has to be both elderly and local. See who you can dig up. That's a joke.'

'Ha ha.' Ingersoll made a few phone calls and eventually produced a middle-aged and Boston-bred FBI agent, Sam McCafferty, who obligingly materialized without wasting any time. He had no trouble identifying the smartly-dressed young woman picked out by Father Hanratty: Edwina Madden, daughter of a well-known bigwig in the Boston Democratic Party, Edwin Madden, a self-made millionaire whose money, it was widely rumoured, had its source in an impressive range of shady dealings, including substantial black-marketeering during the War.

'Madden's still alive,' McCafferty went on, 'at least I haven't seen an obit on him. There would have been a *big* funeral if he'd died, something unmissable because he was really plugged in politically. The thing is, he had a real lulu of a stroke several years ago and he's supposed to be sort of a radish now.'

'Sounds like a poor man's Joe Kennedy,' Ingersoll said.

McCafferty agreed with a disrespectful laugh. 'Yeah. Old Joe Kennedy without Gloria Swanson to give him the pizzazz.'

'What about the daughter?' Kirkwood asked. He had noticed that Father Hanratty's glazed expression hadn't altered by a fraction throughout McCafferty's monologue. Presumably, if he had ever known the Madden woman's name it had left no trace on his memory.

McCafferty screwed up his face to concentrate. 'I don't know anything concrete about her,' he finally said, 'except she had a real reputation as banging all Boston. Town pump. I don't speak from personal experience but it was *said* that she'd blow you in a phone booth if you talked dirty.' He laughed. 'Locker-room stuff, you know, all of us good ole boys passing on tips on who puts out and who whips out a ɔsary if you try to cop a feel.'

Kirkwood steered McCafferty and Ingersoll out of the ɔom. Old Hanratty might be a booze-soaked cretin but McCafferty's breezy dissertation on Miss Madden's friendliness wasn't for clerical ears. 'Christ, McCafferty, I'm not saying you should show any respect for the man but . . . anyway, you know what I mean. Go on.'

'There are two sons,' McCafferty resumed imperturbably, 'both pillars of respectability, which is how come I remember their little sister being anything but. The brothers run the old man's legitimate business, a middling-big stock brokerage. It's called Madden, Madden, Whosit & Whatsie Securities. Look it up in the phone book. Mostly middle-of-the-road sort of business. Pensions and like that. Nothing flashy, nothing too adventurous, not being investigated by the SEC, not *sexy*. Safe enough for all the lace-curtain-Irish widows.'

Kirkwood made a great show of mopping his brow. 'Whew!' he said, 'you FBI guys know everything!'

McCafferty laughed. 'I was at BU at the same time as Edwin Madden, Junior, known to one and all as "Junior", or "June" behind his back. Not 'cause he was a fairy or anything but Jesus he was prissy. We were doing Accounting. He wasn't what you'd call a pal but I knew him. He was a disagreeable little prick. Righteous, you know, and bone-crushingly respectable. Danny, his younger brother, wasn't much better.'

'Edwin Junior and Edwina?' Ingersoll widened his eyes comically. 'You honky Micks take heredity *real* seriously. Do you think my kids would be happier and, you know, like real well-adjusted if I renamed them Winston Junior and Winstonella? Jesus. Edwin Junior and Edwina,' he repeated admiringly, 'musta given poor old Danny a complex. Are we talking tacky here or what?'

'Heredity sure as hell didn't work in this case, Win,' McCafferty shook his head and laughed. 'Maybe the smart chromosomes were out on strike. The Madden brothers haven't got a shred of their old man's entrepreneurial flair, if that's a polite enough term for knowing which palms to grease. They sure as hell aren't the brains of their brokerage house. They hire the brains. And the firm isn't all that successful, anyway. I'd be surprised if they were among the top twenty in Boston. But they really haven't got to make a whole bunch of money since the old man set up trust funds for them and they got their hands on their own little bundles when they turned twenty-five.'

He laughed at Ingersoll's awed expression. 'Just in case you think I've got total recall, I don't but I happen to know the IRS ran an audit on them a few years ago. Someone there wasn't completely happy with their tax returns. I seem to think they had to pay up some back taxes but it wasn't anything spectacular. I think it might have been the usual sort of dodging about with charitable donations being exaggerated. Anyway, ask the tax boys, if you're interested.'

'Perhaps you might like to renew acquaintance with your old buddy June?' Kirkwood suggested. 'Something to do with Boston University's endowment? I've no official interest in what the Madden brothers are getting up to but I'd sure as hell love to know what's become of their sister.' He turned back to the photographs he'd separated out of the pile. 'A good looker.'

'Yeah. I'll see what I can do,' McCafferty promised.

12

'But my dear Prince, of *course* I remember our meeting! How could anyone conceivably forget such a superb lunch in such congenial company?' George was pleased and flattered that the quintessential Italian playboy of Val Sainte-Anne was keeping his promise to look him up. 'Are you in London?'

'Staying with friends near Newmarket,' Ruffo said, 'but I'll be in London tomorrow and I wonder if we might dine together? I was just ringing on the off-chance you might be free.'

'With the greatest pleasure.'

Ruffo laughed with charming self-deprecation; hedging the invitation by asking, 'And your very pretty companion at Val Sainte-Anne? Do you suppose she might be free as well?'

George giggled, not in the least put out by the transparency of the prince's ploy to scratch acquaintance with Camilla. He had a momentary twinge of guilt about Brook: George's worldly old eyes hadn't failed to spot Brook's interest in Camilla. Nor had they failed to notice that she treated Brook like an elder brother.

'Let me,' George stalled, 'scribble down your telephone number. I'll try to reach Camilla and ring you back. She may still be away.'

She was at home, as he knew she would be. She'd barely left her flat since George and Sir Maurice had told her, as gently as they could, of their suspicions concerning Jeremy's activities and the source of all the money he had splashed about with joyous abandon. Camilla had said she'd always assumed that Jeremy had his own money, left him by his sporting quasi-Regency grandfather. She had never thought to ask him about it. There had been such a long list of subjects that she hadn't had the temerity to raise with her husband for fear of provoking fights.

She had been devastated when George told her things about Jeremy she'd never dreamt of, much less suspected. For years she had become bitterly accustomed to accepting that he was a devoted cocksman, a tireless womanizer who had inexplicably found himself married to a woman unable to keep him even superficially faithful. Jealousy had become an ingrained habit, as automatic as swallowing her nightly sleeping-pill, to the extent that she had gradually cut herself off from most of her female friends, convinced that they were sleeping with Jeremy, had slept with Jeremy or were planning to sleep with Jeremy.

Scenes and tantrums had produced nothing but amusement; he didn't even take the trouble to make light of his frequent, unexplained absences. She was shocked that the guardians of the nation's security had been taking an interest in Jeremy. She was even more shocked at her own reaction: she infinitely preferred to know that he had betrayed his regiment and the entire country and not singled her out for unique betrayal. Better a traitor than a philanderer. Camilla had to laugh at herself. What an idiot she was!

'Do say you'll come,' Georgie wheedled.

'Oh God! You're not actually suggesting having a go at match-making me with *the* Playboy of the Western World! I honestly and truly haven't a thing to wear and my hair's in rat-tails and . . .'

'Camilla,' he interrupted, 'do not go on in this vein. I had deluded myself into thinking you were immune to clichés and here you are rabbiting on. You will not skulk about your flat in sackcloth and ashes like Miss Havisham. I'm giving you considerably more than twenty-four hours to get your act together and my advice to you is that you do so without further ado.'

'Yes, Georgie,' she said submissively, putting the phone down. She scrabbled impatiently through accumulated junk in her desk drawer and eventually found the card of a nearby hairdresser all too seldom frequented. She began to feel better and went to commune with that collection of garments charitably known as her wardrobe. The baggy Jaeger skirt and coat clearly wouldn't do. Nothing else would do, either.

With a precautionary but reassuring look at the balance in her current account, she made plans to get to Bond Street when the shops opened in the morning. If all else failed, there were Harvey Nichols, Harrods and Beauchamp Place in a direct line of march, much as she hated the very thought of shopping.

Jeremy Hamilton had been almost certainly a cynical traitor and unquestionably a zealous shit but he had left her very well fixed indeed for money, if an emotional bankrupt. So be it, then. She would spend a small fraction of Jeremy's ill-gotten gains on a dress that would knock this Italian Aly Khan's eyes right out of their sockets.

Mari Shigekawa woke up to find a young woman dozing in an uncomfortable-looking, straight-backed chair drawn up close beside the bed. Mari was vaguely aware that the girl, a complete stranger so far as she could remember, had been there before. She let her eyes fall shut again, trying to assimilate disjointed glimpses that flitted like butterflies at the misty edges of her mind.

She knew she was heavily drugged. She recognized the feeling from a long time ago, when she was a child in Honolulu and had had her appendix removed. By opening her eyes and slightly crossing them she could see a tube running into her nose. There was another tube, attached to a plastic bladder hanging from a metal stand, that went into her arm. The clear liquid sent up little bursts of tiny bubbles to the surface like champagne, hypnotic to watch. A third tube, invisible to her for the present, was in her abdomen and snaked under the bed into a container modestly hidden by the bed-clothes.

She was aware of pain but it seemed a long way off, faintly regrettable, almost melancholic. It was as though someone close to her, someone she was fond of, was suffering. She suddenly felt deeply sad and a single tear oozed down the side of her face, soaking into her hair. Perhaps this tired, pleasant-faced girl beside her was having some trouble, something to do with people milling about and shouting. Mari very much wanted to help her and gently squeezed the hand that lay near her own on the bed.

WPC Helen Tarrant awoke with a start.

'Hello,' Mari whispered.

'Hello,' Helen answered. 'Was I sleeping?'

'I think so. Are you all right?'

Helen was startled by the plain sincerity of the question. 'Yes. Yes I'm fine. How are you?'

Mari thought for a good bit and said, 'I'm not sure, to tell you the truth. You've been here, haven't you?'

'Yes.'

'Do you hurt or is it me? I.'

The brown-haired girl smiled. There was a small gap between her two front teeth which made Mari think of something but it slipped away. 'I don't hurt,' the nice girl said softly, 'so it must be you. I'm only here for . . . well, just in case you were to wake up.'

'Where's Tommy?'

Helen, groggy with fatigue, took a moment before realizing that "Tommy" was unlikely to be anyone but Mr Toshmichi Shigekawa. 'Your husband was here just a little while ago but he's gone to get some sleep. He'll be back again later. I promise.'

'Will you stay a little longer?'

'Of course.'

When Mari woke up again the girl was still there. She began to feel anxious, bordering on crossness, realizing that her grasp of time and place was non-existent. She had no idea if she'd slept for five minutes or five hours. 'What day is this?' she asked querulously.

'Tuesday,' the strange-but-familiar girl said promptly. 'It's Tuesday night.'

'Oh.' She thought about this and eventually asked, 'Is this a hospital?' She felt very stupid. She resented having to ask such a stupid question but she needed to know. Somehow, Mari knew that the brown-haired girl wouldn't lie to her.

136

'Yes. It's the Middlesex. It's an excellent hospital and you're being looked after very well, so don't worry.'

I'm having the baby, she thought. 'I'm having the baby,' she said, wondering why this sounded all wrong. Perhaps she'd spoken in Japanese without meaning to.

The girl squeezed her hand convulsively. 'Something along those lines,' she eventually managed to say. 'Try to go back to sleep.'

Interviewed in their walnut-panelled office, the Madden brothers, disposed on each side of a Victorian partners' desk in possibly genuine leather chairs, were civil enough but not what anyone might term forthcoming. Kirkwood extracted snippets of information from them with difficulty.

They were remarkably alike, both sleek, well-fed, self-satisfied men in their forties with small, snout-like noses and long, supercilious upper lips which made Kirkwood think of camels. Kirkwood mentally dubbed them Tweedledum and Tweedledee, addressing them impartially as "sir", to underline their exalted station in life. This produced a barely-perceptible thaw.

They confirmed that the young woman in the press photographs was indeed their younger sister, Edwina. Her present whereabouts, they insisted, were unknown, at least to the family. Kirkwood was given to understand that neither brother gave a fart where she was, so long as it was not Boston. She had always been, Tweedledum confided, "wild".

'Does she,' Kirkwood asked deferentially, 'have any contact with your parents, sir?'

'Our mother passed away twenty years ago. Cancer,' Tweedledee said, crossing himself and adding, 'God rest her sweet soul.'

'Father suffered a massive stroke some years ago,' Tweedledum volunteered, '*probably* brought on by Edwina's behaviour. That's my opinion.'

'Now, Danny, we don't know that,' Tweedledum remonstrated gently with his younger brother. 'It was God's will.' Kirkwood was sure he would cross himself, too, but he forbore, swivelling around slightly in his chair and gazing out the window with bowed head, no doubt to signify that Kirkwood was adding to burdens already verging on the intolerable.

This wasn't going to be easy, Kirkwood thought. "Wild" could cover a gamut of misdeeds to these pious creeps: Edwina could have converted to Islam or picked up sailors at the Navy Yard or worn falsies. "Wild" could also cover dealing drugs.

McCafferty had made the appointment for him with the Madden Brothers, hinting broadly that Kirkwood was with the CIA ("a government agency with international interests," was what he'd actually said), hoping to give the impression that Kirkwood was battling tirelessly against the godless Commies. 'It would be a very great help to us, sir, if we had an idea where she is now. You gentlemen are both married. Would it be possible that your sister has been in touch with your wives? Even a birthday card would help.'

They both looked aghast at such a possibility being mooted. 'Our wives,' said Tweedledum majestically, 'never cared for her. Frankly, Mr, ah, Kirkwood,' he said, glancing down to get the name from his appointments diary, 'our sister was a great embarrassment to the whole family.'

Kirkwood had done some preparatory mugging up on old Mr Madden's rather lurid background before presenting himself for his audience with the sons and could find few laws, either criminal or ethical, left unbent or unbroken by the vile old turd. Embarrassing such a family as the Maddens would take a pretty dedicated assault.

The line of questioning he'd followed was a dead-end. He regrouped. 'Judging from these photographs, gentlemen, your sister seems to have been something of a mover and shaker in the local Democratic Party. She was working very closely with Senator Kennedy, I read.'

The brothers exchanged quick glances. 'Absolutely nothing in those rumours. I'm at a complete loss to understand how people can put such a filthy interpretation on any little thing that happens. Perfectly innocent explanation for all that,' Tweedledee said, falling silent at a throat-clearing cue from his brother.

Jackpot! Kirkwood thought. 'And,' he took up smoothly, 'she also seems to have held a position of some responsibility in the Noraid hierarchy.'

'She was very brainy,' Tweedledee said, clearly relieved at this abrupt veering away from boggy ground. Kirkwood didn't fail to notice the use of the past tense. 'MBA from Harvard and everything.' He shook his head gloomily, plainly saddened at such a waste of an MBA from Harvard.

'She raised money for Noraid,' Kirkwood guessed.

'Not at all. Not just raised. She managed the money.' There was a note of pride in the correction. Whatever else she may have been, his sister was a chief and no mere Indian. Had been, Kirkwood mentally amended.

'Do you have any idea why she left Boston?'

'Wild,' Tweedledum said again. He was evidently partial to the adjective. 'She was carrying on with some dago.' His lips pursed with ancient disapproval. 'He was at Harvard, not the Business School. History or archaeology, something like that.' This was said in a way to imply that anything other than the Business School was at best an irresponsible waste of time and money and at worst a sink of depravity. 'He was younger than she was. Around four years younger, I think. Wild,' he repeated, whether describing his sister or the dago left unclear.

'And she eloped with him?' Kirkwood prompted.

The brothers shrugged in unison, disclaiming knowledge of, responsibility for and interest in the matter.

'Do you have any recollection of just when this happened?'

'Oh sure. It was just before Christmas, for God's sake! She turned twenty-five in November and got control of her trust fund. She didn't even turn over her portfolio to us so that we could manage it properly for her,' Tweedledee added with a sniff. Then he remembered that he'd already established that Edwina was both "brainy" and an alumna of the B School. 'Not that she wasn't qualified to run her own portfolio but, you know, it seemed like a slap in the face.' He looked aggrieved. 'This business is based on confidence, you know, and people talk. We have competitors. And enemies,' he added darkly.

Kirkwood could well imagine that they might. 'So she took off in December of what year?'

'It was 1976.' Tweedledee was gazing out at the rain clouds again, probably counting the crosses he had to bear.

'And you gentlemen are of the opinion that she was chasing after the boyfriend?'

Tweedledum rattled a pen impatiently. 'Father had a postcard from Italy, giving an address. Then he had this massive stroke. We found the postcard in his desk – he hadn't mentioned it to us; I have no idea why not – and we wrote to her, telling her that the doctors didn't expect Father to live. Well, sir, she never answered and of course Father did live, if you can call it that, not that she seemed to care one way or another. We never heard anything from her.'

'I don't suppose you kept the postcard,' Kirkwood asked hopefully.

The brothers shook their heads, again in unison, more Dum and Dee than ever. 'It was someplace in the North. Not even Rome.' Evidently it was unthinkable that decent folk could frivolously gad about the Italian Peninsula, certainly the atheistical North, beyond the benignly watchful eye of the Vatican.

Tweedledee sighed and marshalled his ebbing strength, recalling that he was dealing with a guardian of the nation's integrity in a world shot through with darkness. He admitted that rumours had reached them from time to time. One's friends, he confided, got around and they had family, in the form of numerous cousins, still living in Ireland.

Over the years since Edwina's "running away"', the brothers had heard variously that she had been killed in a traffic accident in Bangkok, was running a casino on

140

the Riviera, had taken the Buddhist veil in a Kathmandu nunnery and that she had been seen in Colombia, Laos, Manila, Mexico City, Dublin and Sydney. Eventually, these assorted "sightings" had dwindled. The Irish cousins, with whom she had once been so friendly, had lost touch with her. No one had heard anything about her for a long time now. 'Thank God,' Tweedledum added as a pious postscript.

Both brothers declined to speculate about her possible reasons, other than the dago, for quitting Boston. Such an action defied all rational comprehension.

'I've just had Goudhurst on the blower,' Sir Maurice told George. 'Wiltshire. Bodies of two Orientals found in a spinney. They were dug up by a dog.'

'What sort?'

'Jack Russell,' Sir Maurice replied, completely unsurprised that George should ask.

'I meant what sort of *Oriental*, Maurice,' George said, unable to keep himself from laughing. 'Filipino, Indochinese, Chinese Chinese? And which particular sex or sexes?'

'One of each as to sex or sexes. Not sure about the sort of Oriental yet but the Medical Examiner down there thinks Japanese or Korean, tilting slightly towards the former. Early- to mid-twenties. Murder weapon a real executioner's tool, ME thinks: small-calibre pistol, possibly a Smith & Wesson twenty-two.'

'No more stopping-power than a pea-shooter,' George observed with a small frown.

'That's why he said it was an executioner's weapon. Do pay attention, dear boy.' Sir Maurice smiled slightly to obviate the testiness of his rebuke. 'Girl shot through the heart, boy base of skull. Both at extremely close range. They're running tests to see if the victims could've been tied up or drugged. As I said, execution, not heat of the moment. All will be disclosed in time. Bodies being brought up for the tooth fairies to have a good old look. Ought to be able to pinpoint the nationality from the dental work. Amazing what these forensic chappies can

141

do nowadays.'

'Astonishing,' George agreed absent-mindedly, not paying close attention. 'You and Goudhurst are, I imagine, of the opinion that these could be the Hanover Square Gurkhas?'

Sir Maurice took a second to recall the witness Fawnbrake's first impression of the people he'd seen turning into Conduit Street. 'The very same. Not,' he added, 'that finding them murdered gets us much forrader. Moseley's people in Boston seem to have come up against another blank wall with their dim priest and the Madden family but all is not Stygian gloom and doom. For one thing, young Mrs Shigekawa is showing definite signs of improvement.'

'That is good news,' George said, much cheered. 'She may furnish us with a positive ID on the Irish pair, at least, always assuming that's who they are. Gives Goudhurst an excellent shot at extradition if they've scarpered abroad; again, always assuming they can be collared,' he added with diminishing optimism.

'And,' Lyall said, 'Moseley reports that his chum in the Milan Carabinieri has been in touch. Our Mr Castle seems to have arrived there by train. He appeared at the hotel with a porter from the railway station in tow, said porter having one of those buggy things upon which were two large boxes. Heavy, large boxes, the porter said. Castle told him they were samples.'

'Now we know.'

'Indeed.' Sir Maurice looked down at his notes. At least, he thought, little pieces of the puzzle were steadily trickling in. 'The frontier policeman who waved the Renault through the Mont Blanc control post rang up Milan to say his mind has been niggling that the car had a nought-prefix registration. More specifically, zero-four, -five or -six.'

'Where are they when they're at home?' George asked irritably.

'Alps, South of France, logically close to the Mont Blanc Tunnel,' Sir Maurice said, beetling his eyebrows at George.

'Handy for Milan, then.'

'Handy for everywhere. Handy for the Geneva banks. Handy for that skiing place you and Mrs Hamilton were disporting yourselves in.' He almost added 'at the tax-payers' expense' before remembering that the disporting had been at Willie Hibbert's grudging expense. 'Excellent communications by air, rail and road, very much like Milan. Dickie knows a senior chap at the Préfecture in Nice and preliminary enquiries are already afoot. South of France likeliest of the three because of the cocaine, ah, implications.'

'Good job you brought Six in at the off, then.' George sat back in his chair and rubbed his eyes tiredly. 'So what has all this new information told you, Maurice? I confess no pattern seems to be taking shape in my demonstrably senile mind.'

Lyall's eyebrows crept up to where his hairline had once been. 'You surprise me, Georgie,' he said evenly. He hauled a large atlas across the table and opened it to a full spread covering Europe and the British Isles. 'We think we've got a division of labour here. Think of it,' he said, glaring at the atlas, 'as two teams.

'Team One is in Ireland and composed of the standard inept riff-raff, unemployable oiks and blah-blah-blah Sinn Feiners. Local boyos jumping up and down and scoring the odd hit when they're not shooting themselves in the foot.'

'The murdered judge in the Republic being a hit and the abortive attack on the RUC post in Ulster being a miss.' George thought about it further. 'I must say, the gunning-down of the judge came as something of a shock, at least to me. The IRA, so far as the Republic is concerned, has done nothing of late, apart from turning themselves into a gang of Mafia-style thugs. No bank robberies, no kidnappings-for-ransom in yonks. Only their normal extortion, protection rackets, bits and bobs . . .'

'Let's not forget drug-dealing, old boy. Brook's got a Garda drugs specialist he's working with now. Telexing at a terrific clip from Grosvenor Square. May throw up a bit of fresh information.' Sir Maurice shrugged. 'A more recent, hum, enterprise but a nice little earner, cocaine.

The Gardai estimate that the IRA are raking in up to fifteen million pounds a year from their rackets of one sort or another.'

George whistled. 'As much as that! You'd think that with amounts like that coming in they wouldn't bother with anything else.'

'They seldom do,' Sir Maurice said dryly. 'Brook Moseley's Garda friend is of the opinion that murdering the judge was a simple exercise in Sinn Fein public relations.'

'Ah.' George glanced away from his superior and looked instead at the dusty plant struggling for life in a corner of the room. He understood how it must feel. 'Yes, I see. They're perceived by the Irish public as nothing more than gangsters and racketeers so they're scoring the odd hit, to be elegant about it, in order to demonstrate some vestigial traces of political virility.'

'My dear Georgie, talk of elegance!' Sir Maurice chuckled briefly. 'But that's it in a nutshell. Now then, let us turn to Team Two, which is far, far more interesting than those oafish Celtic mafiosi.'

He turned the atlas around to face George. 'Goudhurst has an interesting theory: the IRA cell or cells in mainland Britain are under the control of someone in Europe, not Ireland. An entirely independent and more sophisticated organization, with its own planning and financing. Altogether a higher life-form.'

'A steadier hand which doesn't shoot itself in the foot?'

'Just so.' He pointed to various places on the map. 'Look at Monday's rash of attacks. What pattern can you see, if any?' He drew his great eyebrows together. 'Sorry to catechize but you're extraordinarily good at finding patterns, Georgie, when you set your mind to it, that is.'

George bent over the atlas and pondered. 'Common Market,' he finally said.

Lyall nodded and sat back in his chair. 'Just what Dickie Goudhurst and I were thinking. Glad you've reached the same conclusion. Minimal fuss at frontiers, minimal documentation required to send the bombers and gunmen scuttling about from country to country. Freight traffic at the frontiers too heavy for thorough checking. The Athens Embassy bombing is what tipped us off.'

'Greece being the latest country to join the Common Market. Yes. Police there completely useless, too.' George leant back and shut his eyes. 'No unpleasant goings-on in Switzerland, Sweden, Austria or Cyprus. Accessible as anywhere else, but non-EEC.'

'Precisely. Ditto Hong Kong, America, Australia and lots of other places where they could shoot up our troops or any other species of British life. Fire-bomb our consulates, British banks, cultural what-have-yous, the Rolls-Royce shop, and yet they haven't.'

'So far.' George now felt depressed on top of being tired. 'It's infuriating that all we can do is react. I wish we could find some way to flush them out into the open. Make them react to us instead.'

He stood up and walked to the window, looking down into the quiet street. It was raining again. 'You and Commander Goudhurst assume that Clever Clogs running the operations from Europe ordered a hit to tidy things up here? Unsightly and murderous Japs littering the place; hence the Jack Russell's unearthing of bodies in Wiltshire?'

Lyall merely grunted and George continued to stare down into Curzon Street, empty but for the occasional taxi swishing through puddles, as he thought aloud. 'Clever Clogs was protecting Desmond Reardon, ergo sweeping the excitable and very-visible Japanese gunmen from the board. Gunpersons, I should say. Dear me, how sexist!'

He let the curtain drop and turned away from the window, rummaging for his handkerchief to wipe the grime from the windowsill off his fingers. 'Why can't they clean this place properly?' he complained. 'Is that how you see it, Maurice? Hanover Square adventure gone badly awry. Risk of identification by possible survivors and/or witnesses. Sacrifice the two pawns most easily identifiable and least important in order to protect your rook?'

Sir Maurice sneezed violently. 'For God's sake, Georgie, don't shake those dusty curtains again, I beg you.' He honked loudly. 'In this particular game of chess, your man needed a tight schedule to make a maximum publicity impact: Easter Monday, timing of news bulletins and the like. Buggers time their attacks after careful study of the week's television programming, I shouldn't wonder. Your rook, Reardon, and his charming side-kick Eamonn Cahill move on schedule out of their rustic retreat in Wilts. They have disposed of their highly-visible Japanese auxiliaries, who were likely intended for a third operation which has had to be scrubbed. We're certain they had a car, so possibly the Japanese had been earmarked for a car-bomb operation. In any event, Reardon's two targets override the third, whatever it was to be. He is needed to blow up the shop and the aircraft. Kindly note that Tower Records is the old Swan & Edgar and connected to Heathrow by the Piccadilly Line.'

'So tidy,' George murmured.

'The IRA don't have all that many bomb-making experts, you know. Reardon's one of their best, too, which is why a minder, Cahill, was in permanent attendance on him. Reardon's painstaking and thorough. Always assuming our tentative identification of Reardon is right, that is. Both bombs looked to be his work: Semtex used in both cases, electronic timers, fuses . . .'

'Quick work by Goudhurst's people.'

Sir Maurice nodded. 'He got onto the Home Secretary in a twinkling and virtually had this island sealed off before the dust had settled on the taxiway. But he's fairly certain it was a case of horses and barn doors.'

His brows beetled again. 'A man who might have been Reardon was on a Sabena flight to Brussels, not long before the Belfast plane that blew up was scheduled to leave. Single ticket. Paid for in cash. The bright girl at the ticket desk picked up immediately on his description, the minute the copper suggested the man they were looking for might have a passing resemblance to Arthur Scargill, including the cascade of chins and the bouffant-at-the-sides, swirl-on-top hairdo. You'd think the vain little sod, Reardon I mean, would either change his hairstyle or invest in a hat.

146

Girl apparently had such a fit of the giggles it was hard to get anything out of her for a good five minutes. In any event, he wasn't travelling under the name of Reardon. The young lady seems to think it was something more like Locke or Keyes or something. Passenger list being checked now but I doubt it will get us any further.'

'Belgians notified of course.'

Sir Maurice shrugged. 'Naturally. Doubt he'll have hung about, however. Brussels was no doubt a spur-of-the-moment choice. First flight on the departures board with a destination in Western Europe. Frequent flights from Brussels to Dublin and Belfast. If he went to the transit lounge and jumped on the next plane, it would take an uncommon stroke of luck to track him from Brussels. Come to that, he could just as well have hopped on a train and be anywhere by now: Paris, Amsterdam, Bonn, Copenhagen.'

'Any Common Market country.' George clenched his teeth. 'Which leaves only young Eamonn Cahill.'

'Wrong, Einstein.' Sir Maurice's smile was grim. 'Indeed, there's very little left of Cahill at all. A forearm with hand attached and some fingerprints attached to the hand.'

'Cahill was on the Belfast flight?'

'He was. That much, at least, we are sure of. They're gobbling up their own young, Georgie.' There was a measure of satisfaction in his voice. 'Ginger Reardon planted a bomb on his own minder.'

13

In the course of sifting through the Wiltshire spinney where the two bodies were uncovered, the police found the small cache of arms, Uzis and ammunition, presumed to have been left behind by Reardon and Cahill for future collection. A heavy downpour had caused the earth covering the cache to subside into a shallow rectangular depression, spotted by one of the young police cadets set to work combing every inch of ground for clues. The day grew colder and soon the rain turned to snow. The search was called off and the cadets were issued with mugs of sweet, steaming tea.

Most of the weapons were in their original factory wrappings and carefully sealed into heavy-duty black plastic bags along with their magazines. These were plainly unused. It did not take long for the specialists to establish that only two of the Uzis showed any signs of handling and both had been wiped clean of fingerprints. One, however, had been fired and even before it was test-fired for comparison with the ballistics report on the Hanover Square murders, Detective Chief Superintendent Fry was convinced that this was the weapon they'd been searching for.

As Fry pressed on with the murder investigation, Goudhurst picked away at the putative terrorist connection. His first step was to contact the Japanese police, acting on the assumption that the corpses actually were Japanese, even before the Medical Examiner had really got down to cases. Goudhurst was proceeding on the theory that Japanese terrorists had, for reasons he hoped Mari Shigekawa might be able to furnish, murdered the senior Shigekawas.

His hunch proved to be correct. Photographs and fingerprints taken from the corpses and faxed to Tokyo produced almost an instant reply: the bodies were

148

identified as Mitsu Kawara and Reiko Inoguchi, suspected of affiliation with the Japanese Red Army. Kawara was known to the police: he had been convicted of aggravated assault at the age of eighteen and had served a six-year prison term. The girl had no criminal record in Japan itself but was known to have associated with criminals. The Basque separatists, ETA, had at one time included a Japanese girl but the Guardia Civil in Madrid regretted being unable to furnish either photograph or fingerprints. Both Kawara and Inoguchi were wanted for questioning by the West German police in connection with the murder of an industrialist in Stuttgart two years previous.

Goudhurst quickly telexed all the information he had to the head of the West German anti-terrorist branch, the BKA, who telexed back with his profuse thanks and a cheery "well done", in the mistaken belief his friends at Scotland Yard had gunned the terrorists down. Goudhurst didn't trouble to set him straight for the moment. He had too much on his plate, in addition to keeping everything crossed that Forensics might be able to come up with some solid piece of evidence on the Uzis and their wrappings, even half of a fingerprint. There was still nothing concrete to tie Reardon and Cahill to any of the four murders. Five, he corrected himself, thinking of Mari Shigekawa's unborn baby. He absolutely detested proceeding on guesswork alone, although his instincts had proven sound so far.

A search of the deserted cottage lying almost half a mile from the burial-ground had shown that Reiko was killed there on the bed in one of the two upstairs rooms. Mitsu might have been killed anywhere in the house. The only bloodstains were on a pillow found downstairs, probably used to muffle the sound of the shot and held to his head. Fry's team dusted and sifted through every square inch of the house for fingerprints, hairs, fibres, anything that could give a clue.

The local constabulary, although told as little as possible, were not slow to guess that the enquiry was of interest to shadowy figures who moved on a very elevated plane indeed. A rumour quickly spread amongst them that the Prime Minister was being kept closely informed of developments in the case and they were determined not to be relegated to the uninteresting task of keeping the curious public at bay, eclipsed by the know-it-alls from the Met. Following their own line of enquiry without waiting for instructions from on high, the Wiltshire team blitzed all the estate agents in the area and their efforts bore fruit within the first hour. A small firm in Trowbridge had rented the cottage.

It had been rented in February by post. The lease was for six months and, with several months yet to run, the estate agents had all the documentation readily to hand, in a file-drawer straightforwardly marked "Current Rentals". The puppyish young man, "our Mr Redcroft", who had conducted the transactions, was helpfulness itself and greedily anxious for the police to let drop a few crumbs of inside information.

The man who telephoned to ask about the cottage, our Mr Redcroft recalled, had clearly stated that he had seen the estate agent's advert in *The Times*. Every scrap of paper pertaining to the rental had been xeroxed and stuck into a file flagged "The Meadows, Rudge". Cheques for the rent and deposits for gas and electricity were in sterling but drawn on a Geneva bank, which our Mr Redcroft had found thrillingly smart and exotic. The lease had been in the name of Easter Productions, SA, also the name stamped on the cheques, and the covering letter said that the cottage would be occasionally used by a Mr Charles Banham, who had been commissioned by Easter Productions to write a screenplay for them and needed a quiet retreat. The headed paper gave the address of Easter Productions SA as being in care of the Geneva bank.

The local postman, however, was able to add a piece of potentially useful information. He had once seen a Ford Cortina turning into the track that led to the house but that single sighting had been at least a month previous, possibly a little more. The car had been too far away for the postman to see precisely how many people were in it but there were certainly two in the front. He was, he said apologetically, afflicted with colour-blindness and was therefore unable to provide the police with the car's colour.

Keeping the double murder out of the press was naturally out of the question but Goudhurst succeeded in preventing news of the arms-cache from leaking. There was a slim hope that the IRA would try to recover the dozen new Uzis and the copse, its human grave gaping open and its Uzi grave left looking as close as possible to how it had been left, was staked out from the vantage-point of the cottage itself.

The press-conference was carefully balanced to give away as little as possible without making the Chief Constable appear furtive. He implied that the bodies had decomposed to an extent that made identification difficult, although not in the long run impossible, given recondite forensic examination. This would buy time. As to motive, he cannily did not rule out sex, thus providing the tabloids with limitless scope for lurid speculation on kinky rustic perversions: voyeurism, homicidal jealousy, a wife-swapping ring and the like. The cottage was duly photographed and described as a "blood-soaked rural love-nest", which caused unprofessional hilarity at Scotland Yard.

Mari Shigekawa blackmailed Helen Tarrant into submission by flatly refusing to have any more pain-killers until she could be clear-headed enough to tell her story coherently.

'You'd better do as she says, Helen,' Tommy Shigekawa advised. 'She's a Taurus. She wants to nail the bastards.'

Helen got the tape-recorder working to her satisfaction as Mari and her husband spoke to each other softly in Japanese. Mari was a good witness, sticking to hard fact and elaborating on details as the need arose.

Her glasses had been, as usual, pushed up onto her head, keeping her hair more or less in place. She had seen what she thought of as two Buddha-heads while walking towards them. They had cameras slung round their necks and blue nylon bags, the sort much in vogue for carrying sporting equipment, were at their feet. They were peering up at

151

an undistinguished office block. Buddha-heads, Tommy explained to Helen, were what he and Mari called the type of Japanese tourists one saw everywhere, swarming about the world's principal tourist attractions, unable to observe anything with the naked eye and forever squinting through their view-finders.

Helen smiled and nodded. 'I know what you mean,' she said. 'We English cringe with embarrassment when we're abroad and see our beer-swilling compatriots behaving like cretins. Ours do a good deal of singing and fighting. We wish they'd confine themselves to photography, like yours.'

Mari reached out to grasp her husband's hand for reassurance. She was coming up to the painful part of her story.

As she and Tommy's parents drew closer to the Buddha-heads, she decided that the girl looked familiar. She was very like a girl, Akiko, same no-nonsense hair-style, same height, who was a close friend's secretary at the Dai-Ichi Kangyo Bank in Tokyo when Tommy had worked there. Saying to her in-laws that she knew the girl, she ran forward, calling out to her in Japanese and teasing her for carrying a camera and looking like a Buddha-head. When she got to within a few feet, she moved her glasses into their proper place and realized that she was mistaken; the girl was a complete stranger. Having already accused her of looking like a Buddha-head, common courtesy required an apology and plea of terrible myopia. Two European men who had been standing near the Japanese couple seemed to take a close interest in Mari's voluble, embarrassed apologies.

By then, Mr and Mrs Shigekawa had caught up and were looking on in amusement over their daughter-in-law's evidently having wedged her foot firmly into her own mouth. Mari had smiled nervously at the smaller of the two European men, the one with silly hair, and he had smiled back. He had a gap between his two front teeth. Honour bruised but more or less restored, she prepared to move along with a final apology when suddenly the young

Japanese man had burst into a tirade of shouted abuse. The nicest thing he had called her was "capitalist whore" and worse was to follow.

The three Shigekawas were, to begin with, too shocked to say anything but as the young man warmed to his subject, Mr Shigekawa remonstrated and finally cracked his umbrella hard on the pavement in an uncharacteristic display of temper. With no warning that Mari was aware of, the young Japanese pulled a pistol from his jacket pocket and began to wave it about, screaming that such oppressors of the people as they deserved to die. The taller of the two European men bent down and straightened up carrying what was unmistakably a machine-gun. The other man shouted and tried to stop him but his reactions were slow and the taller one opened fire. She was knocked to the ground, knowing that she had been shot, and she was dimly conscious that Tommy's parents had been shot, too.

WPC Tarrant quickly made notes as Mari sobbed uncontrollably in Tommy's arms. When she was a little calmer, Helen clarified one or two small points, and ran down the passage to report to Prescott at Savile Row.

'Stay there, Helen, but for God's sake tell her that it will take some time to get someone from the Yard to gather together the snaps and get along to the hospital. Make her be a good girl and have the sodding pain-killer!'

'She's stubborn as can be.'

'Bloody hell! Well, use your imagination, girl! Tell her that if she doesn't co-operate with the medicine-men over there, they'll put her off-limits to us entirely and bring the whole bang shoot to a screaming halt. Don't say "whole bang shoot", whatever you do. Perhaps better not to say "screaming", either. Use whatever threats you can think of.'

Prescott and a man from Goudhurst's Anti-Terrorist Squad pitched up about an hour later with their photographs of IRA men and the faxed material from Tokyo on Kawara and Inoguchi. Mari had been persuaded to allow the nurse to give her another pain-killer and was now dozing.

Two hours later, Inspector Prescott had taken over and Mari was sifting through the material and about to give up in disgust. She had made a positive identification of Reiko Inoguchi. About Kawara she was less sure. She had no trouble identifying Reardon from his photographs – again, his ludicrous swirl of lacquered hair gave him away – but, as with Kawara, she couldn't be positive about Eamonn Cahill. She kept returning to his photographs.

'It's so maddening,' she said as she studied Cahill's undistinguished face taken from various angles. 'I'm pretty sure he's the one but I can't swear to it. I'm absolutely positive about two out of the three others but I can't in all honesty nail this son-of-a-bitch. And he's the one who shot us! The male Buddha-head was just waving his gun around and the other two were just like hanging around. Jesus! They weren't even doing anything, just standing there.'

She dropped her head back against the pillows and swore. 'It means you'll never get a conviction. Not if I can't stand there at the Old Bailey with my hand on a Bible and swear that this was the bastard who killed Tommy's parents.' Her face was skewed with impotent anger, her black eyes burning with fury and grief. 'He killed my baby for no reason at all and any defence lawyer would chop my testimony, and me, into little bits. I don't think I could finger him even if you caught him and stuck him into a line-up.' She picked up the photograph and studied it again. 'It's no use. I'm just not sure it's him. He.'

Inspector Prescott looked at her consideringly. He switched off the tape-recorder. Then he took her hand and patted it in a fatherly way, saying, 'There, there, my dear, don't upset yourself. You're an excellent witness. Truly. Hush now.' He cleared his throat. 'I'll tell you a little secret and it will make you feel much better about everything. But first you must promise me that you will tell no one at all, not even Helen Tarrant. Except your husband, of course. You have my express permission to tell him.' He smiled at her, waiting.

154

'All right,' she said, 'I promise,' hope already making her calmer.

Prescott fanned out four photographs and placed them gently on Mari's bed. 'These two,' he pointed at Kawara and Inoguchi, 'your Buddha-heads, are dead. They were affiliated with the Red Army in Japan and we've got positive IDs on them from the Tokyo police.' He smiled at her. 'With me so far?'

'Yes,' Mari said with a slight smile.

He pointed at Cahill. 'This man, the one we're pretty certain shot you, is an IRA gunman. *Was* a gunman. He's dead, too. So no line-up for us to subject you to. His job was to look after this man. Guard his precious life and see to his general well-being.' Reardon's photograph was given a contemptuous flick by Prescott's index finger. 'Cahill was what we in England call a minder and you Americans call politely a bodyguard and impolitely a torpedo.

'Your friend with the funny coiffure, Mr Desmond "Ginger" Reardon here, is a bomber. He's killed many people, a whole *lot* of people for the IRA.' He sighed. 'Unfortunately, he's still at large but, *but*, my dear young lady, his minder isn't because Reardon blew him up.' He grinned wolfishly at Mari. 'Cahill killed your parents-in-law, then he killed Kawara and Inoguchi. Then Reardon here killed him.'

Mari shut her eyes; tears of relief and satisfaction ran down her cheeks. She opened her eyes again. 'Thank you for letting me know all that. I can't tell you what pure pleasure it is to know the filthy scumbag's dead. Oh God it's good to know that!'

'If we're to put our hands on Reardon's collar, it's essential that he and his, ah, associates in the IRA be kept in the dark. If they know that the great white chiefs are looking for Reardon, he'll be kept so far underground that we'll never find him. That's why you can't tell anyone.' He got to his feet and signalled to Mr Shigekawa who was standing by Helen in the passage outside and looking worried. 'Not even Helen Tarrant, mind you.' Mari nodded weakly and smiled reassuringly at him.

'So, madam,' Prescott said briskly, getting the bundles together and dividing the load with the Yard's man, 'the only hard work left for you to do now is to get better.'

'Mr Prescott, I shall. You can count on it. You can even bet on it. I'm going to get well if it kills me.'

'Gotcha!' Goudhurst said when Fry came back from the telephone and told him that Mari Shigekawa had positively identified Reardon.

'Well, not quite, Dickie. He didn't pull the trigger, after all. I mean, at this point, we haven't got enough to put him away for more than a few years. Conspiracy to commit murder's the best we could hope for, even if we had him under lock and key. Which we haven't.'

Waiters and clients at the Star of Punjab were looking at them curiously. The place was a great favourite amongst their colleagues from the Yard and Fry surveyed the openly-eavesdropping men at adjacent tables with disgust. 'Let's pay up and get out of here. I could do with a walk.' He had just consumed an awesome quantity of Our Chef Recommends, which never varied from year to year and was generally believed to consist of minced dachshund from the Battersea Dogs Home, washed down with a pint of lager. Some mild form of exercise would be beneficial to both privacy and digestion.

Goudhurst grunted as he waggled his fingers to get Ali Baba's attention. 'I'd feel one hell of a lot better if we did have him under lock and key.' Ali Baba slid the bill onto the table and expressed smarmy hopes that the meal had been satisfactory to the gentlemen. Goudhurst didn't bother to answer and left a tip calculated to prevent Ali Baba and his minions from pissing in their next meal whilst staving off fulsome expressions of gratitude from their turbanned host.

The two men went out into the cool night air with relief. 'We don't know how much Semtex they had, for one thing,' Goudhurst said, turning down Great Peter Street towards Millbank. 'The bomb experts say that the amounts used for both the shop and the Belfast plane were quite small. If the plane had been in the air when the bomb detonated, it would've blown a hole big enough to bring it down into the sea. Plop. But on the ground, of course . . .'

He paced along thoughtfully for a few yards. 'The missing Cortina is the thing I'd most like to see found at this point. There's every reason to assume its boot has more explosives in it and nothing prevents Mr Reardon from putting its keys and location in the post to another of his playmates here. Travelled to Brussels using the name of Pope, it turns out.'

'Doesn't sound like either Locke or Keyes to me,' Fry observed.

'Odd minds, women. The young lady at Sabena retained Keyes in the old memory bank. Keys of St Peter. Pope. Simple as that. I imagine she's an RC.'

'Or dabbles in heraldry.'

Goudhurst made a growling noise in his throat. 'My guess is that Kawara and Inoguchi had been earmarked for the bomb at Tower Records. Then they would've gone by tube to Heathrow and met Reardon and Cahill. They would have been handed the carry-on bag and been blown up on the Belfast plane. The car should have been left somewhere, neatly packed with the remaining Semtex and another time-delay fuse.'

Fry looked thoughtful. 'All of which tells us that the IRA are going back to tourist targets, designed to scare off people from coming here. If you're right, it's likely that the car's near Heathrow and we'll find it soon.' He shrugged. Everything that could be done about tracing the Cortina had been done. All they could do was to wait.

'But another interesting point is that Cahill couldn't have known anything at all about the plan to blow up the aircraft. He'd have done a runner. The IRA haven't the devotion to suicide bombings that their Muslim brethren-in-terror of the Lebanon have. Thank God.'

'And Allah, who designed them such a nice heaven to go to. Whereas ours is cracked up to be so ineffably dull that even the Irish would want to postpone having a recce . . .'

Goudhurst was not to be sidetracked by Fry's reflections on the Infinite. 'If Eamonn Cahill was an unwitting dupe, it means Reardon's under direct orders from whoever's controlling the operation. No cut-outs.' He fell silent again, brooding.

Fry remembered that Goudhurst hadn't yet seen the lab reports. 'Forensics have been busy. Did their magical number with DNA testing. The unappetising Miss Inoguchi shared her dubious favours with both Kawara and Cahill.' He shivered in fastidious distaste. 'They must've been pretty desperate.'

'Anything else?'

'We've got a positive from Lisburn on the thumbprint lifted from that breadknife in the kitchen I told you about.' The data banks at Lisburn, headquarters for Northern Ireland's Military Intelligence, were capable of disclosing which IRA activist was given to picking fights with his wife over breakfast and likely his nose, too. 'It's Reardon's. No doubt about it. Nice clear print.'

'Still not what the Americans call a "smoking gun" Denis,' Goudhurst said gloomily. 'A print found in a cottage where a murder was committed is a step in the right direction but not a conviction. Puts Desmond Reardon at the scene of the crime at some time, not necessarily when the murder was committed. It's a pity in a way that Mrs Shigekawa is so sure that Reardon wasn't the shooter, although I know she's right. I mean, we've got accessory, conspiracy, what-have-you but not prime suspect, more's the pity. There's nothing, absolutely not one single bloody thing, to link Reardon with those two bombings.'

Fry was rather more optimistic than his colleague. From the point of view of the murder investigation, files could be quietly closed on everything except the bombings, which were Goudhurst's headache. A total of twenty-six people had died so far and another seven were presently classified as either critical or grave. Thank God, he thought for the hundredth time, that the Belfast flight had been queued up for take-off and was still on *terra firma* when the time-delay fuse exploded the bomb. It had been a miraculous stroke of luck, both in human terms of lives saved as well as preserving a few shreds of evidence.

He patted Goudhurst's shoulder, knowing how frustrated he was feeling. 'What's needed now, Dickie, is Reardon making some stupid mistake. He's not a miracle-worker. He's careful, but even the wariest ones make mistakes and don't forget that he's minus a minder now. Got no one to look after him and run his little errands for him. He'll be out in the open more.' He laughed briefly. 'If he'd done the washing-up properly in that cottage like a good lad we couldn't prove he'd ever been near the place.'

Goudhurst refused to be bucked up. 'What I need is a drink, Denis. What I really need is my own miracle-worker.' His brow furrowed in concentration and he narrowly missed stepping in a slick of dogshit. 'I'm sick to death of cleaning up after all these gruesome wholesale killings. I want to make those shifty little buggers jump for a change.' He walked on without speaking.

'What's simmering in your feverish brain?' Fry finally asked, puffing a little as he caught up.

'Miracles!' Goudhurst suddenly stopped dead in his tracks. 'I'm thinking of miracles. By God, Denis, I believe you've given me an idea. What do you think of performing our own little miracle? A good dollop of disinformation can't hurt, now can it?'

'What're you babbling on about?'

Goudhurst paused at some length before answering, examining the idea from all sides. 'We'll raise Cahill from the dead. Our very own Lazarus.' He grinned evilly at Fry. 'It's the least we can do for him, Denis.'

Fry whistled. 'I think I see what you're getting at but it won't be easy to convince the Provos, Dickie. I mean, if you haul in the reptiles for a press conference and spring a surprise witness . . .'

'Not from us.' Goudhurst was thinking aloud as he stared at the flashing yellow light marking a zebra crossing. 'The rumour's got to be given full credence in Ireland if it's to be acted upon by the Provo commanders.'

He prodded Fry gently in the tummy with the ferrule of his umbrella. 'I've got to have a heart-to-heart with Dominic Ryan. He'll know precisely how to set the cat among the pigeons. If we get it right, we can flush Reardon out into the open and possibly the puppet-master, too.' Goudhurst simmered with excitement. 'Let's get back to the salt mine.'

He did a smart about-face and broke into a brisk jog. Ryan was Goudhurst's anti-terrorist opposite number in the Garda Siochana. The man had a formidable network of informers and his methods would give civil-rights campaigners apoplexy if they ever got to hear of them. His hatred of the IRA was legendary and it was widely rumoured that he never left his Dublin office, spinning sticky webs for Provisionals to blunder into.

'My wife will be unforgiving,' Fry wheezed plaintively.

'So go home. My department, not yours.'

'No.'

PART FOUR

14

The brightly-lit television studio was stiflingly hot. The Home Secretary looked across the table and saw that his fellow MP, the Opposition's Shadow Northern Ireland Secretary, was sweating like a horse. The Home Secretary smiled as he turned to his neighbour, a respected and unfailingly jolly journalist from *The Times*, and made an innocuous comment about a sad decline in sandwich-making standards amongst the BBC's catering staff. He was thinking that the Labour spokesman ought to have given the whisky a miss. Alcohol made you sweat and a sweating politician always looked shifty.

As the red lights winked from camera to camera, the show's host introduced the panel in his normal jocular way, causing the Ulster Unionist politician to scowl. Then the questioning began.

'We shall begin this evening's discussion with a question from Mr George McHugh of Warrenpoint, County Down: "In view of the upsurge in IRA violence on Easter Monday, what future tightening of security arrangements do the members of the panel think might now be considered?" I'm sure that the Home Secretary would like to put the Government's position on Mr McHugh's question first.'

The Home Secretary's chiselled features assumed an expression of the utmost solemnity. 'Thank you.

'Mr McHugh is entirely correct in assuming that all our security arrangements have come under intense review during the last few days. It is clear to everyone, I'm sure, that the IRA's tactics have undergone a complete revision. They appear to have resumed a campaign of indiscriminate terror against the civilian population, in addition to diplomatic and military targets. Their failure to get even one Sinn Fein candidate elected to the Dail in the last Irish Parliamentary elections has clearly caused them to abandon any idea of a political victory in either Northern Ireland or the Republic itself. Sinn Fein managed to get somewhere between ten and eleven per cent of the vote in these Irish elections. In Northern Ireland, the Roman Catholics are about a quarter of the population. Polls in Ulster show that about one-third of the Roman Catholics vote for Sinn Fein. To simplify, only eight per cent of the people of Northern Ireland back Sinn Fein. They simply cannot make any claim to widespread public support for their policies.

'But to leave politics aside and return to security, the Garda Siochana in the Irish Republic are committed to keeping order just as any other police force in any other civilized country. Co-operation between them and Scotland Yard has progressed remarkably quickly, even before this last brutal round of atrocities. The Gardai are under no illusion that the Provisionals are anything other than gangsters, masquerading as patriots. Spraying innocent, unarmed people with a machine-gun requires no bravery. Murdering a judge, whether he be in Ireland or Sicily, is the hallmark of vengeful thugs, not freedom-fighters.' He smiled grimly. 'The Mafia started its activities during the Middle Ages as a patriotic organization. So did the Chinese Triads in the seventeenth century and they now terrorize every Chinese community from London to San Francisco.

'The Anglo-Irish Agreement has facilitated the forging of increasingly close links between our two police forces.' This remark produced a snarl of rage from the Unionist MP, to the Home Secretary's satisfaction. 'Close co-operation with the Irish police is having immediate results, which I feel sure,' he turned politely to the programme's host, 'is likely to be the most pressing subject in this evening's discussion.

'We have in police custody here a man who is helping with inquiries about the bomb outrage in Piccadilly Circus, which killed a security guard and a Nigerian tourist, and the tragic deaths of, so far, more than twenty innocent passengers aboard the BA flight to Belfast. This man being held is, not very surprisingly, also wanted by the Gardai in connection with a drug-smuggling ring suspected of at least one murder in the Republic.' He gazed sombrely at the studio audience.

'The parallel I drew with the Mafia was not at all fanciful. What we are dealing with is hoodlums, plain and simple.

'From the standpoint of international police efforts, the IRA will be pursued in the same spirit of co-operation in all the target countries it uses so cynically to publicize its efforts. Security arrangements are not only being tightened here and in Ireland but on the Continent as well.' He permitted himself a wintry smile of satisfaction. 'The rats will find it increasingly difficult to find a cosy sewer.'

Gillon got up from his chair and switched off the television. His first reaction, one of surprised incredulity at the Home Secretary's effrontery, gave way to wariness. He had to concentrate on what he had just heard. What he had just heard defied all rational belief.

There was no point in trying to telephone Desmond Reardon. He had given him strict instructions to answer only at certain set hours, an especially necessary precaution now that Reardon was on his own with no minder. Reardon had always obeyed instructions to the letter. Gillon had impressed upon him the need to keep out of sight, leaving the safe house only to do minimal, essential shopping.

The safe house was an ugly, modest flat in Amsterdam's Osdorp quarter, chosen for its proximity to Schiphol and ease of access by ordinary tram to the Central Station. No taxis, Gillon had specified, aware that Reardon couldn't drive. In addition to the Dutch judiciary's ulcerating deliberations over absolute impartiality in deciding whether to extradite 'political refugees' on their soil accused of terrorist crimes, Amsterdam was a godsend for the IRA because absolutely everyone spoke at least some English. His fellow-Irish, Gillon hadn't failed to notice, seemed congenitally incapable of learning even useful smatterings of foreign languages. The mercenaries he enrolled were far more cosmopolitan: the Japanese pair that Cahill had executed spoke excellent French, the result of their training with Action Directe. It was rather a pity they had to go but they'd served their purpose. They stood out far too much in a crowd for comfort.

Another minder would have to be provided for Reardon to replace poor Eamonn Cahill and the only quickly-available one was Connolly. Besides, he and Reardon already knew one another, despite never having actually worked together, so with any luck there wouldn't be too much friction. Reardon was frequently, Gillon knew from experience, something less than urbane in dealing with his fellows.

Gillon knew that Nedda wouldn't like it but he intended to pull in Connolly to replace the late Cahill as quickly as it could be arranged, no matter how much she objected. There was nothing to be gained in tying up a relatively competent man to keep an eye on Ruffo in London. The recordings of Ruffo's telephone conversations were unexceptionable, having all to do with his son, his horses, his invitations and his sexual conquests. Ruffo did as he was told, no more and no less, because he had no choice in the matter. Gillon considered him to be a charming nonentity, an anachronism, a man with his uses but no real relevance in the modern world. Alexis, of course, was an entirely different kettle of fish.

He picked up his glass and made himself another small drink, then glanced at his watch. It was late but he didn't think Alexis would answer the phone in any event. He dialled the Zürich number and Alexis's voice on the tape gave his telephone number first in French then in Schwyzerdütsch, which invariably made Gillon smile his superior smile. After the voice had bilingually begged him to leave a message, promising to return the call as soon as feasible, Gillon did so, adding that it wasn't urgent, merely a query. He respected Alexis's military training and the experience he'd had in the field as a mercenary during his younger, unmutilated and carefree days. When Gillon led Ireland as its Philosopher King, Alexis would be his right hand, his Belisarius.

Irritably brushing accumulated cigarette ash off his shirt, he sat down once more to sift through various possibilities. He wished he had a tape-machine so he could have recorded *Question Time*. He had known that the liveliest debates were sure to be all about the recent stunning round of IRA activity and he had looked forward to having a satisfying gloat,

166

watching the politicians twisting slowly in the wind as they tried to find some reassuring crumb to throw to the worried public.

But the Home Secretary hadn't been twisting in the wind. He had clearly talked about "a man being held in custody" for the London bombings and just as clearly stated that this same man was the subject of enquiries in Ireland to do with illegal drugs.

He screwed up his eyes, glaring at the blank television screen. Who could it possibly be? Gillon had never been happy about pooling the wholesale cocaine distribution with their other activities but it had been a necessary evil. There weren't all that many reliable people on tap to keep a strict separation between the two sides of the equation, which he would have vastly preferred. An economical approach towards manpower meant tighter security but less flexibility.

Had someone he didn't know about been recruited in Dublin to handle the snow in Cahill's absence? Altdorfer could start making a few phone calls in the morning, no more than casual chats with some of his closer contacts, feeling the water. But the question still niggled: had Cahill struck out on his own in defiance of Gillon's strictest orders, setting up a mini-network to sell the cocaine? Cahill was a revolting specimen. He ought to have been taken out long ago but finding a suitable minder for Reardon was difficult.

Gillon was thinking hard, trying to piece it all together, trying to think like that half-wit Eamonn Cahill would think, if he ever had a thought in his life. When Gillon had ordered Reardon to send Cahill off with the Semtex, Reardon hadn't seemed the least bit put out. There had been no more reluctance for Cahill than there'd been for the Japs, not a trace of hesitation. Reardon had very likely been relieved to be shot of young Cahill.

No. Cahill was out of the question. There was no conceivable way he might have survived the explosion of the Semtex in his carry-on bag. He would have had to store it either in the overhead compartment or under his seat. Either way, he would have been blown to bits, no

167

matter if the aircraft was still on the ground. Desmond had said he'd put about four kilos in that bag.

Could Cahill have found the explosive, perhaps wondering if the bag wasn't on the heavy side, and somehow contrived to get off the plane? A possibility, Gillon thought, but such a remote one that it had to be discounted. How could he have got off the plane without alerting its crew that there was a very compelling reason to do so? Gillon suddenly shot to his feet again and began pacing up and down. By some miracle of good luck, Cahill could have been in the lavatory when the bomb went up. It was so unlikely, though, a one-in-a-million chance.

The Home Secretary had to be lying. There was no other possible explanation.

The morning papers were sure to run articles on the progress, or lack of it, of police investigations in the various countries Gillon had selected for the Easter Monday action. The British press sometimes co-operated with the Home Office in temporarily withholding information but the European press didn't see things quite the same way; D notices were meaningless to them. He would buy the German newspapers and the *International Herald Tribune* first thing in the morning. Until he knew more, there really wasn't a great deal he could do without getting Dublin and Belfast stirred up.

He glanced at his watch again. It wasn't too late to ring Dublin.

Looking up the telephone number in his book, he thought perhaps he wouldn't ring Dessie Reardon in the morning, after all. Best to have as much solid fact as possible before arranging a meeting with him or even putting any questions to him.

The brief telephone conversation they had had when Reardon was at the Brussels railway station on his way back to Amsterdam left Gillon in no doubt that, so far as Reardon knew, everything had gone according to plan. That Reardon could have double-crossed him, given Cahill some sort of warning, was unthinkable. It was completely out of character. Reardon had been brisk and businesslike, his usual laconic self. He had made his report and promised to put the car-keys and chit from the Heathrow car-park in the post on his way to the safe house. The bomb in the Cortina's boot was timed to go off in nine days, as Gillon had instructed. Connolly would be receiving everything within the next day or two.

If, by some freak of nature, Cahill had survived, then it wouldn't do at all to get the wind up Reardon. He would get steamed up, possibly even run, and Gillon hadn't the man-power to track him down before he threw himself into the arms of the police or got picked up by them. Laconic didn't mean the man was stupid. He had sworn to Gillon that he would prefer death to being banged up in the Maze Prison again but, staring the choice in the face, he might change his mind.

Gillon reviewed his plans again. Their logic was impeccable, absolutely impeccable and, really, nothing could go wrong. Nothing had been left to chance. There were random factors, of course; there had to be in any realistic scheme but they had been allowed for, something the morose cattle who ran the IRA in Ireland never bothered to do. If it proved to be a necessary precaution to take Reardon out, then so be it. Bombers weren't easy to come by but they were available if one knew where to look for them and either the good Colonel in Libya would oblige or Alexis would put the word out to the contact in Cannes who acted as the mercenaries' go-between. Reardon was valuable but valuable wasn't at all the same thing as irreplaceable.

Gillon decided that brooding about Cahill's putative survival was something he must put aside for the moment. It served no purpose and Philipp Altdorfer had a good connection in the Garda for inside information. What niggled was that Reardon knew a great deal more than was completely safe. He'd been with Gillon almost right from the beginning.

Reardon knew about Nedda, too, although not in any great detail. The situation there was in need of some tightening up, Gillon knew, but not quite yet. Costelloe wasn't nearly as feckless as Nedda thought on her own

169

and had been encouraged to continue thinking by Gillon himself. But it would take quite a lot more time for Costelloe to master all the access codes for the various bank accounts and further time to weasel his way into Nedda's confidence to the extent where she would reveal the scale and location of the various "projects" in which her Liechtenstein, Swiss, Panamanian, Luxembourg and Bahamian companies held controlling interests. Up to here, she was guarding all of this information with the jealousy of an elderly cuckold over his nubile bride.

It was on-the-job training so that Costelloe would eventually be able to take over completely from Nedda when the time came. He was doing well and had already contrived to take over most of the running of the cocaine trade, claiming that Nedda had far more important matters to oversee. Once Costelloe had assumed control, Nedda herself could be discarded. She was becoming, Gillon thought impatiently, a bore. What was far worse was that her little sexual distractions were very dangerous indeed. The security risks intrinsic to her "harmless relaxations" were horrendous.

Thank God, Gillon thought, Cahill knew nothing of the financial operations at all. If he hadn't been blown up, he could lead the police to Reardon but no farther. He knew Gillon existed. That was all. They had never met.

But Cahill hadn't survived, he couldn't have. It wasn't possible but if he had, somehow, escaped the bomb he'd be spilling his guts out by now. He would have had plenty of time to figure out that the carry-on bag with the Semtex bottom hadn't been given him by mistake.

15

The telephone on the bedside table rang briefly. Ruffo picked it up at once, dropped it on the floor, hauled it up again by its cord and eventually mumbled, *'Pronto?'* There were faint glimmerings of dawn light at the edges of the heavy silk ottoman curtains.

'Good morning, my darling Ruffino,' a woman's voice crooned. Ruffo grunted and squinted at the bedside clock in disbelief. It was six o'clock. 'Don't tell me you've forgotten about little me so quickly.' The voice was throaty, half-teasing, half-annoyed.

'Course not,' Ruffo mumbled sullenly, 'I'm just not awake yet. At this hour,' he added with a heavy hint of reproof.

'I wonder if we might meet later on today,' she said without the least apology, 'at our usual place? Just the two of us.' She sighed gustily and then giggled.

'Ummm,' Ruffo said, trying to throw his brain into first gear. 'I'm not sure that . . .'

'If you pulled yourself together, you could meet me at shall we say a quarter to eight?' The woman's caressing voice held an unmistakably bullying undertone.

'Yes.' He blinked at the clock again in a futile stab at rapid calculation. 'Well, I suppose I could manage it.' His tone was grumpy. 'Seven forty-five it is.' His mind was beginning to function at a subterranean level.

'Good,' she cooed, evidently very much pleased. 'By then I hope you'll be awake. Wide awake.' She gave a brief, sexy laugh. 'See you soon then, *caro*.' The line clicked and the dialling-tone came on. There was a second click.

Ruffo unwillingly dragged himself out of the warm bed and managed after several false starts to overcome the resistance of his Sulka dressing-gown, which gave every indication of having spent the night on an unarmed-combat course. Camilla was still fast asleep.

He was totally exhausted and an incipient hangover nibbled mouselike at the edge of his brain so that he felt slightly anxious about everything. He eyed the toaster with suspicion. Pulling himself marginally together, he took some small comfort in the fact that he would be able to snooze on the train. At such a diabolical hour, it was unlikely to be either crowded or noisy.

He sat down at the kitchen table to compose a note for Camilla to find when she woke up. He hoped the ringing telephone hadn't awakened her. He hadn't kept the phone clamped close to his ear and her head had been close to his own on the pillow. Charlotte sounded terrifically seductive when she had a mind to it and bloody Alexis thought the whole thing hilarious, probably standing at his wife's elbow and egging her on to outdo herself. Ruffo kept expecting her either to break into paroxysms of giggles or to spoil the entire effect by overachieving on her Mae West imitation.

Neither Gillon nor Nedda had any idea that Charlotte existed. They didn't even know Alexis was married, nor precisely where he lived. Ruffo, for that matter, didn't know where Alexis lived, either. It had been agreed between them that it was safer for him not to know. If Gillon or even Nedda were to discover that Alexis seldom went near the office-cum-flat he maintained in Zürich, Ruffo could swear blind, hand over heart, that he couldn't provide Alexis' true address, no matter what unpleasant pressures were applied. When Alexis switched off his answerphone, some other miracle of technology automatically shunted calls to wherever it was that Alexis actually did live, with the caller none the wiser.

On a visit to London, Alexis had had a professional of his acquaintance do a thorough sweep of Ruffo's flat and it had been clean of bugs, except the telephone, as they had suspected. The professional, a solemn, unsmiling man who rejoiced in the improbable name of Mr Albert Chicken, had returned to check for any new developments from time to time but the flat itself remained inviolate,

172

unbugged. Mr Chicken had shown Ruffo how to disengage the bug on the telephone and reconnect it but Ruffo only bothered to take it out when he was ringing Alexis. He was forever afraid he'd forget to put it back, which would alert Gillon and cause unwelcome watchfulness on his part. Nedda would throw herself into a transport of rage.

When Alexis needed to speak to Ruffo, Charlotte always rang on his behalf. It was an ordinary precaution. Why should Gillon or Nedda, one of whom must have ordered the tapping of Ruffo's phone, know how frequently Alexis and Ruffo compared notes, exchanged bits of information?

Charlotte's codes were dead simple. When she said, 'We must talk very soon,' Ruffo agreed that this would indeed be a good thing, rang off, disengaged the bug, rang back, spoke with Alexis, and replaced the bug. When Ruffo was in England and Alexis needed to meet him, the hour Charlotte gave was the approximate departure time of the next train from Victoria to Paris. She always rang to give him enough time to walk from his South Eaton Place flat the short distance to Victoria. There was nothing simpler than spotting a tag during an early-morning walk through deserted streets, unless it was flushing that same tag in a main-line station.

Ruffo inclined towards the theory that Nedda simply liked to keep a weather eye on him. Her legendary paranoia ever alert for hints of betrayal, she would be interested in his comings and goings, looking for any sign that he might be tempted to take the police into his confidence. That Ruffo was in no position to double-cross her without destroying himself and his family did not seem to make her feel any more secure, despite her reiterated threats of massive retaliation, should he so much as flirt with the idea of seeking outside help.

About Alexis she displayed no such qualms. Alexis was in it for the money. Besides, she had no hold over him and could do no more than trust to his greed to keep him on the straight and narrow. It had never crossed her mind that Alexis and Ruffo might conspire against her. She assumed that by sleeping with both men, playing one off against the other, she was maintaining a state of healthy, competitive animosity between them, not unlike rival football teams.

She felt sure that Alexis was in love with her. She needed very badly to believe that. It was, both men had discovered, the only chink in her armour.

Nedda was a lousy judge of character.

Connolly was not by nature an early riser and neither was the prince. This made for a good working relationship, as Connolly had once explained to Eamonn Cahill who had whinged about the out-of-synch hours he was forced to put in as Ginger Reardon's minder.

This morning Connolly had been forced to roll out early and he was consequently in a filthy temper. The little parcel containing car-keys and the ticket for the long-term car-park at Heathrow's Terminal Two had arrived and Gillon had rung to tell him where he wanted the red Cortina stashed. Connolly's displeasure at having been turfed out of his bed so early was compounded by the fact that the entire thing had become an exercise in futility. He had gone by tube, which he detested, out to fucking Heathrow and the red Cortina simply wasn't fucking there. He had thoroughly combed the entire sodding car-park and there was no sign of it, which he'd duly have to report to Gillon later, not something he bloody well looked forward to.

He had then gone back into town by tube, which he loathed even more now that they'd forbidden smoking, to change his clothes. By the time he left his flat for the second time that morning it felt to him like mid-day but it wasn't. He was hungry and resentful. It was rush hour and his bus inched south through dense traffic. Arriving in Belgravia. Connolly carefully manoeuvred 'his' car out of its rented garage in the mews behind the South Eaton Place flat and positioned himself opposite, where he could watch the stinking bastard's comings and goings. He got out from time to time to feed the sodding parking

174

meter. And that was his job, if you could bloody call it a job.

The garage also contained the tape-recorder Reardon had installed there so that the great man's every priceless telephonic word was monitored. Connolly's final chore of the day would be to run through the tape to see if the bugger had spoken to anyone new or said anything interesting, which was never. Connolly despised the wop above any other person in the universe and was only grateful that the flat was used so little.

Connolly's own flat was in Camden Town and he regarded Belgravia with disapproval. It lacked life. Real people didn't live here and the streets were far too quiet, outsiders viewed with suspicion unless readily accounted for. Overcoming that suspicion had been his first task when he'd been assigned to prince-watching and he had accepted Gillon's advice with awed gratitude. Gillon thought of everything. The man was a marvel, no bloody doubt about it. Connolly was sitting in a British racing green Jaguar wearing a chauffeur's uniform, its cap in plain sight on the seat beside him. In this area, no one looked twice at him, not even the police or the goddamn lezzie traffic wardens, as he sat in the Jaguar reading his *Sporting Life*. Following the prince around had, perforce, made a race-goer out of him, just about the only thing on the plus side of this excuse for a fucking job.

At about half-past ten, he looked up from his paper and lowered his window to clear out the accumulated cigarette smoke. A very good-looking young woman, the same tall, toothsome blonde in black silk he'd seen the previous evening, was standing on the steps of the prince's house, looking seriously overdressed in the strong morning sun. Actually it was the prince's half-house, for his flat occupied the upper half. The young woman was the one who'd gone home with his sodding highness last night, Connolly thought sourly. She was a new one. There had been lots of those over the year he'd been assigned to report on the lucky bastard's life, including all his "contacts", if you please, with the female sex. This one seemed uncertain of herself, as well she might, Connolly thought. This assignment frequently made him feel like a voyeur. Perhaps she was looking for a taxi.

He debated the advisability of going up to her, cap in hand, and offering to run her home for a fiver. Then he would be able to find out her address and even, possibly, her name. But the alternative was that he might thereby miss his sodding highness doing something interesting, which would, at least, make for a refreshing change. If the prince were up to something and Connolly were to miss it, Gillon would give him a right bollocking. He might even reassign him to something more arduous if not downright dangerous, which Connolly was anxious to avoid. At forty, he felt himself a bit long in the tooth for knight-errantry and if prince-watching duty was dull at least it enabled him to have a flutter on the horses without being accused of frivolity. He had, in any event, long ago worked out that the simplest method of disposing of the prince would be to wire up his car with a bomb when conveniently left in a racecourse car-park.

She was still standing there, frowning and undecided. Maybe they'd had a fight and she would cave in, ringing the bell to be allowed back into the sacred precincts of his high-and-mightyship's bedroom. A taxi turned into the street and appeared to make up her mind for her. She flagged it down and it squealed to a halt right next to Connolly's Jag. Jesus, what luck, he thought. He watched her in his rear-view mirror. Nothing wrong with a man, humble chauffeur though he may be, looking at a pretty girl. The cabbie caught his eye and winked and Connolly grinned. He had no trouble hearing the address she gave the driver but wrote it down, just to be absolutely sure, the moment the taxi started up.

He sat for a long time staring at what he'd written. Gillon would be most interested in hearing what Connolly had to tell him. The Eyetie's latest was almost certainly on her way home, which just happened to be the same small block of flats in Kensington where he'd recently done a thorough turnover, instructed to find and remove anything of a photographic nature. Well, there you are then, Mr Gillon. You know everything, don't you now.

'Jesus and Mary,' he finally said aloud, wondering at his sudden change of luck, 'thank God for excellent hearing. What a small world it is, to be sure.' His earlier filthy temper had vanished.

He was vastly relieved to have stumbled across something noteworthy to report, especially something that would offset the bad news about bloody Heathrow. Gillon would be highly displeased that the Cortina hadn't been where it was meant to be, although Connolly could hardly be blamed for that. But Gillon was always fair, unlike The Lady. Gillon would take note of the fact that Connolly had used his wits and that this new girl of Prince Monteavesa's was overwhelmingly likely to be the same one whose flat Connolly had searched and that The Lady hadn't been wasting everyone's time when she'd ordered the search.

Connolly had had mercifully few dealings with The Lady but he knew that she would be most interested in this interesting new development, unearthed single-handed, on his own initiative. He worked as hard as he knew how to please her, as would any sensible man.

As Alexis spotted Ruffo's tall figure on the pavement opposite the Brasserie Lipp, he called the waiter and ordered another plate and a second jug of dark beer. The *choucroute* was steaming gently on its platter over a low flame. There was plenty left for Ruffo, who was likely to be half-starved.

The traffic lights changed and Ruffo, turned out in a venerable and immaculately-cut tweed jacket, twill trousers and creamy silk shirt, trotted briskly across the Boulevard Saint-Germain, pausing only to stare after a leggy girl in an unseasonably skimpy dress, who waved jauntily to him as she ducked into a taxi, showing a good deal of leg in the process. He politely stood aside to allow a trio of soberly-dressed businessmen to leave the restaurant and shot through the revolving door.

'I'm famished,' he said predictably.

177

Alexis pointed his fork at the platter and said, 'Thought you might be. Dig in. Got a bit foxed last night, did you? Charlotte said you sounded half-witted on the phone.'

'Impertinent cow,' Ruffo said with a grin. 'I zizzed a bit on the train so I feel rather more human than I've any right to.'

They ate in silence for a few minutes, until Alexis felt he had had more than enough. He sat back in his chair and watched the younger man wolfing another sausage. 'Why don't I talk as you eat? Or does that put you off your food?'

'Nothing puts me off a *choucroute*,' Ruffo assured him. 'Talk away, man.'

'There's something that you and I had better start thinking about,' Alexis began.

'It had better be something deeply serious,' Ruffo said during a brief pause between mouthfuls. 'You hoicked me out of my warm bed in which there was an absolutely adorable creature. Delicious.'

'Your lunch or the girl?'

'Both.' He tipped the rest of the beer into his glass and attacked a piece of smoked pork. 'Don't mind me,' he said as he scraped the platter for the last strands of cabbage, 'as I make a belated effort to preserve a few tattered fragments of health. You have contrived to ruin my day so far. I'm only trying to salvage something of it.'

Alexis carefully smoothed his small, neat moustache with his napkin, an unconscious habit that gave him the look of a large and dangerous but, on the whole fortunately, just-fed big cat, a black-maned lion perhaps. His glass eye – today he had the brown one in; in more frolicsome moods he tended to clap in a baby-blue – was bothering him but he didn't like to take it out and substitute the eye-patch. It was excessively dramatic and attracted too much attention. People thought he was an actor or a model and tended to stare at him, trying to place him, which Alexis felt was something he could do without, given his profession.

178

'Gillon and I had a long chat last night,' Alexis said, once Ruffo's appetite looked like flagging somewhat. 'Things are beginning to go wrong, Ruffo.' He scowled. 'Hello? Hello?'

'I'm listening,' Ruffo said irritably. ' "Things are beginning to go wrong." You had a natter with Gillon. So far I'm with you, oh wise one.'

'Will you have more to eat,' Alexis asked with exaggerated solicitude, 'or shall I order coffee? Perhaps a *tarte tatin*?'

'Coffee, please,' Ruffo said, 'for the moment.' He patted his stomach complacently and belched. 'Maybe we'll have tea and cakes later in that little place in the rue de Buci.' He belched again. 'Why don't I just give up and move to Paris, I ask myself?'

'Because you would get disgustingly fat and spend all your time in cafés ogling women,' Alexis said, 'just as I would.'

As the waiter put their coffee before them, Ruffo observed, 'I suppose we're in for a serious afternoon.' He belched again. 'I ate too fast,' he complained. 'So what did the Philosopher King have to vouchsafe?'

'He wondered if I might pass along word to the Colonel in Cannes to be on the lookout for an experienced, reliable bomber. No urgency about it, he said, but he wanted a good man.'

Ruffo rolled his eyes. 'The mad bastard's hooked on destruction, isn't he? What's he planning to blow up this time?'

Alexis looked at him consideringly. 'I honestly don't know what you'd do without me, old fellow. Doesn't it ever occur to you to read the newspapers? Other than the racing pages, I mean.'

Ruffo eyed his friend without rancour. 'You're much better at reading the signs and portents than I am, Alexis. All that witchcraft you got so interested in when you were living in Brazil, I daresay. So what have I missed?'

Alexis sighed. 'First of all, the bodies of two Japanese in their mid-twenties, a man and a woman, were dug up in

179

the depths of the English countryside. The papers didn't say so, nor did Gillon, but I know that they were two of Gillon's mercenaries. He had me speak with the girl once. She'd been training with Action Directe and her French was miles better than her English. Gillon wanted to make sure that his instructions had been completely understood; said instructions, I might add, having only to do with simple travel and rendezvous arrangements, nothing more interesting than that.'

Ruffo shrugged. 'We both knew he was enrolling mercenaries, Alexis. He must have decided that these two were unreliable or something. Maybe they tried to up their price at a tactless moment.'

'Another interesting item is in this morning's papers,' Alexis went on, tapping the small stack of newspapers on the chair beside him. 'The British have a man in custody to do with the Easter Monday bombings in London. Gillon told me that Reardon had got out of London, no complications, no paper-trail. So that leaves his bodyguard, Cahill, as the man in custody.' He tapped *Le Monde*, which was uppermost. 'Nothing on the various *événements* in Europe but a lot of press speculation about IRA activity in England and Ireland.'

Two men sat down at the table alongside their own and Alexis asked for the bill. 'I think some fresh air would do us good,' he said as he counted out a small tip. 'Let's take to the streets.'

They walked sedately along the Boulevard Saint-Germain in the direction of the Palais Bourbon, Alexis no more than an inch or two shorter than Ruffo, their strides matching like civil servants having a lunchtime stroll through St James's Park. Alexis' limp only showed when he was very tired.

'That's what you meant about things beginning to come apart then?' Ruffo asked. 'I don't really see how, Alexis. Cahill won't talk. None of them ever talks.'

'Let's leave Cahill aside for the moment. But I've also been having to listen to Nedda rave on. And on. She's madder than ever, Ruffo. But above all it's Gillon himself. He never makes the mistake of underestimating the opposition, you know. He's far too clever for that. It's his attitude towards *us* that's dangerous. His own people. He thinks of all of you as being sub-human, incapable of putting two and two together, and I think that's very dangerous indeed.'

Ruffo snorted. 'Gillon thinks you're God Almighty, Alexis; so does Nedda.' He grinned. 'For entirely different reasons, of course. As to me, I play the buffoon with him, as you well know. It's far safer that he consider me an air-head.' He made a wry face. 'As to Nedda's being certifiable, who's in a position to know that better than I? But knowing she's barking mad doesn't make it any easier to get out from under her.' He laughed bitterly. 'As the actress said to the Bishop.'

'Look, Ruffo, the point is that to Gillon we're all as expendable as the Japs he ordered put down.'

'Not you, *mon vieux*,' Ruffo insisted.

Alexis came to an abrupt halt. His tone was one of extreme exasperation. 'Ruffo, Gillon may be many things, most of them disagreeable, but don't ever assume that he's stupid or even uninformed. He needs us for the moment, but only for the moment. His plans for his own eventual golden future do not include us, any of us, not even Nedda. Especially not Nedda.'

He began walking again, Ruffo falling into step beside him. 'I'm all right for the moment but that can't go on forever. He's eventually bound to find out that the Colonel in Cannes doesn't exist and that the small-arms I'm supplying him with come from my existing stocks and not some incredibly complicated deal I've made with shadowy gents in Tunis or wherever. Gillon's extremely capable on his own. He's the only one of that loopy crowd who doesn't whinge for money and contents himself with telling his suppliers precisely what and who he needs for his various projects, where and when he'd like delivery. He doesn't *really* need me, Ruffo.'

Ruffo's expression was mulish. 'But there's still nothing he can do to you. He has no idea where to find you, for

181

one thing, and how on earth could he ever twig to your neatly-laid red herring in the person of the Colonel?'

'At a guess, through the mercenaries, if he ever deigns to question them. Who would know better than they that a retired French colonel of the Paras, living the good life near sunny Cannes, isn't a one-man recruitment bureau for para-military operations?'

Ruffo still refused to share Alexis' apprehensions or, at least, not their intensity. 'But you've supplied him with excellent people. Jacki, for one.'

'And those two crazy Austrian snipers who did the Lisbon job. Bienenstein and Skryanz. I knew them in Biafra. Thank God Gillon didn't have to see them. They're even older than I am, for God's sake! They must be well north of fifty because their first mercenary job was training troops in Katanga, which is a long time ago.'

Alexis saw that he had finally got Ruffo's attention. 'Did you warn them that Gillon might decide they were, ah, not likely to be of any further use to him once the British Ambassador was assassinated? You don't want to be on the shitlist of men like that, Alexis.'

'I warned them to keep the operation strictly independent. Take half the fee up front, do the job, get out, collect the rest and don't tell anyone your plans. I gave them Gillon's phone number and they negotiated the payment themselves. Dealt with Philipp Altdorfer, not the great man himself.' He grinned. 'I told them to pitch it high. Money no object. Gulf prices, not African.' His smile grew even wider. 'I took a cut, of course. From both ends.'

They had crossed the bridge and were walking through the Place de la Concorde with no real destination in mind. Alexis steered Ruffo into the Avenue Gabriel and eventually said, 'You know, don't you, that the only way you'll ever get free from Nedda is to kill her?'

'The thought had crossed my mind. More than once. But I see no way to do it. Not and survive myself, that is.' Ruffo lifted his arms as though supplicating the gods. 'Killing someone is, as who knows better than you, *cher maître*, the

182

easy part. Getting rid of the body and not getting caught are the hard bits. It wouldn't do my poor, long-suffering family much good if they were finally shot of Nedda but I were on Devil's Island or there was a contract out on me lavishly underwritten by the Ayatollah Gillon.'

'That's what we've got to get to work on, Ruffo,' Alexis said. 'There has to be some way out.'

Ruffo shook his head. 'I've thought about little else in the last few years but the entire family can be held to ransom. You don't realize, Alexis, how many people depend on me. My dear father is a game old bird, God knows, but he has a very dicky heart, his blood pressure's high and he can't live many years more. For all intents and purposes, I'm already the head of the family. Too many people rely on me to follow as sensible a course as possible under the circumstances. My hands are too tied to consider some futile, self-indulgent gesture of the gun-spiking sort. My parents, my brother Manfredi and his family, my sister and her family, as well as Guido – they'd all be at risk if I were even to attempt anything against Nedda. Even with your help, which is what I suspect you're leading up to offering, I couldn't risk it. Can you imagine how I'd feel, how you'd feel, if we got rid of Nedda only to find Allegra, Manfredi's little girl, either kidnapped or with her throat cut? Italy's hardly off-limits to Gillon now that he's used Red Brigade people. My entire family is exposed.'

He had been gripping Alexis' arm and now let go. 'Well,' he said in a defeated voice, 'you see how things are. We can't protect everyone at Monteavesa. Even if Gillon were to send someone to kill one of the horses, the message would be the same: a horse this time, but next time it will be one of the children unless you go on working for us.'

Alexis was sympathetic but determined to make his friend fight back. 'I don't think it's a matter of just getting rid of Nedda. It's too late for that. I think we have to plan along the general lines of getting rid of Gillon, too. Neither of us is safe, Ruffo. Believe me when I repeat that it's not only you. I'm safe for the moment but not forever. Gillon, if not Nedda, will realize that I know far too much.'

'How will you know when Gillon or even Nedda, for that matter, ceases to trust you? When will the time come to . . .'

'Strike the first blow?' Alexis laughed and tapped his glass eye with a fingernail, an unnerving habit he had. 'I've a pretty developed instinct for staying alive, dear boy. In the world of the blind, the one-eyed man is king, don't forget.'

'Are you proposing to tell me that you think Gillon and Neda are blind?'

'He is blinded by his own arrogance and she is blinded by her own self-indulgence, coupled with arrogance. A diabolical coupling. Speaking of which, you haven't been rumpling the sheets with her lately, have you?'

Ruffo shook his head.

'I only ask because she boasts of indulging in rather *louche* goings-on of need I add a sexual nature. *Partouzes*, the thought of which is meant to make me crazed with lust. I'd keep away from her bed if I were you. I intend to keep away from her bed if I were me.'

He stopped again, indicating a bench with his walking-stick. They lit cigarettes and watched small children playing pirates in the shrubbery. 'I remember when my two were that age,' Alexis said softly, to Ruffo's astonishment.

'I didn't know you had children.'

'Two. Boy and girl. Fifteen and eleven. The girl, Nina, will be a beauty.' He laughed. 'Thank God she takes after Charlotte, actually Charlotte's mother, and not me.'

'You don't do too badly with the ladies.'

'I am villainous-looking and the ladies like that. But no one could ever accuse me of being a *beau garçon* like you are.'

Ruffo snorted. 'Go back to Gillon and Nedda.'

Alexis blew a smoke-ring and watched it drift upward towards the young green leaves of a chestnut tree. 'You recall I said that we'd come back to Cahill and you said that his being bagged wouldn't matter a damn because he'd

184

never grass. That's completely true. Okay, hang onto the fact that IRA guys don't talk.

'Now, to get back to Gillon – and Nedda by extension but principally Gillon – what's he up to that's new? What's his new *optique* on his chosen rôle of showing the IRA leadership and our Libyan how things ought to be done by an inspired field commander?'

Ruffo wrinkled his brow. 'You mean the mercenaries, Alexis? Hiring them and teaming them with Provos?'

Alexis nodded. 'That's it. Hiring a specialist to get the job done. If things go wrong you tip him into a hole and forget that he ever existed.'

'I see the logic of it,' Ruffo said guardedly. 'Gillon prides himself on being a master logician, after all.'

'There's a hole in the logic, though. At least I think there is,' Alexis said, probing. 'Here's a hint: think of Fact A.'

'Cahill won't talk,' Ruffo said dutifully, tiring of the game. Then light began to dawn. 'I think I see what you're getting at: an IRA man wouldn't talk but a mercenary would. He'd plea-bargain.'

'Good boy! Now do you see why I maintain that none of us is safe? Not even Gillon but he's too fucking arrogant to have looked for any flaws in his own argument. His toy soldiers have an unswerving devotion to The Cause. You can be blackmailed into silence to save your family. But Gillon has no hold on his expendable mercenaries. None whatsoever! Nothing to offer them if they're caught. No inducements or threats.'

'You think he's overreaching himself then?'

'He thinks he's infallible, like the Pope, and Nedda thinks she's the Godfather or some damned fool thing. Hubris.' Alexis sounded depressed. 'You married a rich, manipulating bitch when you were little more than a kid and found yourself in a situation over which you no longer had any control. I was simply greedy for more money. I thought the IRA were such fools I could gradually fob off all my old stuff onto them and retire comfortably on the proceeds.' He shut his eyes and pinched the bridge of his beaky nose. 'We both made a mistake. Now it's up to us to

185

get ourselves out of the mess without putting our families in deep shit.' He stood up.

'What're you doing this evening?' Ruffo asked.

'The girl you saw getting into a taxi as you arrived chez Lipp? She's what I'm doing tonight. Sharpens up the concentration.'

'An excellent specific against headaches, I'm told.'

16

Besides feeling wretched, Nedda was very frightened. She was frightened of Gillon but most of all she was frightened of herself, of what she was doing to herself.

Her hands shook as she picked up the heavy, silver-backed looking-glass from her dressing-table, part of a set given her as a wedding-present long ago, her new initials engraved on the back and surmounted by a coronet. Her face looked puffy; her skin had an unhealthy tinge and there were violet-blue shadows beneath her eyes that resisted all attempts to eradicate them with the liberal application of make-up. She sneezed convulsively and swiped at her streaming nose with a small towel, then rubbed impatiently at the sheen of sweat on her forehead. The way she looked and felt, it was little wonder she hadn't heard a fucking squeak from Alexis, despite having left two messages on his tape, the first pleading, the second peremptory.

She knew she would have to give in, if only to unclutter her mind for enough time to let it get to work on the toughest problems. The smaller matters would have to wait their turn.

Her hands were shaking and she made a deliberate effort to gain mastery over her nerves. With exaggerated care, she took out the little gold jack-knife, "Beware" engraved on its case, and diced up some of the crystals on a square of glass. She laid out two thin lines of coke and hoovered up the first before methodically beginning to set out the third, this time adding a light buff of speed. She could already feel her heartbeat picking up, her blood chugging briskly through her body. Her mouth began to feel frozen and she snorted up the small second line as a chaser. She eyed the third rail and decided to save it for as long as she could. She held her hand out stiff-fingered and the tremor had vanished like a bad dream. Her nerves felt smooth and silky, clean and freshly-ironed.

She was pleased with herself for having made the big decision to cut down. This was better, more like the old Nedda: clear-headed and disciplined, making the coke work for her, and not tipping over into the delicious but unproductive floatiness that made her forget things. Important things, too. She frowned, trying to remember what it was she had to fix.

Her memory had become tricky and she knew that some questionable financial decisions had been made, all too likely due to Costelloe's blundering about, upsetting her concentration. She wished he would go away, vanish. Her giggle was high and girlish and she looked at her reflection again. Her reflection smiled back at her girlishly.

Even if she had made a few mistakes, like that property-development scheme in the Roussillon, she was fairly certain Costelloe was as yet too inexperienced to spot the fact that she'd gambled a substantial amount of IRA money on an extremely long shot. Besides, she'd made the money in the first place and so was entitled to lose a part of it. She couldn't be expected to perform at one hundred per cent efficiency one hundred per cent of the time.

'Win a few, lose a few,' she said aloud and giggled again. There was plenty more and more than plenty coming in. So much cash to be turned into squeaky-clean assets on a balance-sheet.

There were no guarantees in the venture-capital world that even she could not back a winner every time. Money that needed to be laundered quite frequently went into risky ventures. She had condescended to explain some of this to Costelloe. Accounting procedures were elastic, there was no prospectus and no awkward questions were asked if the necessary capital injection arrived in suitcases. Nobody in his right mind could blame her for the fact that the Mediterranean marshland favoured for development had proved to be an intractably undrainable swamp featuring a particularly ferocious strain of mosquito.

But it had been a cautionary tale and it would be extremely foolish on her part to ignore it. These uncharacteristic lapses in judgment were warning signs of a condition she was honest enough to admit had become progressively worse over the past year, maybe even two. She was willing to own up to herself that the cocaine she had been taking in increasing amounts must be a contributing factor, at the very least. There was no point in overdoing things by denying herself any cocaine at all. To keep off it completely, she would have been drinking more heavily than usual and that was unlikely to make things better. Besides, alcohol made her bloated-looking and blowsy, like her inexpressibly dreary sisters-in-law in Boston.

Picking up her little glass straw, she snorted the third rail, feeling the mucus gathering at the back of her throat as her nostril burned briefly then froze.

There was nothing to be gained by getting herself worked up into a state of acute anxiety over the simpleminded priest she'd picked out in her native Boston. Hanratty was too dim to make a dramatic denouncement to the police. He was very likely fuddled with senile dementia from all those bottles of Irish Mist offered up to him by devoted parishioners. If he'd been questioned by the police in Boston then so be it. He would never make a logical connection between his trip to France many years ago and his recent trip to Italy unless some kind-hearted benefactor had treated him to a brain transplant. The problem niggled, however. What could have happened to tip the cops off? The mules returning to the other destinations in America, New York, Philadelphia, Washington, Chicago, Houston hadn't encountered any difficulties whatsoever.

Someone must have talked. There was no other way for the fool priest to be suspected of anything other than terminal gullibility. He was clean. He hadn't been used as a courier since 1973. If Gillon found out that she'd used a mule who could identify her, there would be hell to pay. Gillon was the one person Nedda feared.

As soon as Boston had reported that Hanratty's suitcase contained bags of ordinary baking-soda, Nedda had questioned Costelloe, giving free rein to her gift for vituperation, thinking that he might have decided to earn himself a substantial amount of money by stealing the cocaine allocated for Hanratty and making the substitution. She soon gave it up, however; that Costelloe might disobey her orders was too grotesque a theory to entertain.

She knew perfectly well that he reported everything she did to Gillon, who had put him with her in Monte Carlo for that purpose, as well as being her "assistant", so there was no point in trying to conceal the fact that five kilos allocated to Hanratty had somehow gone missing. Costelloe couldn't have double-crossed her. He was a non-person, an oaf and an errand-boy. For one thing, he had no contact in Milan to buy the stuff. Despite his occasional forays into the red-light district of Nice, he was unlikely to have formed an alliance with the drug barons there, almost all of whom were Mafiosi or Union Corse and virulently xenophobic.

The only person who knew she'd once used Hanratty to run some dirty money into France was Ruffo. That was at the beginning of their affair, when she had badly wanted to impress him. How unbelievably long ago that had been! These days, the only way she sought to impress him was through threats, both veiled and open, and in bed, of course, a stick-and-carrot treatment that had so far worked well enough. She blamed him for everything that went wrong. She chose to ignore the fact that only Costelloe could have told Gillon, Ruffo or anyone else that Hanratty's name was on the list of April mules. The possibility that she might have let something slip in an unguarded moment never crossed her mind.

Feeling ill-disposed towards Ruffo in any event, she was half-convinced that he was plotting against her, possibly with a view to having her out of the way and no longer a threat to re-assume control of their son. According to their separation agreement, it was she who had formal custody of the boy, Ruffo having only visitation rights. Despite never having chosen to have Guido live with her, the agreement remained in legal force and could be exercised if she changed her mind. She had too much power over the family for them to dare to challenge her right to the boy's custody and there was nothing they wouldn't do to prevent that.

There was no doubt in her mind: the wisest course of action for her to take was to have Connolly keep a closer watch on Ruffo whilst he was in London. It would be interesting to know what he got up to in England and he was spending more time there, now that the boy was at Eton. It was the only logical place for him to unburden himself to the police, if that's what he had a mind to do.

The one certainty was that he couldn't be trusted. He had amply demonstrated his unreliability when he'd killed that posturing ass Hamilton. That had, at least, shown some courage and initiative, astonishing enough in anyone as laid-back as Ruffo, but independent action on such a massive scale did not sit well with Gillon, although he had done nothing to discipline Ruffo's intemperate behaviour. Ruffo had never said he'd killed Hamilton but it was Nedda's theory that Hamilton had tried to jack his price up and Ruffo had simply lost his temper. In any event, that whole business had provided Nedda with further ammunition: Gillon would be on her side in any dispute with Ruffo. Gillon didn't at all like people who exceeded their orders.

The sensible thing to do would be to have a long chat with Gillon. He would get the question of Ruffo's loyalty sorted out in his usual brisk way, possibly even sort Ruffo out terminally, should Connolly have any hard evidence to lay before him. The thought of Ruffo's death didn't disturb her much. The family would carry on looking after Guido, as they always had.

Nedda picked up the looking-glass again and smiled at herself with sympathy and some amusement, her round, myopic brown eyes full of tolerant understanding of her own foibles and those of others. She was looking as good as she felt, which was very good indeed. Things would turn out well. She knew it. Gillon would certainly see matters in their proper light and give orders that Ruffo should be taken out. He was remarkably unsqueamish, not at all prone to havering and benefit-of-doubting. Gillon was the best, just as her cocaine was the best, gold on silver, the Château Pétrus of snow.

There was something else, some other problem she had been meaning to sort out but it eluded her, just over the horizon and out of reach. This wasn't the moment to think about any more unpleasant matters. She had to get ready for the evening.

The telephone rang as she was almost dressed and ready to leave. She let it ring as she scrabbled irritably for the clasp on the fourth strand of the large, gunmetal-grey pearls around her neck. The Monteavesa pearls. *Her* pearls. The telephone went on ringing and she finally deigned to answer it. When she heard the voice at the other end, she was glad he'd persisted. It was Alexis, the one person in the world to whom she could confide all her troubles.

She glanced briefly at the carriage clock on her dressing-table as he spoke to her in the caressing, soothing tones of a long-time lover. She would be late and Tiger would be seriously displeased but it didn't matter.

'I am *not* getting my knickers in a twist!' Camilla shouted furiously as George listened with ironic patience. 'How would you feel if you were in bed with the most incredible man in the universe and someone rang at six o'clock in the morning, for God's sake!'

'Camilla, darling, do be sensible. He can't help it if his friends ring at barbaric hours. Calm down. Here, I'll get you a cup of tea.'

'Oh, Georgie, I'm so glad you're here this weekend. We were meant to have gone to the Badminton Horse Trials today and I've never been and it's such a lovely day!' She was verging on tears again and forced herself to be calm. She was behaving like a spoilt child. 'I was so looking forward to meeting his friends and his son . . .'

'But he left you a note, darling, explaining that there was some emergency. Here, have a ginger biscuit.'

She burst out laughing. 'I've never known a man of your advanced years to be so completely sold on the restorative effects of ginger biscuits.' She accepted two without further argument, however. 'God, how boring for you! I'm sorry to sound off, Georgie, but it's all so, oh you know . . .'

'Disappointing, my love, and hurtful. You're right. I do know.' He sat down beside her at his kitchen table. 'You were looking forward to all sorts of little pleasures and he let you down. Men are terrible. You should have kept his note and rushed round here straight away instead of stewing for twenty-four hours. It's made you look quite plain.'

She laughed again. 'I was too busy stewing to talk but I ought to have known better. It does me good to talk to you. Mummy is so logical.' She sighed. 'I wish I were. It's difficult, no, it's impossible to be logical when you've met a man who's so completely dazzling.'

'Don't forget,' George said, Cassandra-like, 'that Jeremy dazzled the knickers off you, too. Or so you told me,' he added primly. 'Not that I disapprove of knickers being dazzled off but sometimes it's far better to hang onto them for as long as you can stand it.' He put his cup down. 'In any event, Camilla, I fail to see what you're on about. His note says clearly he'll only be away a short time and he'll be ringing you. Really, darling, he's hardly done a bunk.'

She reached across the table and patted his hand gratefully. 'You're sweet to listen to my adolescent burblings, Georgie. I know I'm over-reacting. Put it down to lack of practice,' she added with a self-deprecating smile. 'I must confess that I find it extremely difficult to rearrange my opinion of you and think of you as a spy.'

'Good,' George said, 'I want you to think of me as a friend. I have some slight difficulty thinking of me as a spy, too. Actually, I'm not, properly speaking, a spy at all. I'm meant to be incredibly clever and devious and catch them.' He poured out some more tea. 'But you'd best do all your confiding today because Sir Maurice is threatening to send me abroad for a few days, drat the man, to liaise, if you please, a word that fills me with helpless rage on

193

account of its properly being a noun and not a verb.' He gazed out the window. 'This is my favourite time of year to spend hours and hours in the garden.'

His glance strayed to a corner of the kitchen where his new bag of bonemeal was propped against the wall and not sprinkled around the peonies, where it ought to be. 'Well, I'm up for retirement soon, so you needn't think of me as a spy for very much longer,' he said pragmatically, 'or even a counter-spy.'

'What will you do?'

'Go on free-lancing for our Willie as long as he'll have me. I find myself rather enjoying having a crack at the odd scribble about food and hotels and that sort of thing. D'you suppose that elderly spies might be taken on as Michelin inspectors? Such a suitable employment for one.' He became more serious. 'What do you intend to do with yourself, Camilla?'

She sighed, looking rather downcast. 'I haven't really thought. Up to now, I've been going along on a day-to-day basis, waiting for something to happen to me, I suppose. I don't mean to sound quite so weedy. It's only that I knew that things would eventually sort themselves out in my mind, or my life, or whatever.' She shrugged. 'I haven't got a great deal to thank Jeremy for, but at least he's left me fixed well enough so that money isn't a nagging worry.' She looked more cheerful. 'I suppose you think I ought to give it all away. Dirty money and all that. Write a huge cheque to the World Wildlife Fund or the Distressed Gentlefolk's Home. But I don't intend to. Make of it what you like.'

George laughed. 'My dear girl, you do surprise me! Am I really the sort of person who would chivvy you into some absurd, quixotic gesture? It's your money. Do with it what makes you happy.'

He popped a ginger biscuit in his mouth and finally said, 'I wish *I* were a rich and pretty young widow!' His voice abandoned its playful tone. 'Camilla, did you really and truly not know where Jeremy got all the money from?'

'No, Georgie, I really and truly did not know. As I told you and Sir Maurice, all I do know is that he was away

194

a good deal, without telling me anything about what he was getting up to. As I further told you, I jumped to the conclusion that he was poking every female within range. Now will you kindly change the subject. I'm tired to death of all your incessant prying!'

'It's what I'm paid for, Camilla,' George reminded her without apology, but he changed the subject anyway. 'I would respectfully remind you that it was your old Auntie Georgina who positively drove you into the welcoming arms of Valentino for your new dress. Your little number from Saint-Laurent was a triumph, too, and for God's sake don't tell me what you paid for it. Did I tell you how much I liked your new hair, whilst we're on the subject? No wonder our beautiful Prince Charming was snapping your garters!'

'I wonder if the woman who rang at that ungodly hour was his wife. Not likely, I suppose, but possible. Who but a devoted wife would dare?' Camilla asked fretfully. She hadn't the slightest desire to get side-tracked into George's sometimes baroque dissertations on *haute couture*.

George lifted his eyebrows. 'So there's a Princess Charming? I didn't know that, my dear.' He considered for a moment. 'Not that a Principessa makes a great deal of difference, really. They evidently live separately. So civilized, the Italians, when you think of it.'

He smirked at her. 'You don't understand the basic principles involved in playing hard to get, do you, poppet? I mean, I could see with my beady old eyes that you fancied him something rotten when we were having dinner the other night. You two passion's playthings dropped me off and piled straight into bed, didn't you? Admit.'

Camilla blushed violently and was furious with herself. 'Goddamn you, Georgie! I'm not sixteen, you know.'

'On available evidence, I think you aren't much more than that. In your head, I mean. You're *very* developed in your other bits.'

Camilla couldn't take umbrage and laughed instead. 'I don't know why I confide in you but I do.' She looked furtively at George before continuing. 'I did some spying of my own yesterday morning. Well, more like skulking, really. I know so little about him, Georgie. And I confess I snooped about his flat after I was sure that he'd left and wasn't likely to pop back in and find me with his diary in my sticky paws.'

George beamed at her. 'That is progress, my dear. I approve of a completely gloves-off approach in matters sexual. And what did you discover?'

'Nothing, damn him. I don't think he spends much time there. A few bills neatly filed away. The rates, subs for memberships, just what you'd expect to find in a *pied-à-terre*. Diary not of much interest. Things to do with his son for the most part: appointments with the dentist, exeats, sports days, the normal parental preoccupations. I think he must be a widower or his wife must live abroad. He certainly seems to take care of all the boy's bits and bobs.'

She fell silent for a long moment. 'The thing is,' she finally said, adding some hot water to the teapot, 'I don't want to make the same mistakes with this one that I made with Jeremy. Being jealous and shrewish and feeling so bloody wounded all the time. Hard done by and suspicious. Oh, you know what I'm talking about, Georgie, despite your being so vile.'

His eyebrows lifted in surprise. 'But darling, you won't be. It's all part of growing up, of becoming a big person. You're far too intelligent and far, far too practical, no matter how silly you think you are, to make the same mistake twice. Think of it,' he admonished, 'as practice. You're practising on Prince Charming. Practising being a grown-up. Then you can move on to someone else.'

'God you're cynical, Georgie!'

'Now, my angel, you're surely not going to tell me that you want to marry him!'

Camilla bridled. 'Why does that strike you as such a dreadful idea? Not that I'm saying I do, mark you, want to marry him, I mean, but I should think he'd make a sensational husband. He's handsome and charming and rich and excellent company and superb in bed and well-bred and . . .'

'And his wife might object, for one thing.'

'I'm not absolutely positive that the woman who rang this morning actually was his wife. A wife remains a possibility but, on mature reflection, not likely to be his own. Far more probable to be someone else's.'

Georgie's head was at an angle like a bird's. 'Now why should you think that? You said, you wicked girl, that you'd only heard the tiniest bits of their conversation.'

'She sounded too caressing, too seductive to be a wife. Far more mistressy than wifey. Wives don't talk like that,' she added didactically, as he was in no position to challenge any statement she might care to make on wifeliness. 'Wives make arrangements. Meet me at the Ritz at seven o'clock. They don't *cajole*, Georgie.'

'Oh.'

'I'm wondering if I ought to be clever.'

He swiped irritably at some biscuit crumbs. 'That would make for a refreshing change. It's never too late to start, my dear, or so I've heard it said.'

'Don't be disagreeable.' She bit into another biscuit and chewed slowly, ruminating. 'What if he were to get back to London and I simply wasn't here to leap to his bidding? What if I were to ask Willie very sweetly if he'd send me off on a little assignment? Keep Ruffo off-balance.'

'Now who sounds cynical?' George asked peevishly.

17

As he levered his ungainly, short-legged body out of the sagging bed, Desmond Reardon slapped irritably at the Braun alarm-clock on the glass-ringed bedside table, silencing its insistent peeping and scooping it up to add to the other irreducible necessities in the plastic carrier-bag. He checked its contents: spongebag, new shirt, handkerchief, socks, vest and Y-fronts, his best silk tie (a final birthday present from his ex-wife), silk dressing-gown (a final Christmas present ditto) and, on top, a fat thriller, hammer-and-sickle dripping blood down its cover, with four chapters yet to go.

He hoped he would be able to leave by air and that the flight would take off on time because he hadn't anything else to read. The newsstands at Schiphol were well stocked with the more respectable English-language dailies but Reardon didn't want to read them. He knew they would be filled with bad news and he needed to do some constructive thinking about his future. If he were forced to go by train he could browse around the book-stall at the station. It was a good method of spotting followers in any event.

It was unlikely but, no matter how much he disliked thinking about it, still possible that Gillon had quickly manoeuvred watchers into place. The man Gillon sent to kill him would be one of theirs: an IRA man, someone he would welcome without suspicion and not a hired assassin, like those smirking, superior Japs. Gillon might even go one better and send someone he knew well and would welcome with open arms, just to keep him nailed in place and unsuspecting until the killers arrived. It would be one or the other.

Reardon glanced nervously at his watch in the gloom. Time was still on his side but only just. It would be a close-run thing. His first reaction had been an urge to bolt in head-long flight, to make a dash for the Central Station and get on the first train going anywhere. Instead, he had forced himself to be calm and make reasoned, calculated preparations, as he did when he crafted a bomb. Now, he wasn't so sure if he'd chosen the best course. Trying to outwit Gillon could be a suicidal gamble. The bomb could go up in his face.

He didn't dare open the curtains until Gillon's nine o'clock phone call, just in case someone was out there, taking an interest. If not yet someone of Gillon's then possibly, more probably indeed, the Dutch police.

He carefully moved a tiny corner of the curtain and peered out at the street. There were plenty of people but they were all on the move, mostly office-workers heading in the direction of the tram. There were no vans parked anywhere nearby and the cars he could see were all empty, but there could be police just out of sight, hiding around corners. He watched a further ten minutes, to be as sure as he could that none of the office-workers reappeared or that a car he'd seen passing didn't re-pass, possibly cruising the area in a slow circle.

Nothing.

Eamonn Cahill hadn't begun to bleat to the coppers, then. But he wouldn't hold out much longer, Reardon thought grimly. He was probably piddling out the information, drop by drop, and hadn't got to the Amsterdam part yet. If he were in Cahill's position, he would do the same thing: give just enough to maintain their interest in keeping you alive. In any event, there was no love lost between them – Reardon had never bothered to hide his detestation of Cahill – and the young pervert wouldn't have a single qualm about shopping an ex-colleague. He'd be shitting himself to get some protection against Gillon and it wouldn't take him long to spill the location of the safe house, out of revenge for the carry-on bag Reardon had handed him at Heathrow.

Dressing without haste in the Austin Reed grey suit which made him look like the middle-management nonentity that he had once been, Reardon went into the grimy bathroom and carefully adjusted his new brown-flecked-with-grey toupée. It blended in nicely with his own greying hair, at least what was left of it. "Ginger" he would be no more. When he was settled in a job, he could gradually go about changing his appearance to harmonize with the sort of work he'd be doing. He had in mind something like telephone canvassing, something where he wouldn't have to meet large numbers of people, one of whom might recognize him.

He put the Irish passport in the name of Brendan Pope in his inside jacket pocket, along with the thick sheaf of guilders and pounds. The genuine passport he put into an oven pan, its pages fanned out. When the little fire died down, he flushed the ashes down the lavatory and settled down on the bed to wait for the telephone's ring.

'Hello,' he said groggily.

Gillon chuckled. 'Too early for you, Desmond?' Gillon never resorted to nicknames. 'Not like you to sleep late, my friend.'

'What time is it?' he said thickly, rustling the bedclothes and switching on the lamp.

'Nine o'clock, as agreed,' Gillon said patiently. There was a pause. 'Are you awake now, Desmond my boy, or am I talking to myself?'

'Shit,' Reardon said, 'I suppose so.' He yawned loudly, his jaw obliging with an audible crack. 'Go ahead,' he grumbled, 'if you must.'

'Well now,' Gillon said jovially, 'I take it you're feeling a mite frail this morning. Up late with a good bottle, were we?'

'Nothing else to do,' Reardon said in his normal sullen tone.

'Missing even young Eamonn's company, are you?' Gillon asked solicitously. 'Well, help's on the way.'

'Uhnn,' Reardon said, forcing another yawn. He could feel the sweat breaking out in his armpits and prayed his voice didn't betray the state of his nerves. He gripped the phone and allowed a silence to fall, although his instincts screamed at him to put the phone down and get away as quickly as possible.

'Hello?' Gillon finally said.

'Waiting for orders, sir,' Reardon said truculently.

'Ah, now, Desmond, cheer up man! A new assignment that you'll like.' He chuckled again, indulgent, even fatherly. 'I don't suppose you've seen any newspapers?'

'Where would I find English newspapers in this part of sodding Amsterdam?' he growled. 'Can't leave the fucking flat, now can I? Except to buy a few fucking groceries.'

Gillon clucked sympathetically. 'Hard on you, being cut off from news of the outside world and all. But I haven't forgotten about you and help is on the way. Your new helpmate is Connolly. You like him all right, now don't you?' His tone was wheedling.

'He's all right. Yeah,' Reardon said without enthusiasm.

'Well then,' Gillon said, sounding like a dentist with a patient determined to fight back, 'he should be getting into Amsterdam just about . . . now. Yes. His train's due in at nine-three.' Reardon heard a paper being rustled. By now the sweat was pouring down his face as he stared in horror at his own watch. There was no time to lose. Gillon was wittering on about how really admirable Connolly was, how superior in cookery, driving and house-keeping to the late unlamented Eamonn Cahill. How very much happier Reardon would be with his congenial new minder.

Reardon could stand no more. 'Look, Gillon,' he interrupted, his voice hoarse with fear, wildly seeking an out, 'I've got to, got to . . .' Inspiration finally blazed up in his paralysed mind. 'I've got to have a crap.'

'Of course you do, Desmond. So good for you, too. Keep the bowels open. Get rid of all those horrid toxins in the body. *Mens sana in corpore sano.*' He laughed merrily. 'Before you ring off to answer Nature's call though, do tell Connolly I'll ring again this evening at six o'clock. There's a brace of Austrians coming to join you for the next project – very efficient they are, too – and good at . . .'

'Look, Gillon, I've *got* to go,' Reardon said, desperation plain for Gillon to hear.

'Off you go then, you poor man. Bye bye, then, old Desmond.'

Reardon slammed down the phone, collected his carrier-bag and was out of the flat door within a minute. If Gillon rang back within the next few minutes, he would assume that Reardon was glued to the lavatory-seat and unable to answer the phone.

He didn't bother with the lift and went quickly down the concrete stairs, his crêpe-soled shoes making no sound in the stairwell, a monotonously barking dog the only distraction. He blanked out the dog and heard nothing else. A door slammed and he almost jumped out of his skin, blood pounding in his ears. He emerged into the small, dingy lobby and there was still no figure silhouetted against the frosted glass of the street door, no Connolly waiting impatiently to be buzzed in.

Forcing himself to walk slowly, as if setting forth on a constitutional circuit of the Sloterplas, Reardon reached the corner without breaking into a frenzied gallop and crossed the street, his head slightly bent as though unsure of his footing, in case Connolly chose that moment to pass in a taxi or on foot from the Meer en Vaart tram stop. They hadn't seen each other in some years but Reardon wasn't counting too heavily on his toupée to render him invisible. There was a small brick Dutch Reformed church on the opposite corner and Reardon disappeared inside. His line of sight to the safe house was clear and he could check for tags.

He had spent the previous day working out possible escape-routes and he was prepared for virtually any contingency. Reardon was a painstaking man and a patient one when the need arose. He knew that, short of mobilizing the entire Amsterdam police force, whoever might wish to do so couldn't stop him from slipping out of the city and the country with no one the wiser. Even if he had to spend the entire day at the Rijksmuseum, pretending to be transfixed by the genius of Rembrandt, and lose himself in a gaggle of camera-wielding tourists, he had sufficient cash for taxis, planes, trains, buses to shake off a platoon of tags.

As he squinted again out of the slightly-open church door, a taxi pulled into the empty street. Connolly got out, a suitcase in hand, glancing up at the block of flats as he waited for the driver to count out his change. Reardon smiled happily as he stepped out of the church. Connolly was humping his evidently heavy suitcase up the short flight of steps to the block's entrance as Reardon strode jauntily to the kerb and flagged down the taxi just vacated by his new minder.

He slipped in quickly, said 'Schiphol, please,' in passable Dutch to the driver and turned to look out of the rear window as the taxi started up. Connolly was standing before the door, shifting from foot to foot as he waited for Reardon to speak on the intercom and buzz him in.

'Ladies and gentlemen,' the female voice said as the BA flight from Amsterdam continued to roll ponderously along a taxiway, 'we regret that owing to mechanical difficulties we are unable to use the normal arrival gate at Terminal Four. There are buses waiting at the foot of the ramp to convey you to the terminal and the baggage will be available for collection on carrousel five, after you have passed through Immigration. For those of you being met, we estimate that this unavoidable delay will take no more than ten minutes. On behalf of Captain Carmichael and his crew, we apologize for any inconvenience caused and hope to have the pleasure of having you aboard British Airways in the near future. Passengers are requested to check the overhead luggage compartments to make sure they have all their possessions before deplaning. Thank you for travelling British Airways.'

' "Deplaning"!' the woman next to Reardon snorted with annoyance. Across the aisle, the inconspicuous man who had spotted Reardon at Schiphol grinned behind his newspaper. 'Why don't they just say "getting off"? Deplaning! I ask you,' she rabbited on. 'What a nuisance this is! Are you being met?'

Reardon gave her a slight smile and shook his head. He looked out the window as the plane came to a stop and the engine noise faded and abruptly died. There were three red buses pulled up in a neat queue and mechanical stairs were being locked into place. People were beginning to jam the aisles and Reardon was content to sit back and wait until the press of passengers started to shuffle forward. It made for a refreshing change to be neither terrified nor rushed.

He fished his duty-free shopping out from under the seat in front of him, hoicked his carrier-bag down from the overhead storage compartment and draped his old mac over his shoulders. It would be lunchtime soon and he thought he'd go first to Selfridge's and buy a few more bits of clothing and a nylon hold-all to carry his belongings. After lunch somewhere near Oxford Street, he'd buy a *Standard* and see what was available for rent. Some sort of respectable bed-and-breakfast place was what he had in mind, somewhere north of the Park as far as possible from Brixton. Even a flat-share would do him for the moment. He was keeping an open mind: if London didn't feel right to him, then perhaps the Midlands. He was thoroughly sick of living abroad. Once he changed his guilders into sterling there would be well over a thousand pounds in his pocket, enough to keep him going until he found work. British Telecom mightn't be a bad idea.

Smiling pleasantly at the hostess by the door, he marched jauntily down the steps and strode towards the last bus. The first two buses were already pulling away as he noticed two men standing beside a dark-blue Rover saloon. They were looking at him expectantly and he knew that they were policemen.

The lexicographically straight-laced lady who'd been his seat-companion on the journey sniffed audibly behind him, resenting the red-carpet treatment being meted out to such a grubby little man. 'It looks to me as though *you're* being met. Car and driver, too. Collect your bags for you, too, I shouldn't wonder. All right for some.'

He looked around but there was nowhere to run on the concrete apron except back up the steps and into the aircraft.

'Here you are at last,' the taller man said, in the most cordial tones, showing every sign of satisfaction that Reardon had finally decided to join the party. He had a craggy face and extraordinarily pale, deep-set eyes, heavily scored with wrinkles at their corners, that surveyed Reardon with evident pleasure. He raised light-blonde, almost invisible eyebrows and relieved Reardon of his two plastic bags as the other man opened the Rover's door. 'We have so much to talk about, Mr Reardon.' He indicated his associate. 'My friend here will see to your baggage if you give him your ticket.'

The last bus pulled out and Reardon saw his erstwhile companion from the plane still glowering with disapproval at the privileges accorded to some people who were unlikely to deserve any form of preferential treatment. He was paralysed with shock and unable to protest when the shorter, younger man unceremoniously delved into his jacket and retrieved his ticket, passport and money.

Goudhurst riffled through the passport. 'Mr Pope,' he said with a chuckle. 'How nice.' He glanced briefly at the ticket. 'No baggage? Admirable. Travelling light is a far better idea.'

Reardon passively allowed himself to be handed into the back seat of the saloon and Goudhurst got in beside him. He looked down at Reardon's bowed head and patted it approvingly. 'Love the new rug,' he said, beaming, and ran his fingers through his own sparse blonde hair. 'Ever consider a transplant, Ginge? Looks bizarre when it's first growing – like re-seeding a lawn – but there are some chaps who swear by it. Not that it comes cheap, of course,' he said with a considering frown, 'but worth it to some, I suppose.' He laughed again, as though he'd thought of some dubious witticism, perhaps more profitably saved for a better audience.

'Well,' he said as the car was waved through a gate in the high chain-link fence on the airport's perimeter, 'off we go, then.'

'That fucking moron Cahill,' Reardon growled, gradually emerging from catatonic shock.

Goudhurst looked taken aback. 'Ah, now, you can hardly blame him for being the tiniest bit narked that you planted a dirty great bomb on him,' Goudhurst said philosophically. 'Do be fair,' he urged, 'and try to see things his way.' He rubbed his hands together in Uriah Heepish satisfaction. 'I confess I haven't actually felt a collar in years,' he confided, digging Reardon gently in the ribs and ho-hoing like Father Christmas. 'Enjoying it like a copper on his first beat, I don't mind admitting!'

Reardon's mind stuck on the "You have the right to remain silent" part of what he expected to hear and stalled. The Old Bill had unaccountably forgotten to read him his rights. They hadn't charged him with anything, either, two blatant omissions of which his lawyer would immediately be apprised at the first interview.

His decade of training and unswerving loyalty to The Cause nagged at his conscience to do just that: remain silent. And yet, and yet there was the other factor, never mooted as being even remotely possible during all those interminable political wranglings and planning sessions. There had certainly been talk of "terminating" grasses, "eliminating" security risks and outright traitors. But what of those whose loyalty continued firm, unimpeachable even, and were being hunted down by their own side, their comrades, for God's sake, through no fault of their own? Reardon knew he was caught between a rock and a hard place. On the whole, the hard place seemed the better bet. He didn't like to think what Gillon's hired rocks might do to him.

Besides, he reasoned, how could a man remain silent if he weren't asked anything?

'Penny for them?' Goudhurst asked playfully.

Reardon said, 'Fuck off,' without much conviction and continued to stare out the window at the unedifying view of London's western suburbs as rain started to fall. Those were his last words on the subject for the next few hours. He was thinking. He thought all the way to the very private establishment in Hertfordshire and for some considerable time thereafter.

'Get this fucking pooftah away from me!' Reardon roared at the impassive guard who took up position by the door.

'Ooooh,' George said, 'the cheeky old thing!' He rounded indignantly on Brook. 'Did you hear what the naughty, naughty man called me?' he asked rhetorically. 'He's really quite sweet, though. I like the round, cuddly type. Teddy-bearish.' He tried a winning smile with no success. 'Oh dear,' he said plaintively, 'I don't think it likes me. It's growling. You have a go, Dickie. Show it you're not afraid of it.'

Goudhurst smiled and nodded to Brook, who switched on the tape-recorder, giving the time and date.

'Mr Reardon,' Goudhurst began, 'you have indicated to your, ah, handler,' he nodded in the direction of the door, 'that you have re-considered your previous refusal to co-operate. Have you been coerced in any way?'

'No,' Reardon mumbled.

'Will you speak up, please, sir,' Brook said, fiddling with the controls.

'So it's "sir" now the fucking machine's on,' Reardon snarled. 'No is what I said you deaf bastard. No Irishman can ever get a fair hearing in this country so what the fuck's the point of anything? You can shoot me and say I was resisting arrest. I don't notice any offer of legal representation or the Irish Consulate or anything.'

Goudhurst's ice-blue eyes narrowed. 'But Mr Reardon, do be reasonable. You're not here, are you? I mean, here's your passport. It says "Brendan Pope". Mr Brendan Pope *was* here, certainly, but a while ago. He left from Heathrow on Easter Monday.'

He tossed the passport aside. 'Not really worth the paper it's written on, is it? Hot passport, old son. One of a batch of blanks stolen by a clerk at your Foreign Office and sold for an extortionate sum to the IRA in Dublin. Fortunately or unfortunately, the theft was noticed fairly quickly – serial numbers gave the game away – and the much-enriched but very patriotic clerk is enjoying the Irish tax-payers' hospitality in the Mountjoy Prison, I believe.' His smile was wolfish. 'But I digress. Forgive me, do.'

'Look,' Reardon said, visibly deflating, 'let's cut the cackle. I want to make a deal with you.'

'We're anxious to listen, Mr Reardon,' Goudhurst said.

'Who's this berk then?' Reardon demanded, pointing rudely at Brook. 'The pretty boyfriend?'

'Now I see,' Brook said in a mild drawl, 'what you English mean when you speak of Irish charm, fabled in song and legend.' He reached over and switched the tape-recorder to Off.

'A Yank?' Reardon was mystified. 'And what's a bloody Yank doing in this, I'd like to know now?'

'He's a guest, so mind your language,' George said.

Reardon looked sullenly away. 'Look here,' he addressed Goudhurst directly, trying to ignore the others, 'do we make a deal or don't we? Let's get our deal sorted out and quit all this buggering about. I'm knackered.'

And I'm very keen to hear whatever you've got to say,' Goudhurst assured him.

Reardon outlined his proposal, using his fingers as counters. He had had nothing else to think about during the past twenty-four hours. 'One, a new identity, passport, everything. A little plastic surgery, maybe,' he added with a slight smile, 'like the hair-transplant you banged on about yesterday.'

He paused, checking for a reaction, but Goudhurst's expression was unreadable. 'Two,' he went on, 'passage to Australia . . .'

Brook couldn't contain his laughter another second. 'Are you wicked colonialist Brits still transporting convicts to Australia?'

'I believe,' Goudhurst answered solemnly, 'the Australian Government are no longer stipulating a criminal record as a requirement for entry into their country. But Mr Reardon has been living abroad for some time, in heathen parts possibly, and may not be aware of . . .'

'All right,' Reardon said, his teeth clenched, 'stop pissing about. America, then.'

'Now then,' Goudhurst resumed, 'let us review the bidding. You would like a new identity and some new hair and you would like to go to Australia and/or America. Any improvement on America? Do I hear Canada? No? Pity.' He cleared his throat. 'In exchange for the above-mentioned beautification and junketing, what do we get in return?'

'Information.' Reardon looked defiantly at Goudhurst.

'You may start now.'

'What about. . . ?'

Brook looked at him levelly and asked, 'Your hair? Your trip to the land or lands of the free? Let's see how good your information is and then we can talk hair, giving us your poor and your homely and related matters. Or anything else you want to talk about.'

'Tell me what I get in return for the information you want,' Reardon said stubbornly, his expression mutinous. 'Or do you think I'm going to give you something for nothing?' he sneered.

'You know what *I* think?' Brook asked George. 'I think that he thinks that he's a KGB man. That's what I think. For what it's worth,' he added with commendable modesty. He sipped his drink and looked down at Reardon with amused contempt. 'You're not a KGB defector. What you are is an intellectual pygmy who wires up some Semtex and waits, at a safe distance, of course, to see who gets blown to bits. Besides being a coward and a moron, you're a whore who'll sell anything to anyone.' He smiled sweetly. 'You're also wanted in this country on a whole bunch of criminal charges. You know what you have to bargain with?' He held up his hand, making a zero with his fingers. 'Your bargaining position, Reardon, like your IQ and life expectancy if we turned you loose, is unimaginably low.'

Reardon looked at Goudhurst in complete confusion. Goudhurst said nothing.

'Well, creep, you could give us some nice, hard information and maybe you could live a little longer,' Brook said reasonably. 'That is, if you don't just repeat the same old stuff Cahill's already spilled.' He was making himself a gin and tonic, aware that Reardon's eyes were avidly watching every drop he poured.

'That's right,' Goudhurst said. 'Not much point in going over the same ground. Let's begin at the beginning, though.' He shook his head, saddened by human frailty. 'We can't be absolutely sure that Mr Cahill's been entirely truthful.'

' "Live a little longer." ' Reardon's voice rose an augmented fifth. 'Don't try those police-state tactics on *me*!'

'But the thing is, Mr Reardon,' George piped up, 'it's not a bad idea to keep in mind that no one knows you're here. Except us, of course. And we wouldn't tell a soul, would we, gentlemen?'

'My information is much better than Cahill's.' There was desperation in Reardon's voice. 'He's no more than an errand-boy. Where is he? I don't know what he's told you but it's bound to be lies. He'll have told you what he thinks you want to hear.'

I imagine,' Goudhurst said blandly, 'that you'll have heard of Dominic Ryan of the Garda Siochana? I don't know precisely what he's done with Cahill but we turned him over to Ryan for a little while. Just on loan, of course.'

Reardon was pale. 'What do you have in mind for me?'

'It all depends on you, Mr Reardon. Shall we begin?' Goudhurst asked, restarting the tape-recorder. 'George, you're the most experienced of us. Would you like to get things started?'

Yes, I think I shall.' He sat in a chair directly facing Reardon. 'I'd be very grateful if you'd tell me, Mr Reardon,' he said in a strictly neutral voice, 'who killed Major Hamilton.'

PART FIVE

18

'You're not expecting me to underwrite any of your expenses for this Mediterranean adventure, are you, Sayle?' Willie Hibbert regarded her with deep suspicion.

'Willie!' Camilla protested, 'can you imagine that I would do anything so unreasonable?'

'Always keeping firmly in mind the unexampled ferocity with which you scrutinize our accounts,' George pointed out dryly, 'Camilla's offer is entirely sane, Willie. As I expect you're aware,' he added, 'the time and energy required to justify more than a fifty pence bus ticket are so debilitating that only your very poorest employees bother trying to recoup their outlay.'

Willie grunted, not at all sure that his leg wasn't being pulled. 'This is a business, Lacey, not a charity. I know you all think I'm overly careful . . .'

'Frugal, Willie. Cheap, parsimonious, stingy and mean. Cheese-paring, niggardly and penny-pinching. You're a shabby skinflint,' George added in summation.

'I suppose I am,' Willie said, looking on the whole quite pleased that George had actually noticed.

Inspiration seized him. 'Before you go, Sayle,' he said, pawing through the Hibbert Collection, a detritus of bent paper-clips, undisposed-of disposable pens and lighters, broken elastic bands and gnawed pencil-stubs in a decayed cardboard box, 'here's something for you.' He located and proudly proffered a second-class British Rail ticket, Gatwick–Victoria. 'Never had to hand it in, you see. Got through the barrier at Victoria in a gaggle of people.' He looked fondly at the ticket, evidently reluctant to part with his windfall but impelled to do so by an obscure and rare urge towards munificence. It was his idea of a gift.

'Willie, you are *sweet*,' Camilla gushed, 'but it's expired, you see. Here's the date.' She pressed it into his palm and closed his fingers around it, like a tip. 'And I'm leaving from Heathrow, to which I shall be conveyed by taxi. At my own expense, of course.'

'Oh,' said Willie. He returned the ticket to the Collection, not at all displeased to have it back. It was the sort of thing that might come in handy some day. He could always pretend he hadn't noticed the date. Certainly worth a try.

'Thanks for the assist,' Camilla said as George walked with her to the lifts. 'I'm sure he would've insisted on my staying in London to photograph that boring old silver auction at Christie's if you hadn't mentioned tipping people. He's Pavlov's dog, isn't he? Oh, Georgie,' she said fretfully, 'when I come back I think I'll start looking for another job.'

George pecked her on the cheek. 'We can talk about that when you're safely home, darling. Just don't stay away too long.'

Alexis spotted the tag as he walked along the tree-shaded Bruderholzallee towards the restaurant Gillon had appointed. The man was sitting in an ordinary Mercedes taxi, reading a newspaper as though waiting for a fare. Alexis caught a glimpse of a radio as he slowly walked past, exaggerating his limp. There would be a second tag on foot, he knew, who would take up position as he left the restaurant. Perhaps two, if Gillon had managed to scare up enough people. The taxi-driver wasn't likely to be very effective but Gillon had no way of knowing that Alexis wouldn't have come by car. The taxi radio would be used to co-ordinate the pedestrian tags.

As the maître d'hôtel led him to the table booked by Herr Metzler, Alexis pondered that Gillon had chosen their meeting-place with his habitual canniness. The Restaurant Stucki was in a pleasant residential suburb of Basel yet close to the main railway station. A tram-line ran nearby; traffic was sparse and if Alexis were to arrive carless, a fact that Gillon would by now be apprised of, a tall man with a limp and an eye-patch would be highly visible and easily

214

followed, the likelihood of his being able to dodge quickly into a free taxi negligible.

'I am early,' Alexis said.

'Yes, sir,' the maître d'hôtel agreed without much interest. The restaurant and its garden were filling up rapidly. 'An apéritif perhaps or would you prefer to wait?'

Alexis ordered a drink and made inquiries as to the location of the gents. The telephone was nearby and he made a lengthy call to Charlotte. He had warned his wife to stay close to the telephone. There was, he thought grimly, no such thing in life as a free ride and Gillon's faith in him was beginning to crumble.

His cordiality in extending the luncheon invitation had been warm, bordering on effulgent, and Alexis was experienced at reading the signs and portents in Gillon's tone. He was at his most dangerous when he radiated a hearty, man-to-man joviality. Gallows humour, Alexis thought, trying to piece together Gillon's blithe but urgent summons and the presence in the Bruderholzallee of the taxi. A quick look through the lavatory window had shown it was still in place, its driver by the radio instead of doing what any normal taxi-driver would do: taking advantage of the warm afternoon by basking in the spring sunshine as he munched sandwiches or read his newspaper.

There was no insuperable difficulty for Gillon to post a watcher and learn that Alexis seldom went near his Zürich flat/office. Telephone numbers could be matched to addresses, given sufficient inducement in the form of bribes to an employee of water, gas, electricity, telephone companies or the municipality itself, even the canton. Alexis was rather surprised that Gillon had never made any serious attempt to pin down his actual whereabouts, apart from sprightly conversational gambits along the lines of eliciting general information: Alexis' opinions on the amenities of daily life in Zürich, the desirability or otherwise of the married state, other small probes into Alexis' habits, background, likes and dislikes.

But today was to be different. Alexis would be followed as he left the restaurant, the best in Basel, after a pricey and excellent luncheon with an expansive host who would insist on ordering the best food and wine, especially wine.

'Herr Leysin?' the maître d'hôtel asked. Alexis nodded. 'Herr Metzler has telephoned to apologize that he has been slightly delayed but will arrive in ten minutes. Would monsieur like another . . .'

'Thank you,' Alexis smiled, 'but I prefer to wait for Herr Metzler.' He continued to smile after the man had moved away. Gillon's delay was caused by his getting the foot-men into place, now he knew that Alexis was minus transport. And alone, he reminded himself.

Charlotte had instructions to keep trying Ruffo and she would summon him to Paris in the usual way. Hadn't Ruffo mentioned something to do with taking Guido back to school? Alexis hadn't paid strict attention but he knew that Ruffo was in or near London. The message on his answer-phone this morning had announced that he'd be home later. Unless Gillon had fielded an army, Alexis knew that he could slip the foot-men, one by one if need be, somewhere along the way between Basel and the Brasserie Lipp. Had he come by car, he would have had to leave it, which couldn't fail to signal that he knew he was being followed. Tram, train and métro would be best. Stick to what you know.

He was considering his best course when Gillon came up on his blind side. 'I'm most awfully sorry to keep you waiting. Say you'll forgive me.'

'A quarter of an hour is not a serious insult, Gillon,' Alexis answered mildly. 'In the event, I was early, so I ordered a drink without waiting for you.'

'Splendid! Let's have another, shall we?'

Gillon gave the order and settled back in his chair, surveying Alexis with benign approval. 'You're looking fit and well. Ages since we met. We really ought to get together more often. I so enjoy our all-too-rare meetings.'

Alexis agreed with a suitable degree of enthusiasm while noting that Gillon looked tired. Things were clearly not going well. His eyes were shadowed and he was even thinner and paler than usual. 'You're well?' he asked.

Gillon shrugged. 'To be honest with you, my dear friend, one or two small problems have cropped up recently and that is one reason I was delighted you were able to get away from your business affairs at such short notice. Quite apart from the pleasure I derive from your company, that is.'

'I am always happy to be of service to you,' Alexis stated with equal insincerity.

Menus were produced and the two men ordered before getting down to business. Alexis waited patiently as Gillon consulted at elaborate length with the maître d'hôtel and sommelier, playing his chosen rôle of solicitous host to the hilt.

'I'm told the veal is *exceptionally* good here. So kind of you to come,' he repeated unnecessarily, 'and allow me to pick your formidable brain.' He cocked his head in a bird-like, inquisitive gesture, waiting for Alexis to press for details and got nothing but a bland smile in return.

He chuckled delightedly. 'Always hold your cards to the chest, don't you? Well,' he went on, lowering his voice confidentially, 'I've had a busy few days since we spoke last week. Desmond Reardon's vanished.'

Alexis looked mildly interested. ' "Vanished"?'

Gillon's glacial eyes studied him. 'Dropped completely out of sight. You don't seem terribly surprised.'

'You said yourself you thought he might have warned Cahill about the bomb in his bag.'

'He couldn't know the police had Cahill.'

'I don't see why not. Saw that Minister of whosis man on television. As you did.'

'The safe house had no satellite dish. He'd no way to lay hands on British newspapers.' Gillon's expression was grim. Alexis instantly perceived that he was looking for a traitor, a leak.

Alexis laughed briefly. 'My dear Gillon, you can pick up British television in Holland and Belgium with an ordinary aerial, and as to radio, you can get the BBC World Service in Vladivostok, for God's sake.'

'I'd forgotten that,' Gillon said sullenly. He hated being wrong. 'To change the subject, what news of our dear Ruffo?'

Alexis knew there was no change of subject. 'Nothing that I know of. Nedda hasn't mentioned him recently.'

Gillon laughed heartily. 'You rely on your mistress for news of her husband? It's a French farce, isn't it?'

Alexis nodded happily. So it was Ruffo Gillon was after.

Leaning forward on his elbows, Gillon assumed a serious, man-to-man expression and said, 'You're a Swiss citizen, Alexis, and I need your advice. I'm thinking of moving here.'

'There are worse places to live but it's not very *mouvementé*. Cuckoo-clocks and chocolate. Awfully dull. You know, Orson Welles in *The Third Man*.'

'That's more a consideration to you than it is to me,' Gillon said with mild reproof. 'I prefer a life of solitary contemplation, like Montaigne.' The trouble was, Alexis thought, that Gillon really believed that. He nodded, unsmiling, chastened, sympathetic. A welcome distraction in the form of their first course arrived, giving Alexis a chance to assimilate this brisk shift in direction.

'I had thought of becoming your fellow-resident in Zürich,' Gillon announced as he dug into his *ballotine de canard*, 'but, if you'll forgive my saying so, it struck me as being . . .' he waved his fork gently, trying to find an inoffensive word.

'It's not everyone's idea of heaven. Except the Gnomes, of course,' Alexis prompted with an indulgent smile. 'Convenient, of course.'

'Oh, absolutely,' Gillon agreed heartily, 'and for someone in the armaments trade, such as yourself . . .'

'I'm only a very small frog and the arms trade is an immensely large pond,' Alexis modestly reminded him.

'My French is poor,' Gillon admitted with equal modesty, 'so a German-speaking part of Switzerland would naturally be best for me. But I wonder about all this rigmarole with foreigners buying property.'

Alexis appeared to be concentrating on his *bourguignon d'escargots*. 'This is absolutely delicious,' he said to Gillon's inquiring look. 'Want a bite?'

Gillon waved away the offering of snails with his first hint of impatience. 'What I wonder, Alexis, is whether I could buy something through you. Acting as nominee, I mean.' He paused. 'For a fee, of course.'

I'll bet you would, Alexis thought. You'd then be in a position to discover a great deal more about me, legitimately and through the *notaire* who'd be handling the transaction. 'Happy to oblige, my dear fellow. Whatever you decide is fine with me. Frankfurt getting on your nerves, is it?' He didn't wait for Gillon to answer before going on. 'I imagine you've already gone into all the business of residence permits and suchlike, both for yourself and the Altdorfers?'

Gillon looked startled. 'I thought owning property was the only stumbling-block. And having a whopping great bank-balance.'

Alexis laughed cheerfully, mopping up his sauce with a piece of bread, as he'd been strictly forbidden to do when a child. 'The Swiss hedge *everything* with conditions, my friend. You can get an authorization for purchase. Difficult but not impossible. But then there's the sacred residence permit. Unbelievable. The Federal authorities decide on an annual quota and allot them to the twenty-three cantons. The quota goes down every year by about ten per cent. This year it's eighteen hundred, if I recall rightly. Or maybe that was last year and it's gone down yet further.'

'Per canton,' Gillon asked, 'or eighteen hundred per commune?'

'Not a bit of it. Eighteen hundred for the entire country. So you see,' he said with a deliberately annoying grin, 'there's a hell of a queue. And the Swiss police make a very thorough check on each applicant. The Swiss police,' he added superfluously, 'are nothing if not thorough. I'd stick to Frankfurt, if I were you. You've got a German passport among others, I think you told me.'

219

Gillon looked genuinely shaken. 'I can't stay in Frankfurt. It's that bloody Desmond Reardon, damn the man.'

'Oh yes,' Alexis said, as though Reardon's very existence had slipped his mind, 'you mentioned that he'd disappeared.'

Gillon's fists were clenched. 'I rang him on Monday morning. Woke him up. Connolly arrived at the flat ten minutes later and there was no answer. Either lying doggo or bolted but if he bolted he was bloody quick about it.'

'Police?' Alexis murmured sympathetically. He could see from the fixed, unseeing look on Gillon's face that he was turning over possibilities in his mind, looking for logic in a set of incomprehensible givens.

'No time.' Gillon was firm on that point. 'Connolly would've seen them. Hell, he would've been hauled in for questioning himself. And there's no trace of him whatsoever!'

'What about your, ah, colleagues in Ireland?'

'Nothing. It's just possible that he cooked something up with Cahill and they've both gone to ground. But I can't see Cahill slipping the police so easily.' He sighed and sipped his wine. 'Our mole in the Garda reports that Dominic Ryan, a policeman who hates the IRA so violently that we've tried and failed to kill him twice, is looking unaccountably cheerful these days. I say unaccountably because he's got no chance of tracking down the boys who carried out the execution on the judge. What's more, he knows it. What's even more more is that we broke two of our men out of gaol last week. An Irish gaol and that should be enough to send him into an apoplectic fit.'

'You've got a hell of a good intelligence network, Gillon,' Alexis said with admiration. He poured them both more wine, the waiter being out of sight. 'Good intelligence is the key to everything in this game.'

'We find it pays off,' Gillon said, flattered that a man with Alexis' experience in the field should admire his organization. 'We've got someone in the Garda, as I've said, but not highly-placed enough for top-level stuff.' He smiled complacently. 'Nonetheless, we usually get enough in dribs and drabs to keep a step or two ahead of them.' He sipped moodily at his wine again. 'It's a pity we haven't a mole at Scotland Yard. That prime shit Goudhurst is the head of Anti-Terrorist. I'm almost positive it's they who have Reardon and Cahill, not the Gardai.'

'If that's so, then you're wise to abandon Frankfurt. The man who went to check on him . . . ?' Alexis prompted.

'Connolly. There wasn't much he could do. He's not a cracksman; wouldn't know how to begin to pick a lock. Besides, he wasn't about to try. I've no reason to think that Reardon hasn't managed to get his hands on a gun. Anyway,' Gillon nervously drank more wine, 'if someone's trying to gain access to your flat, you've enough time to get to the kitchen and be waiting with a knife.' He fell silent as the waiter brought their main course. He gulped the last of the Côte de Beaune whilst the sommelier uncorked the chilled Meursault.

'I kept trying the phone at the safe house but there was no answer,' he resumed once the field was clear. 'Connolly couldn't contact me. Security.' He looked at Alexis with a wry smile. 'I've got to work out another system – perhaps you might be helpful in that, my friend – so that someone like Connolly can ring if things come unstuck. In this case, he used more commonsense than I was aware he possessed: he couldn't hang about, almost certainly drawing attention to himself, like a lurking child-molester or peeping Tom, so he gave up and trailed back to London.'

'Connolly, Connolly. Do I know him? Sounds like a good man,' Alexis said. 'Practical. Unlike some of the material you have to work with,' he added sympathetically. 'Not an easy job, training people.' He picked the bottle out of the cooler and read the label. 'Excellent,' he said. 'You're a man who knows how to choose a restaurant, Gillon.'

'Connolly's all right for some things,' Gillon said with a laugh, 'but he doesn't exactly melt into a crowd. Bald as a coot and his head's a weird shape. He looks like ET. I couldn't possibly use him in Ireland. Children would follow him down the street, begging him to phone home.' He laughed a good deal and attacked his *paupiettes de langoustines* with gusto, his good humour restored at the thought of Connolly playing Pied Piper to Irish tots.

Our friend Aeschylus has another name and is back in London, Alexis thought, smiling indulgently at Gillon's joke. 'Reardon could be dead, I suppose,' he said dubiously. 'A heart-attack or something.'

'Possible but unlikely,' Gillon mumbled between bites. 'He claimed to have followed my orders and left a car full of explosive at Heathrow. Sent the keys and everything to Connolly but the car's not there. Conclusion: police removed it. Explanation: they discovered it by chance or Reardon told them where to look. Cahill wouldn't have known where the car was to be stashed unless, of course, Reardon told him.' His glance slid away from Alexis. 'Reardon's one of the *dedicated* ones,' he said with heavy sarcasm. 'If he's dead then he topped himself, thinking I might be after him.' A muscle twitched under his left eye. 'Moody and surly as hell but a good man with the explosives. It *is* good, isn't it, this place?' He looked pleased. 'The veal does not disappoint, I trust?'

'A find,' Alexis said placidly, waiting for further revelations. Gillon was not a great one for companionable silences.

'We can get other bombers, of course, but leaving, upping stakes is a trial just at the moment. Another shipment of Nedda's snow due in soon and other plans to make. Nice, big plans.' He winked at Alexis. 'A breakthrough.'

'Well,' Alexis said comfortingly, 'you might not really have to leave. It's so handy and central, Frankfurt. Reardon can't identify you, after all.'

'Oh,' said Gillon airily, nodding to the waiter to pour more wine, 'he knows me by sight. Not my true name; no one knows that.' Except Nedda. Nedda knew, all right. Never mind, he reminded himself, she won't be with us much longer. He and Costelloe would take care of the next batch of cocaine.

Alexis was asking him a question. 'How did Reardon contact you?'

'Only phone numbers I gave him, with a schedule. You know the form: call-boxes, the odd restaurant or café, just like you see in the movies,' he said with a grin. 'Frankfurt and nearby places, Mainz, Wiesbaden. Sometimes not so near, like Mannheim or Heidelberg.' He grimaced in a spasm of irritation. 'If he and Cahill are bleating to the coppers, then they'll know by now the general area I live in and what I look like, nothing more. They'll get full co-operation from the German police, though.'

'Yes, I see.' Alexis nodded thoughtfully. 'I agree that it's wise to make a move, if only as a precautionary measure.' He glanced at his host. 'I expect you to let me know if I can be of any help.'

Gillon put down his knife and fork with regret. 'I can't eat another scrap. Shall we smoke before we face up bravely to the dessert trolley?' They got out cigarettes and Gillon looked contrite. 'But here I've been waffling on about all my little problems and you haven't managed to get a word in. How are things going with Nedda?'

Alexis succeeded in giving the impression of a man sorely tried but too well-bred to complain in any great detail. 'You know how she is, Gillon.'

'Would the word "demanding" cover it?'

Alexis held his hand up like a policeman on traffic duty. 'Please. I think "volcanic" is more apt.' He rolled his good eye up in supplication to the gods. He decided to try a bit of fishing of his own. 'She's undeniably clever but she does get bees in her bonnet. Worse than any other woman I've ever known.'

Gillon snorted with amusement. 'I haven't your – shall we call it "catholic" with a small "c"? – experience of the female sex but even on our strictly platonic basis she's a major handful, I'll grant you.' He shook his head with a fond smile, demonstrating his determination to be broad-minded despite heavy provocation. 'She persists in nagging me unmercifully about Ruffo.'

'Ruffo?' Alexis looked startled. 'One would think that after so many years she had discovered every blemish, every weakness, little blots on his character and escutcheon.'

'She's convinced that he's betraying us somehow. Absolutely no proof, of course.' Gillon was watching him searchingly and Alexis was aware that, although Gillon had drunk the better part of both bottles of wine, he was far from fuddled.

Alexis played with a box of matches on the table, pretending to consider the matter. Finally he shrugged. 'I don't know all the ins and outs of their relationship,' he laughed briefly in self-mockery, 'but I'm in no doubt whatsoever that I wasn't the first man Nedda cuckolded him with and that was a long time ago.' He made a small toast with his wine-glass. 'To adultery,' he said in a half-whisper, leering slightly. Gillon frowned almost imperceptibly. He really was a Puritan, Alexis thought.

'I mean,' he said, elaborating, 'it's entirely possible that he hates her or wants revenge for the dishonour to himself or his family or whatever. So Italian! But then, on the rare occasions that we meet, he's always waffling on about his kid. Crazy about that bloody kid. So if Nedda wants to keep him on the straight and narrow, all she has to do is take the kid back.' He hiccupped slightly and put his hand over his mouth. 'Sorry.'

Gillon slapped ash from his tie and lit another cigarette. 'Difficult to know about Ruffo,' he agreed, 'but the fact of the matter is that he's embarked upon what the vulgar call "a meaningful relationship" with the woman who photographed Jacki's boys as they transported our goodies across the glacier. Connolly saw her leaving his flat one morning and reported straight away.'

Alexis whistled softly. 'Lucky man! I saw her at Val Sainte-Anne. Stunning girl. Turned out to be a magazine photographer. Miss Dale or Hale or some such name.' So that's why Ruffo's in London so much, he thought.

Gillon's cheek twitched again in annoyance. 'Camilla Sayle. Stunning she may be. I wouldn't know. But I do know that it's thanks to her and her little camera that Jacki's glacier route is blown.'

Alexis pursed his lips. 'It's a pity about that, I agree. Still,' he said philosophically, 'it's the sort of thing that

224

happens in this sort of game. Someone stumbles into the picture, if you'll forgive the unintentional pun . . .'

'You say it's a coincidence but Nedda thinks not.'

'Oh, Nedda,' Alexis said, brushing her away with his hand, dismissing her chronic suspicions.

Gillon's smile was chilly. 'I imagine Nedda's confided to you her belief that it was Ruffo who killed Major Hamilton in the parking lot at Ascot. No,' he laughed briefly, 'I see from your expression she doesn't confide in you absolutely entirely.' He chuckled happily, taking pleasure in Alexis' obvious shock.

He signalled for the dessert trolley and set himself to surveying with maddening deliberation what was on offer, knowing that Alexis had an avalanche of questions. To spin out the suspense further, he embarked on another long consultation with the sommelier and eventually ordered a half-bottle of Beaumes-de-Venise. 'Well then,' he eventually said, pleased with himself, 'where were we?'

Alexis smiled blandly, challenging Gillon to continue the game. 'You had posited that Ruffo might have killed Hamilton.'

'So I had. The question is, of course, why. I think we can safely rule out the possibility that Ruffo coveted his neighbour's wife.'

Alexis genuinely looked and felt totally at a loss. Gillon laughed in delight, greedily digging into his chocolate bavarois. 'I forgot to mention that the delectable Miss Sayle is, in her non-professional capacity, the Honourable Mrs Jeremy Hamilton. Interesting, isn't it? Our Ruffo's such a dark horse.'

19

'Calm down, Brook. Calm down and for God's sake sit down. You're giving me a headache.' George scowled with unaccustomed bad temper. 'Watching you pace up and down like a leopard makes my eyes swivel, you silly man.'

Brook's bony frame crashed into an unyielding wooden chair and he winced. 'You'll have to bear with me, George,' he said, unrepentant. 'I'm fighting back a tremendous urge to rush out to Heathrow and get on a plane.'

'To where?'

'Anywhere except here.' Brook's fingers drummed on the tabletop until a quelling stare from George made him stop. He leafed through the file on the table, the entire contents of which he'd been over many times already. 'I'd really hoped we'd get something more useful out of those damned guns. God knows, the Israelis owe us a few favours and these were definitely made in Israel, not Singapore.'

The Israelis had eventually telexed that the dozen mint-condition Uzis from Wiltshire had formed part of a substantial shipment, thirteen years ago, to the South African government, which had, in turn, resold a large number of them to the Brazilian army, almost ten years ago. Both Pretoria and Jerusalem had taken their time about answering and had insisted, in prickly follow-up telexes, that the end-user certificates attached to the purchases had been irreproachable. A priority enquiry to Brazil, giving the Uzis' serial numbers and accompanied by an urgent, high-level request for the Brazilian Government's assistance in the matter, had so far engendered nothing more concrete than polite reassurances that the Uzis and their current disposition were being investigated "with all due speed".

'I wish we could cut to the chase!' Brook snatched at a

yellow legal pad and began to doodle instead, eventually throwing down his pencil and sitting on in sulky silence.

George relented. 'It's all the waiting. I know, Brook, but there it is.' A telephone rang nearby and they both jumped. They looked sheepishly at one another and laughed, breaking the tension.

'We're getting so close,' Brook said softly, 'but we're still not there. Four names, two descriptions, some idea of the organization's basic structure, a general area to look in.' He sighed. 'Thank God the sons-of-bitches went for the Cahill sting. If Reardon hadn't swallowed that and blundered into our web we'd still be nowhere. But nowhere. Not that we're all so far now, even with Reardon's additions, but it all helps.' He grinned suddenly. 'Goudhurst's got to be on Cloud Nine.'

'Could well earn him a K.'

'Okay?'

'Sorry. Knighthood.' George began to feel restless himself. Lisburn's encyclopaedic files on everyone with even a whiff of IRA hanging about them had come up blank on Gillon, Nedda, one Philip, apparently another of Gillon's lieutenants, and one Connolly, based in London, according to Reardon. But it had yielded a name and photograph for "Mr Castle". Signor Buozzi in Milan and the hotel's cashier had both identified the photographs faxed to Milan. Mr Castle was Liam Costelloe, an IRA "possible". But that had been hours ago. 'I wish we could stand over the telex,' he complained.

Brook made a face. 'We haven't got the security clearance, for God's sake. Actually, Jay Rodman could fix it for us but you know how it is: they don't want a bunch of extra people cluttering the place up.'

'It's the same *chez nous*,' George admitted.

'We can't even wait it out at the pub,' Brook said. He laughed again. 'We must look like a couple of expectant fathers.'

George looked at him owlishly. '*You* might but I don't think I could be mistaken for one.' He glared around the tiny room.

227

An uncompromisingly plain young woman came in without knocking and put a flimsy down in front of Brook. As he signed for it, she levelled a glance of deep suspicion at George, then looked away hurriedly, as though she'd seen the ghost of Guy Burgess stalking the land.

'Your fellow Americans,' George observed with a sniff once she'd left, 'automatically assume that every English homosexual with a security clearance, never mind how low, is being rogered at all times of day and night by the KGB.'

'Aren't you?' Brook asked, looking inquisitive. He reread the telex. 'Another tiny piece to fit into the puzzle from my fellow Americans.' He flicked it across the table to George. 'Father Stephen Fahy, SJ was working at the Vatican Radio in the late seventies before taking up a teaching post at the University of Munich. Not exactly a bombshell but what the hell. We can assume that his German's fluent so he could be "Gillon" and he could be living somewhere around Frankfurt. Anyway, I'll shoot all this along to Mallinckrodt at the BKA.'

Goudhurst's opposite number in West Germany was standing by for any leads, no matter how tentative, on the identity of "Gillon". The IRA, behaving as if German territory were an adjunct of Londonderry's Bogside and blithely indifferent when German civilians were murdered alongside British soldiers, had been openly contemptuous towards the German Anti-Terrorist police for so long that Mallinckrodt was grimly determined to nail them.

On a more practical level, even the most sedentary, middle-aged and outwardly-respectable people who had been suspected of terrorist goings-on as far back as the sixties were under surveillance. If "Gillon" tried to recruit his mercenary cohorts in the Federal Republic, Mallinckrodt would know about it.

As Brook chattered away by proxy on the telex to Germany and the National Crime Information Center in Washington, George went over the list of Edwina Madden's circle of acquaintance before she'd shaken the choking dust of Boston from her expensively-shod feet.

Brendan Conklin of Sinn Fein had disappeared, dead or gone underground, according to Lisburn. George studied the photograph taken at the 1973 Noraid fund-raising dinner in Boston, Conklin prominent between Teddy Kennedy and Cardinal Medeiros. He had been prime "Gillon" material, but Desmond Reardon had emphatically denied that they were one and the same. "Gillon", he maintained, was sinister-looking: of slightly-above-medium height, wiry build and with an unblinkingly intense look. Conklin, it had to be admitted, didn't quite fit the bill. Of the right height and colouring, he nonetheless had too open and round a face, little in the way of neck, short arms and legs and the ruddy complexion that could equally be the result of a hearty, outdoor life or a cosy indoor life with good companions and many, many bottles.

George had conducted most of Reardon's interrogations himself and felt fairly certain he wasn't lying, at least on the point of his master's identity. Reardon didn't bother to hide the fact that "Gillon" terrified him: he seemed to know everything. Conklin, judging from the photograph, didn't look as though he understood much more than the usual Sinn Fein cant and the price of a bottle of Bushmill's.

The 1974 photograph of a Democratic Party beano was disappointing. Father Fahy was too much in the background, despite all the photo-enhancement, for Reardon to state with certainty that this was "Gillon". The Jesuit was little more than a grainy shadow photographed in profile and a step behind Cardinal Medeiros, who was having his hand kissed by Joan Kennedy as he chatted with Tip O'Neill. This self-effacement was entirely fitting and proper to his position as the Cardinal-Archbishop of Boston's secretary but it was also the only photograph the Boston people had been able to find of him, suspicious in itself to George's devious mind. Why was he so camera-shy? And, of course, there were no later photographs of Edwina, whom he now thought of as Nedda.

Neither Lisburn nor Dominic Ryan in Dublin had anything on anyone called Gillon, which was why they had assumed it to be a *nom de guerre*. Dominic's formidable menagerie of moles were still scratching diligently away, however. Something more concrete was bound to surface. Someone, surely, must be able to supply more up-to-date information on Nedda, too. Soon, George hoped.

The door opened. 'Jesus! Kirkwood's a persistent bastard. Diligence takes on new meaning,' Brook said, flopping into a chair, this time an upholstered one, 'which is dogged. Shit! The only thing is, I doubt that any of this will be of much use to us.'

He turned his shorthand notebook upside-down. 'Ah.' He looked sternly at George, in fair imitation of the college professor he'd originally claimed he was. 'Do I have your full attention?'

George rolled his eyes up and prayed for patience.

'Wait for it, wait for it,' Brook warned. 'Okay. Evil tongues are saying that Miss Edwina Madden was, as we have already been apprised, no better than she should be *and*,' he lowered his voice dramatically, 'she left Boston to hide her shame. She was in the family way, bun in the oven, knocked up, disgraced! Showing! That's Mrs Edwin Madden, Junior. Mrs Daniel Madden said she wasn't showing yet but it was only a matter of time. I rest my case.'

George shot a disgusted look at Moseley and lit a cigarette without comment.

'The bun would be fourteen now, just turned fifteen tops, depending on the gripping question of showing or not showing when Nedda scampered off to make the Italian boyfriend – the Mesdames Madden refer to him as "that dago" – do the decent thing, assuming he was the lucky father.'

'I thought "dagos" were Spaniards,' George said pedantically.

'Never mind that. Think of the gestation period of the bun.'

'God, Brook,' George said irritably, 'the things you expect one to know. Why must a bun come into play?'

'If Nedda produced the bun abroad, as seems likely, she would have had to register it with an American consulate.

230

Otherwise, the tiny tot would be stateless. A non-person. She couldn't travel with it. See where I'm coming from, fella?'

George perked up. 'But she might have married the child's dear old dad.'

'Dear *young* dad. The Madden ladies, you know, were scandalized that he was a few years younger, although harping on at inordinate length that he was from a very good family. Reassured McCafferty on that point endlessly. McCafferty incredibly relieved to hear it but some pissed off they couldn't remember his very good *name*.'

'The point being,' George said with elaborate patience, 'that if she married her Harvard dago, the child wouldn't be stateless. It would have an Italian passport.'

'Maybe dual nationality,' Brook said with a hint of truculence. 'Well, we'll see. I think you will agree at least on the point that she'd been out in the traffic to an extraordinary degree in one so comparatively tender in years. If the young man was all that young and the very good family was so very good, can you imagine them allowing their dear son to marry a girl like little Miss Madden?'

'*Rich* little Miss Madden,' George pointed out.

Brook pawed through his notes again, ignoring George's cavilling. 'The IRS have her filing in Florida through an attorney, hum, hum, hum, shells out an average of forty, forty-five grand a year in taxes, so she still has major money in the US. Probably all dividend income that she can't get away with not declaring. No point in trying to squeeze an address out of Bernie the Attorney. Not unless we've got a warrant and then he'd start yapping about privilege.' He looked up and grinned irrepressibly. 'Funny, isn't it, how people are scareder of the Internal Revenue than they are of the cops? I mean, here this broad is into cocaine-running, mass-murders and God knows what else but her quarterly taxes are accurate to the penny and bang on time.'

'On the subject of Italians, Brook, is there any chance of a Mafia connection? We've got an Italian boyfriend and drugs, after all. Florida lawyer . . .'

231

Brook shook his head slowly. 'It's what I thought, right at the beginning, with that boozy dimwit Hanratty and Milan. Before I met up with you guys. God that seems centuries ago! I'll tell you why I don't think there's a Mafia angle and that's the size of the drugs thing. Too small for them and the structure's wrong. These people aren't shifting more than a thousand kilos a year. And their cocaine is top-quality, almost certainly from a single source, according to the chemistry lab's analysis.' He shook his head emphatically. 'Miss Madden and Mr Costelloe are running a Van Cleef operation and the Mafia is Woolworth's.'

He slapped a fax down under George's nose. 'Here's what the creative types have decided Nedda might look like now, with fifteen years on the clock.' He surveyed the picture critically. 'I shouldn't think that the lowly Costelloe would be the current love of her life. With her track record she probably wouldn't have settled down with the dago for long, if at all. Probably dropped the child and lit out for pastures green.' He studied the sketch again. 'She's damned attractive still, isn't she? Tough-looking, too, of course, but undeniably sexy.'

'Not a patch on our Camilla,' George said loyally.

'I can't get a look-in with our Camilla, Georgie.' Brook's shrewd expression showed plainly both that he knew George was her confidant and that he was fishing.

'We'll see,' George answered the unasked question placidly. 'Our Camilla needs to get a few things out of her system.'

On the train from Basel to Geneva, Alexis pretended to doze.

He had picked out the two possible tags by the time the train stopped at Biel. One of them, actually the one he'd thought the likelier, got off the train at Neuchâtel, which left the tubby man in the chocolate-brown trilby and short black raincoat, who wore a large gold ring and looked like a bookie.

Having expressly announced his intention of going to

Geneva with a view to furthering Gillon's requirements for his planned "campaign", the "major offensive" which he promised to discuss more fully at a future date, Alexis knew that the bookie would hand over responsibility to someone on the spot. Gillon would be making arrangements for watchers at the Geneva end as Alexis travelled, the bookie's sole shepherding function reduced to flitting along behind him, should Alexis leave the train before his avowed destination.

The only time Gillon sounded a prize ass was when assuming a bluff-soldier pose and military jargon, Alexis thought. And his own most pressing problem had been to treat Gillon's ambitions with the utmost seriousness, the copious amount of wine he had drunk, they had both drunk, giving rise to a dangerous, even suicidal urge to laugh. Gillon thought of himself as a new Napoleon, his minuscule, noisy and half-crazed bunch of Irish patriots and homicidal maniacs the Grand Army of the Republic, spreading the word to the enchained or simply unenlightened. Once in control, Gillon had pointed out, it would be a relatively simple matter to slaughter all those unenlightened enough to resist enlightenment.

There would be no great difficulty in losing the tag or tags. Alexis knew Geneva well, precisely why he was headed there. Indeed, he had occasionally and deliberately allowed his familiarity with the place to creep into Gillon's probing chats, leading him to think that it was not entirely impossible that Alexis actually lived either in Geneva or very close by. The trick lay in slipping his followers without appearing to do so deliberately. It was essential to meet Ruffo in Paris and it was equally essential that Gillon not begin to suspect this, whilst underpinning Gillon's touching faith in Alexis' reliability and general usefulness.

By the time the train pulled into Lausanne, Alexis had made a tentative plan. He examined it thoroughly from every side and his eye blinked open sleepily as they rolled slowly through Geneva's lakeside suburbs. He yawned and stretched, the bookie already in the aisle prepared to alight at the head of the queue. He would be the first off to alert the watchers waiting in the railway station. Alexis struggled into his Burberry wishing he actually had been able to snatch some sleep but at least he now felt entirely sober.

It was pissing with rain, a heavy downpour that sent umbrella-less pedestrians scurrying into the station. Alexis fished a battered khaki hat from the pocket of his mac. He limped slowly across to the taxi-rank, leaning heavily on his stick and politely insisting that others had a prior claim on the available taxis. He thus caught a glimpse of the bookie speaking briefly through the window of a silver-grey Peugeot parked illegally in the Place de Cornavin.

The Peugeot took up station two cars behind as they moved slowly down towards the Rhône in sluggish, early-evening traffic. Alexis was beginning to enjoy himself, his sleepiness forgotten.

Having the fare and Swissly meagre tip ready, he was out of the taxi and hobbling slowly down the Place du Marché in a trice, catching the Peugeot's dry and comfortable occupants very slightly wrong-footed. The interior light flashed on and Alexis knew that the Peugeot's passenger would now be on foot, leaving the driver with no option but to continue on down the one-way Rue de Rive. Apart from getting wet, the foot-man would not be alarmed and would certainly be prepared for such a contingency with a radio link to the Peugeot.

Alexis smiled happily, already slipping off his damp Burberry as he went through the door of the Mövenpick and prodding his hat and eye-patch into its deep pocket. He walked briskly through the large brasserie, already crowded with after-work drinkers waiting for the rain to stop before heading home, and straight out the other door into the Rue du Rhône. Dodging through the creeping traffic, he was across the foot-bridge and on the right bank in less than five minutes, picking up a taxi in front of the Hôtel des Bergues, as his dripping tag finally gave up looking for him and hissed furiously into his small radio.

He directed the driver to take him to Cointrin, not wanting to chance the railway station in case the bookie were hanging about there waiting for a train to take him back to whatever hole he'd crawled out of. It wouldn't do at all to be cornered in the departure lounge but the weather was clearing – the driver had just switched off his windscreen-wipers – and the flights between Geneva and Paris so frequent that the airport represented a far lesser risk.

By the time the plane was approaching Paris, Alexis felt a small stirring of hunger, no more than a reminding trickle of gastric juices, despite his gigantic luncheon. He smiled at his reflection in the dark window as they touched down. There was, he thought, nothing like a bit of scheming to work up a healthy appetite.

20

There was a tentative tap on the door. '*Herein!*' Gillon shouted and Altdorfer entered.

Philipp Aloysius Altdorfer was the product of a German father and Irish mother, the latter parent making him Gillon's first cousin. He combined the efficiency of the Irish with the charm of the Germans. He spoke of himself in the third person, which Gillon found infuriating, and refused to entertain the possibility that any activity not involving actual physical movement constituted activity at all.

'*Ach gut,*' he said, bustling into the sitting-room, 'as we're not doing anything . . .'

Gillon was reading. 'What is it?' he asked wearily.

'Hoepli just called to say he was very sorry but they lost Herr Leysin in Geneva.' He shuffled uncomfortably. 'I, too, am sorry, Stephen. I ought to have stayed on the train with Hoepli instead of getting off at Neuchâtel. Perhaps then . . .'

'I see,' Gillon said evenly and ignoring Altdorfer's apology. 'Hoepli and two auxiliaries failed to keep track of a tall, one-eyed man with a moustache and pronounced limp. I feel sure that he will some day prove invaluable to our little organization.' He looked up at Altdorfer, who smiled ingratiatingly. 'Have you any further news?'

'Philipp always tells Cousin Stephen straight away when there's news. Good or bad.'

'If such is the case, perhaps you'd be kind enough to tell Philipp he can disappear now, like a good little chap. Then I can continue not doing anything.'

Altdorfer grimaced in his own parody of a sycophantic smile and wisely disappeared without further comment. Gillon returned briefly to his book. Glancing at his watch, he saw that it would soon be time to make his nightly call to Connolly in London.

Connolly was a good man: unimaginative but loyal, if a trifle lazy. All he lacked was a little encouragement. Laziness was something that could be cured and Gillon had imagination enough for any number of Connollys.

Gillon planned to reward him soon by bringing him to Europe, as quickly as a new headquarters for the planning and execution of the up-coming offensive could be found. Keeping an eye on Ruffo was an undemanding job for someone as exceptionally devoted as Connolly and one that would cease to exist entirely, in fact, as soon as Ruffo was killed. Very, very soon now.

The side-by-side service flats in Basel's outskirts that the Altdorfers had rented for themselves and Gillon, or Herr Doktor Friedrich Metzler, the name on his Austrian passport, were all right as a stopgap but he needed more staff. There was the security angle to consider, too. This place had a porter in the downstairs lobby and maids coming in twice a week to clean. A house with maximum privacy had to be found as soon as possible, preferably somewhere that was cosmopolitan enough so that a mixed bag of foreigners wouldn't attract undue attention.

He needed people now, to get all the logistics sorted out for the last great offensive against the British, but his as yet inchoate plans could be rolled back two or three weeks, even months, without making serious inroads into the eventual triumphant results. He was in no particular hurry, especially now that Reardon's car bomb had, presumably, been found and neutralized by the British. Gillon's planning was always elastic, to allow for minor setbacks such as the Reardon cock-up and the necessity of a quick move.

He had managed to orchestrate a sudden but efficient evacuation of the house that would raise no questions, unless the local police had excellent photographs and sufficient man-power to comb through the records of every estate agent for the past two years. Philipp had arranged with the bank to pay the final gas, telephone and electricity bills, leaving a small surplus balance and a bogus forwarding address. No trace of Gillon lingered behind in Germany. Everything had been done by the Altdorfers, under an entirely different name and a full portfolio of false papers.

It was a pity about Switzerland, though. With young Liam Costelloe gaining more and more control over the financial side of things, there were further inducements to being in Switzerland but if it was risky, involving thorough police checks as Alexis had been so quick to point out, then another country would do almost as well. Everything these days was done by telex in any event.

What Alexis had told him about the complications of Swiss residence permits and concomitant microscopic police scrutiny had turned out to be true. A single phone call had borne him out. Gillon was aware that he was himself a virgin page so far as Interpol were concerned. However, Ivy Altdorfer's student activities very probably were tucked into some archive in England, France or Germany and he wondered if he needed her computer expertise to keep everything running smoothly. There was no telling what that traitorous shit Ryan in Dublin might have on Philipp. Gillon regretfully decided that applying for residence permits would be unwise, even foolhardy.

He had just learned from Dublin that the Gardai had swooped on yet another arms cache, this one near Limerick. Stocks were reaching a crisis level and Gillon was anxious to find out what sort of package Alexis might come up with. He didn't feel like waiting around for Qaddafi to decide to throw him a few crumbs from his table. It was clear that the British were reeling after last month's orchestrated attacks. One immense, definitive push would do the trick and get them out of Ireland forever. The timeless lessons of history were clear on this point: with the British withdrawal, civil war and chaos would ensue. Out of chaos, order was inevitably born, a phoenix rising from the ashes. Ireland would clamour for order, the stricter, the better.

His new control centre would probably have to be in Holland or Belgium, after all. He would go on a scouting expedition, which was something to look forward to. It wasn't a moment too soon to begin serious planning. A major summer campaign, London awash in tourists, offered serious possibilities, especially in view of the infinite variety of ceremonial occasions on offer. He had a sudden happy inspiration: some large theatre, perhaps Covent Garden, standing room only and a well-placed explosion. He chuckled delightedly. It would bring the house down.

Time to ring Connolly.

'I'm sorry, Gillon,' he said, without preamble, 'I lost his bloody highness at Gatwick.'

'All right,' Gillon said calmly, 'tell me exactly what happened, Patrick.'

'Nothing much to tell,' Connolly said, relieved that Gillon seemed unperturbed that the bird had flown. 'He left the flat about half past one, quarter to two, with a smallish suitcase and briefcase, walked to Victoria, took that shuttle train thing to Gatwick and I lost him in the concourse there. It's very spread out there and awfully big for one man to keep an eye . . .'

'Of course it is, Patrick.' Gillon's voice was soothing. 'Did you have time to note the departures, by any chance?'

'Yes, just as you once told me to look for possibles.' Gillon heard a paper being unfolded. 'New York, Faro, Alicante, Corfu, Houston, Beauvais, Palma, Tunis . . .'

Gillon laughed. 'Slow down then, young Patrick. I can't write that fast now, can I?'

Connolly finished the list of destinations he had conscientiously copied from the departures board for a period of two hours after Ruffo's arrival at Gatwick. Then he gave a précis of the day's telephone conversations and messages left on the princely answer-phone.

'I shouldn't worry about it, Patrick. He's probably gone off somewhere with the new girlfriend, the lovely widow Hamilton. Just to eliminate various possibilities, ring up the magazine and find out where she is, if you can. Or you might deliver flowers to her flat. It gives you an excuse to find out from the porter if she's away and, if so, how long she's expected to be away.'

239

Before ringing off, Gillon thanked him profusely for having followed standing orders. Connolly would definitely be promoted up to one of his own aides.

Alexis had slipped his tags. It could have been pure accident, of course. But Gillon didn't at all like the coincidence of Ruffo's going missing on the same day. He studied the notes he had made.

There wasn't a shred of evidence to show that Alexis and Ruffo were in touch except those infrequent occasions when acquiring some weaponry coincided with the movement of Nedda's sacred snow. And yet, they had much in common, far more than Nedda suspected, perhaps nothing more than an affinity that she was too obtuse to notice. Ruffo's killing of Hamilton, especially strangling the man in a very public place, in broad daylight and with his own necktie, showed a ruthless, vindictive streak in the man's make-up.

There was danger in Ruffo's teaming up with Alexis, Gillon's instincts warned him, but what? If there were some sort of collusion, a possibility that Gillon didn't like to think about, Alexis could not conceivably have warned Ruffo that he, Gillon, wasn't entirely happy with him, Ruffo. All the times of comings and goings were completely wrong, unless there were some sort of prearranged code between them, which wasn't possible when Ruffo's London telephone conversations had never yielded any unexplained contacts or unpleasant surprises of any sort whatsoever.

Connolly's list of Ruffo's calls today was typical and unexceptionable. He had horses in training in Hampshire, a well-known establishment near Andover, and he'd had a mid-morning chat about some upcoming fixtures with the trainer. After that, he'd spoken with his mother in Italy. That couldn't have been Alexis, unless he spoke Swedish, could assume a woman's voice and answered to "Mama". Ruffo had made a June appointment with his dentist; booked two stall seats at the Haymarket three weeks hence; complained to his bank that a new chequebook hadn't arrived. The woman Connolly described as "her with the sexy voice and all" had bitterly claimed that Ruffo was ignoring her and threatened to end their affaire.

Gillon smiled. For all his good looks and charm, Ruffo certainly had more than his fair share of problems with the women in his life. There was much to be said in favour of celibacy.

'Nothing simpler,' Ruffo said happily. 'I lost him at Gatwick, purely by following your precept, oh Master, that you show 'em what they expect to see.'

'Which was?' Alexis asked, amused.

'A man with a suitcase goes to an airport and will naturally go to Departures. I went to Arrivals, back down the stairs to the platform and took the next train to Dover. And here I am. Hungry and curious.'

'In Spain or Greece,' Alexis said, 'you'd be considered unfashionably early.'

'I loathe both Spain *and* Greece. Equally. The only reason they dine so late is that the food is inedible so they put off eating as long as possible.'

They studied their menus, ordered and sipped their drinks. 'My last meal,' Alexis said conversationally, 'admittedly some hours ago now, was taken in the rivetting company of Gillon. He and Nedda are convinced that you killed Major Hamilton.'

'Ah.'

'Did you?'

Ruffo shook his head vigorously, his mouth full of bread. 'Why should I?' he finally asked.

'Nedda's precious twenty kilos of virgin snow he had in his car were never recovered, that's why. I needn't tell you how much that little lot was worth. Gillon is of the opinion that you killed Hamilton and stole the cocaine both for the money and to erase the inconvenient fact that it was packed into Monteavesa Vineyards wineboxes. You'll ruin your appetite.'

Chewing on another piece of bread, Ruffo mumbled, 'Doesn't make any sense.' He swallowed. 'Not on either

241

of those two grounds. If I'd wanted Nedda's stupid snow, all the wineboxes I turned over to Hamilton would've contained nothing but wine. Especially if I thought the cops or Customs might be onto him. Why should I give him the stuff and then kill him to get it back? Stupid idea. I thought our Philosopher King was supposed to be a master logician.'

Alexis smiled. 'Gillon picked that hole himself, so don't get uppity. Nedda, on the other hand, thinks either that you killed Hamilton because he wouldn't turn over the boxes without being paid more than the agreed amount *or* that you quite simply coveted his wife to such an extent that you were overwhelmed with a primitive urge to have her entirely for yourself. Nedda thinks Biblical.'

Ruffo looked interested. 'Didn't know he was married. Never mentioned a wife. Mark you, he'd no reason to. We weren't on a very matey footing. Couldn't stand him, to tell you the truth. He seemed to think he was the Scarlet Pimpernel of the cocaine trade.' He smiled. 'He didn't know that I had a wife, unless Nedda took him into her confidence, probably in bed.' He dug hungrily into the large platter of oysters the waiter had just put down in front of them.

'You don't know then,' Alexis said, keeping his tone neutral and buttering a thin slice of brown bread.

Ruffo reluctantly put down his fork and said, 'Alexis, can we do without the mystery, please?'

'The "delicious creature", I believe you called her, who is the subject of your recent gallantries is the widow Hamilton, Ruffo. The pretty photographer who was watching Jacki's troops moving guns and dope across the glacier and down into France.' Alexis regarded him severely, his glass eye somehow looking fiercer than his real one. 'What's more, Nedda believes her to be a copper. A nark.'

'*Camilla?*'

'None other.' Alexis sipped his wine, watching Ruffo. He popped another Belon into his mouth and chewed it slowly. 'I also discovered that the fellow dressed as a chauffeur who looks like a tortoise was dropped on his head is called Connolly. He saw Camilla leaving your flat one morning. Two and two were put together, Ruffo. Do leave a bit of bread for me,' he said with some irritation.

'What's clear,' he went on judiciously, having demolished his last oyster, 'is that both Gillon and Nedda think you're co-operating through Camilla with the police, that she's your contact. That you're being blackmailed by them on a possible murder charge. That Hamilton could have been a plant, a double-agent, reporting every move back to MI5, Scotland Yard, the CIA, Buck House, for all I know. What Gillon didn't say, but I think highly probable, is that he's going to kill you. He was being unusually *insouciant*.'

'Yes. Well, thanks for the vote of confidence.'

Her mother-in-law picked up the phone on the first ring. The old bag was probably already in bed before eleven o'clock, Nedda thought.

'I do hope I didn't wake you up, Margareta,' she said with bogus solicitude, implying volumes of disapproval that her mother-in-law had nothing better to do than to sleep.

'No,' she answered serenely, 'you didn't. I was reading.'

'I was wondering if you'd heard from Ruffo lately.' Nedda vaguely resented having to ask but Gillon was most insistent.

'Yes, I have.'

There was a long silence. 'How is he?' Nedda finally asked, knowing that Margareta would not be volunteering any information.

'He's extremely well, thank you.'

After another pause, Nedda asked, 'Did he call you from London?'

'I don't know. He didn't say.'

The conversation, such as it was, began to get on Nedda's nerves. 'Do you think you could bring yourself to venture a guess?' She found it obscurely irritating that her mother-in-law refused to utter her name, as if she were a person of no consequence whatsoever, an importunate door-to-door salesman, perhaps.

243

She heard Margareta whispering. 'Who's with you?' she demanded suspiciously.

'My husband. I was simply telling him that it was nothing important.'

Two can play that game, you dreary old bitch, Nedda thought. 'I absolutely can't wait to see Guido in his quaint school uniform!'

Margareta didn't rise to the bait as she normally did, which infuriated Nedda. She had more than enough things on her plate to deal with than this doting, foolish old Swedish broad who thought of nothing but her family.

Another long silence had developed and Nedda was beginning to lose her temper. 'Look, Margareta, I want to know where Ruffo is.'

'Perhaps you didn't hear me. I told you I don't know.'

'Well, find out! I'll call you tomorrow morning.'

She slammed the phone down and began to shake.

Margareta was displaying a very bad attitude. She would never be so calm unless Ruffo had promised her that their troubles would soon be over, that her daughter-in-law would soon be swept off the board, perhaps? It would be interesting to know how Ruffo intended to put her safely behind bars without spending the rest of his own life breaking up rocks on Dartmoor. And destroying the family in the process. Even their wine trade would fall off. Respectable wine-merchants didn't like doing business with convicted criminals.

But meanwhile where was Ruffo? She would have to call Gillon back and tell him she was working on it. Going over the list Gillon had given her of Ruffo's possible destinations, she thought he could be almost anywhere.

He could have gone to New York and on to Kentucky. The Derby was being run on Saturday and Ruffo had a host of fatuous cronies in the racing world who would be only to happy to put him up. Horses reminded her of something else: the airport at Beauvais was the one used by the Chantilly racing set. He could have gone there. She was pretty sure that the Beauvais plane also went to Deauville, either before or after Beauvais, she couldn't remember which. He could be with Cristina and Antoine in Normandy.

She suddenly thought of the charter pilot, a Frenchman, that Ruffo used to transport his fucking horses from place to place. He sometimes gave Ruffo flying lessons.

She smiled with satisfaction, her thoughts going back to Connolly's bungling. It was a way to get back at Gillon. He thought Connolly was just dandy, excellent material to train up to a position of responsibility in the IRA pecking order, just like Costelloe, whom she had come to hate with unparalleled ferocity. Nedda was willing to bet that Gillon's protégé Connolly hadn't had the brains to look for Ruffo in the private section of Gatwick, which was where the flying horse-box would be parked. So okay he hadn't talked to the pilot on the phone but they could have met somewhere or Ruffo could've called him on someone else's phone, for God's sake. She grudgingly recognized that it never failed to annoy her when Gillon praised anyone else's abilities; this would give her a perfect opportunity to underscore Connolly's manifest shortcomings.

One thing she could no longer put off telling Gillon was the worrying fact that nothing had been heard from Pereira in Brazil. If she hadn't been so jumpy and strung out lately, which was entirely Ruffo's fault, she wouldn't have forgotten to do something about that. Her concentration was suffering from the constant worry that Ruffo was either betraying the entire organization to the police or planning to do so.

She had finally noticed that the postcard from Manaus hadn't arrived, that it should have arrived at least ten days ago, more like two weeks, and that she was losing track of time. The cocaine shipment ought to be at Belém right now. Pereira had never been late before, not in all the years they'd been doing business. It was true that the heat was on in Colombia but there hadn't been any suggestion in the press that anything was going on in Brazil.

It was long past the date when she ought to have brought Gillon's attention to the possibility that something was potentially out of kilter, faraway in Brazil, where there

245

was little they could do about it. Conway's old rustbucket was steaming up towards Belém now. He had sent a telex from the shipping agent's at Montevideo. What the hell were they to do if the snow wasn't there, waiting to be transferred from Pereira's launch to the cargo ship?

Gillon would be furious. She could claim that she'd been waiting from one day to the next for a letter or postcard to arrive from Brazil, thinking there must be some delay with the mails or that Pereira had had some difficulty with his launch. It was vital to know far in advance of the *Caribbean Pearl*'s arrival on this side of the Atlantic how many one-kilo bags of snow would have to be dealt with. This was apart from the precautionary measure of knowing the precise weight, just in case Conway tried to short-change them by more than the kilo or two he blandly assured her was due to "spillage".

It was all too much. Mules would have to be organized but she didn't know how many they'd need, when or where they ought to be herded into place or if, God forbid, they'd ever again be needed at all. The thought of being without her wonderful, beautiful snow, even temporarily, made her sweat. Other sources for cocaine would have to be located and vetted to avoid stepping on any Mafia corns. Colombia, Peru and Panama were definitely out. Gillon would insist on going out to South America, no doubt taking Alexis along for some hearty male companionship as well as his knowledge of the country and language, keeping her out of things.

She glanced at the clock. It was almost midnight in Brazil and the shipping agents in Belém would have long been shut. She would call them tomorrow and leave an urgent message for Conway. If she remembered. She had to start remembering and scrawled a note to herself: Conway. Under that, she wrote, Guido.

Tears of self-pity began to well in her eyes. How could she be expected to do everything? Gillon was planning a major offensive and she had sworn the money would be there as and when it was needed. Taking advantage of Costelloe's absence on some obscure errand of Gillon's,

Nedda had sat down at the computer, only with great difficulty and many false starts remembering various access codes and cross-references to work out roughly that their liquidity position could be better. Much better. She ought to have paid more attention to hedging the dollar. The fucking dollar kept going down and she had counted on its clawing some of the way back up against the pound, the yen and various European currencies. What did those Treasury clowns in Washington think they were doing? A major move into sterling and yen was too late now.

She walked into the kitchen, opened the freezer and poured out half a tumbler of Finlandia vodka, treacly from having been iced for a day, and added a few cubes of ice.

It wasn't fair, she thought, wiping her eyes angrily. Gillon, for all his much-trumpeted giant intellect, simply had no conception of the complexities of world financial markets. There wasn't an unlimited supply of cash she could lay hands on at a moment's notice but some really major investments she'd made were just about to come to fruition, trebling the original outlay, at a conservative estimate. If only she dared explain it all to Gillon without feeling so defensive, as though she'd made a terrible mistake.

Deciding that she might have some fresh insights into the present situation, she wandered bare-footed back through the huge apartment to her dressing-room. Opening the wall safe with shaking fingers, she brushed aside the jewellery and cash and found what she was looking for. She got out a bag of cocaine and began to work away with the little gold jackknife, ignoring its engraved warning: *Beware*.

She eventually looked pensively at the knife, open in the palm of her trembling hand. This had been a gift from Ruffo, an innocuous little offering for her birthday in that first, happy year of their marriage. As she got busy chopping the beautiful creamy crystals, she wondered vaguely what instinct had prompted him to choose it for her.

21

'Saddle Balloon for me please, Trevor,' Barbara said to a startled stable-lad who was busily doing the first of his two.

'I think his Lordship has her, m'lady.'

'Dragonfly, then.'

'He's awfully fresh, m'lady,' the lad said dubiously. 'He hasn't been out in . . .'

'Good. We could both do with the exercise, then.' Barbara strode back into the house and ran upstairs. She changed into breeches, thick socks and a heavy sweater; then ran back down to rummage for her boots and the old waterproof mounted policeman's cape she wore on wet days.

Dragonfly was feeling frisky in the damp chill of the early morning and she rode him hard to the all-weather gallops where Nicholas was watching the second string as the work-riders listened attentively to his instructions.

'Nicky,' she said as she reined up beside her husband, 'I've got to talk to you. Urgently.'

He looked at her with considerable surprise but didn't argue. With a few economical instructions to Hamish, his young assistant, he dug his heels into Balloon's fat flanks and cantered off after his wife. She eventually persuaded Dragonfly to slow to a walk.

'Sorry, Nicky, but Ruffo just phoned.'

'He's up early. For Ruffo, I mean.'

'He's in Paris,' Barbara said with a slight smile. 'It's an hour later there. Look,' she began, 'he's in some difficulties and . . .'

'Nedda?'

Barbara said grimly, 'Nedda. It's always Nedda when there's trouble. But it's bigger trouble than even you and I have ever thought, darling.'

She paused before taking the plunge but there wasn't any way to tell Nicky what had to be said without sounding absurdly melodramatic. 'This is all rather involved so try to bear with me. Nedda's with the IRA. Always has been, since even long before she and Ruffo were married. She's pretty high up in their "inner councils".' The last words were pronounced with heavy irony.

'My God!'

She laid her hand on her husband's arm. 'Nicky, there's more and worse: Ruffo's been working for them, too. He's had to.'

'To protect Guido from her?'

'That and something else. Something far less important that he said would take too long to go into for the moment. But Guido's definitely Nedda's hold. The reason Ruffo called us for help is that he's convinced that Nedda's going to take Guido out of school, which she's got every legal right to do, and hang onto him until Ruffo sees things her way.'

Nicky was totally speechless and Barbara thought a bit before adding, 'Ruffo isn't trying to exonerate himself, Nicky. He said outright that he ought to have gone to the police long ago. But he was sucked into IRA shenanigans bit by bit – a favour here, keeping his mouth shut there, ignoring that; enough involvement to put him firmly behind bars – and before he knew it he was in too deeply himself to know what to do.'

'If Ruffo were behind bars, my darling heart, Nedda would be lumbered with Guido.'

'No, she wouldn't at all,' Barbara countered firmly. 'Nedda doesn't want Guido. Margareta and the rest of the family would continue to have him for school holidays. Us, too, of course.'

'All right, Bar. You've given me the background. Now tell me what Ruffo wants us to do.'

'Take Guido away from Eton and hide him. Ruffo said that the immediate problem is that Nedda and her "boss", I quote there, are convinced that Ruffo's double-crossed them in some way. He says he hasn't but there's no way

249

he can make them believe him. In Paris, he's safe enough for the moment but when Nedda and the Boss discover that they can't find him, that leaves Guido exposed. Guido can be pulled in to force Ruffo out into the open. Do you follow?'

'Oh yes, my dear, I certainly follow.' Nicky's voice was harsh, his mind working fast. 'There's a further problem, though. After we take him away from Eton, then what do we do with him? Nedda will know he's here, Barbara.'

He saw from her expression that she hadn't thought that far. Or perhaps she had and assumed that a trainer's yard, with thirty lads to hand and state-of-the-art security, was sufficient protection against the thugs sent by the IRA.

'Darling, a sniper at the gallops . . . What I'm saying is that the IRA wouldn't necessarily have to come after the boy to take him away. Any and all the horses are vulnerable; the lads, us. One dead body, or not even dead but simply missing, whether two- or four-legged, would do the trick. We'd have to go to the cops; the insurance people would be all over the place if they went for one of the horses or set fire to the stableyard. You know perfectly well that the IRA don't jib at anything, Barbara. My God, how many times in the past year have they slaughtered completely innocent people, people who just happened to be passing at the wrong time, and then gone on television to say how dreadfully sorry they are for the silly mistake? Neither Ruffo nor Guido could be shielded in any way here. I mean, I'm afraid it all sounds timid and I-don't-want-to-be-involved, but bringing Guido here quite frankly wouldn't do either him or Ruffo an atom of good.' He looked pleadingly at his wife. 'You do see that, don't you?'

She nodded. 'Ruffo said he was willing to face up to prison, Nicky. All he asked for was that we get Guido out of the line of fire – those were his very words and I don't mind telling you my blood turned to ice – until he and a friend of his could "neutralize", again I quote, the unutterably ghastly Nedda. On form, he said, she was unlikely to dawdle before pouncing on poor Guido. She's not what you'd call the contemplative type. If she's decided on a course of action, she moves.' She swiped impatiently at a strand of light-brown hair that had blown into the corner of her mouth and Dragonfly danced fretfully, sensing his rider's agitation. 'God only knows what she'd do with him if she had him, Nicky. I shudder to think of it.'

'You don't think she'd harm her own child!'

'I certainly wouldn't put it past her and *certainly* not if Guido were underfoot in some way. But I think it's vastly more probable that the boy would be turned over to some IRA hearties for security against Ruffo's continued co-operation. Or to lure Ruffo out of hiding so he could be killed without causing too much inconvenience.'

'You're sure Ruffo is in actual fear of his life? Barbara, you don't think for a moment he's simply being, well, a bit paranoid?'

'No. I don't.' Barbara looked evenly at her husband. 'We both know Nedda. Do *you* think it possible that Ruffo's overstating the case?'

Nicholas shook his head and jerked impatiently on the reins. Balloon had stopped to graze. 'Eton is the first place Nedda will send her friends to look for Guido. Then Monteavesa. Then here.' He kicked Balloon on.

Barbara felt savage. 'I wish Ruffo weren't such a damned fool! He's very far indeed from being a stupid man but he's a throwback, an anachronism. He struck some sort of deal with Nedda; he's stuck by it and expects her to follow suit. He's playing by the rules and he simply can't understand that Nedda isn't. What's more, she never intended to.'

Nicky nodded his agreement, thinking. 'Nedda's always understood that about him, too, and taken full advantage of it. She sees it as weakness and, in a way, I suppose it is, really.' He pushed Ruffo out of his mind and concentrated on the immediate problem. 'We'll take Guido away from Eton as soon as we can get there but we'll have to think of something to tell his housemaster. We'll lay a false trail to buy time. Then, darling, what do you think of the Swedish cousins?'

Barbara looked startled, then giggled. 'Ruffo's cousins? What a good idea, darling! I hadn't thought of them.' She frowned, biting her lip. 'You don't suppose Nedda would think of going to Sweden? No, I agree. Normandy yes, as Guido was in school there and Cristina and Antoine would do their utmost to hide him, but I'm fairly certain she wouldn't consider Sweden.'

'We'll suggest it, then leave it to him to decide. Do you have Ruffo's telephone number in Paris or is he ringing you back?'

'No. I'm to ring him. He's staying in an hotel on the Left Bank under the name of Monsieur Raphael Cavallesi. The friend who's helping him is there, too. I've got the number written down at home.'

'Let's go then,' Nicholas said, whacking the lazy Balloon across the shoulder with a switch he'd snapped off just to remind her that he expected to be obeyed. She whinnied in protest at the indignity and shuffled into a reluctant trot.

'There must be some mistake,' George Routledge said evenly, his tone gelid.

'What mistake?' Nedda demanded. 'I should have thought my wishes were clear enough. I'm only asking to see my son. I have already produced my passport for your inspection, to prove to you that I am who I say I am.'

She despised this place, this man, this entire country and race. The less time she spent here, the happier she'd be.

Routledge was aware that Guido's, Guy's, parents were separated. Now he saw why. 'I'm quite sure, Princess, it's nothing but a slight breakdown in communication.'

'What sort of breakdown?' Nedda countered with growing impatience.

The housemaster regarded her evenly. He'd formed a highly unflattering opinion of her on sight. 'Prince Monteavesa rang me this morning.' He deliberately avoided saying "your husband" or "Guy's father" in order to preserve a maximum formality and distance from this highly disagreeable woman; over-dressed, over-made-up, over-scented. He took an unconscious step backwards,

252

away from her, knowing he was being snobbish, judg-mental, and not caring a damn. 'All the arrangements were made.'

'Arrangements for what exactly?' Nedda asked, her teeth clenched.

'I imagine for precisely the same reason you've come. The prince did not confide in me the exact nature of the family crisis but said he was ringing from abroad and that Lady Nicholas Millardale would be coming to collect Guy and take him to Heathrow.'

'And when, may I ask, are you proposing to hand my son over to Lady Nicholas?'

'I'm afraid that . . .'

'Surely my presence here overrides any verbal orders you might have had. If you're uncertain, I'm sure that the Headmaster will see things my way.'

'If you would permit me to finish, Princess, I was about to tell you that Guy has already been fetched. Not so very long ago, in fact.' It gave him considerable satisfaction to see the expression of frustration and fury on her hard face. 'I offered to run him to Heathrow myself but the prince insisted. The Millardales had some of Guy's clothes that he would need and so they kindly . . . '

'Heathrow? Where were they taking him?'

'Again, madam, the prince did not take me into his confidence. The Millardales were a little pushed for time when they arrived. Lady Nicholas had telephoned well in advance and I had no wish to delay them. There was no opportunity for chit-chat. I assume the travelling arrangements to be the same as for the Christmas holiday.'

'Refresh my memory,' Nedda ordered, loathing this man, despising everything he stood for. She felt his antipathy towards her radiating out from him and was warmed by it. The English ought instinctively to hate and fear her.

'A flight to Milan, where they're to be met.' Routledge was unaccustomed to being spoken to as though he were being had up for shoplifting but he managed to control himself and answered her with a modicum of civility.

'They? The Millardales were going along for the ride?'

'Only their son, Edward, or so I gathered. He's Guy's best friend.' He smiled at her politely. 'If there's nothing else . . .'

'There is. What time did they leave?'

'Oh,' he answered vaguely, 'some little time before luncheon.'

'Where's your phone?' she asked abruptly.

'What I'd like to know is this: how do you *really* feel about being killed?' Alexis asked with a lop-sided smile.

They had booked into a two-bedroomed suite, choosing a large, impersonal hotel in the Boulevard Raspail. Alexis was drunk. In all the years they had known one another, Ruffo had seen Alexis in many moods but never outright drunk. Jolly and relaxed, yes, and not infrequently. But knee-crawling drunk: never.

'I've seen you in many moods but never drunk, *mon vieux,*' he said.

'It seemed, seems, the right thing to do. I'm tired,' he admitted, 'but I think we've got a plan. Finally. If it works. If I can get Gillon and Nedda to bite. My few remaining brain-cells are buzzing too much to go to bed, at least not right now.'

Ruffo yawned, more from nerves than drowsiness. 'At least Guido's safe.' He was feeling a little tight himself. He poured out two large glasses of Contrexéville. 'Here, drink this. Otherwise you'll be seriously overwhelmed with a headache tomorrow morning.'

'There are many massive ironies in our lives,' Alexis said with drunken solemnity, 'not the least of which is you and I, conspiring over a bottle of whisky late at night,' he peered at his watch, '*fairly* late at night, to do in your wife.'

'Alexis, why are you doing this? You're safe enough from Gillon.'

'Only for the moment, Ruffo. He's already harbouring suspicions about me; you can bet on that.'

He bent far over and put his head between his knees. 'Gillon's nothing if not thorough and he'll eventually succeed in tracking me down. I've postponed the day of reckoning by promising to do what I can to supply him with some grown-up weapons for his new "offensive".' He straightened. 'God knows what goes on in Gillon's obsessive brain,' he eventually said.

'Father Fahy,' Ruffo murmured.

'What?'

'Father Fahy,' Ruffo repeated. 'Gillon. He's Father Fahy. Nedda introduced me to him in Boston, when we first started to be an item. I think she was trying to impress upon me that she was a good Catholic girl and, therefore, entirely suitable to be my wife. She introduced us at a party of some sort – I think it was a wedding reception – and neither of them thinks that I remember.' He laughed again. 'It's fair to say I was a bit pissed at the time.'

Alexis took a while to digest this new piece of information. 'Real or bogus?'

'Oh, real enough I should imagine. Had done time in Rome. Spoke really quite good Italian. With a marked Roman accent.' He shrugged. 'When Nedda reintroduced us, many years later, he'd become Gillon and by then it seemed prudent to avoid an inconvenient display of total recall.'

Alexis lapsed into brooding silence, chasing a line of conjecture. 'At a guess, I think your Father Fahy might be intending to begin all over again with a clean slate. I would tread very warily if I were Nedda.'

'You're both useful to him.'

Alexis snorted. 'That's not what he thinks nor is it how he thinks.' He got up and stretched.

'I feel like moving around,' Ruffo said impatiently. 'I'll bring up another bottle of water. I hope the night-porter's got cigarettes.'

Alexis picked up the notes they'd made during the evening as Ruffo left the room. It was only with considerable difficulty that he managed to focus on his own crabbed hand and Ruffo's careless scrawl. He looked at the letter he'd been working on earlier and added a few more sentences. Tomorrow, he'd try to borrow a typewriter for a few minutes from the highly-impressionable young lady he'd smiled at in the hotel manager's office.

Ruffo came back into the room and opened the new bottle of mineral water, poured some out and put two packets of Disque Bleu filter-tips on the table. He peered with open curiosity at the messily-scrawled sheet of paper Alexis was studying with such obvious satisfaction. 'What's that?' Ruffo asked.

'My next *billet-doux* to MI Five or Six or whoever gets them,' Alexis said smugly, 'if anyone gets them at all and they don't get tossed in the rubbish, that is.' He shrugged. 'I've been doing this for ages. Sending them hints as to what our Irish friends are up to.'

'You've been *what*?' Ruffo was stunned.

'Just hints, Ruffo,' Alexis said defensively. 'Call it enlightened self-interest. Sound marketing strategy. Good Harvard Business School stuff.' He sipped at his glass. 'I've never made any formal approach to them or passed along very much. Mark you, I haven't known very much *to* pass along. You will see the reason for them when you recall that I've been, for some little time now, selling a modest assortment of weaponry to our Provisional friends. It stands to reason, therefore, that the law of supply and demand comes into play.'

'For God's sake, Alexis . . .'

'Tut tut! See it from my standpoint. If the British or Irish fuzz can, shall we say, *neutralize* a bunch of IRA goodies – expensively supplied by me – the more they are forced to buy as replacements. It's very sound business practice.'

Ruffo rolled his eyes up. 'No wonder Gillon had you followed.'

'That was only his nasty suspicious mind at work. Your old pal the priest subscribes to the principle of guilty until proven innocent and he's confided in me rather more than is strictly necessary or even prudent. I haven't passed along anything that could possibly indicate that I was the source.' He handed Ruffo the letter. 'Instead of bleating like an outraged nun, read the letter.'

Ruffo quickly scanned the few paragraphs, read through them again more slowly the second time and then put the paper back down on the table with a contemptuous look at Alexis. 'It makes absolutely no sense at all,' he said firmly. 'Why not give them Nedda's whereabouts, which we know nearly enough, instead of waffling on about Gillon? Nedda could be clapped up smartly in a French prison and I doubt they'd get much useful information out of her but her fangs would be pulled. She's the one who's out to get us. Me, at least.'

Alexis was rapidly sobering up. 'Because Gillon is out to get certainly you and eventually me. Take Nedda out, slam her up for years, and that still leaves Gillon, an even more dangerous and vindictive Gillon. It wouldn't take him forever to figure out that Nedda was right all along and you're the, forgive the expression, nigger in the woodpile. You have absolutely no protection at all. You are the only one with a sound reason to betray Nedda to the cops.'

Ruffo opened his mouth to voice another objection but Alexis forestalled him. 'I know what you're going to say. What small intelligence you possess is of the simple, straightforward variety. For an Italian, Ruffo, you're disappointingly lacking in pure, Machiavellian deviousness. What you were about to suggest is that we take out Nedda and then go after Gillon.'

Alexis laughed at the mulish expression on Ruffo's face. 'The problem there is that we don't know where Gillon is. We can't get in touch with him, find him except through Nedda. So, given a great deal of careful planning, blinding flashes of genius from me and a heavy dash of luck, we bag 'em both at once.'

'What about Frankfurt? You've got his phone number there. Why not give his phone number to the readers of your *billet-doux* and let them get on with smoking Gillon out. We let them catch Gillon, then we tell them where to go looking for Nedda.'

'You're awfully gullible, Ruffo. Just because Gillon told me that he was thinking of moving to Switzerland you believe him to be still cosily tucked up in Germany.

My dear fellow, he's already left Frankfurt! He wouldn't have breathed a word to me about Switzerland had he not thought he could use me as a nominee to buy a house. He would never have told me anything to do with Frankfurt if he hadn't already shut up shop there.'

He yawned again and got to his feet. 'I must leave you and get some sleep. But I'd like to send you off to your bed with another stately irony of life to brood on.'

'What's your stately irony?'

'The valedictory stately irony is as follows: it occurs to me that if you and I were to go this very minute to the coppers and tell them everything we know, we could get our prison sentences somewhat reduced in recognition of our co-operative attitude, your being coerced, my *billets-doux, und so weiter*. With me so far?'

Ruffo nodded impatiently. 'We've been over that ground about a million times already. Arguments for, arguments against. I must say, the prospect of prison sounds no more appealing than it did before.'

'Ah, but you've not heard the ironical bit yet. Consider the fact that we'd likely get ten years for this and that, cut in half if we behaved ourselves inside. But, if we manage successfully to, hum, liquidate Gillon and Nedda, and are caught, then, *mon vieux*, we're looking at life sentences. Maybe twenty years if we behave.'

He smiled beatifically at Ruffo. 'Just something to sleep on. Goodnight and sweet dreams.'

PART SIX

22

'Popeye?'

Brook smiled in spite of himself. No sooner had he jumped at the chance to come down to the South of France than Jay Rodman had renamed him "Popeye", after the New York cop in *The French Connection* who had smashed a heroin ring in Marseille. Brook only prayed that the joke would eventually pall and his nickname wouldn't stick to him for the rest of his allotted span.

'Hi, Jay. If I'm Popeye, doesn't that make my ex-wife Olive Oyl? There's more than a passing resemblance, to tell you the truth.'

Jay chuckled. 'How're ya doing chasing snow all over the Riviera? Lucky bastard! Weather in London really sucks.'

Brook glanced apologetically at his French colleague before saying, 'They're working on it hard, Jay, but so far there's nothing more than a whisper about some exceptionally high-grade blow available if you know the right people. There's no rap sheet on Costelloe, Nedda or the dark-blue Renault, at least not until we get better IDs on them.'

'Listen, a hell of a lot of stuff just came in from Rome. Mostly deep background, but it could come in handy. Background, my ass; it's *gossip*. At least it tells you if you're on the right track. I've already relayed it to the guys at Six so don't call 'em up on the Frog taxpayer's nickel. Got a pencil?'

'Shoot.'

'Okay. Here we go. First, we have Father Fahy of the Society of Jesus. This is all stuff from the horse's mouth, by the way. The Vatican, no less.'

'Great God Almighty,' Brook said, impressed. 'The long arm of the Inquisition *and* the CIA at work?'

Jay laughed. 'Stop making with the jokes and let's get

down to business. You already know that Fahy worked for Vatican Radio, which is entirely a Jez operation. Well, a book published in the early 1980s is generally thought to be either Fahy's work or at least partially his. It created something of a stir and blew the lid off all *sorts* of juicy scandals to do with the Banco Ambrosiano and God only knows what-all.'

Brook whistled. 'Your Vatican sources think that this radio Jesuit and barer of Curial skeletons is the same guy as our Gillon?'

'So they say. The putative authors of this book are Stephen Urquhart and Edward Gillon. The jacket blurb says they're journalists but that's all. Nobody in hack circles here has ever heard of 'em and there's absolutely no doubt in those selfsame hack circles that those two names are pseuds.'

'Remarkably reticent for a jacket blurb. I mean, if the authors were for-real. Keep going.'

'That's it, I'm afraid, except for deep background. Maurice Lyall called to say that Lisburn hasn't got a scrap on Stephen Fahy, Stephen Urquhart or Edward Gillon. Meanwhile, back at the ranch, we know Fahy was born in Londonderry in 1936 and that he got his first passport, British of course, when he was twenty and already under the Jesuits' wing, to go abroad and study. He'd already done a couple of years at Oxford. Not another thing on him.'

Brook grunted as he scribbled and finally said, 'No idea of current whereabouts? A rumour? An educated guess?'

'No such luck. Not even a postcard to his old buddies in the Society of Jesus, for Chrissake.' Jay laughed. 'If you'll pardon the expression. He hasn't been unfrocked or exorcized or whatever it is they do nowadays to naughty priests. You can bet he wasn't flavour of the month around Rome when that book came out. I mean, no dishonourable discharge from God's army, so he's entitled to baptize godless heathens like you and me if he feels like it.' He laughed again. 'You still there?'

'Just thinking, not that it's getting me anywhere.'

'Well, think later. I've got more,' Jay warned, 'and,

believe it or not, other little problems to sort through before I can get out of here at the end of my weary day of guarding the nation's integrity.'

Brook heard the dry rattle of paper being shuffled about. 'Pencil still poised? This'll really impress you. I bet you didn't know that the CIA has tentacles that reach deep within the Almanach de Gotha, not to mention every *piano nobile* of every palazzo in Rome.'

'Fire away,' Brook said, laughing.

'Your lovely friend Miss Edwina Madden married into a very snazzy family, originally from Rome, it won't surprise you to hear, given that I now know everything that's ever happened there since Alaric the Goth decided he didn't much care for the place.'

He cleared his throat. 'The family name is Cavallesi.' He spelt it. 'Some no-good Prince Cavallesi in the late nineteenth century got himself into a hell of a bind and had to sell the family palazzo and leave town real quick, creditors and/or outraged husbands in hot pursuit. The family had a summer place up by Lake Garda so he moved in there and married the local heiress. He attached her name to his, in order to please her rich daddy, so now the family is called Cavallesi di Monteavesa.'

Brook laboriously wrote it out. He said, 'So charming Nedda is or was the Princess Cavallesi di Monteavesa. Got it. Anything more on her?'

'Only that she presented her new family with an heir. A son. Name unknown. According to whatever titled old cat my guy in Rome got all this from, your friend Nedda didn't stay the course. The Cavallesi family aren't too interesting, at least not to someone like her. They breed racehorses and grow wine, probably play golf, for Chrissake. No bright lights. The mother is a Swede and a countess in her own right. The whole family takes off for Sweden in August. That's after the horses finish fucking until next year and before the grape harvest. Life of the family governed by Old Mother Nature, if you follow. Ottavio, the father, is apparently the handsomest man who ever lived. Now you know everything.'

'So Nedda got bored with the simple joys of motherhood and country life and slipped the traces. She got in touch with her old buddies and took up her former, more challenging, employment with the IRA. From what Kirkwood in Boston got out of her brothers and their wives, it all fits. Thanks, Jay. I really mean it.'

'Glad to oblige, Popeye. Anytime one government agency can lend a helping hand to . . .' He suddenly thought of something else. 'Oh, I almost forgot, Brook. Lyall called earlier, like I already told you. It's not mouth-watering enough to spend the Brit taxpayer's nickel but he told me to tell you that another Paris Embassy letter arrived. He said you'd know. Anyway, he said it was mostly about Gillon, how he speaks German and they think he might have once been a priest. Also, at least some of the banking is done through Monte Carlo. Only useful to corroborate what we've already found out but he said to be sure to tell you that the author is emphatic on one new point. Hang on a sec. Here it is: the IRA had absolutely nothing to do with Major Hamilton's murder.' Jay laughed. 'Can you imagine old Uncle Maurice's bushy eyebrows knitting away like mad over that?'

'Hmm. That *is* interesting. What did George Lacey have to say on the subject?'

'Dunno. He's in Germany, ditzing around with Mallinckrodt of the BKA, trying to get a line on Gillon. Listen, Uncle Sam needs me. I gotta go. You know where to find me if you need me, sweetheart.'

Before killing the Altdorfers, Gillon made careful preparations.

More than anything else, Gillon wanted to make a clean beginning when he left Basel. The chances of Reardon's giving the police anything really useful were negligible. It was doubtful he'd ever known the Altdorfers' name, much less be able to describe them. They therefore didn't absolutely have to be killed, in the sense of categorical imperatives, but he wanted no further encumbrances and they were all of that.

He thought that his fresh, new organization would be far easier to live with than the present unsatisfactory arrangements. Patrick Connolly and Liam Costelloe would be his lieutenants. They were both excellent men, neither too young nor too old, seasoned without being rash or blasé, good at following orders and not given to mindless paroxysms of ill-timed rage, a failing in so many men Gillon had worked with. Neither of the two men was a genius, but then neither was virtually brain-dead, like the obnoxious Cahill, or a dedicated drunk like so many IRA hotheads Gillon had tried and failed to shape into some semblance of professionalism.

The essential was to build the new organization along the lines of the Templars and Hospitallers. He wondered idly if the Teutonic Knights were celibate, too. Very probably they were. In any event, women would no longer be tolerated. They caused too much trouble and the lads could refresh themselves *extra muros*, as it were.

He was attracted by the idea that a most practical course of action was to allow the Altdorfers to lay the groundwork and participate in their own executions.

He began by telling them that he was leaving Basel the following morning in order to find a nice house where they would all be far more comfortable. 'I'll go down by train and stay at Vence. That's the general area we want, I believe, close enough but not too close to Nedda. Convenient to Nice Airport. Excellent rail connections to Italy and Spain.'

He stood up and went to the tiny kitchen to refill his coffee-cup. Yes,' he said, as though just coming to a final decision, 'the area is good for us. Marseille is the recruitment base for the Foreign Legion and we can do a spot of recruiting of our own. We can offer far better working conditions than the Foreign Legion.

'As soon as I've found a house, I'll ring you and you can fly down to join me.'

He almost left to return to his own adjoining flat but appeared to remember something and turned back, his hand outstretched, palm up. 'Your pistol, Philipp, please, and the silencer.'

Philipp momentarily looked confused, perhaps even wary. 'Why?'

Gillon chuckled. 'Silly boy. Everyone's baggage goes through a snooping machine when travelling by air. Anything metal shows up, even your wife's lovely diamanté hair thingummies.'

'Don't be so silly, darling,' Ivy chided her husband. 'Give clever Cousin Stephen your gun. He's perfectly safe to carry it in his suitcase as he'll be travelling in the train. You know perfectly well that you daren't try to smuggle it into France. Stephen will give you your toy back when we join him in the South of France, won't you, Stephen?'

'Of course I shall, dear Ivy. You know how I hate guns but I'm just carrying it for Philipp. So Philipp will be happy in his new home with all his favourite things.'

The connection was atrocious and Costelloe could only hear about one word in three. Conway's voice drifted in and out, heavily overladen with furious atmospheric crackling.

It gradually became clear that Pereira had missed the rendezvous with Conway and the *Caribbean Pearl*, deliberately and forever. Conway had stayed in Belém for as long as he could, discovered as much as he could, and would shortly be putting to sea, bound for Trinidad.

He had picked up information, all negative. He had elicited from the chatty manageress of Pereira's habitual hotel that Senhor Pereira hadn't been in Belém since February, when Captain Conway had himself last seen him. No other Belém hotel had been granted Pereira's custom and his launch hadn't been seen, either. Keeping to his line of concerned friend, Conway had contrived to elicit hard information from Pereira's bank manager. Captain Conway need have no fears for Senhor Pereira's health; the esteemed gentleman had written a letter of instruction, closing his account and authorising the transfer of funds to a place the bank manager could not bring himself to divulge, not even to the much-loved Senhor Pereira's dearest chum. Despite considerable fine-tuning of the old Irish charm, Conway couldn't squeeze out of the bank manager either the geographical origin of Pereira's letter of instruction, nor the destination of the transferred funds. It looked as if their supplier had fled the coop. He promised to ring from Port-of-Spain for further instructions.

As he put the phone down, Costelloe wished, for the first and no doubt only time in his life, that Nedda were on hand to cope. He didn't know what to do, not that there was anything he or Nedda or even Gillon could do with the *Caribbean Pearl* putting to sea minus the usual three to four hundredweight of cocaine.

He had no idea where Nedda had gone and Gillon was due in later. Costelloe would be leaving later to collect him at the railway station in Nice. He thought it might be prudent to have a chat with Philipp Altdorfer, just in case Nedda had rung there. He let the Basel number ring countless times before giving up. Costelloe brooded about the entire situation, wishing this day had never dawned.

He switched on the television and watched the end of *I Colby*, then tried the Altdorfers' number again but there was still no reply. He was unenthusiastically considering going to Nice a little early for a relaxing half-hour with Chantal or Soleil when he heard the flat door slam. Nedda shouted for him.

'Ah and here's yourself. Where . . .?'

She gave him a murderous look. 'I've been looking for people. My husband and son, to name but a few. They've both vanished into thin air. Make me a drink.'

'Gillon's coming tonight,' he said, thinking she would be greatly cheered by this unexpected good news.

'Oh Christ,' she said, putting her face in her hands.

'And Conway rang from Belém,' Costelloe swept on. 'There isn't any snow.'

23

When she heard Ruffo's voice her heart lurched and she felt the palms of her hands go slippery. In a moment, however, she realized it was not Ruffo himself but his answer-phone.

'Ruffo,' she began in what sounded to her own ears like a moronically high-pitched whine, 'it's Camilla Sayle speaking. Uh, I'm in, oh God where am I, oh yes, Marbella, of all places, but I'm leaving tomorrow for the South of France.'

Her tone became more brisk, business-like. 'You said that I would be welcome anytime at Monteavesa, I mean to photograph the place and the winery and the horses and everything,' she hastily added, thinking of the all-too-likely female companion, 'and I wondered if you might be there in a few days, say next weekend or the following week.'

She glanced at the date on her watch. It was Tuesday. If he were in Italy, she could spend Wednesday and Thursday photographing in Monte Carlo and then continue on from there.

'Uh, I won't give you my number here, as I'm about to leave. But I'll ring you when I get to the South of France. Bye bye,' she said, putting the phone down.

It had been Georgie's suggestion that she go on from the Costa del Sol to the South of France which, in addition to providing extremely fertile ground for a bumper crop of nouveau-riche, high-life grotesqueries, would have the advantage of "someone to play with, darling" in the person of Brook. Brook, George told her, had nothing much on his plate, having passed from the euphoria of progress in London to what might prove to be a dead-end in Nice. Brook would have to do, at least for the moment, Camilla thought.

She simply couldn't bear the thought of having to sit down to one more solitary dinner. Roving males had made it impossible for her to enjoy a peaceful drink in the bar, even when armed with a book on Moorish architecture. She wanted to be with people but not these people. She was feeling good, what with the change of scene and a few hours of painless exercise in the hotel pool, and she knew she looked good, a light tan giving her a healthy warm glow.

It seemed that Brook, George had assured her, not being overwhelmingly busy in Nice, would welcome her company as a much-needed change from the unending shop-talk of policemen working on a weak lead combined with guess-work. The trail had gone cold on whatever he was chasing with the French narcotics people.

Picking up the phone again, she dialled the number George had given her. Monsieur Moseley was not there but the policeman she had been put through to said he would take a message with pleasure.

She was surprised to feel a sharp pang of disappointment that Brook had been elsewhere. At least, she thought, he hadn't gone trailing back to London, which was some measure of comfort to her. She realized that what she was feeling was nothing more than stark loneliness, which was obscurely encouraging.

She had cut herself off from people for far too long, putting herself behind a thick wall, and now the wall was beginning to crack. Georgie had been right after all; getting away on her own had taught her an object lesson: there was no virtue in loneliness.

She tried to ring her mother in Bath but there was no reply.

'My *dear* Gillon!' Alexis laughed heartily, 'one sees that your years in America were not entirely spent demurely sipping Earl Grey.' He laughed again, this time from an attack of nerves: was he meant to know that Gillon had ever lived in America? Yes, it was all right. Gillon had once mentioned that he had developed a strong taste for

269

Mexican food, at least as it was prepared in America. 'When I'm offering you Stingers, I mean the splendid little hand-held, ground-to-air missile variety, not that very potent cocktail. I'm sure that their having the same name is not at all coincidental.' He laughed again and forced himself to relax.

Ruffo stood up and left the room, afraid that even the smallest noise, lighting a cigarette, picking up his glass, might betray the presence of another person to the ever-watchful Gillon. There was nothing to be gained by hanging nervously about, making Alexis nervous by contagion. What made both of them more nervous than anything else was the fact that Gillon was suddenly in Monte Carlo. Not only in Monte Carlo but in Nedda's flat.

Gillon's laughter was long and he sounded relaxed, comradely, at his folksiest. 'Sure and I'd wondered where you were keeping yourself, my friend. I was wondering whether you'd abandoned me at a time of great need for your unique services.'

'I got your message and I'm ringing you back now I've something concrete to offer you,' Alexis said reasonably.

Gillon's voice held no hint of menace. 'Stingers. Hmmm. We had some Russian SAM-7s, you know, thanks to our good friend in Tripoli, but they were disappointing.'

'The advantage of the American Stinger,' Alexis parried, as though anxious to clinch the deal then and there, 'is that your operator doesn't have to be behind the target aircraft's heat-source. He can fire at an oncoming target.'

Gillon chuckled appreciatively. 'Always the sales-pitch, Alexis. You arranged for the undrinkable Stingers in Geneva, did you?'

Alexis laughed briefly and said, 'Only once I'd managed to avoid your friends, Gillon. You know, I'm sure, to which of your friends I refer,' he teased. 'I've no doubt you tore strips off them for losing me but the man I've been dealing with is *very* cautious. He would have been most displeased if I had met him like a comet, trailing a plume of dirty ice in my wake, but let's get down to business,' Alexis said, to forestall further witticisms, his own or Gillon's. He was growing tired of so much relentless joviality. 'The only difficulty in arranging a demonstration of the Stinger's capabilities is where to do it.'

'And, basically, *how* to do it. We can't very well hang about Heathrow, potting away at passing airplanes, now can we?' Gillon found this idea highly entertaining, too. 'Well, it's a nice little weapon. And with such a good reputation. Perhaps it's premature to discuss price and delivery at this early stage but I shall certainly discuss the matter with my good friend across the Mediterranean.'

'I have no doubt he could supply you with the Russian version, Gillon,' Alexis suggested helpfully. He was well aware that Gillon wasn't entirely delighted with the Russian products supplied by his Libyan source.

Gillon abruptly changed the subject. 'I'm afraid that the dozen Uzis we bought from you as a trial sample are a write-off.'

'I test-fired one myself and I know they were mint. Am I to assume your people in England have had difficulties with the Uzis or with the police?' Alexis asked.

'Alas, the failure is due to the asinine bungling of my own people. They, ah, disposed of some bodies, dead bodies I mean, in close proximity to your excellent weapons so I'm afraid that, for all practical purposes, they are compromised. Perhaps recoverable at some future date but for the moment, I believe, not available.' He sighed, a man troubled by the short-comings of his inferiors. 'That cell has now been disbanded but any new cell in Britain will need new equipment. You have a substantial number more, I seem to recall your saying?'

'As many as you need.'

'The price was, if I remember correctly, five hundred dollars each.'

'What a good memory you do have, Gillon. You're very nearly right: it was five hundred pounds. Including the magazines, if you recall, and transport to Paris.'

'But, Alexis, surely for a bulk order? One naturally expects some small discount for sizeable numbers.'

271

'I'm entirely willing to negotiate the matter, Gillon, but the order would have to be a very large one for me to consider cutting the price.'

'You're a hard man to do business with, to be sure.' Gillon sounded melancholy but Alexis knew he was enjoying the game.

'As to getting some fresh stocks on the ground in England, I can supply you with anything from fragmentation grenades to rocket-launchers. Perhaps, Gillon, a shopping-list would do the trick. If you tell me what sort of operation you have in mind, I might be able to make a few helpful suggestions as to matériel. As to delivery, you have another "shipment" due in shortly, so we could work around that date and whatever means of transport Nedda and Ruffo have worked out. Obviously, I don't know how quickly you would need to establish your stock-piles but something can be arranged.'

Alexis sensed that something was severely out of kilter. He could think of no combination of factors cataclysmic enough to stampede Gillon into quitting a German-speaking country, where he blended chameleon-like into the background, for Nedda's high-profile base of operations in Monte Carlo.

When Gillon finally answered, Alexis thought he sounded a touch evasive. 'I'll think about what you've said and get back to you on it, if I may.'

'Fine. Do that, Gillon, any time that suits you.' He took heart from the fact that Gillon seemed slightly off-balance, unusual enough in itself. 'You're the customer, after all.'

'I take it you'll be around then? No more little trips?'

'Not unless you'd like me to meet you somewhere for another of our delightful chats.'

'By the bye, Alexis, you don't happen to have heard from Ruffo, have you? Just by any chance?'

'No.' He sounded amused. 'Nedda having trouble tracking him down?'

'Let's just say she's curious. He doesn't seem to be in any of his usual haunts.'

'Well,' Alexis said indulgently, as if he were speaking of a child known for his chronically wayward behaviour, 'you know how Ruffo is during the flat-racing season. If you don't, Nedda certainly knows. He could be anywhere, I imagine: Ireland, Kentucky, Paris. He'll pitch up in London again like the proverbial bad penny. I'd leave a message on his machine, if I were you,' he advised, dismissing the question of Ruffo's whereabouts as being of little importance.

'I'll do that. And I'll ring you back soon. In the meantime, thank you, old son.'

Thank God Koepfli spoke excellent English, George thought as he watched the various police specialists go about their allotted tasks in almost perfect silence. It was late at night and the flat was cold, as cold as the grave.

Mallinckrodt of the BKA was with him, his English even better than Koepfli's. Mallinckrodt had introduced him as "a friend from England", which left Koepfli free to draw his own conclusions. George had no legal or diplomatic right whatsoever to be here and doubted if the Belgian or Dutch police would have been as courteous as this taciturn Swiss from the Stadtpolizei.

Koepfli was issuing terse instructions in a low voice and a tall, bald, angular man nodded briefly and left. 'Truebner will be in charge of interviewing all taxi-drivers and persons of that nature,' Koepfli explained. 'Herr Metzler had no car. Not that is known. I neglected to thank you for faxing the man's likeness so quickly,' he said politely to Mallinckrodt.

Mallinckrodt looked uncomfortable, his hands shoved down deep into his jacket pockets, his collar turned up. He was cold, too, and had arrived coatless, like George. Koepfli spoke to a young man with ruddy cheeks who went around the flat shutting all the windows and switching on the electric heaters. The bodies had been removed to the Kantonsspital; the fingerprint man had finished dusting and there was no reason why the men remaining in the flat should be forced to freeze.

273

For the millionth time, George wished that a better photograph of Stephen Fahy were available. The computer wizards at Lisburn had sifted through the vast database in an effort to find a family connection, a school photograph, even a casual friend who might be willing to furnish some pointers for a composite likeness, never mind how incomplete, and had found nothing useful. There was still only the grainy image of a man in clerical subfusc lurking behind the Cardinal-Archbishop, courtesy of *The Boston Globe*, upon which Reardon had grudgingly offered some few improvements: very even teeth and a thinnish mouth, hairline slightly higher, eyes very pale, cheekbones sharp, pronounced. But the result was lifeless, the essence of the man, his energy and intellect, conspicuously lacking.

George whispered to Mallinckrodt who spoke on his behalf to Koepfli. 'It is possible,' Mallinckrodt said, going along with the official posture that George had no actual existence, 'that Herr Metzler had an Irish driving licence. The licence a forgery, with an Irish passport, not a forgery but a stolen blank appropriately filled in, to support it, as well as a legitimate, by which is meant un-forged or genuine, credit-card in the name of Gillon. Either Gillon Something or Something Gillon.' George whispered again. 'Also possible is Urquhart,' Mallinckrodt spelt it, 'Stephen Urquhart, or Fahy,' further spelling, 'Stephen Fahy. A perfectly genuine British passport in the latter case but it is not very likely that he would have used this.'

George whispered again to Mallinckrodt. 'A Libyan passport and other documentation are not out of the question.' Koepfli registered no surprise at this, a complete shot in the dark on George's part. After all, why not? Fahy had pale-blue eyes but brown contact lenses cured that. Put a dark-haired, brown-eyed man into an ill-cut, preferably shiny grey suit and no Immigration official in Western Europe would look twice. If the man were coming in, a searching look was altogether likely; going out, it was more a matter of good riddance.

Mallinckrodt winked at George and said to Koepfli, 'It is late, but if your responsibilities would permit, I would

274

like to offer you a glass of something at our hotel.' Koepfli had booked them two modest rooms at the Trois Rois, an expensive hostelry but only a few paces from Koepfli's office in the Petersgasse.

As the car turned left under a railway bridge and an elevated highway, Koepfli gestured up to the right. 'Your friends were evidently unwilling to leave German territory far behind them. The frontier is less than a mile up that road.' They could see a glow of sodium lights at the frontier post reflected back from low clouds. 'And our airport, as you saw, is in France.'

Koepfli looked resigned to the fact that Basel, in a corner of Switzerland with virtually unsealable frontiers, presented a strong lure for international drug cartels, financial fixers and assorted terrorists, at least for those with sufficient self-discipline to avoid breaking any Swiss laws. Only moments after it had been established that the two corpses in the Fasanenstrasse were possibly West German nationals, Mallinckrodt had been apprised of the double murder. Swiss memories of the Red Army Faction, the imbecilic agitprop posturings of Mao-quoting, Che-worshipping "students", had not faded with the convenient speed that had been exhibited by the police in the Low Countries.

The night-porter at the Trois Rois obliged with a bottle of Dézaley and the three men sat in the gloom of the lounge, frugally lit by a single lamp, bringing Willie Hibbert's economizing to George's tired mind. Koepfli outlined the facts of the case, perforce based almost entirely upon supposition at this early stage, a few helpful but inconclusive facts added by Mallinckrodt.

'We begin with last Thursday,' Koepfli said, taking a small sip of his wine, 'with the woman, Frau Kellner, notifying the management that Herr Doktor Metzler in the adjoining apartment would be vacating the place the following day. She specifically said that Herr Metzler would be leaving early, so that the maid could change the linen and ready the place for the next occupant. The manager thanked her and checked his accounts. The rent on both apartments had been pre-paid until the end of the month but Frau Kellner said that she understood that there was no refund for an early cancellation.' He checked his notebook. 'So far so good.'

'The woman?' Mallinckrodt asked.

'Dumpy, "floury" was the adjective used by the porter,' Koepfli answered with a slight smile. 'Fiery-red metallic hair, dyed, not a wig. You hadn't arrived when the bodies were taken to the Kantonsspital but you'll see tomorrow that she clearly wasn't the self-effacing type.'

He glanced at his notebook again. 'The manager says that she spoke good, grammatically-correct High German, not Schwyzerdütsch, but with a strong foreign accent. He declined to speculate on the sort of foreign accent. The man, presumed to be her husband, sounded like a Rhinelander, the manager thought, and looked to be several years younger. Apparently, she did all the shopping, the porter seeing the husband only occasionally and Metzler only once or twice. Metzler is very thin. The porter thought he might have Aids.' He glanced at the two foreigners, his eyes twinkling. 'We Swiss are deeply shocked by Aids and find it endlessly fascinating, in a smug sort of way.

'The maid, a Portuguese woman, duly gave Metzler's place a thorough cleaning on the Friday morning . . .'

'Fingerprints?' Mallinckrodt interrupted.

'Not a hope. We fingerprinted the maid for a match, of course, but in addition to her, the apartment was re-rented almost immediately.' He checked his notes again. 'On Sunday. To a blameless businessman, insurance, from Stockholm, here for only five days and not entirely pleased at being fingerprinted and rousted out of his flat while the forensics lads gave the place a thorough going-over.

'After doing Metzler's flat, the maid intended to do the Kellners' but there was a "do not disturb" sign on their door. She thought nothing of it until today, when the sign was still there.' His lips tightened. 'Unfortunately, she forgot, at first, that she hadn't done the apartment on the Friday. It wasn't until she was changing to leave for the day and checking her work-sheet to hand into the building manager that she noticed that apartment number six had a cross beside it, which means that the flat wasn't done on a particular day at the tenant's request. The flats are normally only cleaned on Tuesdays and Fridays, you see.'

'Didn't she have a pass-key, like hotel chambermaids?' George asked.

'No. The manager has that. So . . . a good-sized pistol was used. Possibly a .38. Both victims shot from behind at point-blank range below lower occiput.' Koepfli put his notebook down on the table and reached for the wine resting in its bucket. 'More detail on that tomorrow morning,' he said, pouring into the three glasses after carefully wrapping the bottle in its napkin. It looked like a bandage, George thought, as he lit a cigarette and blew a plume of smoke up towards the lamplight on the ceiling.

'How do you see it?' Mallinckrodt asked.

'An extremely cool and competent job,' Koepfli said with admiration. 'Carefully planned, virtually every factor taken into account. The owner of the shop where Kellner bought the champagne on Friday morning said that the gentleman told him there was a small celebration for a friend who was leaving.' He sat back in his chair and steepled his fingers. 'What we might assume is that the killer sent Kellner out on this small errand, giving him a clear field to shoot the wife, then the husband upon his return. He then coolly goes about switching off the radiators, opening all the windows and taking with him all the Kellners' papers, not forgetting the computer discs. He leaves the building by the service door and, this is my own guess, goes to one of the two railway stations to collect his other baggage from the *consigne*.' He shrugged. 'It sounds simple enough put as a series of actions but it all requires an amazing degree of self-control and calculation of risks.'

He turned to George. 'Herr Lacey, does all of this accord with your man?'

'Without any doubt,' George said firmly. 'This case entirely conforms to pattern: nothing left to chance, no untidy loose ends left lying about. Above all,' he summarized, 'no hard evidence to support any sort of case against him. Even in the unlikely event that your people were to find his fingerprints in the murder flat, it gives you no case. The "Kellners" or, to give them their true name, the Altdorfers were openly associated with the reclusive Herr Metzler, Stephen Fahy to give him his real name.' He puffed on his cigarette and then irritably stubbed it out. 'Your Medical Examiner won't be able to produce more than an approximate time of death.'

Koepfli nodded gloomily. 'I rather thought the killer had deliberately turned the heating off and opened all the windows to keep the temperature in the flat as low as possible. Warmer weather is expected tomorrow and the smell would have alerted . . .'

'Quite,' George said. In his particular line of work, he was less hardened to the physical realities of death than the two policemen. They exchanged an amused look and grinned at him.

'The reason,' George continued, acknowledging his squeamishness with an apologetic smile, 'that we are here is that for the first time there's a relatively fresh trail to follow.'

'My department,' Mallinckrodt took up, 'is concerned with the possibility that Fahy has doubled back into Germany, minus his appendages, the Altdorfers. They are the ones who handled all the day-to-day arrangements when this charming little *ménage* lived at Bad Homburg.'

'How did you trace them there?' Koepfli asked curiously.

'Through the banks,' Mallinckrodt answered promptly, 'after a good deal of searching.' He laughed at Koepfli's slight frown. 'Ours in the Federal Republic are rather more, what's the word, "helpful", I suppose, than yours. With terrorists, there is always the balance-sheet. Terrorism is a capital-intensive business. Frankfurt is our New York and many of the people in my department are accountants, after the useful example of the FBI in America.' He laughed again. 'People tend to forget that Al Capone was eventually trapped by unexciting, pedestrian tax-evasion, not a glamorous shoot-out in Chicago's mean streets.'

Koepfli looked dubious. 'I shouldn't think this man, Fahy, would want to be in Germany in this case, especially now he's without these people he employed, presumably as cut-outs. And why bring his minions here to kill them?' he asked with an understandable hint of peevishness.

'It is unfortunate but true,' Mallinckrodt countered, 'that the Federal Republic is an extremely fertile recruiting-ground for mercenaries.' His expression registered some of the disgust policemen feel towards politicians. 'We have many "refugees" of various nationalities, including the Middle East, and some of the Red Army Faction are now trickling out of our prisons, deemed to have spent sufficient time to atone for their crimes and become model citizens.'

'And you believe him to be raising a mercenary army?' Koepfli asked, intrigued.

'So we believe,' Mallinckrodt said with a nod to George.

'We think that Fahy simply hadn't enough time to get rid of the Altdorfers until they all arrived here. We have in custody the leader of a cell Fahy had established in England, a noisome character and skilled bomb-maker called Desmond Reardon. Once Reardon disappeared, Fahy would know that it wasn't going to take forever for the BKA to get on his trail.' He smiled at Mallinckrodt. 'Klemens is not known for cherishing compassionate, understanding attitudes towards men with machine-guns and electronic timers.

'As to Fahy's reasons for killing the Altdorfers, well, to him it would seem a childishly simple logical imperative. They were no longer necessary to deal with day-to-day matters; they were not entirely unknown to the police; therefore it was expedient that they be removed from the scene. He ordered the execution of an IRA man and two Japanese mercenaries in his employ in England for the same simple reason: just as a precaution. As a planner, he is a formidable adversary, a fact that you, Herr Koepfli, recognized straight away. The Easter Monday killings on the Continent are ample proof of that.' He laughed briefly.

279

'The misfiring of the attack on our Athens Embassy is, we think, due to a laughably simple error. If the men he hired to do the job there were Greeks, as seems probable, their Easter is later than ours and they would not therefore know that the date assigned was our Easter Monday, a holiday, and that the Embassy would be shut.'

Koepfli was sitting on the edge of his chair, completely rapt, nodding from time to time. 'Your Mr Fahy employs specialists, then, to do the chores. Specialists, my friend, do not, what is the expression, fall out of trees.'

'My Mr Fahy is supplied with an enormous amount of money,' George explained, 'and there would be no financial impediment to his raising and equipping hundreds of mercenaries if he so chooses. Fahy's millions are derived from the cocaine trade, a nice little earner for him. Thirty, possibly even forty million. A year. Pounds, that is. A man with that sort of financial muscle is extremely difficult to stop dead in his tracks.'

'So.' Koepfli, who had been about to make his good-nights, relaxed back into the deep armchair. 'Drugs. Profitable but somewhat risky for someone as careful as Fahy.'

'The cocaine is handled by a separate organization, headed by an American woman called Edwina Madden, known as Nedda. We assume that she is the paymaster, in overall charge of laundering the cocaine money and keeping the operational groups topped up with cash. I must ring the office tomorrow to see if anything's come in about her, if you'll be good enough to remind me, Klemens. The profits are, as you say, Herr Koepfli, immense but the risks, in this particular instance, less so. All we know so far is that Nedda is probably based in France. Her hall-mark is low volume – by low I mean as compared to the Mafia – and excellent quality. Perfectly sound economic practice: find the hole in the market and fill it.

'Our only lead so far was an African, Senegalese, actually, who was a part-time dealer in a very modest way and full-time male prostitute in Villefranche. Alas, he has recently succumbed to his own addiction and died of a lethal cocktail of heroin and cocaine. He died in his own flat, while the French police had him under surveillance. They're still hoping to track down his contacts but,' he shrugged, 'you gentlemen know better than I how it goes in police work.'

'Bad luck,' Mallinckrodt murmured. 'With prostitutes, the contacts tend to be painfully shy about giving information.'

'Sometimes, Herr Lacey,' Koepfli said solemnly, 'you must trust in fate or even God, if you're so inclined, to put matters right.' He got tiredly to his feet and shook hands all round. 'Good night, gentlemen, and sleep well. The sleep of the just,' he added, with a slight smile.

24

Ruffo was deeply frightened, now the commitment had been made. He was ashamed to admit it to Alexis, who showed no sign whatsoever of nerves. Indeed, having made the plans and set everything in motion, Alexis gave every appearance of enjoying himself thoroughly. Perhaps, Ruffo reasoned, it was because Alexis had more to do, more to keep his mind off the unpalatable but inescapable possibility that they could easily all be dead by Sunday evening. Ruffo felt useless. Worse, he had nothing to occupy him except multiplying at an exponential rate the rich variety of things that could so easily go wrong.

He made a third circuit of Charlotte's delightful terraced garden and perched on the edge of a bench, gazing moodily at the lake. The lights of Porto Ceresio on the Italian side of the water were beginning to wink on and the soft May breeze carried the sounds of people enjoying the *passegiata* in the lovely arcaded streets of Morcote, just below the outer wall of the Leysins' terraced garden. He felt profoundly melancholy and rummaged for a cigarette, then made a determined effort to shrug off his listlessness and marched briskly into the house, bracing himself for the call he had to make to Gillon.

Jacki and Alexis looked up as he came through the French windows into the dining-room. The table was almost entirely covered with maps and they were making lists. Of what, Ruffo didn't know. He was just a subaltern now, following Alexis' terse orders, otherwise keeping out from underfoot. Ruffo found the parade-ground atmosphere oddly comforting, responsibility in all but small matters lifted from his shoulders and entrusted to experts.

Alexis looked at his watch. 'Better get it over with now,' he said. 'Then we can all relax and have a drink. Jacki and I think we have lift-off,' he added with a grin.

Gillon's welcoming voice came on the line right away. 'Is it you, my dear Ruffo?' he asked. 'We've been so worried about you. You got my message, I see. Are you back in London then?'

'No,' Ruffo answered evasively, 'not yet.' There was no way of knowing if Gillon's spy was back on duty in South Eaton Place.

'How did you know to ring me here then?'

'I have one of those remote-control thingummies that plays the message tape. You left Nedda's number,' he reminded Gillon, 'saying to ring you at any time of night or day. I quote.'

Gillon's rich, deep laugh made Ruffo angry. Alexis made a fingers-spread, palms-down gesture, enjoining calm. 'And so I did, young Ruffo, so I did now. Where have you been on your travels?' he asked chattily. 'It's your lovely wife who was wanting to know.'

'I've been hiding my son from my lovely wife,' Ruffo answered, keeping his voice neutral.

There was a slight pause. 'So we gathered.' Gillon's voice was tight, angry. Ruffo was intrigued, despite his fear. It was heartening to know that Gillon was capable of ordinary human emotions and weaknesses.

'Look, little princeling,' Gillon swept on contemptuously, rage gathering within him, 'I know you think you're such a clever little boots, taking that boy of yours away from Eton. You thought that would make you safe from Nedda, didn't you? *Didn't you?*'

'I thought it was certainly a step in the right direction,' Ruffo said calmly, rather surprised by his own sang-froid. Anger was there, deep inside him, but it was containable, working for him.

Gillon's laugh was harsh. 'You thought wrong. You miscalculated, boyo. Now I know you're an untrustworthy bloody traitor! We have more than one string to our bow. Bowstrings are for strangling as well as shooting. Keep that in what passes for your uniquely juvenile mind. Everything at Monteavesa is open to us, my dear Ruffo: your parents, Manfredi, his charming wife, his winsome children, the horses . . .' He laughed again. 'But I needn't go on about that, I'm sure. You do catch my drift, don't you? *Answer me!*'

'Yes. I do.'

'Good. Very good.' Gillon's voice reverted to its usual blandishing tone. 'Alexis has very kindly arranged to demonstrate some unusual new items he has for sale. This coming Sunday. In Switzerland. Do you suppose you might be able to fit that into your dizzying round of social engagements?'

'I think I might manage it. An invitation it would be unwise to refuse, I take it,' Ruffo answered blandly.

'Yes. I'm glad, very glad you can make time to join us.'

'I imagine you'd like me to arrange something to do with Captain Kerrien?' There was a silence. 'Our Breton trawler-captain, if you remember. For the incoming "shipment" from Brazil and getting Alexis' things into England.'

'Leave all of that to me, Ruffo. Alexis will give you all the details on where we're to meet. Here is his telephone number.' He reeled off the Zürich number of Alexis' office. 'Got that?' Ruffo stolidly repeated it back to him. 'Good, good. But before I ring off, Ruffo dear, I would like to hint gently to you that it would be very silly to bring along any unexpected, ah, friends or associates of your own. It would be taken by me as an insult, a very unfriendly gesture, and it would be terrible for poor little Guido to be an orphan at his tender age.'

'Does Nedda know you intend to kill her, Father Fahy?' Ruffo asked, keeping his tone entirely conversational.

The phone clicked. Ruffo didn't know if the reverend father had heard his question or not.

'Blast the bloody man!' Goudhurst ran his fingers through his thin, grey-blond hair.

'I imagine, Dickie, he's trying to track the girl down.' Sir Maurice was unruffled. He'd worked with George for so long he knew they would hear from him the moment he had anything to say. 'George will try to locate Mrs Hamilton and find out from her what, if anything, she knows about

Prince Monteavesa's current whereabouts. Considering her relationship with the prince, I think it might be tactless to ask her about the man's wife.'

Goudhurst's shoulders slumped. 'Sorry, Maurice. I'm only being vile-tempered. It's all futile in any event. Everything we know about him – and he's a man who leads an extremely, even excessively, public life – confirms that he's been separated from the ineffable Nedda for at least six years. No divorce but firmly separated. They are never seen together and he makes no effort to conceal his, ah, romantic attachments.'

'Presumably both RCs. Papal annulments cost the earth in greased Curial palms and take time. Years. No point to it, really, unless you intend to remarry. Nedda's clearly a career girl. As to the prince, he has a son to inherit everything in the fullness of time, money, position, lovely ladies *en masse*.'

'Lovely ladies, singly or *en masse*, cannot be passed on from father to son under the current laws of inheritance,' Goudhurst observed testily.

They stopped before an immense fountain, transfixed by its colossal blue-tiled ugliness. Camilla snapped away as Brook stood by, avidly studying the architectural havoc surrounding them, the result of the House of Grimaldi's fathomless greed, or so he had been assured by Commissaire Lombroso. Monte Carlo's charmingly rococo buildings, sun-bleached pinks with sinuous ironwork and Beaux-Arts balconies, had been ruthlessly extirpated to make way for office- and apartment-buildings resembling concrete-and-glass chests of drawers with all their drawers inexplicably left open.

'Got enough?' Brook asked.

'Sure.' She put her arm through his, pleased that he had taken the trouble to pump his French policeman friend for useful tips. 'Now, then, you were telling me how you came to be a nark.'

'It's not very noble.'

'Go on, Brook,' she urged him, lightly pinching his arm.

'When I got out of college, Yale, I really didn't know what I wanted to do so I spent a year in Geneva, at the Institute for Advanced International Studies . . .'

'My God, that sounds impressive!'

Brook grinned. Camilla noticed that his normally very regular features became charmingly crooked when he smiled. In his khaki cotton jacket and pale-blue Brooks Brothers button-down shirt, he looked exactly the part he'd originally assigned himself: a professor in a small New England college. It was his true profession that seemed outrageous, scarcely credible.

'I'm glad you're impressed because I worked my ass off there. Economics and politics. I even impressed myself but I still didn't know what I wanted to do so I went back to Yale. They gave me a job as a dean, a baby dean, and I farted around for another couple of years with some more graduate courses, getting more and more interested in Latin America. The CIA came sniffing around – they've always had a soft spot for Yalies – and I was sort of interested but then the DEA kind of interested me more.'

'What you're doing then, I mean your side of things, is to follow the slime trails that the drug barons leave behind them?' she asked, genuinely intrigued.

'Exactly. The biggest, fattest slugs don't dirty their own hands, to mix metaphors, but they leave a money trail behind them. After all, they're in it to lead the good life as far away as they can get from the source of their wealth. And we're talking big bucks, as you know. Now there's legislation in place to seize all their assets, too, and that includes yachts and houses and whatever turns them on.' He laughed briefly. 'It wouldn't surprise me at all if a fair proportion of the people you saw living high on the hog around Marbella had some connection or other with drug trafficking. Even here.' He flapped his hand towards the line of monstrous apartment-buildings lining the sea-front, a faithful, line-for-line replica of Miami Beach.

She laughed. 'But, at the risk of prying, Brook, when do you have time for your own life?'

286

'I haven't really got much of one, to tell you the truth. My wife left me for a guy who works at Treasury. They have a baby now. He even goes home for lunch. What she minded more than anything is that I didn't mind when she left.'

'Didn't you really?'

'No, really not.' Camilla could see that he was being honest. 'She sulked a lot but I decided not to notice. I guess that was wrong of me – staging some sort of showdown is considered healthier – but I knew something would happen sooner or later and I'm a patient man.' He looked at her intently and smiled. 'Maybe I'm even too patient but you really have to be in my job.'

Her eyes held his and she smiled but said nothing. 'What's next on our agenda?'

'Peach champagne. A regional specialty. I thought we'd spend an instructive half-hour or so people-watching on the terrace at the Café de Paris, next-door to the Casino. My new best friend in Nice, Antoine Lombroso, says we've got to have an experimental guzzle.' He laughed. 'Commissaire Lombroso of the Nice Police.' He hissed like a snake on the sentence. 'He of the ill-fitting false teeth. Commissaire Lombroso, or Hissssing Ssssid.'

'How's it going?'

He made a slightly-fed-up face at her as they ambled uphill towards the Casino. 'It's police work, Camilla. And police work is slow. We've got a lead through the dead Senegalese I mentioned to you on a guy here in Monaco but right now that's a matter of softly softly catchee monkey. Patience, you remember? The guy works just down there in the Condamine. He runs a restaurant owned by some bizarre Belgian woman. But he's a Monégasque and, although you may have leave to doubt my word on the matter by looking around here, Monaco is a police state. The only equivalent I know of in the Western World is Beverly Hills.'

'How do you mean?'

'The cops here don't like outside cops muddying their waters. Lombroso says they're very prickly about their own territory. All Lombroso can do is inform the cops here, in the spirit of professional courtesy, that a Monaco citizen is mixed up in some pretty minor drug deals. Then, all he can do is sit back and hope that the Monaco police return the favour. They do things their own way here and their own way doesn't include any effete notions of firm evidence or proof. You could die of old age waiting for the Monaco police to read you your rights. They don't like the looks of you and next thing you know you're hustled into a police car and whisked out of the Principality to be as nasty as you like on someone else's patch.'

'Did your Nice policeman drop them a hint about possible terrorist connections?'

Brook shrugged. 'So far as we know, this Renato has kept his nose clean, so Lombroso has nothing concrete to lay before the local cops. All he can do is to sit back and wait for Renato to set a foot wrong on French soil before he can take him in for a little questioning. Even then, he can't let the questioning get too, how shall I phrase it, "insistent". All he can do is shake the guy up a little and try to keep him under discreet surveillance so that the Monaco fuzz don't get on a high horse.'

Camilla shook her head. 'Georgie gave me the outline of this operation, Brook, but without meaning to pry, I wonder if you could explain one or two things to me that just don't make any sense. At least, not to me. Perhaps I'm being obtuse.'

'Fire away,' he said with a grin. 'You've got a right to know pretty much everything, so far as I can see, considering what you've been through.'

'Well, the IRA leader, this Gillon that controls the European operations. What I don't understand is what he aims to achieve with all of the killing and bombing. I mean, if he could intimidate and murder his way into being, if not Prime Minister of Ireland, then the power behind the throne, all his sins would come home to roost. I'm not saying immediately but someone, sometime would be bound to spill the beans and stand up in the Dail or on television and say "this man is an Uncle Joe Stalin clone".

He's a killer, Brook!' She gnawed at her lip, her head bent, her dark-blonde hair hiding her face.

'That sounds stupid, I know.' To her astonishment, she realized she was in a rage. Her hands were shaking and she shoved them into the pockets of her skirt. Brook took her elbow and steered her to a front-row table where they had an unobstructed view of the comings and goings at the Casino and, across the Esplanade, the Hôtel de Paris. Several people were looking at Camilla with interest but she noticed nothing.

Brook reached across the table and took her hand in his own. 'As they'd say in California, Camilla, I know where you're coming from and I really relate to what you're saying. I respect your commitment.' She giggled nervously and removed her hand from his, fumbling for a cigarette as a pretext. A waiter stood superciliously by as Brook took his time with the wine list and finally ordered a half-bottle of Lombroso's favourite tipple.

He waited until they'd been served before he answered her unasked question. 'There are two factors that you may not have thought about. The first is the dry-as-dust economic one. Apart from Greece, Ireland is the second poorest country in the Common Market. The country's in desperate financial shape and that makes voters do a lot of clutching at straws.

'But the second factor is the purely political one you raise.' He squeezed her hand. 'Camilla, think: the current Prime Minister of Israel . . .' He popped a fistful of peanuts into his mouth, chewed, swallowed. 'He has been freely elected as Prime Minister and he makes absolutely no bones about having been in the Stern Gang and cheerfully murdering the maximum possible number of British diplomats or soldiers all in the name of liberty. Maybe with equality and fraternity thrown in, for all I know. Not a squeak of protest, so far as I'm aware.'

She sat back in her chair and smiled. 'It's the old formula, isn't it? I am a patriot; you are conducting a television interview; he is a terrorist.'

'Got it,' Brook said with a slight smile. 'Not just the Israeli Prime Minister, either, but a fair number of his Cabinet are up to their elbows in blood. And the patriot, being interviewed, will unblushingly speak of the stone-throwers as "terrorists". High moral tone and everything. I am a freedom-fighter, he is a terrorist, just as you said. That's despite the fact that the Israelis are considerably more hard-headed, less romantic, if you will, than the Irish. Yet they elect a terrorist, and the current incumbent is hardly the first terrorist they've elected. And don't forget Arafat. People listen to him with respect, even deference. Politics, my dear. South African black leaders are on the record as approving of the most gruesome murders of their fellow-blacks, all in the name of unity. Unity in the sense that whoever disagrees must be killed. That doesn't make any sense, either, and no one says anything.

'As to Father Fahy, our Jesuit friend who calls himself Gillon, why should he see things any other way? He's far too smart to have ignored the political lessons of the Middle East. God knows, terrorism's been amply proven to work. Once you're in power, all you have to do is plead that the other guy wasn't kosher. And there's that inevitable coda about the end justifying the means.' He took a sip of champagne and said, 'Oh, that *is* good!'

Camilla smiled. She stubbed out her cigarette and tilted her head back, her eyes shut, enjoying the gentle touch of the late-afternoon sun on her skin. 'Okay, so much for explaining Ireland's answer to Lenin. Now, what about the deeply mysterious Nedda?'

'Ah. Progress has been made there. Well, a little forward movement, but not much. At least we've got a name for her now.'

'That is good news. Now you'll be able to bring her to book, at least.'

'Well, let's not count our chickens, Camilla,' he said, knocking the wooden table. 'Such a resplendent name, too, redolent of the Almanach de Gotha and rolling trippingly off the tongue. She's the Principessa Cavallesi di Monteavesa.'

25

Connolly gave the taxi-driver the address, carefully written down on a scrap of paper in phonetic French, and fumed as they made their slow way around the Place du Casino, filled with coaches that had disgorged trippers for an evening out.

Connolly hated Monaco. He couldn't understand why Gillon was here, nor why he had ordered him to come here. So far, nothing had been given him to do and he had asked to have the afternoon off, simply to stretch his legs and get out of Nedda's horrible flat. The atmosphere in there was dreadful and Connolly wasn't accustomed to being cooped up all the day long. And certainly not accustomed to being cooped up with three people who, in varying degrees, absolutely loathed one another, without any attempt to disguise the fact.

The concierge looked at him disapprovingly but he was in too much of a hurry to give a damn. He stabbed several times at the lift-button and the wretched thing finally opened its doors, disclosing a clutch of chattering, lavender-rinsed females with Midlands accents and clearly in no great hurry to vacate the lift. The automatic doors kept trying to shut themselves as the biddies gave little shrieks of mock alarm, plainly feeling no strong urge to decide the matter by moving.

'I shall hold the doors open if you ladies would leave,' Connolly volunteered, to looks of indignation from the ladies at such unseemly haste.

He let himself into the flat with the key Costelloe had grudgingly given him for his afternoon's dereliction of duty. 'You're back early, Patrick,' he remarked, as Connolly shot breathlessly into the flat. Costelloe quickly reached for the television's remote-control and the snooker quarter-finals beamed from Reading played on in perfect silence.

'Where's Gillon?' Costelloe demanded.

'He and Nedda have gone out to have a drink and an early dinner. They have important matters to discuss,' Costelloe said, 'in private.' He stared rudely at Connolly's bald, saddle-shaped dome, heavily beaded with sweat. 'What business is it of yours anyway where they are?' Costelloe didn't like him. Connolly was a useless turd, chronically underfoot and underemployed, capable of nothing more important than skulking about, spying and eavesdropping on Nedda's equally useless, blood-sucking, capitalist lackey of a husband.

'Where've they gone to?'

'They didn't take me into their confidence,' Costelloe said with ponderous irony.

Connolly hated him equally, but he was bursting with the need to tell someone his shattering piece of news. 'I've seen that bloody girl!' he blurted out.

'And what girl might that be?' Costelloe remained unimpressed with the importance of Connolly's news, but vaguely curious as to why anyone would wish to tell Gillon about a girl. Any girl.

'Nothing to do with you,' Connolly said with tit-for-tat contempt. 'The one who photographed everybody in the fockin' Alps if you must know,' he said, reconsidering. 'The one who's walking out with his bloody highness. The one whose flat I turned over looking for the missing fockin' film. The one whose flat Eamonn Cahill turned over looking for the missing fockin' snow, you stupid git! The one who's a copper, whose husband his bloody highness done in under the fockin' Prince of Wales's fockin' eyes. That's who.'

'And what about her?'

'She's here in Monte Carlo. That's what, you arse-licking moron! And she's brought her camera, too, to photograph your ugly mug.'

292

'I feel such a socking great fool!' George said furiously. 'A man of my advanced years – perhaps that's the problem, Maurice – but for someone with my experience not to have twigged is ludicrous.'

'Do shut up, Georgie,' Lyall said. 'You're hardly the first man whose head's been turned by a pretty face.'

George snorted rudely. 'I'm the one who waffles on about my intense suspicion of coincidences, yet I failed to spot a glaring one. When Monteavesa walked into that restaurant, he'd followed me there. I already knew Camilla's hotel room had been given a cursory search. I'd seen him the previous evening, dining in our hotel and giving Camilla the glad eye. I was delighted when he followed up on our luncheon and rang me in London. I not only introduced him to Camilla but made her rush about buying new clothes. I came as close as dammit to tucking them up in bed together!'

'My dear fellow, at that point you thought it was nothing more than demon sex, his interest in Camilla. My friend, it was you who spotted something amiss with those skiers. If it weren't for you, we'd have no line on these people at all. So kindly cease and desist with beating your scrawny old breast and let's get down to cases.'

They went the first few miles in almost complete silence, Alexis merely giving Ruffo basic directions to negotiate around Lugano, its airport, its suburbs and eventually out into open country. The road would take them into the Autostrada that went to Milan.

They had been in the midst of an acrimonious conversation when the telephone rang. Alexis had then chattered away endlessly and Ruffo had removed himself from earshot once he realized that it must be Charlotte, ringing from Göteborg. Some time later, Alexis had found him mooching about the garden and marched him wordlessly up to the garage, handing over the car-keys and strapping himself into the passenger seat.

Alexis said, 'Listen, Ruffo, I'm not saying that there's any iron-clad certainty that we'll get out of this alive. We know that Gillon will bring along plenty of support. I'm guessing at how his men will be deployed. I have no idea how they'll be equipped. The Libyans have even gone into making mustard gas recently, for God's sake. Gillon might have a dainty little tactical nuke to throw at us. But I'm betting that he'll have a few riflemen, an automatic or two and a few side-arms. He's not sure what *we* have.'

'Not much is what we have.'

'Nonetheless,' Alexis swept on imperturbably, 'I think we stand a good chance.'

'How good a chance?'

'Around fifty-fifty.'

'Swell. I'm not a betting man, it may surprise you to know, but it doesn't sound very encouraging.' Ruffo glanced at his speed and eased up on the accelerator.

'Here's the way Jacki and I see it: Gillon, Nedda and maybe two or three "soldiers" will openly present themselves for this Stinger demonstration.'

'Which you don't happen to have in your possession. If you did happen to have one, our troubles would be over. We could loose off a round, or whatever the wretched thing looses off, and blow up Nedda's goddamned armoured car.'

'Oh, I don't know. I think we stand a better chance with our own little gadget. If it works, that is,' he added cheerfully, 'or if Jacki doesn't get blown up with the damned thing in his car as he bumps along to his house. However, that's in the lap of the gods. Our problem is a straightforward one: escape. They're bound to have two cars, more likely three, so even if we had an anti-tank gun, we'd still have cars two and three to worry about. This isn't a comic-strip or Rambo silliness, so pay attention.

'It looks certain that Gillon has hired Bienenstein and Skryanz – someone's hired them because neither is virtuously at home with the wife and kiddies – and they're both crack shots. They'll be posted in the trees with their telescopic sights on our backs. Therefore, Jacki's people will have to be posted around the clearing, where my wonderful demonstration is meant to take place, to neutralize the Austrians.

'What we have to work on is surprise. In order to surprise we have to think as Gillon thinks. He will have made his dispositions by studying the maps, just as we did. He will know that the only road in is, obviously, the only road out. What we've got to assume is that it won't have occurred to him that we can continue on up, up and over the pass. But we've got to move very fast.'

'Don't lose sight of what you told me, Alexis. Something to the effect that a battle-plan is no good once the first shot's been fired. I sincerely hope you're not counting on your Austrian friends laying down their elephant-guns when they see it's wonderful good-old-buddy you they've got in the cross-hairs.'

'Your grandmother and my eggs,' Alexis said rudely. 'Bienenstein and Skryanz aren't likely to have been told who the targets are. That's One. Two is that I'm not paying them. Shit, Ruffo, what do you think the definition of mercenary is?' he asked impatiently. 'Gillon will base everything on having us surrounded, therefore we base everything on not being surrounded.' He threw up his hands. 'The entire point of the exercise is that we've chosen the ground and Gillon's agreed.'

'How did you sell that? I meant to ask you but I forgot, what with one thing and another.'

'Oh,' Alexis said airily, 'I told Gillon that I had a good rapid-fire light machine-pistol I wanted to try out for him. Czech manufacture. So he said that we couldn't very well blast away at targets on a peaceful Sunday afternoon and I said for goodness' sake that's all you hear on a peaceful Sunday afternoon in Switzerland. Shooting practice, weapons training, all scrupulously entered in every Swiss soldier's pay book, is compulsory. And every Swiss soldier includes the entire male population of the country up to the age of fifty. We Swiss take national service seriously.'

'And he went for it? He actually believed you?'

'Course he did. It's true, Ruffo. We all blast away like mad, having a fine old time. That's why I'll be wearing my own Landsturm kit and Jacki's getting a Landwehr uniform for you.'

'Now that we're practically at Malpensa, do you suppose you might trust me with the identity of the person or persons we are collecting there?' He flung the fistful of coins Alexis handed him into the basket and waited for the light to turn green.

'Barbara.'

'*What?*'

'You heard me. Barbara. I thought it best to avoid mentioning her until we had come to a halt.'

'Oh, Jesus, Alexis, how on earth . . .' He clashed the gears furiously.

'Maintain calm, I beg you. Entirely her own idea, *mon vieux*. The vocabulary that woman has! I simply can't wait to meet her. I did try to talk her out of it,' he said reasonably, 'but she threatened to go to the police. Said she didn't trust you not to get yourself killed which meant that she would be stuck with the problem of hiding Guido until he reached his majority so that Nedda couldn't get her hands on him and that she didn't at all fancy the idea of moving to Mexico or Rarotonga.

'What exactly is Barbara meaning to do?' Ruffo's voice was tight with fury.

'Follow my orders,' Alexis said modestly. 'She is replacing your father. She said that your father's age, blood-pressure and heart did not make him the best possible choice for cavorting about over high Alpine passes. Your sainted mother has, it appears, told her everything, the "everything" pregnant with meaning, to coin a phrase. All she'll be doing is to hold your horses. Hold your horses, geddit?'

'Ha ha.'

'I am merely passing along what she said to me. I really don't see that we have any choice in the matter, to tell you the truth.'

'How do I explain it to Nicky if she gets killed?'

'She said that she'd already taken care of that. Keep a look-out for SAS. She's on the flight from Copenhagen. I cannot tell you how much I hate this airport.'

26

Camilla's long walk around the aquarium up on the Rocher had made her feel a good deal calmer, her emotions pacified by watching the aimless circling of vivid fish.

She had left Brook looking hurt and bewildered, promising to dine with him, promising that she would explain everything. She wanted to talk to Georgie before saying anything to Brook about Ruffo, about her brief but intense involvement with Ruffo. Georgie would never have introduced Ruffo to her if he had had the least suspicion that Ruffo's wife or ex-wife, whose very existence they had only recently speculated about over tea and ginger biscuits in Georgie's kitchen, was connected with this horrible business.

The prospect of discussing everything with Georgie made her walk faster as she got to her hotel. She pushed her way through the revolving door feeling almost light-hearted.

'I'm expecting a friend at around seven,' she told the smiling Italian concierge. 'Could you please ask him to come straight up to my room,' she said, 'and have some ice sent up to my room then.' She remembered that the Michelin was partial to a restaurant that was practically on the hotel's doorstep. 'Would you also be good enough to book a table for two at the Saint-Benoît for eight o'clock?'

'On the terrace?'

'Yes, if at all possible.'

'With pleasure, Madame Hamilton,' the man said, writing. He handed over Camilla's room-key and said, 'Oh. There's a gentleman waiting to see you, Madame Hamilton. An English gentleman.' He gestured.

Camilla turned and saw a slightly stooped man, thick, dark hair and a face of startling pallor, getting up out of an armchair in the small lobby, at this hour filled with elderly tax-exiles drinking late tea or early gins. The man carefully folded a newspaper and stashed it in the pocket of his mac. His eyes were fixed intently on her and she had no idea who he might be.

'Mrs Hamilton?' he asked, advancing, his overlarge black coat swirling about his slight form. There was something vaguely donnish about him, she thought, although the impression could have been due to the black folds calling to mind an academic gown. She noticed a scattering of cigarette-ash across his chest, at which he brushed absent-mindedly.

'I'm Camilla Hamilton,' she said, leaning on her Christian name. Hamilton was a common enough surname and the hotel, its clientele more residential than transient, was as solidly British as if it were on the front at Brighton.

He bowed stiffly. 'My name is David Gwyn-Evans, Mrs Hamilton.' His speech was precise, reinforcing the donnishness, but without any Welsh lilt.

'Have we met, Mr Gwyn-Evans?'

'Only very briefly, I regret to say. At Major Hamilton's funeral, but I'm sure you won't, ah.'

'No, I'm afraid . . .' She was embarrassed, looked away.

'I thought I recognized you earlier this afternoon, crossing the road,' he said hastily, 'and I took the liberty of inquiring to see if you might be stopping here. The thing is, Mrs Hamilton, my conscience has been pricking me ever since, ever since . . . Well, it's to do with Jeremy's, ah, to do with that ghastly business and I was rather thinking that better late than never, don't you know. I've allowed almost a year to pass, you see.' He looked with apprehension around the well-populated room. 'Oh dear. This is rather awkward. Do you suppose we might speak privately? In your room, perhaps? I can assure you that I wouldn't dream of taking up more than five minutes of your time, Mrs Hamilton. It *is* something that I, that I . . .'

She glanced impatiently at the clock above the concierge's desk. Brook would be coming in little more than an hour's time and she wanted time for talking to Georgie as well as a soak in the bath. She was about to plead overwhelming urgencies of various sorts but suddenly remembered that London was an hour earlier. Georgie wouldn't be on his way home yet. The mournful Welshman's anxious eyes made her change her mind. She could have a quick shower instead of a bath. 'All right, Mr Gwyn-Evans, but I'm really a bit pushed for time. I'm dining early this evening with a friend and taking the morning plane to London.' She smiled at him. 'If you don't mind telling me whatever it is as I start my packing . . .'

'Oh, thank you, Mrs Hamilton.'

She led the way to the lift. 'How fortunate, for me that is, that I happened to see you, Mrs Hamilton.' He flapped along behind her in silence as she went down the corridor and opened the door to her room.

The chambermaid had drawn the curtains and she was reaching for the light-switch just inside the door when Mr Gwyn-Evans broke her collar-bone.

Waves of nausea and pain engulfed her and she slid down the wall, her head lolling, her eyes shut tight against the blackness. She sat on the floor, breathing hard, and vomited bile. Her ears sang and she thought she might have fainted for a few seconds because now his legs were in front of her and the voluminous black coat gone.

His voice was entirely neutral when he spoke. 'I shall help you to a chair, Mrs Hamilton. Support your left arm with your right. That's it.' She whimpered and fainted again from the agony as he half-lifted, half-dragged her into the small bedroom. He left her sitting on the floor, propped up against the foot of the bed like a floppy doll, and placed the chair from the dressing-table in front of her with neat, precise movements. 'Now, then, Mrs Hamilton,' he said, peeling off his brilliant yellow rubber kitchen-gloves and sitting down, lighting a cigarette, 'we can have our chat. Your packing will have to wait. Such a boring task, packing.'

He giggled and negligently elbowed aside the pistol he'd used to smash her collar-bone.

'Why?' Camilla croaked.

'It saves time, I find. Cuts out useless speculation of the will-he-or-won't-he sort. The threat of pain is less immediate than the actuality of it, you see. You and I both know that all I need do now is to reach forward and tweak your left arm even *slightly* . . .'

Camilla shrank back as far as she could, silently crying, unable to stop retching. 'No. Please,' was all she could say.

'There you are. QED. Now then, you said you were pushed for time and so am I. Let's get started. Where is my dear old friend Ruffo?'

Camilla's head was swimming, her breathing shallow and ragged. 'Ruffo. I know nothing . . .' She gave a half-strangled shriek as the pistol-butt crashed down onto her kneecap, propelling her into a red void of searing agony.

She was forced back into consciousness as the smell of brandy filled her head like a balloon. A bright-yellow hand held a glass to her face. 'Drink,' he ordered. 'I took advantage of your temporary absence to raid the mini-bar.' His other hand was clutching her hair, forcing her head back. She gulped convulsively and choked but some of the brandy went down, burning its way to her stomach. She retched weakly and he tipped more into her mouth. She felt obscurely grateful to him.

'That's better, isn't it?' he asked, smiling slightly.

'Thank you,' she heard herself saying, knowing he was insane.

He sat in his chair once more, this time keeping the rubber gloves on as he sipped daintily at a second glass. He frowned, added another drop of mineral water, sipped again and lit another cigarette. He gazed at her, his expression neutral.

'We are making no progress,' he eventually said, the words tumbling out in a sudden, rapid burst. 'Your late husband had my cocaine in his motorcar, Mrs Hamilton, as you undoubtedly know. *Twenty kilos of it, Mrs Hamilton!* Pure.' He sighed deeply and visibly collected himself. 'Both vehicle and cocaine vanished after his death. To be plain with you, I've no interest in either. What I want

301

is information, Mrs Hamilton. You and Ruffo have been conspiring against me.' He sat back, waiting, his eyes once more empty of emotion.

To her surprise, she realized that despite her body's agony her mind was beginning to function again. She had no idea how much time had passed but Brook was always punctual. She had asked for ice to be delivered, too, she remembered. Someone would come. She looked up into the man's mad, pale, immobile face and knew, with sudden, jolting certainty, that this was Gillon. The knowledge terrified her and she shut her eyes against it.

'Mrs Hamilton,' he said sternly.

'I haven't seen Ruffo, Mr Mr,' she said. 'I haven't either seen him or heard from . . .'

He sighed deeply again and she rushed on, saying everything, anything, to keep him from hurting her more. 'Jeremy's CO came to see me, the day of the funeral. He said, oh God please don't, he said someone wanted to buy Jeremy's car.'

'And where was it? You and Ruffo had it.'

'No no no. I don't remember oh wait, wait. *He* had it! That's what it was. Please, you must you must I need to think. I can't think *please* if you if you . . .'

He put the pistol down and took another sip of his drink, nodding. 'Your husband's commanding officer told you that he had the car. How did it come to be in his possession, Mrs Hamilton? You must see that I cannot bring myself to believe you. What is your connection with the police? How much has Ruffo told them?'

She took a deep breath, thinking hard. 'Jeremy's CO was there. At Ascot. I remember now.' She shut her eyes, feeling faint again. 'I don't know if Ruffo was there or not. I don't know what it is you want me to say.' She began to cry helplessly. 'May I have more brandy, please?' she whispered.

He helped her to drink. 'Thank you,' she said once more, willing herself to ignore the pain and speak rationally to this irrational man. 'The Colonel told me that the police finished with the car and released it to him, so that he

302

could give it to me, drive it back to London, you see, and . . .' She looked up at him. 'Ruffo and I have never even discussed Jeremy's death. You must believe me.'

'Sorry, Mrs Hamilton,' he said, shaking his head sadly, as though she were a continuing disappointment to him. 'You and Ruffo sold my cocaine. That is one possibility. The second possibility is that Ruffo kept it and the wineboxes handed over to Major Hamilton not far from here, now I think of it, to be transported to England actually contained nothing but Ruffo's sadly indifferent wine.' There was further melancholy head-shaking but then his tone sharpened. 'But that hardly provides a convincing reason for Ruffo to kill poor Major Hamilton.' He pursed his lips. 'Unless, of course, your husband and Ruffo had conspired to defraud me of my cocaine and then the thieves had subsequently fallen out, as thieves so often do. Well, that is neither here nor there. You persist in trying to protect Ruffo . . .'

'Please,' she begged, 'I don't know . . .'

'*I need that money!*' He was leaning forward, glaring at her with icy intensity. 'And I need to know what Ruffo knows and where he is!'

'You must believe me.' She kept repeating, pleading, willing him to listen to her, cringing away from his stare. 'I'm telling you the truth, if only you'd . . .'

'What is truth? How can I believe you, Mrs Hamilton? I'm mystified by your continuing association with Ruffo. So very unwise.' He smiled at her, his head to one side. 'I confess, however, to being lamentably ignorant in matters of the heart. Perhaps you and Ruffo, the romantic, shall we call it, attraction was so strong that . . . Well, we have David and Bathsheba and Uriah the Hittite, don't we?'

'I didn't know Ruffo then, Mr –' She was trying to make herself very small, like Alice.

His gaze was neutral, weighing, judging, assessing. 'So you say, so you say. Well, then, the only interpretation possible is that you and Ruffo are collaborating with the police. If such is the case, both my cocaine and my money are beyond reach and my only option is to use you to flush out Ruffo. You do see that, don't you?' he asked, grinning. 'Now I wonder where that young devil is hiding himself. It would be useful to know what he's been getting up to but I imagine you might be able to tell me something of his . . .'

The sound of voices came from the hotel corridor. He took a metal object from his pocket and reached for his pistol. Camilla began to sob helplessly, unable to speak, even to move. It was a silencer.

There was a sudden knock on the door.

'Brook,' she mumbled, almost inaudibly.

'Your friend,' Gillon said. 'How nice.' He screwed the silencer onto the end of the pistol-barrel.

Brook knocked once more, calling, 'Camilla. It's Brook. The waiter gave me the ice.'

Gillon leant forward and shot Camilla through the heart. Then he got up from his chair and went to open the door.

A hand was shaking George's shoulder. He was in the toils of an absurd but terrifying dream of being trapped underwater by an immense spider. His eyes flew open and he looked up at the duty officer, who was putting a steaming mug of tea on the chair beside George's cot. George smiled his gratitude for both the tea and the abrupt termination of the dream.

'Morning, sir. Awake?'

George nodded and almost scalded himself on the tea. He hastily spat it back into the mug. 'Sorry,' he said.

'Should've warned you, sir. Blow on it a bit.'

'What time is it?' He was too tired to fumble for his watch.

'Just gone ten, sir. The DDG said let you sleep as long as possible.' He laughed. 'Said he needs a fresh, rested mind because his is decomposing at a terrific clip.'

'Kindly tell him that I'll be as quick as I can.'

'Razor, towels, toothbrush all laid out for you, sir. Next along to the left.'

'I remember,' George said, still smiling. 'Thanks very much, Viney.'

By the time he joined the Deputy Director General, George had collected a second mug of tea on his way and was feeling better for his five hours of sleep.

'Maurice, you look awful.'

'Your honesty does you great credit, Lacey.' Lyall's cold look softened. 'At least one of us got some sleep. I simply cannot make heads or tails of all this, Georgie,' he said plaintively.

'Put me in the picture.'

Sir Maurice gulped his tepid tea and said, 'Lombroso, the Nice copper, spent the entire night in deep conclave with the Monaco Chief of Police. Lombroso says the wretched man finally agreed to some limited co-operation at around eight o'clock, seven our time.

'Then what happens?' Sir Maurice's expression curdled as he stared into his mug, searching the oily surface for clues. 'It now looks a hundred per cent sure that the birds have flown but what in the name of *God* put the wind up them and made the entire bunch break cover at once?' He was slumped in a hard chair, a huge Michelin road-map of France spread out before him.

'Someone on the Monaco police force was on Nedda's payroll?' George ventured.

'I don't know. I just don't know. Possible, I imagine, but the conference was at such a high level it seems inconceivable. Well. No use speculating, I suppose. What's done is done.'

He took a deep breath before continuing. 'The Mercedes registered to Princess Monteavesa *may* have crossed into Italy sometime between half-past eight and nine on the coast road. According to Lombroso, a tremendous number of Italians from the San Remo area work in Monaco and that area of France. There are only the two roads crossing the frontier, so the traffic builds up. Academic, in any event, because the car's registration number didn't even reach the frontier police until after nine. A French cop thinks a Mercedes with Monaco registration could have gone through. He merely half-remarked that it was early for the pampered rich to be on the road. Vague as that, I'm afraid.'

George twitched the French map away and studied the Italian one that lay underneath. 'They could,' he said after a long moment's scrutiny, 'be headed for Turin, Milan or Genoa. All three have airports.' He looked up. 'D'you recall, Maurice, we always rather fancied Genoa as the likeliest landing-place for the cocaine?'

'Yes, of course.' Sir Maurice was clearly exhausted. 'It's possible that another shipment of cocaine is due to come in somewhere nearby.'

He knitted his brows and threw up his hands. 'I'm beginning to feel that we're right back where we started from, a month ago. Chasing our tails. It seems incredible after entire geological ages of stones have been turned and examined under the microscope. But the fact remains that we have no idea what they're doing, much less where they are. We have one man under lock and key. One man!' He rubbed his eyes. 'You don't suppose there's any point in asking the obnoxious Reardon if he has any ideas . . . No.'

'We're not quite at square one,' George murmured. 'We now have names and faces, certainly one car's registration number. . .

'All of that can be disguised, George. Change the licence-plates, change the passports, disguise the appearance.' He hauled himself upright and opened the door. 'Viney!'

'Sir?'

'More tea, please, quick as you can.'

'Sir.'

He was back, empty-handed, in less than a minute. 'Tea's on the way, sir. There's a telex on its way up from Signals for you, Mr Lacey. From Switzerland.'

'Koepfli,' George said to Sir Maurice. 'Good. Perhaps he's traced Fahy's movements.'

He waited at the top of the stairs and scribbled a signature on the clipboard the messenger held out to him. He walked back to Sir Maurice's office as he read.

'Anything?'

'Well, yes and no. Koepfli circulated Costelloe's photograph on our behalf and he may be in the navy Renault and he may have crossed the border about,' he glanced at his watch, 'an hour ago at St Julien-en-Genevois. Two men in the car; it had the zero-six prefix. The driver, it says here, was certainly not Costelloe. He had a bald head with a depression running across the top.' He looked up at Sir Maurice. 'Doesn't strike any familiar bells, does it?'

'Not to me.'

'The other man was curled up on the back seat, sleeping or pretending to. That one could be Costelloe: thin, dark, etcetera. Both men had British passports.'

They bent over the French map. George traced a line with his finger up from the south. 'They could have been in Monaco and driven all night, taking it in turns.'

'Geneva.' Lyall straightened and shrugged. 'I give up trying to work out any reason why Costelloe should go to Geneva and his dear colleague Nedda should then leave for Italy, many hours later, unless she's seeing to a cocaine pick-up and he's cashing a cheque at the bank.'

George was still bent over the map. 'I wonder,' he said.

'What do you wonder?'

'The Mercedes could be going to Geneva, too. By a different route. Look here, Maurice. The autostrada from Turin goes along to Aosta. From there you have a choice between the Mont Blanc Tunnel into France and the Saint-Bernard into Switzerland. Both will take you on to Geneva.'

'Get on the blower to your friend Muesli, George, and get yourself onto a Geneva flight. They'll wake me if anything comes in.'

PART SEVEN

27

Stephen Fahy sat in the front seat beside the driver because he didn't want to have to talk to Nedda any more than was strictly necessary. The driver, a gunman from Derry's Bogside called Kevin Quinlan, appeared to disdain the benefits to mankind of soaps or deodorants and Fahy rolled down his window, breathing in the intoxicatingly pure air of the Alpine spring.

Nedda sat sullenly in the back seat, pointedly refusing to acknowledge occasional inane remarks made to her by Quinlan's younger brother, Terence, who had never been out of Northern Ireland in his life, except for a week or so of weapons-training just across the border in the Republic. Kevin, on the other hand, made few attempts at conversation, concentrating with the limited amount of intelligence available to him on keeping to the right-hand side of the road. The autostrada had not presented an insuperable challenge but on the smaller roads he tended to drift to the left. A road junction at Sembrancher had given them all several harrowing moments. The Quinlans were last-minute draftees, dregs scraped from the bottom of the barrel.

Something was slightly off-key and Fahy didn't like it. He was relieved that he'd thought to have the Brothers Quinlan liberate a pair of licence-plates from a crowded car-park at a shopping mall near Turin. The MC sticker on the rear-window of the Mercedes had scraped off easily and the Monaco plates had been removed. Nedda had been on the verge of objecting to pointless, time-wasting precautions but she had looked thoughtful when the Swiss police seemed to be taking more than a passing interest in all the cars going through frontier controls at both ends of the Great St Bernard Tunnel. Nedda had used her Italian passport, Fahy and young Terry Quinlan the French ones bought in Nice and Kevin his own British passport. There hadn't been time to find him a suitable replacement that matched his general physical description and age.

Another factor that kept turning over in Fahy's mind was a conversation overheard in the bar of their hotel at Martigny. Two Austrians, judging by their accents, had been discussing the tailback on the road out of Geneva, the police ostensibly spot-checking for the roadworthiness of occasional cars. But Connolly and Costelloe had noticed nothing untoward. They had followed instructions, travelling along the French side of the Lac Léman. The Renault had crossed back into Switzerland at St Gingolph without encountering any difficulty.

Nonetheless, Fahy didn't at all like the picture these small, possibly insignificant, fragments of mosaic were making. Once Ruffo, Alexis and, above all, Nedda had been safely disposed of, he would naturally kill the Quinlan brothers. They were of no use to him. The snipers would be paid off and vanish once they had transported him into Austria. He would then meet up with Costelloe and Connolly, all the help he really needed to pull the pieces of his operation back together, the bank accounts and any other assets that were recoverable.

It had done him a great deal of good to kill that stupid English bitch and her friend. His mind was working with unusual clarity and he was looking forward to shooting Nedda. He smiled, thinking how surprised she would be. It was a pity Alexis had to go. He quite enjoyed chatting with Alexis but leaving him alive was too risky, not worth a few minutes of sprightly conversation.

He began to go over his plan of escape once more. He could see no logical flaw in it. He would leave Switzerland with Bienenstein and Skryanz in their hired car. He would travel with them as far as Innsbruck, he thought as he glanced down at the Swiss road-map in his lap, and continue on by train to Munich, using his German passport.

He relaxed in his seat, anticipating with pleasure a return to his former, semi-solitary, scholarly existence in Munich.

He had spent his days in reading, his evenings in café conversations amongst the rococo splendours of the town's liveliest meeting-places or the profoundly tranquil beauty of the Bavarian countryside, dotted with comfortable inns warmed by extravagantly baroque porcelain stoves.

A teaching-post in some small but excellent establishment would suit him admirably, but he doubted he would actually need to find work, work that paid more than a pittance. His mind catalogued the pleasant aspects of living to a schedule in a slightly monastic, but not unnecessarily rigorous, atmosphere. If Costelloe couldn't manage to recover all of Nedda's investments, then so be it. There was still a respectable amount of money squirrelled away in a Zürich bank and, in any event, his needs were modest. But it would be naturally preferable to control the millions heaped up in other banks as well, numbers and access codes neatly docketed on the discs in Costelloe's boxes, safely stashed in the boot of the Mercedes.

Perhaps he would take up writing again. He had enjoyed the discipline involved in writing, quite apart from the intense pleasure he had derived from setting the red-fanged cat amongst the unsuspecting Vatican pigeons. Some reflections on politics and power: a series of essays, perhaps; certainly to be published pseudonymously – he had neither need nor desire for celebrity – and in German, the proper language for modern philosophical speculation.

Having decided on the shape his new life would take, he looked back over the experiences of the last several years and concluded that they gave no cause for regret over time wasted, nothing with which to reproach himself.

His experiment could not be seen as failure, not even by the troglodytes that made up the IRA's "active service units", much less the windy Sinn Fein ideologues. The success-rate of his operations had made their own botched efforts look like seaside circus-acts. They would never have the imagination to envisage how close he had come to establishing his dominion over an entire country, a poor place but his own, almost his own given a little more time.

Any intrinsic failure in his planning or methods could be demonstrably proven to stem from the inadequacies of ham-fisted associates, human error and folly carried to unimaginable extremes.

Stephen Fahy was entirely content. There really was nothing whatever to be held against him; even the police forces of Europe working in concert would come up against insuperable difficulties in building any sort of a case against him. He had done nothing wrong, unless ridding the world of Philipp and Ivy could be construed as wrong, which he doubted. The Englishwoman and her friend were complete nonentities. Any chance of finding him was slim to the point of emaciation and would vanish entirely within a matter of weeks as he assumed a cloak of invisibility, a protective colouring to provide exquisite camouflage against his new background.

He day-dreamed contentedly about buying a small chalet with a book-lined room and a cosy porcelain stove somewhere in the Bavarian Alps. In his mind's eye, he sat at his desk, placed under a window that afforded a magnificent view of majestic peaks rising in the background, and worked at his essays on the nature of political power.

Snow, he thought, beautiful clean, sparkling Alpine snow, unsullied by urban filth both physical and spiritual. St John Chrysostom had described the inhabitants of Antioch as "meditating on endless deceits". All of that would soon be behind him.

He smiled and sighed with contentment, much to Kevin Quinlan's surprise.

Ruffo paced back and forth as Alexis murmured inaudibly into the radio from his vantage-point farther up the track. Ruffo's eyes were hypnotically fixed on the small patch of track below, where he knew the eight-kilo land-mine, looking so innocent in its gay blue plastic carapace, like two frisbees stuck together, had been reverently lowered into its grave by Jacki and Alexis. It had looked about as lethal as a child's beach toy.

The minuscule and equally toy-like village of Ferret lay just below the flower-covered meadow, old stubborn patches of pock-marked winter snow now forced to retreat back into the shadiest corners. Cows grazed placidly amongst the Alpine pansies and gentianella. The metalled road ended above Ferret, although the track that continued on up the few hundred yards to where they waited was kept in excellent condition by the villagers. There was no reason for Gillon and his troops to abandon their cars and proceed on foot.

Ruffo tore his eyes away from the meticulously-smoothed grave. He checked for the sound of cars making their slow way up the valley in second gear and heard nothing. A kilometre uphill, hidden from the track by a thick belt of larch and Norway spruce, was the even tinier settlement called Les Ars and the barn where Barbara was meant to be waiting with the three horses. Jacki had adamantly refused a mount for the trek up and over the Grand Col Ferret.

The track ended at Les Ars and shrank into the narrow path that led, in a comparatively easy climb, to the old Great St Bernard road, still snow-bound in places and shut at this time of year. If they were chased by Gillon's men, perforce slowly and on foot, the followers might reasonably assume them to have gone that way. But a little above Les Ars, a sharp turning to the right and across the ice-cold, fast-flowing Dranse de Ferret was another path that would take them by a far steeper route to the col and over into Italy.

If they made it that far. If they hadn't been gunned down first.

At least Barbara and the horses would be able to get away, Ruffo thought for the hundredth time. He wouldn't die with innocent deaths on his conscience. Jacki and whatever helpers he had enrolled were on their own manor and could double back to their houses. Alexis' unique basement, which looked to Ruffo like the Den of the Forty Thieves, had yielded up radios and Jacki would be in communication with Barbara giving her the signal to move.

315

Alexis ambled over, as relaxed as though sitting on his garden bench watching the boats tacking across the lake.

'Jacki reports three cars. The first one pulled up under the old watch-tower and Bienenstein and Skryanz got out. The other two are a goodish way behind and well spread out.'

'How does Jacki know? I mean, he's never seen them . . .'

Alexis smiled. 'He described them to me. They've got their rifles with them, in those cases that look like the ones fishermen carry their rods in. 'They're probably moving into place right now,' he said cheerfully. 'They're probably watching us.'

Ruffo's throat constricted. All he wanted to do was dive for cover behind the untidy clutter of ice-cracked rocks dotted about the clearing. He eventually managed to croak, 'What makes you think they won't shoot us right now?'

Alexis laughed. 'Because they'll have been told to wait for Gillon's signal. He'll want to see what he can get out of me first, like a Stinger or two and the Czech machine-pistol, plus whatever else I might have brought along to try to sell him.'

He shuffled about, kicking at a pebble. 'Look unsuspecting, unconcerned, Ruffo. Nonchalance, dear fellow; that's the general line to follow.'

He looked at his watch and then peered down the track with a slight frown, the quintessence of a busy man being forced to wait for an unpunctual business acquaintance. 'Can't radio any more and risk having them hear us banging on. We don't know how close they are.' He shrugged indifferently. 'They may have radios, too, for all we know.'

Their own Uzis were hidden behind a large glacial boulder a few yards away. Alexis had given Ruffo a couple of hours of training with them during the morning. He had chosen a meadow above Les Ars, in case Gillon decided to do a recce on the proposed site for the Stinger demonstration. Jacki's wife had kept watch in their own village of Branche, half-way down the valley, but Gillon

316

had evidently found the precaution either unnecessary or the risk of giving himself away unacceptable.

'*Don't*,' Alexis hissed, 'keep glancing at the fucking boulder, Ruffo.' His face broke into a delighted grin for the benefit of the snipers. 'Nedda, Gillon and two other men are in Nedda's Mercedes, which is now the lead car, thank God. It's all going according to plan so far, Ruffo, so relax.'

Their nightmare had been the strong possibility that Gillon might send another car ahead of his own, to spy out the land. Instead, he was having his reinforcements bring up the rear. Sound, textbook military disposition of troops. The Austrians concealed in front, the commander and his guard in the centre, the better to order up his reserves in case of need.

The reserves were, Alexis told Ruffo conversationally, two men in a navy Renault and, according to Jacki, didn't look up to very much. 'It seems possible that one of them is your watcher, or Connolly, as we must learn to call him. Seems a pity if we have to kill him,' he added without any convincing sign of deep regret.

He paused and listened, head to one side. 'Here they are,' he said and strode without hesitation to where the clearing met the track, in order to welcome the advancing Mercedes and wave it on.

When it happened, it wasn't in the least like Ruffo's imaginings.

There was a deep booming sound. It was as if an immense drum, an entire tympani section of a huge Wagnerian orchestra had been struck, the reverberations rolling in Götterdämmerung sonorities around the bowl of towering mountains. This doom-laden soundtrack lagged fractionally behind the action. In uncanny slow motion, the big car reared back on its hind wheels and a second explosion came on the heels of the first as the petrol-tank burst into flame.

All four doors sprang open but the driver was already dead. The man in the back seat screamed in piercing agony as fragments of searing metal lanced into his face. He was soon engulfed by the flames, hands still held in terror to the place where his eyes had been. Somehow, the other person managed to drag themselves a few yards clear, leaving behind a thick trail of blood on the fresh young green of the meadow. It glistened hypnotically in the sunlight.

Alexis was already at the boulder, diving to retrieve their two Uzis. Ruffo's eyes were locked on the figure lying near the Mercedes, which was now well alight and sending an oily pall of dense, smothering black smoke gusting across the small meadow towards the surrounding trees. At least one shot was close enough for him to feel the slight rush of air from its wake against his face but he heard nothing, the fiery car blanketing all other sounds.

Most of the figure was naked, naked as Ruffo had never seen and hoped never to see again, the skin flayed from large sections of the body like a proto-Christian martyr or Aztec fertility sacrifice. What remained was female and Ruffo knew it couldn't be anyone but Nedda.

He was pulled to it but had to avert his horrified gaze as he drew close. Rich, brilliant-red blood rhythmically spurted from terrible wounds as other, smaller injuries oozed more lethargically. Tallow-coloured subcutaneous fat, the dead white of bone, the pinkish red of muscle tissue were exposed in a spectrum of ultimate indecency. He could hear it moaning deep in its throat, even above the dull crackling of the fire, already beginning to burn itself out but sending out more choking fumes than ever as the upholstery smouldered. The head rolled back and forth in the grass as Ruffo watched, rooted to the spot.

He could hear the intermittent crackle of single-shot gunfire, staccato bursts from a machine-gun and the distinctive sound of a bullet ricochetting off rock, whining harmlessly away somewhere closeby. He continued to stand, head bowed, mesmerized by the figure, as though they were alone on the planet.

He fell to his knees beside her, his body cracking under the crushing weight of overwhelming pity. An immense sadness bowed him to the ground and, oblivious

318

to everything, he almost took the gruesome, outstretched hand with his wedding-ring on it in his own.

'Nedda,' he finally managed to say.

'Ruffo.' Her voice was almost unrecognizable, coming from deep within her throat.

He vaguely heard Alexis yelling his name but ignored him.

'Don't leave me alone,' Nedda said. She tried to say more but it took a moment for Ruffo to understand her. The word was "please".

He shook his head and knew she couldn't see him. 'No. I'm here, Nedda.' He hunkered back on his heels, prepared to wait, his eyes tightly screwed shut against the paralysing sight. He knew that death would not be long in coming.

He thought he saw Nedda's body jumping and twitching and he clutched his head, knowing he was going mad. An explosion beside his ear deafened him and he thought he'd been shot. A single word flashed through his mind: "fitting".

He opened his eyes as a powerful arm dragged him upright, a foot encouraging him none too gently with a sharp kick to his posterior. 'Follow me! *Run*, you stupid bastard!' Alexis screamed, cuffing him on the side of the head with his left hand as the right clutched the Uzi in a white-knuckled grip.

Ruffo dutifully broke into a dazed jog, eyes down, following Alexis blindly. His mind tried and failed to assimilate a series of images flashing before his eyes like stroboscopic lights. Bells continuously rang in his ears, actually more of an arhythmic, dull clanking, peppered with the abrupt cracks of rifle-fire. The Uzi bumped against his back as a timely reminder and he unslung it as he ran, beginning to pick up a bit more speed as naked instinct assumed command over his numbed brain.

Alexis was racing ahead of him up the track, looking back over his shoulder from time to time to make sure that Ruffo was following, that he hadn't completely collapsed from shock. The hideous scene in the meadow was now blocked by trees from his view as he turned for a final look.

What he saw instead jolted him back into the real world: a small herd of benign, brown-and-white cows were coming up the track, their bells clanking discordantly, urged on by a pair of twins, identical smiles on their jaunty sunburned faces. Jacki's boys, Ruffo thought as he waved to them, dispatched to block the narrow track against any pursuing car and making it difficult even for men on foot.

He fumbled at the switch for automatic fire and gave Alexis a thumbs-up signal, still speechless but relatively rational. He felt the reassuring weight of the spare magazine. If it came to some sort of ludicrous shoot-out with whatever troops of Gillon's might still be alive and kicking, the terrain offered a choice of cover. For the first time in longer than he chose to remember, he felt he had a chance of emerging from all of this alive.

A figure broke almost silently from the trees to their left and he brought the Uzi up to firing position but saw, in the nick of time, that it was Barbara. 'Thank God,' she said, joining the two men for the final sprint up the track to the barn.

'I think I bagged Gillon, and I *know* I got your minder,' Alexis managed to gasp as they pounded up the last few hundred yards.

Ruffo's chest felt as though it were caving in but his mind was beginning to function more or less clearly again. He willed himself not to look for where the trees ended and their horses waited, hidden out of sight unless one were, almost literally, on top of them.

Barbara reached the barn first and Alexis and Ruffo hurtled in behind her, both gasping for breath and weak-legged. 'Jacki?' Ruffo managed to get out.

Alexis grinned despite his heaving chest. 'Let's try him, shall we?' He propped his Uzi against a bale of hay and spoke breathlessly into his radio, laughing with delight as he switched it off. 'Jacki got one, too. Saw him go down. He said to go on ahead.'

Ruffo was securing his horse's girth and nodded as Alexis went on. 'Jacki will circle round to make sure no one's following and meet up with us farther along.' He did some quick calculation on his fingers and said, 'Let's do an inventory.' He held up fingers. 'I'm pretty sure we got the four in Nedda's car. Two at least wounded, mine and Jacki's. That leaves Bienenstein and Skryanz and they may or may not come after us but they're the most dangerous. Let's haul ass out of here!'

'Wrong,' Gillon said from the door. His face and hair were caked with blood and he stared at Ruffo with incandescent hatred, ignoring Alexis and Barbara. He braced his back against the door-frame and slowly raised the heavy pistol until Ruffo was staring down the barrel.

There was a shattering amount of noise as Gillon spun insanely, erupting into a fountain of blood. The horses screamed and plunged, terrified. Alexis lowered his still-smoking pistol. The sudden silence was almost worse than the noise.

Barbara was the first to calm her horse and mount. She moved into the open without speaking or looking back. Giving Alexis a leg up on Vino Rosso, Ruffo managed to haul himself with difficulty onto Pinot Grigio, shaking so violently he could barely pick up the reins. His head ached abominably.

Out of the dark barn, the warmth of the late-afternoon sun felt wonderful but unreal, inconsequent. Ruffo glanced at his watch. The sun would soon dip behind the Mont Dolent and the air temperature would plummet within minutes, as it had the previous evening. That a mere half-hour had passed since the Mercedes nosed up the track seemed incredible to him.

Casting an expert eye over the two horses ahead, he was relieved that they appeared to be fully recovered from their terror in the barn as well as the previous day's nine-kilometre uphill excursion from Praz-de-Fort. They had taken it in easy stages to keep them from getting winded in the thinning air. Luca hadn't dared to attempt manoeuvring the big horse-box any farther up the narrow and steepening road.

Barbara had seen to the three stallions' comfort, keeping them rather better rugged up than the humans. She was still very pale but she gave Alexis the thumbs-up signal when he asked if she were all right. Then he turned around and waved at Ruffo, reining Vino Rosso in for Ruffo to catch up.

'What did I tell you, Ruffo?'

'What did you tell me what?'

'That I'm Switzerland's answer to Clint Eastwood is what,' he answered, nettled, 'tall in the saddle and everything.'

Ruffo began to laugh, hearing a strong note of hysteria in the laughter but unable to stop himself. He was just sane enough to know that his maniacal mood and light-headedness were the result of shock combined with a general shortage of oxygen. Barbara reined in and stared at him worriedly. Then she, too, broke into a smile that became a laugh. The horses put their heads down and began to inspect the sweet new grass beside the path. Their riders seemed to have forgotten their previous hurry. What a completely mad picture we must make, Alexis was thinking as he, too, got infected by the laughter.

'*Alors, les enfants*,' Jacki called out to them, rounding a bend in the path and trotting up without a sign of breathlessness, 'you have chosen a beautiful moment to do the night-club act!'

'What's happening below?' Alexis quickly asked him, instantly sober and trying to read Jacki's expression.

'For that, one must wait. What I myself know is that the two riflemen went to earth in the woods.' He grinned at Alexis, white, uneven teeth flashing in his dark face. 'One of them seems to have suffered a slight wound but only to the arm.' His smile faded abruptly. 'I think I heard the sound of some motors coming up the valley. Maybe the police. Maybe anyone. Maybe more Irish.' He shrugged. 'We must radio to find out certainly but there's no time to lose.'

'They can't get up here in cars,' Alexis pointed out reasonably.

'Once they see what a great big damage your pretty blue toy has done, my old friend,' Jacki retorted with a show of exaggerated patience, 'and should the visitors be the police, a helicopter may be sent to inspect. Go on up as quickly as you can. Choose carefully where you cross the stream because the snow melts very quickly in the afternoons.'

Ruffo looked over to his left and was almost blinded by the sun's reflection from the snowfields on the jagged-topped peaks towering into the clear sky. He tried to regain his vision by focusing on a rock. Black dots danced before his eyes.

'Your horses are fresh. There is a hut about a kilometre up. It will be on your left. It is very difficult to see from the path so keep a sharp eye. Wait for me there and get your horses inside. The hut is still uninhabited so early in the season so have no fear.'

'And you?' Alexis asked.

Jacki's weather-beaten face broke into another grin. 'I can make myself invisible from helicopters. You cannot. Do as I say. I'll radio from here and see what the situation is below. Keep your own radio switched to receive.'

He slapped Pinot Grigio on the rump and ducked into the cold shade of a boulder. They set off again, the horses picking their way nervously through unaccustomed terrain with patches of loose scree making the going difficult underfoot. Ruffo tried to listen for the sound of car engines but the rushing of the stream leaping over boulders blotted out all extraneous sounds.

They were above the tree-line and there didn't appear to be much cover available. Yet, when Ruffo looked back from no more than thirty yards along the path, Jacki couldn't be seen.

28

'Stuff your thanks, you silly, *fatuous* ass! Don't you understand *anything*, Ruffo?' Her voice rose an octave in her fury. 'You . . . you . . . bloody little stupid . . . *gentleman*!'

The force of Barbara's rage was making her visibly tremble. Ruffo just stared at her open-mouthed, struck completely dumb. He looked to Alexis for enlightenment.

'I think, Ruffo,' he said seriously, looking at his friend with profound understanding, 'that what Barbara is trying to point out to you is that you ought to have shot Nedda. In fact, it was Gillon who shot her, not me, not Jacki, not Barbara. I saw him do it, just as I winged him down in the meadow. I ought to have shot him again then, just to make absolutely sure.'

Barbara had regained some mastery over her rage. 'Don't you ever learn about that odious woman? What a fool you are, Ruffo,' she said contemptuously. 'Will you never be able to assimilate what a monster she is? Was,' she amended, 'God be praised. You could have got all of us killed because you couldn't bring yourself to do what was right. *You* ought to have been the executioner!'

She took a deep breath before going on, measuring her words with elaborate care. 'The reason she begged you to stay beside her is that she *knew*, even with the life draining out of her, that you would be killed if you lingered behind. Ruffo,' she said gently, suddenly coming off the boil and taking his cold hand in both her own, 'her mind was still working, calculating, as it always did. She was aware that one of her people would kill you if she could keep you out in the open.'

She took another deep breath. 'Whatever was happening to her *physically*, she was clinging to the fact that there were snipers hidden nearby in the trees and the others close behind, whose assignment was to make sure that none of you left that meadow alive. By delaying you, even for one or two *minutes*, Ruffo, or as long as it took her to die, she was determined that you should die, too.'

She laughed harshly. 'Believe me, my friend, I am not the person to put Nedda out of her misery. I wouldn't have hesitated to leave her there in torments, which is what she, God knows, richly deserved. Gillon did the job for all of us, God knows why. Maybe compassion. But you would have gone on sitting there, waiting to be picked off. A sitting duck.'

She dropped his hand and poked a finger through a neat hole in the pocket of her Barbour. 'They were *shooting* at us, poppet.'

She waggled the finger through the bullet hole and burst into a gulping paroxysm of tears, eventually rubbing vigorously at her blotchy face with her shirt-tail. From the mutilated pocket, she produced a book and some pieces of paper. The back of the book had a deep score running its length, a sheaf of half-pages neatly amputated. 'I hope this is still readable,' she said, looking at it worriedly as she carefully stored the cut-off bits in the book's intact middle. 'I'd only got through about two chapters. I might fix it with sellotape, I suppose, or . . .'

'Here it comes again,' Ruffo announced from his coign of vantage by the hut's only window. He pulled back into the darkness of the room. That helicopter would have men in it and the men would be looking for anything unusual. A face at a hut window, the hut lying immediately below an Alpine pass, and in this premature season, could easily be construed as something unusual.

His voice sank to an absurd whisper, as if the clattering helicopter could hear him. 'This ought to be their last sweep. The light's beginning to go.' Down in the valley, night would have already fallen but up here on the roof of Europe the sky was still bright. It was becoming bitterly cold in the hut but they couldn't risk lighting a fire until enough darkness fell to hide the smoke.

Thank God, he thought, the rocky path showed no sign

of their scrambling ascent. The helicopter's first pass had come just as they got the horses into the basement or cellar or undercroft; whatever the damp, murky space below them was called. Anyway, downstairs. The horses had moved about nervously, stamping and whickering, alarmed by the machine's deafening noise which had been magnified by the unrelieved stone of the hut's lower floor.

He wondered idly if it were a police or army helicopter, not that it made much difference now. He prayed that no one would think to send up another helicopter at dawn tomorrow. As soon as the helicopter had moved off enough for him to make himself heard, he said, 'I didn't dare to use the damned binoculars for fear of a flash, which would give us all away in a twinkling, ha ha, pun intended.'

He started to gather up all their weapons and looked around the bare hut for a hiding-place. 'Before we leave in the morning, make absolutely sure you have *nothing* remotely incriminating on you. Check your pockets and saddlebags. We'll check each other. If the fuzz, and I mean on either side of the frontier, get curious and stop us, we're clean. God knows it's not normal for three people to be cavorting around the Alps on thoroughbreds at this time of the year, at *any* time of the year, but we can try to brazen it out if . . .'

The radio crackled and they heard Jacki's voice. He had had to go on up the final ascent and transmit instructions to Luca from the top of the col. After having left them the previous day, Luca was supposed to have driven back through the Great St Bernard Tunnel into Italy and should now be waiting for them with the horse-box at Lavachey, on the Italian side of the Val Ferret. Luca and safety lay no more than eight kilometres from the Alpine hut. The radios Alexis had unearthed from his hoard of arcane equipment were line-of-sight and wouldn't carry over the col.

'From up here I see you are now in comparative darkness, Alexis. Tell the others it's safe to go out now and water the horses at the stream before it gets pitch-dark. On my way down to you. Over.'

'Go carefully, my friend. No broken legs. We'll wait

until you come to start the fire. Any sign of the Austrians? Over.'

'Nothing of them but my wife reports the valley is swarming with police. Over.'

'Anything on the two that you and I bagged? Over.'

'No ambulance. No stretchers. It's already dark down there so they won't start looking for anyone until morning. It's entirely possible they will bring dogs so we must be moving before dawn. Luca is going now to telephone Lenfant. I'm switching off now. Over and out.'

Alexis switched off his own radio and looked pensive. 'I think, my friends, we needn't concern ourselves about the Austrians.'

'But you said they knew their mountains,' Ruffo objected. 'Why wouldn't they come after us?'

'Franz and Gerhard are mercenaries, Ruffo, not woolly revolutionaries like Gillon's IRA canaille,' he said, dismissing them contemptuously. 'They've been paid to do a job and they can't fail to know that their paymaster's dead. Mercenaries tend to want to live to fight another day, another battle, another war, if the pay and, above all, the insurance coverage are okay. There's no earthly reason for them to come after us.' He grinned and elaborated, 'There's no money in it. We'll take turns to stand guard tonight, just to be on the safe side, but I doubt it will prove necessary.'

He blew on his cold hands, wishing he could get a fire started now. He paced about to keep warm and said, 'It sounds to me as though our principal worry for the moment is that Luca will not manage to track down your *Capitaine* Lenfant. When we fail to make the rendezvous on time at the Turin airport, he could decide to fly off without us.'

Ruffo shook his head firmly. 'No, Alexis. Lenfant will wait for us, even if Luca doesn't find him. I know Lenfant well. He's not the sort to panic. He'll just assume we've been delayed. He'll be there tomorrow, a Gauloise stuck in his face, so worry about something else.'

'Oh goodie, I'll worry about the cops then. Jacki's wife will radio if they bring dogs in.' He thought a minute about dogs. 'They can't possibly do that until tomorrow. They have no way of knowing there's anyone to be tracked.' He barked with laughter. 'Good idea of Jacki's, sending those cows lolloping up in our wake. What with both cows and horses, the dogs won't have an easy time of it.'

Alexis peered out of the hut's window again and decided the time had come. As he busied himself with the arrangement of logs in the rough stone fireplace, Barbara and Ruffo walked slowly with the agitated stallions, picking a careful path through the scree down to the stream. The horses had sweated up a little, whether from fear or exertion it was impossible to tell, and were even now breathing more heavily than usual. The col was at a trifle under nine thousand feet, Barbara thought, calculating the risks they would face in the morning, and the climb up to it gradual enough. The south side was trickier, steeper, according to Jacki. They would start out in the faint light of pre-dawn and set an easy pace going up. The more taxing descent could be negotiated in full morning light.

She prayed that the police wouldn't think to summon an air-survey of the area again, at least not in Italian air space. If the helicopter crew should also prove to be early risers, there could be trouble. Jacki had warned them that there was an altiport near Courmayeur, uncomfortably convenient to where they would, perforce, be making their slow way down to the relative security of Luca and the horse-box. There was certainly at least one helicopter there, frequently called out for Alpine rescue drills and the like, and regarded with respect by Jacki and his happy little troupe of smugglers. The horses could so easily panic and bolt, harming themselves or their riders. Jacki had warned them, the evening before when they were doing a final review of the escape route, that the first stand of trees thick enough to hide them all lay at least an hour's ride down the Italian Val Ferret.

It was useless to speculate on the comparative amenities of Italian and Swiss prisons and she concentrated instead on the immediate present, firmly blocking out the uncertain future. There was a sparse covering of grass near the stream and the three stallions tore at it without any great show of appetite. She wasn't very hungry herself. It would do the horses little harm to sleep one night on fairly empty stomachs. Luca had loaded the big van with enough fodder for the entire Horse Guards.

The delicious smell of woodsmoke drifted into her nostrils and she could see the faint glow of the hut's single Coleman lamp Alexis must have set in the window as a beacon for them. 'Let's go, Ruffo,' she said, picking up a pail and half-filling it in the stream. He had perched on a boulder to see that none of the horses strayed in search of more succulent grasses.

'Not for a moment, if you don't mind, Barbara.'

He filled the other pail while he could still see what he was doing, then sat down again and patted the rock beside him. She meekly sat down, too, thinking about the fire that would be starting to warm the hut a little, and fished her cigarettes and lighter out of the pocket that hadn't been holed. They smoked in silence for a moment, then Ruffo asked, 'Sometimes I wonder if you're a sorceress. Or a sibyl. They're nicer, I believe. What prompted you to disobey Alexis' order to stay with the horses?'

She looked up at the sky, the light leeching slowly away, and thought before answering. 'To be honest, I didn't think that you would be able to bring yourself to the point of killing her, or, indeed, anyone else,' she answered. 'Alexis, yes. You, no.'

'You're right, of course,' he said without rancour, 'but you risked getting yourself shot – you very nearly *were* shot – just to make sure that I got away. Why?'

'Because Nedda was a poisonous creature, a scorpion with a tough shell. Hard to kill. She would never have forgotten that Nicky and I helped you. She fed on hatred, Ruffo, and I had to know she was dead. You must make yourself understand that, so that you won't ever be tortured by any regrets over what happened here today. Even if *you* were dead, she would have pursued Nicky and me for vengeance, had she survived. Tracking Alexis down would have taken too much time and patience, so it would have fallen to Nicky and me to atone. Or the children,' she added with a shudder.

Her voice in the semi-darkness sounded exhausted. 'The only thing that kept her going was a grinding need to destroy or abase everything more or less conventional, what we lesser mortals would term normal or comfortable. She despised your family as much as mine, or as much as Charlotte and *her* children, had she known of their existence. She respected Alexis, just at a guess, because he appears on the surface to be *so* unconventional but I expect she would have been just as contemptuous of him had she known of his domestic arrangements.'

She turned to face him, a smile barely visible in the gathering darkness. 'Nedda was fabulous in bed, wasn't she?'

'Fabulous.'

'Talk of sorceresses,' Barbara said with a derisive snort. 'During the first few years that you were married, she had you completely under her thumb. Or some other portions of her anatomy. The way you used to look at her, Ruffo!' She shifted uncomfortably on her granite perch. 'Well, if we hadn't been in something of a rush, I believe I'd have sharpened a wooden stake to hammer into her heart. Isn't that how witches were dealt with?'

Ruffo laughed briefly. 'A turbulent priest and a sorceress conspiring together and dying together. Wooden stakes and silver bullets. I can't remember which was required for witches and which for werewolves.' His cigarette glowed brightly as he puffed on it. 'I wonder what made her that way. That urge to destruction must have been in her before she ever met the turbulent priest. Don't you ever wonder what it was that made her so malevolent?'

'Not really, no. Who knows, Ruffo? Living constantly on a knife-edge was an actual, physical craving for her. At least,' she finished up with a shiver, 'that's what I think.'

'You're cold. Let's round up the boys and go inside,' he said, putting his arm around her shoulder. 'About the knife, living on the edge of it, I mean: I think you're right again. But then, you usually are.' He pecked briefly at her cheek and said, 'Anyway, thank you for everything you've done. For Guido, too. We must, some time soon, discuss what we're going to say to him about, about today.' He sighed and looked searchingly at her, hoping for reassurance. 'If I go to prison, if the cops round up some of Gillon's boyos who can brighten their dreary lives by filling in the details about Nedda's cocaine operation . . .'

'Guido will be all right, Ruffo. You'll see. He's a highly intelligent boy, my godson,' she said with a fond smile, 'having plainly inherited *her* brains. But not her unique disposition,' she added hastily. 'I asked him about her once, just to try to get some idea how he really felt about his mother, and he told me that as a small boy he'd been frightened of her but that now . . .' she shrugged, 'he simply found her tiresome. Odd, isn't it, seeing your own mother as a strident bore?'

Abruptly changing the subject, she said, 'Come on, the geegees are getting cold and so am I.'

They picked up their pails and led the tired, unprotesting stallions up to the hut. 'It's funny that you mentioned knives just now,' he said as they walked. 'I gave her a little gold penknife once. It was a birthday or anniversary present years ago, when we were first married. I saw it in a Bond Street shop, Cartier's or Asprey's I think, and I *had* to buy it for Nedda. I don't know what moved me to buy it for her but I did. A charming, useless little trifle. "Beware" was engraved on it, writ large.'

'You see, Ruffo,' Barbara said with a slight smile, 'even you knew. You knew but decided not to know.' She sighed. 'I wonder if there's anyone on earth who'll mourn Nedda.'

Ruffo was silent.

'Not anyone who knew her well,' Barbara said with finality, answering her own question.

29

'You look a good ten years younger, Maurice. At *least* ten years younger.'

'Kind of you to say so, Dickie, but at my age it's a matter of ten years younger than whom? God, I expect. Still, going to bed with a clear conscience does wonders for the outlook. You must try it sometime,' he said with a laugh.

'Another gong for you, Maurice, I shouldn't wonder,' Goudhurst speculated.

Lyall cancelled the putative honour with a dismissive wave. 'Operation not confined to our department, Dickie. Yours put up a tremendous show, then there's Six, not that they did much but use up an immense amount of money keeping their useless cauliflower ears to the ground in Europe. Jay Rodman's Pontifical associates were extremely helpful and those other Yanks, poor Brook's drugs lot, were vital, God bless 'em. Lisburn's data banks. Eyeties, Frogs, Huns and Switzers. Or do I mean Gnomes?'

Goudhurst pondered the semantic pros and cons of the matter. 'I believe,' he answered judiciously, 'that the term "Gnomes" refers specifically to the inhabitants, native or otherwise, of Zürich but I have no wish to be pedantic and I shall retain a completely open mind on the subject.'

'Noted,' Lyall said and continued with his own honours list. 'Let's not overlook the Home Secretary who deserves some sort of award for his television performance. Played Ophelia at Eton, he confided. Endless, really. Even Interpol, for God's sake, did their bit, too, and you know how useful they generally are.'

He snorted and swiped at a pigeon with his umbrella. 'Filthy things. Vermin. Flying rats,' he said loudly, glaring at an old man sitting on a bench and feeding the flying rats. The man ignored him, clutching a brown paper bag which obviously contained some edible substance the pigeons fancied something rotten; he cooed maniacally back at his feathered friends as they massed round his bench in a solid pearl-grey phalanx.

St James's Park in the late morning was peaceful, the tourists far more interested in pointing their cameras at the Changing of the Guard than the Park's permanent population of birds and strolling civil servants.

'Lacey's still out there?'

Sir Maurice nodded briefly, thinking about George's grief and guilt over Camilla's murder.

'He's coming up for retirement soon, isn't he?'

'Sadly, yes.'

'Tough man to replace,' Goudhurst said sympathetically.

'Not easy,' Sir Maurice agreed. 'Still, I have an idea or two.' He swiped at another flying rat who waddled off at its own sedate pace, looking slightly aggrieved although on the whole accustomed to the slings and arrows of an unfair, man-infested world. 'Gong for *him*, certainly. George, I mean,' he clarified with a smile.

'Who did the actual blowing-up?' Goudhurst asked curiously.

Lyall shrugged, not really caring very much. So many deaths. 'That honour is very much up for grabs. Could be the pair of men believed to be mercenaries. Middle-aged, Bavarian or Austrian by accent, according to the inn-keeper at Martigny. Spoke proper German, not Swiss. Could be Jugs, of course, the Jugoslav frontier right there. Some Jugs are fluent German-speakers, Hapsburg territory and so on. Abandoned the car they arrived in, hired at the Klagenfurt airport, near Jug border. They either had another car stashed somewhere nearby or they managed to get a lift from a passing lorry or they legged it, if they were fit enough. Very rough country they were in, although a far cry from the north face of the Eiger. Still, it's possible to do, given sturdy legs and a decent pair of lungs.'

'Stolen driving licence and credit card given to car hire company?'

333

'Right.' He spied a free bench and pointed imperiously to it with his umbrella. He got out his handkerchief and fastidiously spread it before sitting down. 'Mind the birdshit,' he warned Goudhurst, 'probably pigeonshit.' Goudhurst wondered briefly if Maurice had less objection to swiftshit or eagleshit but obediently did as he was told.

'Two of the corpses,' Lyall went on, 'the shot ones, not the bits of blown-up ones, were, as you know, low-level Provos, Liam Costelloe and Patrick Connolly, both involved with the IRA practically from the cradle but neither known to be a gunman. Might have picked it up along the way.' He shrugged, losing interest in Costelloe and Connolly, but suddenly brightened again. 'The one interesting thing to be said for them is that on the basis of medical evidence, they may have been murdered. Executed. Finished off, like Nedda herself.'

He caught Goudhurst's look of profound shock and knitted his eyebrows. 'Not by the Swiss police, Dickie, but by their own side, no doubt to prevent them from talking. Possibly the mercenaries, if, indeed, mercenaries they were. We're unlikely ever to know one way or the other.'

'How "executed"?'

Sir Maurice lit a cigarette, addressed a flattering remark to a questing duck and apologized handsomely to it for his failure to provide any sustenance. Finally he said, 'Both of the men had been wounded. The medical examiner out there specified that neither died of the wounds, however, but were shot in the heart at point-blank range some time later. High-velocity rifle. They really had to dig for the bullets, practically to China. Nedda got herself done in with pistol-shots to the head and neck. Close range but not point-blank. Bullets match the gun found in Gillon's hand. Gillon himself shot several times and his body was found in a barn farther up the mountain. Said barn had also recently sheltered some horses.'

'Wait a moment, Maurice,' Goudhurst said. 'Let's go back a bit. The IRA people were all wounded first, then lived long enough to finish one another off?'

'Something like that. Two professional-assassin-type rifles with those high-powered telescope attachment thingummies were considerately left lying beside the men, wiped clean of fingerprints,' Lyall said vaguely, losing interest again. 'There is absolutely no way we shall ever know precisely who shot whom. Just as we'll never know the identity of the writer of helpful hints sent to our Paris embassy.'

He looked about with contented approval. It was a beautiful day, the light breeze carrying the sound of band music from The Mall. Something to lift the souls and cameras of the Buddha-heads, he thought and laughed aloud.

'You'll be feeding the bloody pigeons next, Maurice,' Goudhurst warned with a puzzled glance.

'Sorry. I was thinking about Mrs Shigekawa's Buddha-heads. I don't know precisely why but it suddenly struck me funny. And not only me: the DG has adopted the term as his own. Oh dear,' he said, starting to laugh again.

'The dead Provos in the armour-plated Mercedes had just flown out to the Continent, clearly a rush operation,' Lyall said cheerfully, grinning. Goudhurst was beginning to suspect Lyall of gross impropriety, getting at the gin at a shockingly early hour.

'Lacking the two mysteriously vanished, German-speaking, middle-aged gentlemen of Klagenfurt and having no less than six bodies on their hands, the good Swiss are doing their nuts.'

'Course it was nothing even remotely like that, Dickie, but it's as far as we're ever likely to get.' His face became sombre and he gazed fixedly at a pretty girl strolling with an attentive young man. 'The tragedy is Mrs Hamilton, poor girl.'

'And Moseley.'

'And Moseley, yes, but he, at least, died quickly and cleanly. A bullet through the head. The ballistics people out there are working with the Swiss and it seems entirely likely that it was Gillon's weapon. The concierge from Mrs

Hamilton's hotel has identified him in the morgue.' He took a deep breath. 'It's Camilla Hamilton who suffered. Georgie's going to go and stay with her mother, in Bath. I need hardly say that his version of events will be highly edited. Can't have the poor woman know her daughter was tortured.'

He shrugged off his gloomy thoughts and glanced at his watch. 'I'll be off soon but I shall leave you with an absolutely delicious morsel to chew on: one of those coincidences that Lacey tends to be so severe about.

'The Swiss fielded a helicopter the evening of and the morning following the, ah, incident under present discussion. Evening of: nothing. Morning following: still nothing on the Swiss side of the Val Ferret but, from the bird's-eye view afforded by their being up in the air, they saw three people leading horses down an extremely difficult path, just below the summit on the Italian side of the mountain.'

He lit another cigarette, bent over double and blew smoke out at a pigeon. He straightened and glanced slyly at Goudhurst. 'I thought that would get your attention,' he said with some pardonable complacency. 'They hover there, just hanging about above the frontier, and radio for instructions. Horses clearly upset by noise but their two-legged friends steadfastly refuse to look up, shake their fists at hovering helicopter, whatever. They plod on doggedly, as though nothing were happening right above all of their heads, eventually coming to an easier, level patch of the trail and mounting.'

'Did the helicopter have a camera?' Goudhurst interrupted.

'Certainly, and it was rolling but, as I told you, they didn't look up so no faces. One of them could have a moustache or a very big nose that casts a heavy shadow. Woolly hats. The horses were big ones, not ponies; one grey, the other two horse-coloured. Black-and-white film, you see. Anyway,' he went on, 'Swiss helicopter hovering in its own air-space as the riders continue down the valley, apparently unconcerned. Eventually lost to sight of Swiss, owing to clouds, them above, riders below, wisps of soggy mist, don't you know. The Italians send in their own helicopter in the fullness of time, sweeping up the valley to rendezvous with the Swiss and take over from it. Blah blah blah on the radio. The Carabinieri have seen nothing but there are thick stands of trees lower down, where a fine rain is now falling, to add to their troubles.

'Further problem is the non-cosiness of the locals. The entire area is positively aswarm with smugglers, a genetic trait in that part of the world, Georgie tells me, all of them sworn enemies of the Carabinieri and pretending not to understand one word of Italian.'

'But I thought you said this was Italy.'

'It is, dear boy, but the Val d'Aosta is French-speaking. Let's not get into folklore; I've got to bugger off in a moment, so no further interruptions, please.

'The Italian machine sweeps up and down and eventually gives up and goes home. Consternation all round. It finally occurs to a bright young spark, some considerable time later I might add, that if the horses are no longer in the Val Ferret despite a concerted effort to find them, they must be elsewhere. Furious burst of activity. French police alerted to be on the watch for a horse-box at the Chamonix end of the Mont Blanc Tunnel.'

He laughed. 'As you've no doubt guessed, it becomes literally a matter of horses and barn doors, or horse-box doors, in this case. A large horse-box has trundled its unmolested way down through Aosta and thence onto the autostrada.'

'Don't tease, Maurice, you terrible old man!'

'That is all that is definitely known about one particular horse-box and there is naturally no way of knowing what, if anything, that one particular horse-box contained.' He smiled beatifically as Goudhurst squirmed with impatience. 'The coincidence is, Dickie, that there was a big race-meeting at Turin. Lots of equine to-ing and fro-ing from the airport there. Perfectly normal, that. One of those flying-stable aircraft, you know the kind I mean, flew out that afternoon. As did several others, needless to say.'

'And?'

'Its destination was Verona.'

'*And?*' Goudhurst repeated, his teeth clenched.

'Prince Monteavesa's stables aren't all that far from Verona *and*,' Lyall went on, forestalling Goudhurst, 'he had no runners entered for the Turin meeting.'

Goudhurst blew out air as though he'd made a fast circuit of the lake. 'Is anyone going to do anything about it?' he finally managed to ask.

Sir Maurice threw up his hands. 'What would you suggest, Dickie? There's no law against loading some horses onto an aircraft which is in an airport which is near a town at which there is a race-meeting in which the aforesaid horses are not making an appearance.' He laughed. 'If you follow.'

Goudhurst nodded gloomily. 'The Carabinieri might at least ask politely what Monteavesa was doing there.'

'They did. He implied that it was absolutely none of their business but as they seemed interested, he had flown the brutes to Turin so that his brother-in-law could have a look at them.'

" 'His brother-in-law",' Goudhurst echoed in a defeated voice.

'A French trainer of the highest respectability. Trains at Chantilly, had a runner at Turin. He and his wife, Monteavesa's elder sister, also have a stud in Normandy. Their entry had been flown down by the same pilot, a Frenchman, who flew Monteavesa's three to Verona. No coincidence there so don't make yourself go red by holding your breath, Dickie,' Sir Maurice warned. 'Pilot chap, called Lenfant, used all the time by Monteavesa, his brother-in-law and other pillars of the racing establishment all over the Continent.'

'I see,' Goudhurst said, as Sir Maurice got regretfully to his feet with another worried glance at his watch. 'Entire bloody Jockey Club providing one another with alibis,' he said morosely.

'What are clubs for, Dickie?' With a jaunty wave, he strode briskly off towards St James's.

338

He reached his own club in St James's Street somewhat out of breath and was told by the porter that his guest had already arrived and was waiting in the library.

Trust the military, Lyall thought, to be ruthlessly punctual. He was unavoidably delayed by a quick visit to the lavatory and apologized effusively to his guest as he collapsed into the chair beside him, a little breathless.

'I'm most frightfully sorry to have kept you waiting, Colonel.' There was a handsome Waterford sherry decanter on the table with a plateful of cheese biscuits. 'Glad you didn't wait for me, at least, and they took care of you.'

Lieutenant-Colonel Dalgleish had risen, his lightly-built and immaculately tailored figure almost standing at attention. He put down the *Country Life* he'd been looking at and resumed his seat. 'I can never resist an orgy of masochism by looking through the country properties on offer. Queen Anne manor-houses. Who can possibly afford them, I ask myself.'

'Oil sheiks and the Soviet Trade Mission,' Lyall said promptly, pouring himself a glass of sherry. 'I'm so glad you were able to join me, Dalgleish. It's a refreshing change for an old fart like me to have a chat with the younger generation.'

Dalgleish's expression was tinged with cynicism. 'You forget the Army, Sir Maurice. I am on the old-fart list or I shall be very soon. It's a colonelcy and Camberley for me next, teaching baby colonels. Instructor there for a few years, then retirement and a job in the City, I suppose. That is, if the Stock Market doesn't bark its shins again.' He sipped his sherry. 'I'm afraid that all sounded rather sour but it's a soldier's lot and soldiering on isn't for the over-fifties.'

'Surely you're nowhere near that,' Sir Maurice said, genuinely surprised.

'Not yet. I'm forty-four next month and a few months later, a new chap will be taking on my job and I'll be down at Camberley. Well, it's better than a posting to the MoD. I'm afraid I'd be hopeless in Whitehall.'

'It's not everyone's dish of tea, I agree. Well,' he said, getting down to cases, 'it's your future I wanted to have a chat about. You'll be bumped up to full Colonel somewhere between here and Camberley and probably up to Brigadier when your retirement comes up.'

'That's the usual form, yes,' Dalgleish said. He held his hand up in warning. 'You're not going to offer me a job, are you? Don't forget, Sir Maurice, I'm only too well aware of your, shall we say *professional* connection? I really can't make any sort of claim to expertise in code-cracking and invisible ink and that sort of thing.'

'Yes, well, we have plenty of people to handle that side of our business. Dons and chess-playing types, you know,' he added vaguely. Sir Maurice blinked, as though he'd just remembered something. 'When last we met, it was to do with Major Hamilton, if you recall.' His smile was ingenuous.

'Of course,' Dalgleish said in a neutral tone.

'It's a year ago now and, sadly, my memory isn't what it was but I'm sure you'll put me straight if I've got something atrociously muddled. It seems to me that we had intimations of security leaks, not strictly limited to the Brigade of Guards, of course, but including regiments that had recently served in Northern Ireland. I seem to think that there were certain irregularities to do with Hamilton, not exclusively him; not by any means was the finger of suspicion pointed directly at him, but he was on a shortish list. Is that about right so far?'

'Yes. You asked me to keep information out of his reach to do with troop movements, leaves and that sort of thing. Training schedules and transport and the like. Anything that could possibly be of aid and comfort to the enemy. You told me you were at a stage in your, "investigation" was the term you used, Sir Maurice, when you were merely trying to narrow down your list to "possibles",' Dalgleish quoted helpfully.

'Of course. Thank you. What an excellent memory for detail you do have, Colonel. We had unearthed several officers with access to information useful to the IRA who were, sadly, in a position to be blackmailed: sexual irregularities, a bit of embezzling, an unfortunate man addicted to poker, a very silly game, I've always thought. Never mind. Just because a man's blackmailable does not, of course, inexorably lead to his being blackmailed and enrolled by the IRA. In any event, Major Hamilton seemed to have none of these more blatant failings but had unaccountably managed to lay hands on considerable sums of money. Splashed it about lavishly, too, which, had he been under the control of any professional foreign organization, such as the Russians or the Chinese or what-have-you, wouldn't have been tolerated for a second.' He nibbled at a cheese biscuit and reached for the sherry decanter to top up their glasses.

'And your government department were keen to find out the source of Hamilton's unexplained source of income, you told me.'

'And it was *you* who found it,' Sir Maurice said, beaming with approval at the younger man. 'Clever you. Hamilton was an obscene disgrace to the regiment. Good riddance, I say.'

'You give me too much credit, Sir Maurice,' Dalgleish said politely. His blue eyes were cold as he studied his host.

Lyall looked at him quizzically. 'Dear boy, you don't think I'm "wired", do you?' He pronounced the word with majestic irony. 'I should electrocute myself. Hopeless with gadgets. Wife takes care of plugs and, and . . .' he searched for a word to convey the ultimate in electronic sophistication, 'the *toaster*.' He sat back in his chair, pleased at having pinpointed a satisfactory noun.

Dalgleish remained stubbornly mute and Sir Maurice swept chattily on. 'You do recall, I hope, that the department by which I'm employed has no power of arrest, much less prosecution. Criminal proceedings are a matter for Scotland Yard.'

'Yes, I'm aware of that.'

Sir Maurice looked at the soldier indulgently. 'If you prefer, we could totter down to the RAC and have a paddle in the pool. That way, Colonel, you could see with your own eyes that there is no microphone secreted about my person.' The idea of it struck him very funny but met with no reciprocal amusement. 'Well, perhaps that isn't such a splendid idea; food there not anything like up to our kitchen, although considerably improved, I'm told.'

He tried a different tack. 'Actually, all I'd really like to satisfy my curiosity about is this: where did the late unlamented Hamilton have the cocaine stashed?'

'In his car,' Dalgleish replied promptly. 'In the boot. It was in large wineboxes. It was cleverly done. Those bladder things actually contained wine. But the bladders were much smaller, three litres, at a guess, than the boxes. The point is that had the Customs men shaken the boxes, they would've heard liquid sloshing about inside. Actually, Hamilton could easily have pushed the button on the spigot and wine would have flowed. It was absolutely ingenious.' He spread his hands out and, for the first time, favoured Sir Maurice with a slight smile. Although a very far cry from warm, his manner was thawing.

Lyall relaxed in his chair, steepling his fingers. 'Ah. Of course. You got the car-keys out of Hamilton's pocket and simply drove the car away. No one thought to wonder how Hamilton had arrived at Ascot. So easy to jump on a train at Waterloo, of course.'

He mused in silence for a moment and said, 'I don't suppose you happened to notice if there were any identifications on these wineboxes that might indicate their, ah, origin.'

'Alas, no,' Dalgleish replied blandly, not caring tuppence if Sir Maurice knew him to be lying. He laughed harshly. 'I am aware that these questions are to allay some lingering suspicion that Hamilton was conceivably expunged, if you will permit the euphemism, to cover up my being in partnership with him. I can only give you my word that I was not. When I told him I suspected that he was selling information to the IRA, he actually tried to brazen it out. He said he had graduated to smuggling and offered to cut me in.'

'Without specifying what it was he smuggled?'

'No no no. He said it was drugs.' He sipped his sherry, his hand trembling slightly from remembered rage. 'Then he laughed at me, told me that he was about to resign his commission and quit whilst he was ahead. Those were the words he used. I was not in collusion with him in any way but I had no hard evidence to lay before the police. He told me I had no proof and he was right. I had nothing. I guessed that the drugs were in his car. That's why I took the keys and drove the car home to have a look. If I'd found nothing in the car, I would've simply driven it somewhere and abandoned it. Left it in a London street to be stolen. In the event, I found the drugs. Then I told Camilla that I had the car and I offered to get it sold for her. She told me to keep it, that it was of no use to her and I was welcome to it. What's become of her?'

'I'm deeply sorry to say that she's dead, my boy. Murdered by Hamilton's IRA man.'

'Oh my God,' Dalgleish whispered. 'I ought to have come to you, Sir Maurice.' He looked down at the floor. 'I thought that Jeremy's death would end it all.'

'Might-have-beens are a waste of time,' Lyall said grimly. 'I was sure you were not in any way collaborating with Hamilton but I am happy to have it confirmed nonetheless.' He nodded several times and beetled his brows. 'And the eventual dénouement, Colonel? Forgive me for pressing but I'm a fussy old man who intensely dislikes untidiness of any sort. I merely wish to warn you that, ah, storage of these wineboxes would be unwise in the extreme.'

Dalgleish smiled briefly. 'They no longer exist, Sir Maurice. The white stuff, whether heroin or cocaine I neither know nor care, was scattered, literally, to the four winds. A breezy afternoon, I remember, and it settled on the grass like snow. It melted away, too, with the first spit of rain later on the same evening. I don't suppose the Ministry of Ag. and Fish. would be best pleased with the ecological implications but there you have it.'

'And the wine, Colonel?'

343

Dalgleish lifted his pale-blonde eyebrows in astonishment. 'My wife and I drank the wine, Sir Maurice. Finished off the last of it at a summer barbecue. Jolly good it was, too. Fresh and fruity, quite like a Beaujolais.'

Sir Maurice appeared to be lost in thought. 'Do I take it,' Dalgleish eventually asked, 'that what all of this is in aid of is a roundabout sort of job interview?'

'Well, yes, I suppose it is,' Sir Maurice admitted.

'An offer I can't refuse,' Dalgleish specified with a wry smile.

'Oh, as to that, dear boy,' Lyall said with an airy wave, 'we can discuss it all over luncheon. I do hope you like lamb. Pink, of course. The thing is, you see, that I'm losing one of my best men. To retirement,' he added hastily, dispelling any implication of a more melodramatic loss, 'and I'm most anxious to replace him. Someone with initiative, don't you see, rather like yourself. You'll find that we're nothing like the MoD, my boy. Some pettifogging inevitable, of course, but really quite mild in comparison. Much more fun than instructing baby colonels at Camberley. Dreadful town, Camberley.'

He bestowed an avuncular smile on his guest. 'I believe,' he said, rising slowly, 'they've collared a lobster for us as a starter. Shall we go through?'